For more information on Steven Erikson and his books,
see his website at www.steven-erikson.org

The Second Collected Tales of
BAUCHELAIN &
KORBAL BROACH

www.penguin.co.uk

The Second Collected Tales of
BAUCHELAIN &
KORBAL BROACH

Steven Erikson

BANTAM PRESS

LONDON · NEW YORK · TORONTO · SYDNEY · AUCKLAND

TRANSWORLD PUBLISHERS
61–63 Uxbridge Road, London W5 5SA
www.penguin.co.uk

Transworld is part of the Penguin Random House group of companies
whose addresses can be found at global.penguinrandomhouse.com

Penguin
Random House
UK

This edition first published in Great Britain
in 2018 by Bantam Press
an imprint of Transworld Publishers

A CIP catalogue record for this book
is available from the British Library.

ISBNs 9780593063965 (cased)
9780593063972 (tpb)

Typeset in 11.5/14 pt Sabon by Jouve (UK), Milton Keynes
Printed and bound in Great Britain by Clays Ltd, Elcograf S.p.A.

Penguin Random House is committed to a sustainable
future for our business, our readers and our planet. This book
is made from Forest Stewardship Council® certified paper.

1 3 5 7 9 10 8 6 4 2

Contents

THE WURMS OF
BLEARMOUTH

'BEHOLD!' ARMS SPREAD WIDE AND BRACED AGAINST THE wind, Lord Fangatooth Claw the Render paused and glanced back at Scribe Coingood. 'See how this bold perch incites me to declamation, Scribe?' His narrow, hawkish features darkened. 'Why are you not writing?'

Scribe Coingood wiped a drip from his nose, worked his numb fingers for a moment, and then scratched out the one word onto the tablet. Here atop the high tower, it was so cold that the wax on the tablet had chipped and flaked beneath the polished bone point of his scribe. He could barely make out the word he had just written, and the biting ice in his eyes didn't help matters. Squinting against the buffeting wind, he hunched down, pulling tighter his furs, but that did nothing to ease his shivering.

He cursed his own madness that had brought him to West Elingarth's Forgotten Holding. He also cursed this insane sorcerer for whom he now worked. He cursed this rotting keep and its swaying tower. He cursed the town below: Spendrugle of Blearmouth was a hovel, its population cowering under the tyranny of its new lord. He cursed the abominable weather of this jutting spur of land, thrashed by the wild ocean on three sides on most days, barring those times when the wind swung round to howl its way down from the north, cutting across the treeless blight that stretched inland all the way to yet another storm-wracked ocean, six days distant. He cursed his mother, and the time when he was seven and looked in on his sister's room and saw things – oh, what was the point? There were plenty of reasons a man had to curse, and with infernal intimacy he knew most of them.

His dreams of wealth and privilege had suffered the fate of a lame hare on the Plain of Wolves, chewed up and torn to bits; and the wind had long since taken away those tattered remnants: the tufts of blood-matted fur, the wisps of white throat-down, and the well-gnawed splinters of bone. All of it gone, scattered across the blasted landscape of his future.

Chewing on the end of his graver, Coingood considered setting that description down in his secret diaries. *A lame hare on the Plain of Wolves. Yes, that's me all right . . . was that me or my dreams, that hare? Never mind, it's not like there's a difference.* Not when he was huddled here atop the tower, miserably subject to his lord's whim, and Hood knew, a manic, eye-gleaming whim it was.

'Have you written it down now, Scribe? Gods below, if I'd known you were so slow I would never have hired you! Tell me, what did I say? I've forgotten. Read it back, damn you!'

'M-m-master, y'said . . . er . . . "Behold!"'

'Is that it? Didn't I say anything more?'

'S-s-something 'bout a bold p-p-perch, m-m-milord.'

Lord Fangatooth waved one long-fingered, skeletal hand. 'Never mind that. I've told you about my asides. They're just that. Asides. Where was I?'

'"Behold!"'

The lord faced outward again, defiant against the roaring seas, and struck a pose looming ominously over the town. 'Behold! Oh, and note my widespread arms as I face this wild, whore-whipped sea. Oh, and that wretched town directly below, and how it kneels quivering like an abject slave. Note, too, the grey skies, and that fierce colour of . . . grey. What else? Fill the scene, fool!'

Coingood started scratching furiously on the tablet.

Watching him, Fangatooth made circular, tumbling motions with one hand. 'More! Details! We are in the throes of creativity here!'

'I b-b-beg you, m-m-milord, I'm j-j-just a s-s-scribe, n-n-not a poet!'

4

'Anyone who can write has all the qualifications necessary for artistic genius! Now, where was I? Oh, right. Behold!' He fell silent, and after a long, quivering moment, he slowly lowered his arms. 'Well,' he said. 'That will do for now. Go below, Scribe, and stoke up the fires and the implements of torture. I feel in need of a visit to my beloved brother.'

Coingood hobbled his way to the trapdoor.

'Next time I say "Behold!",' Fangatooth said behind him, 'don't interrupt!'

'I w-w-won't, m-m-milord. P-p-promise!'

'There he was again!' Felittle hissed through chattering teeth. 'You seen him too, didn't you? Say you did! It wasn't just me! Up on that tower, arms out to the sides, like a . . . like a . . . like a mad sorcerer!'

Spilgit Purrble, deposed Factor of the Forgotten Holding yet still trapped in the town of Spendrugle of Blearmouth, at least until winter's end, peered across at the young woman now struggling to close the door to his closet-sized office. Snow had melted and then refrozen across the threshold. He'd need to take a sword to that at least one more time, so that he could officially close up for the season and retreat back to the King's Heel. As it was, his last day maintaining any kind of office for the backstabbing mob ruling the distant capital and, ostensibly, all of Elingarth, promised to be a cold one.

Even the arrival of Felittle, here in these crowded confines, with her soft red cheeks and the overdone carmine paint on her full lips, and those huge eyes so expansive in their blessed idiocy, could do little to defeat the insipid icy draught pouring in past her from around the mostly useless door. Spilgit sighed and reached for his tankard. 'I've warmed rum in that kettle, mixed with some wine and crushed blackgem berries. Would you like some?'

'Ooh!' She edged forward, her quilted coat smelling of smoke, ale and her mother's eye-watering perfume that Spilgit privately called *Whore Sweat* – not that he'd ever utter that out loud. Not if he wanted to get what he wanted from this blissful child in a woman's body. And most certainly never to that vicious hag's face. While Felittle's mother already despised him, she'd not yet refused his coin and he needed to keep it that way for a few more months, assuming he could find a way of stretching his fast-diminishing resources. After that . . .

Felittle was breathing fast as Spilgit collected the kettle from its hook above the brazier and poured out a dollop into the cup she'd taken down from the shelf beside the door. He considered again the delicious absence of guilt that accompanied his thoughts of stealing Felittle away from her tyrant of a mother; away from this miserable village that stank of fish all summer and stank of the people eating that fish all winter; away from her mother's whores and the sordid creatures that crawled into the King's Heel every day eager for more of the old wick-dipping from that gaggle of girls only a blind man would find attractive, at least until the poor fool's probing fingers broke through the powdery sludge hiding their pocked faces. Away, then, and away most of all, from that deranged sorcerer who'd usurped his own brother to carve out, in broken bones, spilled blood and the screaming of endless victims, his private version of paradise.

Oh, there was no end to the horrors of this place, but Lord Fangatooth Claw sat atop them all like a king on a throne. How Spilgit hated sorcerers!

'You're still shivering, darling,' he said to Felittle. 'Drink that down and have another, and come closer. Now, with only this one chair, well, sit on my lap again, will you. That's surely one way to get warm.'

She giggled, swinging her not-ungenerous backside onto him and then leaning back with one arm snaking round the back of his neck. 'If Mother saw this, she'd hack off your mast and roast it on a fire till it was burnt crisp!'

'But my sweetheart, are we not dressed? Is this not entirely proper, given the cold and the cramped conditions of this office?'

'Oh, and who else do you do this with?'

'No one, of course, since you are the only person to ever visit me.'

She eyed him suspiciously, but he knew it to be an act, since she well knew that he entertained only her. Felittle missed nothing in this village. She was its eyes and ears and, most of all, its mouth, and it was remarkable to Spilgit that such a mouth could find fuel to race without surcease day after day, night upon night. There were barely two hundred people in Spendrugle, and not one of them could be said to be leading an exciting life. Perhaps there was a sort of cleverness in Felittle, after all, in the manner of her soaking in everything that it was possible to know in Spendrugle, and then spewing it all back out with impressive accuracy. *Indeed, she might well possess the wit to match a . . . a . . .*

'Blackgem berries make me squirt, you know.'

'Excuse me?'

'Squirt water, of course! What else would I squirt? What a dirty mind you have!'

. . . sea-sponge? 'Well, I didn't know that. I mean, how could I, since it's such a . . . well, a private thing.'

'Not for much longer,' she said, taking another mouthful.

Spilgit frowned, only now feeling the unusual warmth in his lap. 'You call that a squirt?'

'Well,' she said, 'it's just that it got me all excited!'

'Really? Oh, then should we—'

'Not you, silly! Fangatooth! On the tower, with his arms spread wide like I said!'

'Alas, I didn't see any of that, Felittle. Busy as I was in here, putting things in order and all. Even so, for the life of me I can't see what it was that excited you about such a scene. He does that most mornings, after all.'

'I know that, but this morning it was different. Or at least I thought it was.'

'Why?'

'Well,' she paused to drink down the rum, gusted out a sweet sigh, and then made a small sound. 'Oops, it's all going now, isn't it?'

Spilgit felt the heat spreading in his crotch, and then his thighs as it pooled in the chair. 'Ah, yes . . .'

'Anyway,' she continued, 'I thought he was looking at the wreck, you see? But I don't think he was. I mean—'

'Hold on, darling. A moment. What wreck?'

'Why, the one in the bay, of course! Arrived last night! You don't know anything!'

'Survivors?'

She shrugged. 'Nobody's been down to look yet. Too cold.'

'Gods below!' Spilgit pushed her from his lap. He rose. 'I need to change.'

'You look like you peed yourself! Hah hah!'

He studied her for a moment, and then said, 'We're heading down, darling. To that wreck.'

'Really? But we'll freeze!'

'I want to see it. You can come with me, Felittle, or you can run back to your ma.'

'I don't know why you two hate each other. She only wants what's best for me. But I want to do what her girls do, and why not? It's a living, isn't it?'

'You're far too beautiful for that,' Spilgit said.

'That's what she says!'

'And she's right, on that we're agreed. The thing we don't agree on is what your future is going to look like. You deserve better than this horrible little village, Felittle. She'd as much as chain you down if she thought she could get away with it. It's all about her, what she wants you to do for her. Your ma's getting old, right? Needing someone to take care of her, and she'll make you a spinster if you let her.'

Her eyes were wide, her breaths coming fast. 'Then you'll do it?'

'What?'

'Steal me away!'

'I'm a man of my word. Come the spring, darling, we'll swirl the sands, flatten the high grasses and flee like the wind.'

'Okay, I'll go with you!'

'I know.'

'No, down to the wreck, silly!'

'Right, my little sea-sponge. Wait here, then. I need to go back to the Heel and change . . . unless you need to do the same?'

'No, I'm fine! If I go back Ma will see me and find something for me to do. I'll wait here. I wasn't wearing knickers anyway.'

Well, that explains it, doesn't it. Oh darling, you're my kind of woman.

Except for the peeing bit, that is.

The hand gripping his cloak collar was hard as iron as he was dragged from the foaming, icy surf. Hacking, spitting out sea-water and sand, Emancipor Reese opened his eyes to stare up at a grey, wintry sky. He heard gulls but couldn't see them. He heard the war-drums of the waves pounding the rocks flanking this slip of a bay. He heard his own phlegmatic gasping, punctuated by the occasional groan as that hand continued dragging him up the beach, across heaps of shells, through snarled knots of seaweed, and over sodden lumps of half-frozen driftwood.

He flailed weakly, clawing at that hand, and a moment later it released him. His head fell back with a thump and he found himself staring up at his master's upside-down face.

'Will you recover, Mister Reese?'

'No, Master.'

'Very good. Now get up. We must take stock of our surroundings.'

'It's made up of air, not water. That's enough of the surroundings I need to know.'

'Nonsense, Mister Reese. We seem to have lost Korbal Broach, and I could use your assistance in finding him.'

At that, Emancipor Reese sat up, blinking the rime from his eyes. 'Lost? Korbal's lost? Really? He must be dead. Drowned—'

'No, nothing so dire, I'm sure,' Bauchelain replied, brushing sand from his cloak.

'Oh.' Emancipor found himself staring at the wreck of the ship. There wasn't much left. Fragments were being tossed up to roll in the surf. 'What is it about me and the sea?' he muttered. Amidst

9

the flotsam were more than a few bodies, their only movement coming from the water that pushed and pulled at their limp forms. 'It's a miracle we survived that, Master.'

'Mister Reese? Oh, that. Not a miracle at all. Willpower and fortitude. Now, I believe I spied a settlement upon the headland, one that includes a rather substantial fortification.'

'No,' moaned Emancipor, 'not another fortification.'

'Prone to draughts, I'm sure, but more suited to our habits. We shall have to introduce ourselves to the local lord or lady, I think, and gauge well the firmness of his or her footing. Command, Mister Reese, is a state of being to which I am not only accustomed, but one for which my impressive talents are well-suited. That said, and given our record thus far when assuming positions of authority, even I must acknowledge that trial and error remains an important component in our engagement with power.'

'Now here's a miracle,' said Emancipor as he pulled out his pouch of rustleaf. 'The hawker claimed it would be watertight, and she was right.' He found his pipe, blew the wet and sand from it and began tamping the bowl. 'Life's looking up already, Master.'

'The lightening of your spirits is most welcome, Mister Reese.'

'Show me a man who can't smoke and you're looking at the end of civilization.'

'I'll not argue with that assessment, Mister Reese.'

The crescent beach they'd found banked steeply above the waterline, and high ragged cliffs rose beyond, but Emancipor could make out a trail. 'There's a way up, Master.'

'So I see, and if I'm not mistaken, we will find our companion in yonder village.'

'He didn't wait for us?'

'He elected wings to effect his escape from the sinking ship, Mister Reese. I would have done the same, if not for you.'

'Ah. Appreciate that, Master. I really do.'

'My pleasure. Now— Oh, we have company on the way.'

Emancipor saw, too, the three figures making their way down the trail, hunched over against the buffeting wind. 'Are they armed, Master? This could be a wreckers' coast.'

'Armed?'

'My eyes ain't what they used to be, Master.'

'No, Mister Reese. Not excessively so. I assure you, to us they pose no danger.'

'Glad to hear it, Master.' Emancipor was starting to get cold, or, rather, he was starting to feel it. His dunk in the seas had numbed things up pretty fast. Glancing over at Bauchelain, he saw that the tall necromancer was not even wet. Mages, he concluded, were obnoxious in so many ways it was almost pointless listing them.

Now shivering, he studied the three strangers making their way down the trail.

Hordilo Stinq's pirating days were behind him now. He liked the feel of solid ground under him, even as that terrible sea still held him close, within reach, stubborn as an ex-wife whose sole reason to breathe was the conviction that she was still owed something by the fool she'd tossed away, and it didn't matter how many years had passed since he'd last wallowed in her icy arms. The watery witch never let him wander too far from her thrashing shores. These days, it was nothing to step outside to begin his daily patrol, and feel on the wind the wet spray of her bitter spite. Aye, an ex-wife, spitting like a cat and howling like a dog. A hoary, wild thing with venom under her long nails and dead spiders in her hair.

'You ain't answered me, Stinq,' said Ackle, who sat across from him and was, thankfully, not looking Hordilo's way, busy instead plucking clumps of old mud from his deadman's cloak. 'Ever been married?'

'No,' Hordilo replied. 'Nor do I want to be, Ackle. Want no ex-wives chasing me down everywhere I go, throwing snotty runts at my feet I never seen before and sayin' they're mine. When they aren't. I mean, if my seed produced anything as ugly as that – well, gods below, I've known plenty of women, if you know what I mean, and not one of them ever called me ugly.'

Ackle paused, examining a long root he'd pulled from the

woollen cloak. 'Heard you like Rimlee,' he said. 'She can't see past her nose.'

'Your point?'

'Nothing, friend. Just that she's mostly blind. That's all.'

Hordilo drained his tankard and glared out through the thick, pitted glass of the window. 'Feloovil's whores ain't selected for how good they look – see, I mean. How good they see. But I bet you wish they wasn't the smelling kind, don't you?'

'If they smell I remain unaware of it,' Ackle replied.

'That's not what I meant. They smell just fine, and that's your problem, isn't it?'

At that Ackle looked up – Hordilo could see the man's face reflected blurrily, unevenly, in the window, but even this distorted view couldn't hide Ackle's horrible, lifeless eyes. 'Is that my problem, Hordilo? Is that why I can't get a woman to lie with me no matter how much I offer to pay? You think so? I mean, my smell turns them, does it? Are you sure about that?'

Hordilo scowled. Out on the street beyond he saw Grimled stump past, making the first circuit of the day. 'You don't smell too good, Ackle. Not that you could tell.'

'No, I couldn't. I can't. But you know, there's plenty of men in here who don't smell too good, but they get company in their beds upstairs anyway, every night if they can afford it.'

'Different kind of smell,' Hordilo insisted. 'Living smell, if you know what I mean.'

'I would think,' said Ackle, straightening in his seat, 'that my smell is the least of their concerns. I would think,' he went on, 'that it's more to do with my having been pronounced dead, stuck in a coffin for three days, and then buried for two more. Don't you think it might be all that, Stinq? I don't know, of course. I mean, I can't be sure, but it seems plausible that these details have something to do with my lonely nights. At least, it's a possibility worth considering, don't you think?'

Hordilo shrugged. 'You still smell.'

'What do I smell like?'

'Like a corpse in a graveyard.'

'And have I always smelled that way?'

Hordilo scowled. 'How should I know? Probably not. But I can't really say, can I? Since I never knew you before, did I? You washed up on shore, right? And I had a quota to fill and you were broke.'

'If you'd let me lead you to the buried chest you'd be rich now,' Ackle said, 'and I wouldn't have been strung up because your lord likes to see 'em dance. It could've gone another way, Hordilo, if you had any brains in that skull of yours.'

'Right. So why don't you lead me to that damned chest you keep talkin' about? It's not like you need the coin anymore, is it? Anyway, the whole point you're avoiding is that we hanged you good, and you was dead when we took you down. Dead people are supposed to stay in the ground. It's a rule.'

'If I was dead I wouldn't be sitting here right now, would I? Ever clawed your way up out of the ground? If that coffin lid wasn't just cheap driftwood, and if your ground wasn't so soft and if your gravediggers weren't so damned lazy, why, I would never have made it back. So, if there's anyone to blame for me being here, it's all of you in this lousy village.'

'I didn't dig the grave though, did I? Anyway, there ain't no buried chest. If there was, you'd have gone back to it by now. Instead, you sleep under the table, and that only because her dogs like rolling on you to disguise their scent. Feloovil thinks you're funny, besides.'

'She laughs at my dead eyes, you mean.'

Hordilo glanced into the tavern's main room, but Feloovil was still sitting behind the bar, her head barely visible, her eyes closed. The woman stayed up till dawn most nights, so it was no surprise she slept most of the day every day. He'd watched that useless Factor, Spilgit Purrble, slink past her a while earlier, and she'd not raised a lid, not even when the man returned from his upstairs room only moments later, and wearing a change of clothes. There'd been a suspicious look on the Factor's face that was still nagging Hordilo, but for the moment he didn't feel like moving, and besides, with Feloovil asleep it was no difficult thing to draw the taps for a flagon or two, on the house as it were. 'Lucky you,' he finally said, 'that she's got an uncanny streak in her. Unlucky for you that her girls don't share it, hah.'

'With what they must see in a man's eyes every night,' said Ackle, 'you'd think they'd welcome mine.'

'Lust ain't so bad t'look at,' Hordilo said.

'Oh indeed. Why, it charms a woman right out of her clothes, doesn't it? I mean, it's just like love, isn't it? Love with all the dreamy veils torn aside.'

'What veils? Her girls don't wear veils, you fool. The point is, Ackle, what they see every night is what they're used to, and they're fine with that. Dead eyes, well, that's different. It puts a shiver on the soul, it does.'

'And does my reflection in the window keep you warm, Stinq?'

'If I had an ex-wife, she'd probably have your eyes.'

'No doubt.'

'But I don't need reminding of what I've been lucky enough to avoid all these years. Well, sometimes, but not all the time. I got a limit to what I can stomach, if you get my meaning.'

'I get your meaning, Stinq. Well, sometimes, but not all the time, as you're such a subtle man.'

Hordilo grunted, and then frowned. Grimled should have been by already, second time around. It was a small village, and doing the circuit was what Grimled did, and did well, since he didn't know how to do it otherwise. 'Something funny,' he said.

'What?'

'Fangatooth's golem, Grimled.'

'What about it?'

'Not "it". "Him." Anyway, he showed up as usual—'

'Yes, I saw that.'

'The rounds, right? Only, he ain't come back.'

Ackle shrugged. 'Might be sorting something out.'

'Grimled don't sort things out,' Hordilo replied, squinting and wiping at the steamy glass. 'To sort things out, all he has to do is show up. You don't argue with a giant lump of angry iron. Especially one carrying a two-handed axe.'

14

'It's the bucket head that I don't like,' said Ackle. 'You can't talk to a bucket, can you? Not face-to-face, I mean. There is no face. But that bucket's not iron, Stinq.'

'Yes it is.'

'Got to be tin, or pewter.'

'No, it's iron,' said Hordilo. 'You don't work with Grimled the way I do.'

'Work with it? You salute it when you pass it by. It's not like you're its friend, Stinq.'

'I'm the lord's executioner, Ackle. Grimled and his brothers do the policing. It's all organized, right? We work for the Lord of Wurms. It's like the golems are milord's right hands, and I'm the left.'

'Right hands? How many does he have?'

'Count it up, fool. Six right hands.'

'What about his own right hand?'

'All right. Seven right hands.'

'And two left?'

'That's right. I guess even the dead can count, after all.'

'Oh, I can count, friend, but that doesn't mean it all adds up, if you understand my meaning.'

'No,' Hordilo said, glaring at the reflection, 'I don't.'

'So the bucket's iron. Fine, whatever you say. Grimled's gone missing and even I will admit: that's passing strange. So, as executioner and constable or whatever it is you say you do, officially, I mean, and let's face it, you chirp something different every second day. So, as whatever you are, why are you still sitting here, when Grimled's gone missing? It's cold out there. Maybe it rusted up. Or froze solid. Go get yourself a tub of grease. It's what a real friend would do, under the circumstances.'

'Just to prove it to you, then,' said Hordilo, rising up and tugging on his cloak, 'I'll do just that. I'll head out there, into this horrible weather, to check on my comrade.'

'Use a wooden bucket for that grease,' said Ackle. 'You don't want to insult your friend, do you?'

'I'll just head over to the Kelp carter's first,' said Hordilo, nodding as he adjusted his sword belt.

'For the grease?'

'That's right. For the grease.'

'In case your friend's seized up?'

'Yeah, what is it with these stupid questions?'

Ackle held up two dirt-stained palms, leaning back. 'Ever since I died, or, rather, didn't die, but should've, I've acquired this obsession with being . . . well, precise. I have an aversion to vague generalities, you see. That grey area, understand? You know, like being stuck between certain ideas, important ideas, that is. Between say, breathing and not breathing. Or being alive and being dead. And things like needing to know how many hands Lord Fangatooth has, which by my count is seven right hands and two left hands, meaning, I suppose, that he rarely gets it wrong.'

'What in Hood's name are you going on about, Ackle?'

'Nothing, I suppose. It's just that, well, since we're friends, you and me, I mean. As much as you're friends with Grimled . . . well, what I'm saying is, this cold slows me up something awful, I've found. Maybe I don't need grease, as such, but if you see me out there sometime, not moving or anything. I guess the point I'm making, Stinq, is this. If you see me like that, don't bury me.'

'Because you ain't dead? You idiot. You couldn't be more dead than you are now. But I won't bury you. Burn you on a pyre, maybe, if only to put an end to our stupid conversations. So take that as a warning. I see you all frozen up out there, you're cordwood in my eyes and that's all.'

'So much for friendship.'

'You got that right. I ain't friends with a dead man I don't even know.'

'No, just lumps of magicked iron with buckets for heads.'

'Right. At least we got that straight.' Hordilo pushed the chair back and walked over to the door. He paused and glanced back to see Ackle staring out the window. 'Hey, look somewhere else. I don't want your dead eyes tracking me.'

'They may be dead,' Ackle replied with a slow smile, 'but they know ugly when they see it.'

Hordilo stared at the man. 'You remind me,' he said, 'of my ex-wife.'

Comber Whuffine Gaggs lived in a shack just above the comber's beach. He'd built it himself, using driftwood and detritus from the many wrecks he'd plundered as lost traders struck the sunken reefs that were noted only on the rarest of maps with the grim label of *Gravewater*, and which the locals called *Sunrise Surprise*. Indeed, the night storms on this headland were nasty, blood-thirsty, vengeful, cold and cruel as a forgotten mistress, and he'd made his home a doorstep from which he could view her nightly tirades, wetting his lips in the hope of something new and won-derful arriving in splintered ruin, and faint, hopeless cries.

But it was a cold squat, here above the beach, the wooden walls gritted in the cracks and polished like bone by the winds, and so he'd made of those walls two layers, with a cavity in between into which, over the course of three decades, he'd stuffed the cuttings from his scalp and beard.

The smell of that stuffing was, admittedly, none too pleasant to the guest or stranger who paid him a visit, if only to look over the loot he'd scrounged up from the wrack, and such visits had become increasingly rare, forcing him to load up his handcart for the morning market that sprang up in Spendrugle's centre square every few weeks or so. That journey both exhausted him and left him feeling depressed; and it wasn't often that he came back at the day's end with anything more than a handful of the tooth-dented coins of tin that passed for local currency.

No, these days he was inclined to stay at home, especially now that a mad sorcerer had taken over the Holding, and strangers had a way of ending up with a hanged-man's view of the scenic sites that made Spendrugle such a charming village. So rare had his visits become he truly feared that one day he might be mis-taken for one of those hapless strangers.

He'd heard the ship come in this past night, striking the reef like a legless horse sliding across a dhenrabi's bristling hide, but the morning had broken unruly cold, and he knew that he had plenty of time in which to explore, once the sun climbed a little higher and the wind whipped back round.

The lone room of his shack was bright and warm with a half-dozen ship's lanterns, all lit up and hissing from the occasional drop of old rain making its way down through the roof's heavy, tarred beams. He was perched on the edge of an old captain's chair, its leather padding salt-stained but otherwise serviceable, and sat leaning far forward to make sure every hair he scraped off his jaw and cheeks, and every strand he clipped from his head, fell down to the bleached deerskin he'd laid out between his feet. He had been mulling notions of adding a room . . .

It was then that he heard voices drifting up from the beach. Survivors were rare, what with the rocks offshore and the deadly undertow and all. Whuffine set down his blade and collected up a cloth to wipe the soap from his face. It was simple decency to head down and offer up a welcome, maybe even a cup of warmed rum to take the chill from their bones, and then with a smile send them on their way to Spendrugle, so Hordilo could arrest them and see them hung high. It wasn't much by way of local entertainment, but he could think of worse.

Like me, dangling there beneath the overhang atop Wurms' stone wall, with the gulls fighting over my tender bits. No, he wouldn't find that entertaining at all.

Besides, delivering such hapless fools had its rewards, as Hordilo gave him the pickings from whatever they happened to be wearing and carrying, and the fine high leather boots he now pulled on reminded him of that, making this venture out into the bitter cold feel worthwhile. He rose from the chair and drew on his sheepskin cloak, which was made of four hides all sewn together in such a way that the heads crowded his shoulders and the hind legs hung like dirty braids past his hips. He'd been a big man, once, but the years had withered his muscles, so that now his frame was all jutting bones and stringy tendons, wrapped up in skin like chewed leather. He didn't have many tender bits left, but he knew the damned gulls would find them, given the chance.

Pulling on his fox-fur hat, made of two skins with the heads hanging down to protect his ears, and the bushy tails pulled into a warm fringe round the crown of his dented skull, he gathered up his knobby walking stick and set out.

The instant he emerged from his shack he halted in surprise to see two bent-over figures hurrying down the trail. A man and a woman. Gaze narrowing on the man, Whuffine called out, 'Is that you?'

Both villagers looked up.

'Why, I'm always me,' Spilgit Purrble said. 'Who else would I be, old man?'

Whuffine scowled. 'I ain't as old as I look, you know.'

'Stop,' said Spilgit, 'you're breaking my heart. I see you're getting ready for a day of picking through bloated corpses.'

But Whuffine was studying the sands of the trail. 'See anybody on your way down?' he asked.

'No,' said the woman. 'Why?'

Whuffine glanced at her. 'You're Feloovil's daughter, ain't you? Does she know you're here? With him?'

'Look,' said Spilgit, 'we're going down for a look. You coming or not?'

'That's my beach down there, Factor.'

'The whole village takes its share,' Spilgit countered.

'Because I let them, because I've been through everything first.' He then shook his head, making the fox heads flap and the sharp canines run eerily along his neck – he shouldn't have left in the upper jaws, probably. 'Anyway, look at the ground here, you two. Someone's come up the trail – Hood knows how I didn't hear that, or even see it, since I was at the window. And if that's not enough, there's more.'

'More what?' Spilgit asked.

'Whoever it was passing me and my shack, it was dragging bodies. Two of 'em, one to each hand. Makes for a strong person, don't you think? This trail's steep and dragging things up all this way ain't easy.'

'We didn't see anyone,' Spilgit said.

Whuffine then pointed down towards the beach. 'I just heard voices below.'

Felittle gasped. 'We should go and get Hordilo!'

'No need,' said Whuffine. 'I was going to send them up, anyway. It's what I do.'

Spilgit spat but the wind shifted and the spittle whipped up and plastered his brow. Cursing, he wiped it away and said, 'You all have blood on your hands, don't you? That tyrant up in the keep found himself the right people to rule over, all right.'

'You're just saying that,' said Whuffine, 'because you're sore. What's it like, eh? Being made useless and all?'

'That's a usurper up there in Wurms.'

'So what? His brother was, too. And that witch before him, and then that bastard son of Lord Wurms himself – who strangled the man in his own bed. And what was he even doing in that bed with his stepfather anyway?' Whuffine shrugged. 'It's how them fools do things, and us, why, we just got to keep our heads down and get on with living and all. You, Spilgit, you're just a Hood-damned tax collector anyway. And we ain't paying and that's that.'

'I don't care,' Spilgit said, taking Felittle's arm and pulling her along as he trudged past Whuffine. 'I quit. And when the Black Fleet shows up and an army lands to bring down in flames Wurms Keep and that mad sorcerer with it, well, I don't expect there'll be much left of Spendrugle of Blearmouth either, and the gods of mercy will be smiling on that day!'

During this tirade, voiced as Spilgit marched on, Whuffine fell in behind the two villagers. He thought about pushing past them both, but with living people on the beach, maybe it paid to be cautious. 'Anyway,' he said, 'why are you two going down there, now that you know there's survivors? You ain't going to warn them off or anything, are you? If you did that, why, Hordilo and Lord Fangatooth himself wouldn't take kindly to it. In fact, they'd have to find somebody else to hang.'

Ahead, Spilgit paused and swung round. 'I'm surviving one more winter here, Whuffine. You think I'd do or say anything to jeopardize that?'

'I like the hangings,' said Felittle, offering Whuffine a bright, cock-stirring smile. 'But aren't you curious? How did anyone survive that storm? They might come from mysterious places! They might have funny hair and funny clothes and talk in gibberish! It's so exciting, isn't it?'

Whuffine flicked a glance at Spilgit, but couldn't read much from the man's expression, other than the fact that he was shivering. To Felittle, Whuffine smiled back and said, 'Aye, exciting.'

'Aren't you cold?' she asked him. 'You don't look cold. How come you're not cold?'

'It's my big kindly heart, lass.'

'Gods below,' Spilgit said, swinging round and pulling Felittle with him.

They rounded the last bend in the trail and came within sight of the beach. And there on the pale strand stood two men, one tall and dressed in fine clothing – black silks and black leathers, and a heavy burgundy woollen cloak that reached down almost to his ankles – and beside him a more bedraggled figure, a man Whuffine guessed was a sailor by the rough clothes he wore and the way he stood on those bowed legs. Beyond these two, the surf was crowded with corpses and detritus. Out on the reef the wreck had already been battered to pieces, with barely a third of the hull remaining, and only the foredeck, over which was wrapped the tangled remnants of a sail that looked partly scorched.

Spilgit and Felittle had both paused upon seeing the strangers, proving once again the pith behind the bluff when it came to that tax collector. Whuffine edged past them and continued down to the strand. 'Welcome, friends! Mael and all his hoary whores have looked kindly upon you, I see. To think, you seem to have escaped unscathed from the furies, while your poor companions behind you lie cold and nothing but meat for the crabs. Do you give thanks for such mercy? I'm sure you do!'

The taller man, fork-bearded and with his hair slicked back from his bared head, frowned slightly at Whuffine and then turned to his companion and said something in a language the Comber didn't understand, to which the man grunted and said, 'Low Elin,

Master. Seatrader tongue. Eastern pirates. Sailor's Cant. It's just the accent that's thrown you. And by that accent, Master, I'd say we've hit the Headland of Howling Winds. Probably the Forgotten Holding, meaning it's claimed by the Enclave.' This man then turned to Whuffine. 'There's a river other side of the keep, right?'

Whuffine nodded. 'The Blear, aye. You know well this shore, then, sir. I'm impressed.'

The man grunted a second time and spoke to his companion. 'Master, we're on a Wreckers' Coast here. That heap of sheepskin and furs with all his happy words and big smile, he's eager to start stripping corpses and picking through the wrack. See those boots he's wearing? Malazan cavalry officer, and he ain't no Malazan cavalry officer. If we was badly hurt he'd probably have slit our throats by now.'

Spilgit laughed, earning a glare from Whuffine, who was struggling to hold onto his smile.

The tall man cleared his throat, and then spoke in passable High Elin. 'Well then, let us leave the man to his task, since I doubt our dead comrades will mind. Alas, as we are hale, there will be no throat-slitting just yet.'

'The villagers won't be any better,' the other man then said, eyeing Spilgit and Felittle.

'Do not be so quick to judge us,' Spilgit said, stepping forward. 'Until recently, I was the appointed Factor of the Forgotten Holding, and as such the official representative of the Enclave.'

The sailor raised his brows at that, and then grinned. 'A damned tax collector? Surprised they ain't hanged you yet.'

Whuffine saw Spilgit blanch, but before he could say anything, the Comber cleared his throat and said, 'The lord is resident in his keep, good sirs.' Then, shifting his attention to the taller man, he added, 'And he will be delighted to make your acquaintance, seeing as you're highborn and all.'

'Is there an inn?' the sailor asked, and Whuffine noted how the man shivered in his sodden clothes.

'Allow us to escort you there,' Spilgit said. 'This young woman with me is the daughter of the innkeeper.'

'Most civilized of you, Factor,' said the highborn man. 'As you can see, my manservant is suffering in this weather.'

'A warm fire and a hearty meal will do him wonders, I'm sure,' said Spilgit. 'Yet you, sir, appear to be both dry and, well, proof against this bitter wind.'

'Very perceptive of you,' the man murmured in reply, glancing about as if distracted. A moment later he shrugged and gestured towards the trail. 'Lead on, Factor.' Then he paused and looked to his manservant. 'Mister Reese, if you would, draw your sword and ware our backs, lest this Malazan cavalry officer falter in his wisdom, and do note the knife he hides in his right hand, will you?'

Scowling, Whuffine stepped back, sheathing his knife. 'The blade's for swollen fingers, that's all. In fact, I'll be on my way then, and leave you in the hands of Spilgit and Felittle.' And he hurried down the beach. He didn't like the look of that highborn or the way the manservant was now handling that shortsword with unpleasant ease, and all things told, Whuffine was glad to be rid of them.

Coming down to the wrack, eyes scanning the corpses, he paused upon seeing the ragged bites taken out of most of them. He'd seen the work of sharks, but that was nothing like what he looked upon now. Despite his sheepskin and fox-furs, Whuffine shivered. Glancing back, he saw Spilgit and Felittle leading the strangers up the trail. *Could be a bit of trouble washed up here today, eh? Well, I doubt Fangatooth and his golems will have anything to worry about. Still . . .* He eyed the nearest, chewed-up corpse. Some of those bites looked human.

The crabs were marching up from the sea in scuttling rows, and through the moaning wind he could hear their happy, eager clicking.

I'll set out the traps once they've fattened up some.

Hordilo Stinq felt Ackle the Risen's dead eyes tracking him as, bucket of whale grease in one hand, he walked up the street opposite the King's Heel. Most strangers did the proper thing and died after being hung, but not Ackle. If Hordilo was a superstitious man, why, he might think there was something odd about that man.

But he had more practical concerns to deal with right now. Adjusting his sword belt with one hand while tightening his grip on the iron handle of the wooden bucket, and doing his best to ignore how the icy wind stole all feeling from his fingers, he set out up the street. The ground was frozen hard, the edges of the wheel ruts slippery and treacherous, the puddles filling those ruts frozen solid. For all of that, Grimled's progress was mapped out before him in cracked impressions, the golem's iron boots leaving dents already leaking turgid water that pretty much froze as soon as it bled out. His gaze tracked them up to the front street's end, where the footprints turned right and disappeared behind Blecker's Livery.

Hordilo continued on. Those damned golems unnerved him. Ackle was right in that one thing, Hood take him. Offering up a nod and maybe a muttered greeting as one trudged past wasn't what anyone in their right mind could call a friendship. But they were Lord Fangatooth's creations, stamp-stamp-stamping his authority on Spendrugle and everyone calling it home, and if any acts of kindness on Hordilo's part, no matter how modest, could alight the glint of sympathy in such abominations, well, he had to try, didn't he? Besides, the few times there'd been trouble with some stranger, one of them would show up to sort things out right quick, and that had saved Hordilo's skin more than once.

So in a way he owed them, didn't he? And if it wasn't in a walking lump of iron to feel anything about anyone, Hordilo was flesh and blood, with genuine feelings and even a heart that could break if, say, some hag of a wife he'd once loved went and did the nasty on him, and not just one animal, either, but all kinds of animals, and then told him about it with shining eyes and that soul-cutting half-smile that said she liked what her words were doing to him and besides, Ribble had been *his* dog, dammit! If something like that had ever happened to him, which of course it hadn't, why, his heart might break, or at least start leaking.

Because a man without feelings was no better than a . . . well, a golem.

Reaching Blecker's Livery, he paused for a moment to utter a soft prayer to the memory of old Blecker, since remorse always came afterwards and never went away, when the fury of knowing that Blecker knew everything with his nickering stallion and all, well, that faded after a time, and that ex-wife he didn't have was a seductive woman when she wanted to be, not that Ribble cared much either way, with his endless panting and witless but knowing eyes, but Blecker himself had seen plenty, hadn't he, with his damned menagerie and all. But whisper a prayer anyway, because Hordilo knew that that was what a decent man did, but not much of a prayer, since Blecker had never known a thing about decency and nobody had complained much when he swung from the gibbet, except when they saw Hurta riding off on that stallion with Ribble chasing after them, none of them ever to be seen again – oh, there was plenty of disappointment about that, wasn't there? That said, Feloovil had cleared his tab at the Heel and spotted him free drinks for a whole week afterwards, which was peculiarly generous of her. This was the kind of mess having a wife would have given him, and was it any wonder he was having none of that?

Rounding the livery, Hordilo halted in his tracks. Twenty paces away, Grimled was lying motionless on its back. A large black-cloaked man was kneeling beside it, his hands deep in the golem's chest. Strange fluids were spraying out past the man's forearms. A few paces beyond them lay two bloated corpses.

'Hey!' Hordilo shouted.

But the man ripping pieces out from Grimled's chest didn't look up.

Hordilo set down the bucket and then drew his sword. 'Hey!' he yelled again, advancing. 'What have you done to Grimled? You can't do that! Step away from him! By the lord's command, step away!'

At last, the stranger looked up, blinking owlishly at Hordilo.

Something in the man's piggy eyes made Hordilo slow down

and then stagger to a halt. He lifted the sword threateningly, but the blade wavered in his numbed grip. 'The lord of Wurms Keep will see you hang for this! You're under arrest!'

The stranger withdrew his hands from Grimled's chest. They were black and dripping. 'I was trying to fix it,' he said in a high, piping voice.

'You broke it!'

'I didn't mean to.'

'Explain that to Lord Fangatooth! Get up now. You're coming with me.'

The stranger's uncanny eyes slipped past Hordilo and fixed on the distant keep. 'There?'

'There.'

'All right,' the man replied, climbing slowly to his feet. He looked over at the two corpses. 'But I want to bring my friends with me.'

'Your friends? They're dead!'

'No, not those ones.'

The man pointed and Hordilo turned to see a group appearing from the beach trail. *That's where Spilgit was going, and Felittle with him! She must have seen a ship on the reef and snuck out to the Factor, so they could get a first look. Gods below, will the treachery never end?*

'But I want these ones, too,' added the stranger. 'I'm saving them.'

Licking his lips, his mind in a fog, Hordilo said, 'They're past saving, you fool.'

The stranger frowned. 'I don't like being called a fool.'

The tone was flat, unaccountably chilling. 'Sorry to tell you, those two are dead. Maybe you're in shock or something. That happens. Shipwreck, was it? Bad enough you arriving uninvited, and if that wasn't enough, look what you did to Grimled. Lord Fangatooth won't be happy about that, but that's between you and him. Me, well, the law says I got to arrest you, and that's that. The law says you got to give account of yourselves.'

'My selves? There is only one of me.'

'You think you're being funny? You're not.' Stepping back, trying to avoid a peek into the inner workings of poor Grimled – not that they worked anymore – Hordilo shifted his attention to the newcomers as they arrived.

The tall one with the pointed beard spoke. 'Ah, Korbal, there you are. What have you found?'

'A golem, Bauchelain,' the first man replied. 'It swung its axe at me. I didn't like that, but I didn't mean to break it.'

The man named Bauchelain walked over to study Grimled. 'A distinct lack of imagination, wouldn't you say, Korbal? A proper face would have been much more effective, in terms of inspiring terror and whatnot. Instead, what fear is inspired by an upended slop bucket? Unless it is to invite someone to laugh unto death.'

'Don't say that, Master,' said the third stranger, pausing to tamp more rustleaf into his pipe, though his teeth chattered with the cold. 'What with the way I go and all.'

'I am sure,' said Bauchelain, 'that your sense of humour is far too refined to succumb to this clumsy effort, Mister Reese.'

'Oh, it's funny enough, I suppose, but you're right, I won't bust a side about it.'

Spilgit was almost hopping from one foot to the other behind the newcomers. 'Hordilo, best escort these two gentlemen up to an audience with Lord Fangatooth, don't you think? We'll take their manservant to the Heel, so he can warm up and get a hot meal in him. Spendrugle hospitality, and all that.'

Hordilo cleared his throat.

But Korbal was the first to speak. 'Bauchelain, this man called me a fool.'

'Oh dear,' said Bauchelain. 'And has he not yet retracted his misjudged assessment?'

'No.'

'It was all a misunderstanding,' Hordilo said, feeling sudden sweat beneath his clothes. 'Of course he's not a fool. I do apologize.'

'There,' said Bauchelain, sighing.

'I mean,' Hordilo went on, 'he killed one of the lord's golems.

Oh, and he wants to bring those two bodies with him up to the keep, because they're his friends. So, I don't know what he is, to be honest, but I'll allow that he ain't a fool. Lord Fangatooth, of course, might think otherwise, but it's not for me to speak for him on that account. Now, shall we go?'

'Hordilo—' began Spilgit.

'Yes,' Hordilo replied, 'you can take the manservant, before he freezes solid.'

Bauchelain turned to his manservant. 'Off with you, then, Mister Reese. We'll summon you later this evening.'

Hordilo grunted a laugh.

'All right, Master.' Mister Reese then glanced down at Grimled and looked over at Hordilo. 'So, how many of these things has your lord got, anyway?'

'Two more,' Hordilo replied. 'This one was Grimled. The others are Gorebelly and Grinbone.'

Mister Reese choked, coughed out smoke. 'Gods below, did the lord name them himself?'

'Lord Fangatooth Claw the Render is a great sorcerer,' said Hordilo.

'I'm sorry, Lord what?'

'Go on, Mister Reese,' ordered Bauchelain. 'We can discuss naming conventions at a later time, yes?'

'Conventions, Master? Oh. Of course, why not? All right, Slipgit—'

'That's Spilgit.'

'Sorry. Spilgit, lead me to this blessed inn, then.'

Hordilo watched them hurry off, his gaze fixing with genuine admiration on Felittle's swaying backside, and then he returned his attention to the two strangers, and raised his sword. 'Am I going to need this out, gentlemen? Or will you come along peacefully?'

'We are great believers in peace,' said Bauchelain. 'By all means, sheathe your sword, sir. We are looking forward to meeting your sorcerer lord, I assure you.'

Hordilo hesitated, and then, since he could no longer feel his fingers, he slid his sword back into its scabbard. 'Right. Follow me, and smartly now.'

Scribe Coingood watched Warmet Humble writhe in his chains. The chamber reeked of human waste, forcing Coingood to hold a scented handkerchief to his nose. But at least it was warm, with the huge three-legged bronze brazier sizzling and crackling and hissing and throwing up sparks every time his lord decided it was time to heat up the branding iron.

Weeping, spasms clawing their way through his broken body that hung so hapless from the chains, Warmet Humble was a sorry sight. This was what came of brotherly disputes that never saw resolution. Misunderstandings escalated, positions grew entrenched; argument fell away into deadly silence across the breakfast table, and before too long one of them ended up drugged and waking up in chains in a torture chamber. Coingood was relieved that he had been an only child, and the few times he'd ended up in chains was just his father teaching him a lesson about staying out after dark or cheating on his letters and numbers. In any case, if he'd had a brother, why, he'd never use a bhederin branding iron on him, which could brand a five year old from toe to head in a single go. Surely an ear-puncher would do; the kind the shepherds used on their goats and sheep.

Poor Warmet's face bore one end of the brand's mark, melted straight across the nose and both cheeks. Fangatooth had then angled it to sear first one ear and then the other. The horrid, red weal more or less divided Warmet's once-handsome face into an upper half and a lower half.

Brothers.

Humming under his breath, Fangatooth stirred the coals. 'The effect is lost,' he then said, lifting up the branding iron with both hands and a soft grunt and then frowning at the burning bits of flesh snagged on it, 'when it is scar tissue being scarred anew. Scribe! Feed my imagination, damn you!'

'Perhaps, milord, a return to something more delicate.'

Fangatooth glanced over. 'Delicate?'

'Exquisite, milord. Tiny and precise, but excruciatingly painful?'

'Oh, I like that notion. Go on!'

'Fingernails –'

'Done that. Are you blind?'

'They're growing back, milord. Tender and pink.'

'Hmm. What else?'

'Strips of skin?'

'He barely has any skin worthy of the name, Scribe. No, that would be pointless.'

Warmet ceased his weeping and lifted his head. 'I beg you, brother! No more! My mind is snapped, my body ruined. My future is one of terrible pain and torment. My past is memories of the same. My present is an ending howl of agony. I cannot sleep, I cannot rest my limbs – see how my head trembles in the effort to raise it? I beg you, Simplet—'

'That is no longer my name!' shrieked Fangatooth. He stabbed the branding iron into the coals. 'I will burn out your tongue for that!'

'Milord,' Coingood said, 'by your own rules, he must be able to speak, and see, and indeed, hear.'

'Oh, that! Well, I'm of a mind to change my mind! I can do that, can't I? Am I not the lord of this keep? Do I not command life and death over thousands?'

Well, hundreds, but why quibble? 'You do indeed, milord. The world quakes at your feet. The sky weeps, the wind screams, the seas thrash, the very ground beneath us groans.'

Fangatooth spun round to face Coingood. 'That's good, Scribe. That's very good. Write that down!'

'At once, milord.' Coingood collected up his tablet and bone graver. But the heat had melted the wax and he watched the letters fade even as he wrote. This was not a detail, he decided, worth sharing with his master. After all, there was another set of chains in this dungeon, and the wretched figure hanging from them was if anything even closer to death than poor Warmet Humble. A quick look in that direction revealed no motion from that forlorn victim.

Some strangers had arrived and proved too obnoxious to simply hang. For a time then, his lord had taken great pleasure in rushing from one prisoner to the other, and in a foul fug of burning flesh the screams had come from both sides of the chamber, along with spraying fluids that dried brown on the stone walls. But it could not last. Whatever uncanny will to live that was burning in Warmet's soul was evidently unmatched by that other victim in this dungeon. 'Done, milord.'

'Every word?'

'Every word, milord.'

'Very good. Now, take note of this, and in detail. Dear brother, your life is in my hands. I can kill you at any time. I can make you scream, and twist in pain. I can hurt you bad – no, wait. Scratch out that last one, Scribe. Twist in pain. Yes. In agony. Twisting agony. I can make you twist in twisting agony. No! Not that one, either. Give me some more, Scribe. What's wrong with you?'

Coingood thought frantically. 'You've covered it well, milord—'

'No! There must be more! Burn, pull, cut, impale, kick, slap. Slap? Yes, slap slap slap!' And Fangatooth walked up to his brother and began slapping him back and forth across the face. The man's head rocked to either side, sweat spraying from the few remaining clumps of hair on his pate. Fangatooth then kicked his brother's left shin, and then his right. Suddenly out of breath, he stepped back and swung round to Coingood. 'Did you see that?'

'I did, milord.'

'Write it down then! In detail!'

Coingood began scribbling again.

'And note my exultant pose, will you? This stance here, see how it exudes power? Somewhat wide-legged, as if I might jump in any direction. Arms held out but the hands hanging like . . . like the weapons of death that they are. Weapons of death, Scribe, you got that? Excellent. Now, look at me, I'm covered in blood. I need a change of clothes – wait, are you writing all that down? You damned fool. It was an aside, of course. That bit about my clothes. Tell me you've washed and dried my other black robe?'

'Of course, milord. Along with your other black vest, and your other black shirt and other black leggings.'

'Excellent. Now, clean up around here. I will meet you in the Grand Chamber.'

Coingood bowed. 'Very well, milord.'

After Fangatooth marched from the room, Coingood set down the tablet and studied it ruefully for a moment, noting how flecks of ash had marred the golden sheen of melted wax. 'No wonder my eyes are going,' he muttered.

'For the blessed gods of mercy, Coingood, release me!'

The scribe looked over at the wretched figure. 'Them slaps weren't so bad, were they? The kicks to the shins, well, that must've smarted. But you have to agree, sir, today's session was a mild one.'

'You're as evil as my brother!'

'Please, milord! I am in his service, and take my pay the same as the maids, cooks and all the rest! Does this make us all evil? Nonsense. What is evil, sir, is you inviting me to hardship and discomfort. I need to eat, don't I? Food on my table, a roof overhead and all that. Would you deny me such rights? In any case, how long would I survive defying your brother? Oh no, he wouldn't just fire me, would he? No, he'd *set* me on fire! Why, I'd be up in those chains, screaming myself hoarse. Do you really wish that on me, sir? All for a few moments of blessed freedom?'

Warmet's bleak eyes remained fixed on Coingood throughout the scribe's reasoned defence. Then he said, 'My flesh is in ruin. My soul cries out in unending torment. The joints of my arms rage with fever. The muscles of my neck tremble with this effort to hold up my head. I was once a hale man, but look at me now, and wait to see me tomorrow, when I will be even worse. So, you will not lift a hand. Then I curse you, Coingood, as only a dying man can.'

'That was cruel! Spiteful! I am not to blame! It is your brother who commands me!'

Warmet bared bloodstained teeth. 'And there we are indeed different – you and me, Coingood. Look at me and know this:

despite these chains, my soul remains free. But you . . . you have sold yours, and it came cheap.'

There was a moan from the direction of the other man hanging in chains, and both Warmet and Coingood looked over that way, to see the prisoner stirring, drawing his legs under him and then slowly, agonizingly, standing to relieve the weight of his chains. His terribly scarred face swung to them, and the man said, 'It's green and comes in all sizes, but that's all I'm giving you, Warmet.'

Warmet's sweat-beaded brow wrinkled above the red weal of burnt flesh. 'All right, give me a moment. Coingood's still here.'

'Green—'

'I'm having a conversation, damn you!'

'You're down to four questions, Warmet!' the man sang.

'Shut up! I'm not ready to start again!'

'Four questions!'

'Bah! Solid or liquid?'

'Both! Hee hee!'

Coingood collected up his tablet and hurried from the chamber.

'Wait, Scribe! Where are you going?'

'I can't!' Coingood cried out. 'Don't make me stay, milord!'

'You have gore, shit and piss to clean up – your master commanded it!'

Coingood halted almost within reach of the door's latch. 'Unfair!' he whispered, pushing the scented cloth against his nose. But Warmet spoke the truth, damn him. He swung round. 'Hot or cold?'

'You can't ask questions!' the other prisoner shrieked.

'Hot or cold?' Warmet shouted. 'That's my next question!'

'In between!'

Sighing, Coingood said, 'Snot.'

'Cheaters!'

'Snot?' Warmet asked. 'Is it snot? It's snot! Snot! I win!'

Feloovil Generous adjusted her breasts beneath the stained blouse and then sat down opposite the sailor with a heavy sigh. 'We don't get many strangers visiting,' she said, 'for long.'

The man shrugged, hands wrapped tight around the tankard of hot rum – a rather excessive amount of rum, but then he'd dropped a clean silver coin onto the tabletop before she'd even finished pouring it, so she wasn't of a mind to advise him on medicinal portions – the man was chilled down to the marrow in his bones. She could see that. 'Wreckers' lot,' he said in a low, unsympathetic rumble.

'Well now,' she replied, leaning back. 'No reason to be unkind and all. Let's start anew. I'm Feloovil Generous, and I own the King's Heel.'

'Happy for you,' the sailor replied. 'My name's Emancipor Reese. Not that you'll need to remember it, since we won't be here long. I hope.'

'As long as you got the coin,' she said, 'you'll be welcome in here, is what I'm saying.' She glanced over at Spilgit, who shared the table with the sailor, and scowled. 'Take heed of that, Factor, since you got rent owing and the winter ahead's long and cold.'

Spilgit leaned closer to Emancipor. 'That's why she calls herself Generous, you see.'

'Oh I'm generous enough,' she retorted, 'when it's appreciated. One thing I ain't generous about is some fool showing up calling himself a damned tax collector. We built this place up ourselves and we don't owe nobody nothing! Tell that to your prissy bosses, Spilgit!'

'I will, Feloovil, I will, and that's a promise!'

'You do just that!'

'I *will* do just that!'

'Go ahead, then!'

'I will!'

Ackle spoke from the window. 'What's he doing with those bodies?'

Only Emancipor did not turn at that, still hunched over his steaming tankard and breathing deep the heady fumes.

Feloovil grunted her way upright and walked over to the inn's door. She pushed it open a crack. Then quickly drew her head back and swung to Spilgit. 'That the one who killed the golem?'

'He was tearing out its insides when we come up,' Spilgit said.

'How did he kill it?'

'No idea, Feloovil, but he did it and without getting a scratch!'

She realized she was having a conversation with the tax collector and quickly looked away, edging the door open a little further to watch Hordilo leading his two prisoners up the street towards Wurm Road. Spilgit showing up with her sweet daughter had been enough to make Feloovil want to slit the man's throat right then and there. But that kind of public murdering was bad for business, and more than a few of her girls would be pretty upset with her and that was never good. Instead, she'd sent Felittle up to her room to await a proper hiding. For the moment, that little slut-in-waiting could stew for a while longer.

Ackle edged up beside her and she recoiled slightly at his smell. 'He's a bit too possessive for my liking,' he then said, squinting up the street. 'About those corpses, I mean.'

She pulled him back inside and shut the door against the cold. 'I told you, Risen, y'can sit at that one table since it's the smallest one here and out of the way of the others, and y'can keep my dogs happy, too, but you ain't a proper customer. So stop wandering around, will you? I swear I'll lock you out, Ackle, and leave you to freeze solid.'

'Sorry, Generous.' The man stumped back to his seat.

Thinking, Feloovil returned to Emancipor's table and sat down again across from him. 'Spilgit, go away,' she said. 'Find another table, or go upstairs and say hi to the girls.'

'You can't order— well, I suppose you can. All right, then, upstairs I go.'

She waited until she heard his steps on the creaking stairs, and then leaned forward. 'Listen, Emancipor Reese.'

He'd drunk half the rum and when he looked up his eyes were bleary. 'What?'

'Golems. They're sorcery, right? Powerful sorcery.'

'I suppose.'

'And Lord Fangatooth Claw's got three of 'em.'

The man snorted. 'Sorry, can't help it. Three, you said. Right. Two now, though.'

'Exactly,' she replied. 'That's my point, right there.'

He blinked at her. 'Sorry? What was your point? I somehow missed it.'

'Your masters – one of them went and killed one of those golems. That can't be easy, killing a heap of iron and whatnot.'

'I wouldn't know,' Emancipor said. 'But take it from me, Korbal Broach has killed worse.'

'Has he, now? That's interesting to hear. Very.'

'But mostly it's Bauchelain you should be worried about,' Emancipor went on, taking another deep mouthful of the rum.

'That the other one?'

'Aye. The other one.'

'Sorcerers?'

The man nodded. And then laughed again. 'Fangatooth!'

She shifted her considerable weight on the chair and tried leaning even closer, but her breasts got in the way. Cursing, she lifted one and thumped it down onto the tabletop. Then did the same with the other. Glancing up, she caught the look in Emancipor's eyes. 'Aye, lovely, ain't they? I'll introduce them to you later. Your masters, Emancipor Reese—'

'Mancy will do. Call me Mancy.'

'Better, less of a Hood-damned mouthful anyway. Mancy. They sorcerers?'

He nodded again.

'They're heading up to the keep, all on their own. Are they stupid?'

Emancipor lifted one wavering finger. 'Ah, now that's an interesting question. I mean, there's all kinds of stupid, izzn't there? Ever seen a ram butt its head against a rock? Why a rock? Why, 'cause there's no other ram around, thaz why. Your Fungletooth up there, been standing on that rock all this time, right? All on his lonesome.'

She studied him, and then slowly nodded. 'Ever since he imprisoned his brother, aye.'

Emancipor waved carelessly. 'Up there, then, maybe they'll all butt heads—'

'And if they do? Who comes out on top?'

'—and maybe they don't.'

'You're not getting it, Mancy. Butting heads sounds good. Butting heads sounds perfect. I like butting heads. You think it's fun living in fear?'

The man stared across at her, and then grinned. 'Beats dying laughing, Floovle.'

She rose. 'Let's get some hearty food in you. So you can sober up. We got more talking to do, you and me.'

'Do we?'

'Aye. Talking, and from talking we'll get to bargaining, and from bargaining we'll get to something else, something that'll make everyone happy. Sober up, Mancy. I got girls for you aplenty, and they're on the house.'

'Kind of you,' he replied, squinting up at her. 'But girls just make me feel old.'

'Better, 'cause then you got us.'

'Us?'

She hefted her tits. 'Us.'

From a few paces away, Ackle flinched back when Feloovil proffered the sailor her breasts. 'But then,' he whispered, 'if there's any good way to go . . .' He glanced across at the other patrons, regulars one and all, of course, and he supposed he was a regular now, too. Sort of. Funny how all the things he longed for in life just up and tumbled right into his lap now that he was dead.

But that was, in some ways, typical, wasn't it? Greatness was happiest with an ashen face, cloudy eyes and a demeanor unlikely to make any sudden unexpected moves. Even a mediocre man could climb into greatness by the simple act of dying. If he thought about history, these days, he saw in his mind's eye a whole row of great men and women, heroes and all that, and not one of them alive. No, instead they stood guard over great moments now long gone, and through it all stayed blind to whatever legacy their deeds left behind. It was selfish, in a way, but in a good way, too. Dying was a way to tell the world to just . . . *fuck off. Go fuck yourselves, you fucking fucks! Fuck off and fuck off forever and if you don't know what fucking forever is, take a look at us, you fuckers, we're fucking forever and we don't give a fuck about any of you, so just fuck . . . fuck . . . fuck off!*

He contemplated the possibility, in the wake of these thoughts, that he had some anger issues, which seemed pointless, all things considered. *It should hurt swallowing, shouldn't it? That rope didn't break my neck, well, maybe it did, who knows. Anyway, it was the choking that killed me. Suffocation, turning blue in the face, tongue poking out, eyes bulging. That kind of suffocation. So swallowing should hurt.*

Fuck, do I want to kill them all? Hmm, difficult question. Let's mull on it some . . .

It's not like I've got anything else to do.

Still, that big, fat man, dragging those corpses. That's troubling all right. For a man like me, I mean. Dead, but not dead enough.

Between a rope and a pair of giant tits, I know which I'd rather suffocate from, and I doubt I'm alone in my learned opinion here. I doubt it sincerely. Ask any man. Ask any woman, too, for that matter. We're all heroes, so why not go out like one?

I should be standing in that line, back there in history, with a big fucking smile on my fucking face. But it doesn't hurt to swallow. Why is that?

Fuck!

Red, the lizard cat, bewildered once again by vague, troubling memories of walking on two feet and wearing clothes, stared at the two figures sitting side by side on the bed. He owned one of them, the one with the soft belly and the soft things above it that he liked to lie across when she slept. The other one, with his hands that slithered and his smells of lust wafting from him in pungent, whisker-twitching clouds, he didn't like at all.

Among his memories was the even stranger notion that once, long ago, there were more of him. He'd been dangerous back then, capable of ganging up on and then dragging down and killing men who bellowed and then shrieked and screamed that they wanted their eyes back, until jaws closed around the poor fool's throat and ripped and tore until it was all bloody and in shreds, with air bubbles frothing out and spurts that came in quick succession only to slow down, and finally fade into trickles. That was when he would feed, every one of him growing fat and torpid and eyeing places to lie up for a day or two.

Red wanted to kill the man on the bed.

What made things all the more infuriating, the lizard cat understood everything these two-legged creatures said, but his own fang-filled mouth ever failed to speak, and from his throat came nothing but incomprehensible purrs, hisses, moans and wavering wails.

Lying atop the dresser, Red was silent for the moment, eyes unblinking and fixed on the man's throat. Every now and then his thin, scaled tail twitched and curled.

The pink-throated man with the slithering hands was speaking. '. . . not thinking clearly, that's for sure. Hah hah! But there's no telling how long it'll last, Felittle.'

'You can always hear her on the stairs, silly. Besides, we're not doing nothing, are we?'

'I shouldn't be in here. She's forbidden it.'

'When I live in Elin, in that city, where you're taking me, there won't be nobody to tell me I can't have men in my room. So I will! Lots and lots of men, you'll see.'

'Well, of course you will, darling,' the man replied, with a tight smile that made Red's scales crackle down the length of his serrated back. 'But then, you know, you might not want that.'

'What do you mean?'

'One man might be enough for you, is what I'm saying, my love.'

Felittle was blinking rapidly, her carmine lips parted in the way that always made Red want to slide his head between them, to look into the cavern of her mouth. Of course, his head was too big for that, but still, he longed to try. 'One man? But . . . no woman wants just one man! No matter how much he pays! Where's the . . . the . . . variety? One man!' She yelped a laugh at her companion and punched him on the shoulder.

Such gestures were appallingly useless, with the nails folded in like that. Far better, Red knew, if those short claws lashed out, slicing that shoulder to ribbons. There was no doubt in the lizard cat's mind that she needed proper protection, the kind of protection that Red could give. He rose slowly, affecting indifference, and lazily stretched out his back.

But the man noticed and his eyes narrowed. 'Your damned cat's getting ready again. I swear, Felittle, when we go it's not coming with us. If it attacks me again, I'll punch it again, hard as I can.'

'Oh, you're cruel!' cried Felittle, jumping from the bed and hurrying over to take Red into her arms. Over her shoulder, the lizard cat met the man's eyes and something passed between them that both instinctively understood.

By the time the flying scales and bits of flesh settled, one of them would stand triumphant. One of them, and only one, would possess this soft creature with the wide eyes. Red snuggled tighter and stretched open his mouth in a yawn, showing his rival his fangs. *See them, man-named-Spilgit?*

The display stole all colour from the man's face and he quickly looked away.

She snuggled Red closer. 'My baby, ooh, my baby, it's all right. I won't let the big man hurt you again. I promise.'

'It can't come with us,' the man said.

'Of course he will!'

'Then you'd better forget about having lots of men in your room, Felittle. Unless you want them all sliced up and enraged and liable to take it out on the both of you.'

Cooing, she slipped her hand to the back of Red's round head and held him so that she could peer into his face, only whiskers apart. 'You'll get used to them, won't you, sweetie?'

Used to them? Yes. Used to killing them. Bellows, shrieks, screams about the eyes and then gurgles. But this elaborate and detailed answer came out as a low purr and a snuffle. Red exposed his claws and batted one paw in the man's direction.

At that he grunted and stood. 'The problem with lizard cats,' he said, 'is that they kill the furry kind. Angry neighbours are never good, Felittle. In Elin, why, someone will strangle this thing before the first week's out.'

'Oh, you're horrible! Not my Red!'

'If you want him to live for, er, however many years lizard cats live, you should leave him here. That's the best way of showing your love for Red.'

No, the best way is tying you up and leaving you on the floor while she goes down for supper. I don't need long.

'Then maybe I won't go! Oh, Red, I so love your purring.'

'You don't mean that.'

'Oh, I don't know anymore! I'm confused!'

During this, Red had been gathering his limbs under him, moving slowly up onto her shoulder. Without warning, he launched himself at the man's face.

A fist collided with Red's nose, and then he was flying sideways, into the wall. Stunned, he fell to the floor beside the dresser. Something buzzed in his skull and he tasted blood. As if from a great distance, Red heard the man say, 'You know, if that thing had any brains to speak of, it would try something different for a change.'

Red felt hands slip under him and then he was lifted into the air, back into her arms. 'Oh, you poor thing! Was Slippy mean to you again? Oh, he's so mean, isn't he?'

Something different? Now there's an idea. I need to remember this. I need to . . . oh, she's so soft, isn't she? Soft here, and soft here, too, and . . .

Whuffine Gaggs hummed under his breath as he pulled the silver ring from the severed finger and then tossed the finger into the spume-laden surf. It rolled back onto the sands with the next wave, as if trying to make a point, and then joined the others, jostling like sausages in a mostly even row above the fringe. A brief glance at them made his stomach rumble. Sighing, he squinted at the ring, which was thin but bore runic sigils running all the way round its surface. He saw the mark of the Elder God of the Seas, Mael, but little good that prayer had done the poor fool. Glancing down at the now-naked corpse at his feet, he studied her fleshy form for a moment longer, before shaking himself and with a muttered curse turned away.

A sharp grating sound made him look up to see a battered boat grounding prow-first against the wrack twenty paces up the beach. It looked abandoned, its oar-locks empty and the gunnels mostly chewed away, as if subject to frenzied jaws. Waves thumped into its stern, foamed over its square splashboard.

Grunting, Whuffine made his way over. As he drew near, cavalry boots crunching smartly in the sand with the jab of the walking stick making sweet punching sounds, he saw a man's head rise into view, and then a bandaged hand lifted in a frail wave. The face was deathly pale, except where a burn had taken away half the beard. Rimed in salt, the man could have crawled out from a pickling barrel.

'Ho there!' cried Whuffine, quickly pocketing the ring as he hurried closer. 'Another survivor, thank Mael!' His free hand slipped beneath the sheepskins and deftly palmed the knife.

Red-rimmed eyes fixed on him, and then the man straightened. A short sword was belted to his waist, and he now settled a hand on it. 'Back off, wrecker!' he said in a snarl, using the sea-trader's cant. 'I ain't in the mood!'

Whuffine halted. 'You look done in, sir! That's my shack up on the trail. Nice and warm, and I have food and drink.'

'Do you now?' The man suddenly smiled, but it wasn't a pleasant smile. He looked down and seemed to nudge something with one foot. 'Up, my love, we found us a friend.'

A dark-skinned, mostly naked woman rose into view. Her left breast, brazenly exposed to the chill wintry air, was white as snow, but this absence of hue was uneven, its edges like splashes of paint. The look she settled upon Whuffine was full of suspicion. Moments later a third figure stirred upright in the boat. Blood-stained bandages covered most of his face, leaving only one eye clear, along with the lower jaw. 'Thath's a wrecker all right,' this man said, pausing to split and then lick his lips with a forked tongue. 'I bet thath thack of hith ith a damned gallery of murder and worth, and crowded with loot bethideth.'

'Just my point, Gust,' said the first man. 'We could do with some new gear, and stuff to sell, too.' He then clambered over the side and stood on the sand. 'Brisk, ain't it?' he said to Whuffine. 'But it ain't no Stratem winter, is it?' He then drew his sword. 'Put the knife away, fool, and lead us up to the shack.'

Whuffine eyed the weapon, noting the savage nicks along both edges. 'I'm not going to take kindly to being robbed, and since the only town for leagues in any direction is just up the trail, where I have lots of friends, and where the Lord of the Keep is stickler about law and order, you'd be making a terrible mistake doing me harm, or cleaning me out.'

The one-eyed man loosed a laugh verging on hysteria. 'Lithen to him, Heck, he'th threatening uth! Hah hah hah! Ooh, I'm thcared! Hah hah!'

'Stop that, Gust,' snapped the woman. 'The point is, we gotta get going. Those Chanters ain't all dead, you know, and I bet they'll want their lifeboat back—'

'Too late!' shrieked the man named Gust.

'They went down, Birds,' said Heck. 'They must've! There was fire and screamin' dead men and demons and Korbal Broach and the sharks – gods the sharks! All with Mael's own storm crashing down on us! Nobody survived that!'

'We did,' Birds reminded him.

Heck licked his lips, and then shook himself. 'It don't matter, love.' He rubbed at his face, wincing when his fingers touched the weal of the burn. 'Let's go and get warm. We can plan over a meal and a keg of ale. The point is, we're on dry land again, and I don't mean to ever go back to sea. You, wrecker, where in Hood's name are we?'

'Elingarth,' Whuffine replied.

'Nothing but pirates,' hissed Birds, 'the whole lot of them. Who's up in that keep, then? Slormo the Sly? Kabber the Slaughterer? Blue Grin the Wifestealer?'

Whuffine shook his head. 'Never heard of those,' he said.

'Of courth you didn't,' said Gust. 'They all been dead a hundred yearth! Birdth, thothe thailor taleth were old when you were thtill farming clamth with your Da.' He waved a bandaged hand. 'We don't care who'th up at the keep, anyway. It'th not like we're getting an invite to dine, ith it? With the lord, I mean.'

'Oh,' said Whuffine, brightening, 'I expect the lord will indeed invite you into his keep. In fact, I'm sure of it. Why, he's already entertaining your companions—'

'Our what?' Birds asked.

'Why, the elderly nobleman with the pointy beard, and his manservant—' He stopped then as Heck was clambering back into the boat.

'Push us off!' he screamed.

'Excuse me?'

But all three were scrabbling back and forth in the boat, as if by panic alone they could make the craft move.

'Push us off!' shrieked Heck.

Whuffine shrugged, walked over to the prow and set his shoulder against it. 'I don't understand,' he said between grunts. 'You've been saved, spared by the storm, good people. Why risk another, and you so unprepared for any sort of sea voyage—'

The tip of Heck's shortsword pressed up against Whuffine's neck, and the man leaned close. 'Listen to me if you value your life! Get us off this cursed beach!'

Whuffine gaped, swallowed delicately, and then said, 'You'll all have to climb out and help, I'm afraid. You're too heavy. But I beg you all, don't do this! You'll die out there!'

The bandaged man laughed again, this time in the jabbering grip of hysteria. The other two scrambled from the boat and began tugging and pulling and pushing, feet digging deep furrows in the wet sand. Whuffine resumed his efforts and together they managed to dislodge the craft. Heck and Birds leapt back in and Whuffine, wincing at what the salt water would do to his boots, edged out into the waves and gave the boat a final shove. 'But you have no oars!'

Hands paddled furiously.

The surf battled against their efforts, but after some time the boat was clear of the worst of the swells, and at last making headway out to sea.

Whuffine stared after them for a time, confused and more than a little alarmed. Then he returned to the corpses on the strand, and cutting off fingers and whatnot.

The sea was a strange realm, and the things it offered up on occasion passed comprehension, no matter how wise the witness. There was no point, Whuffine knew, in questioning such things. Ugly as fate, the world did what it did and never asked permission either.

He moved to the next body and began stripping the clothes away, eyes darting in search of jewellery, coin-pouches or anything else of value. Like his father used to say, the sea was like a drunk's mouth: there was no telling what might come out of it. Or go back in.

Hordilo Stinq made a fist and pounded on the thick wooden door. He was slightly out of breath from the climb, but the effort had warmed him up some. As they waited, alas, he could feel the cold seeping back in. 'Normally it's not a long wait,' he said. 'Lord Fangatooth has sleepless servants, ever watching from those dark slits up there.'

The man named Bauchelain was studying the massive wall rearing up to either side of the gatehouse. The remnants of a few corpses still remained, hanging from the hooks they had been impaled on. The heads, still bearing tufts of weathered hair and a few sections of dried skin, were all tilted at unnatural angles and the effect, from directly below where stood Hordilo, was that of being looked down upon, with toothy smiles and empty eye sockets. At the foot of the wall more bones were jumbled in disordered heaps.

'This keep is very old indeed,' Bauchelain then said. 'It reminds me of the one I was born in, to be honest, and I find this curious detail most enticing.' He turned to his companion. 'What think you, Korbal my friend? Shall we abide here for a time?'

But Korbal Broach was stripping down the two corpses he'd

dragged all the way from the beach, flinging the sodden, half-frozen garments aside and prodding exposed, pallid flesh with a thick finger. 'Will they keep, Bauchelain?' he asked.

'In this cold, I should imagine so.'

'I will leave them here for now,' Korbal replied, straightening. He walked up to the heavy door and closed his hand on the latch.

'It's locked, of course,' said Hordilo. 'We must await the lord's pleasure.'

But the huge man twisted until the iron bent, and then there was a muted snapping sound from the door's other side, followed by something striking the floor. Korbal Broach pushed the door open and strode inside.

Appalled, Hordilo rushed after the man. They crossed the broad, shallow cloakroom and emerged into the main hall before Hordilo was able to interpose himself in the man's path. 'Have you lost your mind?' he demanded in a hoarse whisper.

Korbal Broach swung round to Bauchelain. 'He is in my way,' he said. 'Why is he in my way?'

'I would expect,' Bauchelain replied, stepping past and adjusting his cloak momentarily, 'that this constable serves his lord from a place of bone-deep fear. Terror, even. I for one find the relationship between a master and his or her minions to be ever problematical. Terror, after all, stultifies the higher processes of the intellect. Independent judgement suffers. As a consequence, our escort finds his position most awkward, and now fears his potential demise as a result.'

'I have decided that I don't like him, Bauchelain.'

'I am reminded of Mister Reese, on his first day in our employ, as he stood belligerent against an intruder in defence of our privacy. See this man before you, Korbal, as a victim of panic. Of course you may kill him if you wish, but then, who would make introductions?'

Heavy footsteps were drawing nearer, each plod rumbling like thunder through the stone tiles of the floor.

'A golem approaches!' gasped Hordilo. 'Now you've done it!'

'Do step aside, sir,' Bauchelain advised. 'It may be that we are forced to defend ourselves.'

Eyes wide, Hordilo backed to the wall beside the entranceway. 'This has nothing to do with me! Not anymore!'

'Wise decision, sir,' murmured Bauchelain, sweeping clear his cloak to reveal a heavy black chain surcoat and a longsword strapped to his belt, the bone handle vanishing inside a gauntleted grasp as the man readied to draw free the weapon.

His companion now faced towards the sound of the approaching footsteps.

They were all startled by a voice from the other side of the chamber. 'Hordilo! What in Hood's name is going on? Go close that damned door! It's chilly enough in here without the added draught!'

'Scribe Coingood!' Hordilo gasped in relief. 'I arrested these men – that one there killed Grimled! And then he broke the lock on the door and then he—'

'Be quiet!' Coingood snapped, setting down the bucket he carried and then leaning his mop against a wall. Brushing his hands, he strode forward. 'Guests, is it?'

'They killed Grimled!'

'So you say, Hordilo, so you say. How unfortunate.'

'I would certainly describe it in just that manner,' Bauchelain said. 'And I trust, good sir, that your master will not hold it against us.'

'Well, as it took him five months to animate the thing, I expect he'll be somewhat upset,' Coingood replied.

At that moment the golem arrived. By the rust rimming its pail-shaped head Hordilo knew it to be Gorebelly. Hinges squealing, the abomination thumped to a halt and slowly raised its halberd.

Impossibly, Korbal Broach was suddenly standing in front of it, plucking the heavy weapon effortlessly from the golem's iron hands and flinging it aside. He then reached up and twisted off Gorebelly's head. Fluids gushed from the gaping throat. The headless apparition staggered back a step, and then toppled. Its impact on the floor shattered tiles.

Still clutching the dripping iron bucket, Korbal turned to face them, a deep frown lining his brow. 'It broke,' he said.

'See!' Hordilo shrieked, rushing towards Coingood. 'That's what he does!'

The scribe was very pale. Licking dry lips, he cleared his throat and said, 'Ah, well. I had best summon my master, I think.'

'Sound judgement,' said Bauchelain.

'I'll go with you!' Hordilo said.

'No. Stay here, Sergeant. I won't be but a moment, I assure you.'

'You can't leave me with them!'

Sighing, Coingood turned to Bauchelain. 'I trust you can constrain your companion, sir, and so assure the sergeant here that no one will tear off his head or anything.'

'Ah, we are ever eager for assurances, it's true,' Bauchelain replied. 'Only to invariably discover that the world cares nothing for such things. That said, I am confident that the sergeant will get to keep his head for a while longer.'

Hordilo stepped close to Coingood. 'Please, don't leave me alone with them!'

'We'll be right back. Show some courage here, damn you!'

Hordilo watched the scribe hurry off. Although they were now inside the keep, still he shivered. Setting his back against a wall, he eyed the two men opposite. Korbal Broach had upended the golem's iron head and was shaking out the last few rattling bits left inside it. Bauchelain was removing his gauntlets one finger at a time.

'Dear sergeant,' the tall man then said. 'About your lord . . .'

Hordilo shook his head. 'That won't work.'

Brows rising, Bauchelain shrugged. 'Simple curiosity on my part, nothing more.'

'I've done my part and that's all I'm doing.'

'Of course. But now . . . do you regret it?'

'The only one regretting anything will be you two. Lord Fangatooth Claw is also known as The Render, and it's a title well earned!'

'Surely it should be "The Renderer"?'

48

'What?'

Sounds from the corridor drew their attention. Korbal Broach dropped the golem's iron head and the clang echoed shrilly in the chamber.

Moments later Coingood appeared and a step behind him was Lord Fangatooth.

Hordilo saw his master's eyes fix on the decapitated golem lying on the broken tiles. His expression revealed nothing.

'Korbal, my friend,' said Bauchelain, 'I believe you owe the lord an apology for your mishandling of his golems.'

'Sorry,' Korbal said, his flabby lips strangely stained by the fluids from the golem, as if he had but moments earlier licked his fingers.

'Yes, well,' said Fangatooth. 'Their sole purpose, of course, was to instil fear in the villagers. Now, as I understand it, but one remains. I see a busy winter ahead.' He swept his black cloak back from his shoulders. 'I am Lord Fangatooth Claw, Master of the Forgotten Holding, High Sorcerer of the Lost Gods of Ilfur, Seneschal of Grey Arts, High Mage of Elder Thelakan and last surviving member of the League of Eternal Allies.' He paused, and then said, 'I understand that you are survivors of an unfortunate shipwreck.'

'We are,' replied Bauchelain. 'This is a fine keep, sir, in which every chill draught evokes nostalgia. As a child I once haunted an edifice quite similar to this one. This has the feel of a homecoming.'

'I am pleased,' Fangatooth replied with a tight smile. He then turned to Coingood. 'Scribe, be sure the best rooms are prepared for our guests. Furthermore, you will attend our supper this evening with all the wax tablets at your disposal, for I anticipate a lively discourse.'

'Our manservant,' said Bauchelain, 'is presently recovering from his ordeals at a tavern in the village.'

'Sergeant Hordilo will collect him,' Fangatooth said. 'Although I assure you, my own staff can see to all of your needs.'

'Of that I have no doubt, sir, but I am partial to Mister Reese.'

'Understood. Now, by what titles are you two known?'

'Such titles as we may have accrued in our travels,' said Bauchelain, 'are both crass and often the product of misunderstanding. Our names should suffice. I am Bauchelain and my companion is Korbal Broach.'

'Yet of noble blood, I presume?'

'Most noble, sir, most noble. But we have travelled far—'

'In the company of misfortune, it seems,' cut in Fangatooth, finally showing his teeth in the smile he offered his guests.

Bauchelain waved one pale, long-fingered hand. 'If the past pursues, it is leagues in our wake. While the future holds only promise, and should that promise be nothing more than one foot following the other, pray it continues without end.'

Fangatooth frowned, and then he said, 'Yes, just so. Please, my dear guests, shall we retire to the sitting room? A fire burns in the hearth and mulled wine awaits us, in keeping with the season. Scribe? I trust you have recorded this momentous . . . moment?'

'I have indeed, milord.'

'Excellent!'

'I wonder, good sir,' ventured Bauchelain, 'if this keep has a spacious kitchen?'

'It has. Why do you ask?'

'As I said earlier. Nostalgia. It was in the kitchen where I skulked the most as a child, and where, indeed, I learned the art of baking.'

'Baking? How curious.'

'I would be delighted with a tour later.'

'I don't see why not.'

Bauchelain smiled.

'What wuz I drinking?' Emancipor asked, as the room tilted back and forth, as if he still stood on a deck, amidst rolling swells. The walls bowed in sickly rhythm, the floor lifting and falling beneath him.

'Rum,' said Feloovil. 'You're celebrating.'

'I am? What's happened, then, for to be celerbating. Brating. Celeb . . . rating.'

'The death of Lord Fangatooth Claw, of course.'

'He's dead?'

'About to be.'

'Is he sick, then?'

She scowled. 'Listen, sober up, will you? You got half a pot of stew in you, damn me, and that wasn't for free neither.'

'I'm sober enough. It's you who ain't making any sense.'

'They're up there, right? In the keep. All together, the three of them. Blood will spill, and who will be left standing when it's all done? You told me—'

'Oh, that.' Emancipor spread his legs wider to keep his balance. Feloovil swayed before him.

'They'll kill him, won't they?'

'Probbly.'

She smiled. 'That's what I like to hear, friend. Oh yes, and for that, why, it's time for your reward.'

'It's my birthday,' said Emancipor.

'It is?'

'Must be. Celerbating, rewards, but then, how do you know it's my birthday? I don't even know what day this is, or month for that matter.' He shook his head. 'You probbly got it wrong, which is typical, since everyone does. Or they forget. Like me. Is there any more rum? I'm not warmed up yet.'

'Let me warm you up,' Feloovil said, stepping closer. 'Here, grab these. No, one for each hand. No, you keep missing. How can you miss these?'

'They won't sit still, that's why.'

'I named them, you know.'

'You did? Why?'

'Now that's my secret, only you're about to find out. Just you. Only you. It was a gift, you see. From Witch Hurl, who ruled here years back—'

'What happened to her?'

'No one knows. She just vanished one night. But that don't matter, Mancy. It's what she gave me. She had this statue, right? Very old. Some earth goddess or someone. She took all her power from it, for her magicks. In any case, whoever carved that statue could've been using me as a model, if you know what I mean.'

'I thought you said it was old. How old are you, then?'

She scowled. 'No, it wasn't me. But it could've been. Especially my friends here – no, don't look around, you idiot. The tits you're holding. This one here, her name's Stout, on account of her staying firm the way she does. And the other one's Sidelopp, on account of . . . well.'

'You've named your tits?'

'Why not? They're my friends.'

'As in . . . bosom companions?'

Her eyes thinned. 'Oh,' she said, 'I never thought of that one before. Thanks. Now, let go of them so I can get this tunic off, so you can see what she did to them. To make them just like the statue's tits.'

'I thought you said they already were.'

'Almost, but now, aye, they are, Mancy.'

He watched while she turned her back, as if suddenly succumbing to modesty, and shrugged and tugged her way out of the heavy, stained tunic. Then she turned around.

Her breasts had no nipples. Instead, in place of them, were mouths, with soft, feminine lips painted bright red. As he stared, both tits blew him a kiss.

'They got teeth, too,' Feloovil said. 'And tongues. But they can't talk, which is probably a good thing. I think it's a good thing, at least. Watch while I make them lick their lips.'

Emancipor spun round, staggered to the nearest corner of the room and threw up.

'Hey!' Feloovil shouted behind him. 'That was half a pot of my best stew, damn you!'

Spilgit leaned away from the wall. 'She yelled something,' he whispered. 'And then started berating him. Something about thinking he was a man of the world, only he isn't. And then there were footsteps and someone trying to get out of the room.'

'Only Ma's locked it,' Felittle said. 'He can't get out.'

Spilgit frowned across at her. 'She's done this before? What's she doing to him? She locks men in her room? Why do they want to get out? Well, I mean, I would, but then I'd never go into her room in the first place. But he did, so he knew what was coming, more or less, didn't he? But I swear I heard him gag, or something. It sounded like a gag – wait, is she strangling him or something? Does she kill them, Felittle? Is your mother a mass murderer?'

'How should I know?' she demanded from where she sat on the bed, her lizard cat sprawled across her thighs, the creature watching Spilgit with unblinking, yellow eyes. 'Maybe I've seen her bury a body or two, out back. But that happens. It's an inn, after all, with people in beds and old men trying to die smiling, and all that.'

'She's buried people out back?'

'Well, dead ones, of course. Not like Ackle.'

'Ackle wasn't dead.'

'Yes he was.'

'Not a chance. The noose strangled him bad, that's true, and probably killed bits of his brain, which was why he looked dead to everyone. But he wasn't, and that's why he came back. Gods below, I can't believe the superstitions you have here in this wretched backwater. No, you've not treated him well since then, have you? It's a disgrace.'

Felittle blinked at him. 'Backwater? Are you calling Spendrugle, where I was born, a backwater? So what am I, then? A backwaterian? Is that what I am to you, Mister Big Smelly City?'

Spilgit hurried over, recoiling at the last moment from Red's savage hiss and raised hackles. 'Darling, of course not. Every dung heap has a hidden gem, and you're it. I mean, if I didn't find you lovely and all, would I offer to help you escape? And,' he went on, still trying to get closer but Red was now on its feet, dorsal spines arching and ears flattened and mouth opened wide, 'if you didn't think this was a backwater you wouldn't want to get away, would you?'

'Who says I want to get away?'

'You do! Don't you remember, my sweet?'

'It was you who wanted to steal me away, and I listened and all, and so you convinced me. But maybe I like it here, and once Ma lets me start working with the other girls, I'll—'

'But she won't, Felittle,' Spilgit said, looking for something he could use as a weapon on the cat. 'That's just it. She'll never let you do that. She'll see you stay a virgin, a spinster, all your life. You know it, too.' He found a brass candlestick on the dresser and collected it up.

'But then you said you weren't going to let me have lots of men in the city, so what's the point of me going with you anywhere? You'll end up just like Ma, chaining me in some cellar! What are you doing with that?'

He advanced on her, hefting the candlestick. 'Is that how you really want it? You want me to hire you out for the night, to who-ever's got the coin?'

'Oh, will you? Yes, please! What are you doing with that candlestick?' she backed up on the bed. 'How many bodies have you buried behind the tax office, that's what I'm wondering now!'

'Don't be silly. Tax collectors want people to live forever, of course. Getting older and older, so we can strip from them every single hard-won coin.'

'Put that thing down!'

'Oh, I'll put something down all right. Count on it.' He raised the candlestick.

Red leapt at his face.

He swung with all his strength.

Emancipor Reese clawed fruitlessly at the lock on the door. Behind him, Feloovil laughed a deep, throaty laugh. 'It's no use, Mancy, we've got you for the night, and when I say we're going to cover your body in kisses, I do mean it, don't I? Kisses and bites and nips and—'

'Open this damned door!' Emancipor snarled, spinning round and reaching for his sword.

But Feloovil had raised one hand. 'Shh! Listen! I hear voices in my daughter's room! Voices! Gods below, it's Spilgit!' She collected up her tunic from the floor and began pulling it on. 'That's it, he's a dead man for this. And I'm calling in his tab, too. Can't pay, can't leave, ever. Can't pay, it's the backyard for you!'

Edging away from the door as Feloovil produced a key from somewhere beneath her tunic, Emancipor drew his shortsword. 'Good, open it, aye. Before things get ugly here.'

'Ugly?' She barked a laugh. 'You're about to see ugly, Mancy, like no ugly you've ever seen in that miserable, sheltered existence you call a life.' She unlocked the door.

They were startled by a loud thump on the wall, followed by broken plaster striking the floor beside Feloovil's bed.

Something had come through the wall, halfway to the ceiling. As the dust cloud cleared, Emancipor saw a lizard cat's head, its nose draining blood, its eyes blinking but not synchronously. It seemed to be winking at them.

With Feloovil standing motionless, staring at the cat's head, Emancipor made his move, pushing hard to get past her and into the corridor. Without a look back, he rushed for the stairs. Behind him he heard Feloovil bellow, and someone else was now screaming. Reaching the stairs, Emancipor plunged downward – and coming fast behind him was another set of footsteps. Growling a curse, Emancipor looked back over one shoulder. But it was Spilgit who was on his way down, with Feloovil thundering after him.

Reaching the ground floor, Emancipor ran down the length of the bar to the door.

It opened then, revealing Hordilo, who pointed a finger at Emancipor and said, 'You!'

Despite the bitter cold, the half-frozen sand Whuffine turned over with his shovel stank of urine. He'd already excavated a decent hole, and had begun to wonder if his memory had failed him, when his shovel struck something hard. Redoubling his efforts, he quickly worked the object loose, and lifted into view a pitted and suitably stained stone idol. Grunting, he heaved it out of the pit and set it down on the sand for a closer look.

It had been a few years since he'd buried the thing beneath his piss trench, but the chisel work now looked centuries old. Come the spring, after the winter's hard weathering, he could load it onto his cart and take it into the village. If anything, this one was better than the last effort, and hadn't Witch Hurl paid a bagful of silver coins for that one? For all he knew, Fangatooth might be just as happy to kneel in worship before an idol from the Ancient Times.

The creation of true art had a way of serendipity, and if he hadn't snapped off a nipple on the final touches with the last one, he'd never have found the need to rework it into a mouth instead, and then do the same to the other nipple, inventing a whole new goddess of earth, sex, milk and whatever. This time, he had elaborated on the theme, adding a third mouth, down below.

Hearing more voices from the beach, he climbed out of the stinking pit and brushed gritty sand from his hands.

The boat was back, and this time the three sailors were piling out to scrabble their way up towards the trail, the bandaged one limping and already falling behind the others.

Collecting his shovel, Whuffine awaited them.

'Come to your senses, did you? No wonder. There's another blow coming in . . .'

But the three simply swept past, gasping, moaning and whimpering as they hurried up the trail. Whuffine stared after them, frowning. 'I've got warm broth!' he shouted, to no effect. Shrugging, he set down the shovel again and collected up the idol. He'd walk it down to the water, off to the left of the sands where the rocks made ragged spines reaching out into the bay. Lodged amidst those rocks, the idol would sit, gnawed by salt and cold and hard waves day and night for the next few months.

Whuffine was halfway to the spines when he saw the other boat, coming in fast.

Gasping in pain, Spilgit limped up the street. If Feloovil hadn't stumbled at the last moment, that knife would have found his back instead of his right calf. Shivering with shock, he approached his office. It took a strange person to decide to become a tax collector, and over the past month he had come to the conclusion that maybe he wasn't cut out for it.

He thought back to his days in Elin, when he was first apprenticed to the trade. Taxation in a city ruled by pirates was a bold notion, to be sure, and its practice was a vicious affair. They'd all trained in weapons and the detection of poison, and a few of his fellow apprentices had indeed plunged into the grey arts. On one day each year, the day that taxes were due, not even the Enclave bodyguards attached to each and every collector could be trusted. Spilgit's final year in the city had seen almost sixty per cent losses in the Guild, and more than one chest of tax revenue disappeared in the chaos.

He'd thought this distant posting would be a welcome escape from the horrors of Elin's Day of Blood and Taxes. He'd displayed few of the necessary talents to imagine a long and prosperous life in Elin as a tax collector. He wasn't coldhearted enough. He lacked the essential knot of cruelty in his soul, the small-minded descent into arbitrary necessities upon which collectors founded their arguments justifying blatant theft and the bullying and threats essential to successful extortion. Instead, he had revealed a soft ear for sob stories, for terrible tragedies and sudden house fires and mysterious burglaries and missing coin. He wept for the limping man tottering on his stick, for the snotty runts clinging to a destitute mother smelling of wine and sour milk, for the wealthy landowner swearing that he had not a single coin in his purse.

The worst of it was, he had actually believed that the taxes he collected went to answering worthy needs, and all the necessities of governance and the maintenance of law and order, when in truth most of it filled the war-chests of gouty nobles whose only talent was hoarding.

No, this journey into the empty wastelands out here in the realm's dubious borderlands had taught him much, about himself, and about the world in general. Feloovil's attempted murder would go unpunished. She offered too essential a service in Spendrugle. He, Spilgit, was the unwanted man.

Pushing open the door to his office, he staggered inside and made his way to the lone chair. The wood-stove still emanated remnants of heat and he fed more scraps of driftwood onto the coals. *But that was all before today. I'm not the same man I used to be. I'm not soft anymore. I am now capable of murder, and when I return to Elin, with that idiotic lovely cow in tow, why, I will sell her and feel not a single qualm, since she'll be blissfully happy.*

And I will be a tax collector. With iron for eyes, a mouth thinned to a dagger's edge, straight and disinclined to warp into anything resembling a genuine smile. No, this upturn of this here mouth, it signals the delightful pleasure of evil.

Evil: the way it flows out from the deed, the way it spreads its stain of injustice. Evil: smelling of sweet lies and bitter truths. We own the tax laws. We know every way around them, meaning we never pay up a single sliver of tin, but you do, oh yes, you do.

He struggled to wrap a cloth around his wounded calf, cursing his numbed fingers. At least, he consoled himself, he had killed the cat. There was no way it could have survived, despite its twitching body, or the way it sank its claws into the wall, spread-eagled as it tried to pull its head free, tail curling like a wood shaving to the flicker of flame. Oh, who was he kidding? The damned thing still lived.

And if the roads fall into ruin, and the city guards starve without their bribes; and people live on the streets and need to sell their children to make ends meet. And if the judges are all bought off and the jailers sport gold rings, and everything that was once free now costs, why, that's just how it is, and which side of the wall do I want to be standing on?

He understood things now. He saw with utter clarity. The world was falling into ruin, but then it was always falling into ruin. Once that was comprehended, why, the evil of every moment – this entire endless realm of *now* – made perfect sense. He would join the others, all those bloated greed merchants, and ride the venal present, and to Hood with the future, and to Hood with the past. The Lord of Death awaited them all in the end anyway.

The door scraped open and Spilgit bleated, reaching for his knife.

'It's just me,' said Ackle, peering in.

'Gods below!'

'Can I join you? I brought some wood.'

Spilgit waved him in. 'Try and close that behind you. Funny you should drop by, Ackle. It occurs to me that we have something in common.'

'Aye, we're both dead men.'

Spilgit sighed, and then rubbed at his face. 'If we stay in Spendrugle all winter, we are.'

'Well, I could stay around. Unless I freeze solid. Then Hordilo will burn me in a pyre and I saw the look in his eyes when he said that. It's all down to Feloovil being nice to me, and that's why I'm here, in fact.'

'What do you mean?'

'I mean, all is forgiven. And if that's not enough, why, Feloovil has decided to wipe clean your tab. And you still have your room.'

Spilgit studied the man levelly. 'You should be ashamed of yourself, Ackle.'

'The dead are beyond shame, Spilgit. That said, I admit to some qualms, but like I said, I need somewhere warm for the winter.'

'She actually expects me to go back to the Heel with you? Arm in arm?'

'Well, it's hard to say, honestly. She is a bit beside herself at the moment. Poor Felittle is distraught, with what you did to her.'

'I didn't do anything to her! The cat attacked me and I defended myself.'

'Then it went and attacked Feloovil, too, once it got its head out of the wall. And then the damned thing attacked just about everybody else – all the customers and half the girls, and down in the bar, well, it was chaos. The place is a shambles. Two dead dogs, too, their throats ripped out. I take that bit hard, by the way.'

Spilgit licked his lips, and then pointed a finger at Ackle. 'Didn't I warn them? Didn't I? Lizard cats can't be domesticated! They're vicious, treacherous, foul-tempered and they smell like moulted snakeskin.'

'I wasn't aware of any smell,' Ackle said.

'Did they kill it?'

'No, it got away, but Feloovil swore she'd skewer it if it ever tried to come back, which made Felittle burst into tears again, and that got all the girls going, especially when the customers started demanding their money back, or at least compensation for wounded members and such.'

'What was Hordilo doing during all of this?'

'Gone, escorting that manservant up to the keep. He said he'd never seen such a scene since his wife left. Not that he was ever married.'

'Before my time,' Spilgit muttered, shrugging and looking out the small window, peering through patches in the ice. 'Anyway, if I go back with you, she'll kill me.'

'At least it'll improve her mood.'

'And this is proof of how people just look out for themselves! Which is precisely why they all hate tax collectors. It's the one time when someone is asking something of you, from you, and you get that murderous look in your eye and start blathering on about theft and extortion and corruption and all the rest. Take any man or woman and squeeze them and they start making the same sounds, the same whimpers and whines, the same wheedling and moaning. They'd rather bleed themselves than give up a coin!'

'I'm sorry, Spilgit, but what's your point? In any case, it's not like you can tax me, is it? I'm dead.'

'You're not dead!'

'Just what a tax collector would say, isn't it?'

'You think we don't know that scam? Faking your death to avoid paying? You think we're all idiots?'

'I'm not faking anything. I was hanged. You saw it yourself. Hanged until dead. Now I'm back, maybe to haunt you.'

'Me?'

'How many curses do you imagine are hanging over you, Spilgit? How many demons are waiting for you once you die? How many fiery realms and vats of acid? The torment you deliver in this mortal life will be returned upon you a thousandfold, the day you step through Hood's gate.'

'Rubbish. We sell you that shit so we can get away with whatever we damn well please. "Oh, I'll get mine in the end!" Utter cat-turd, Ackle. Who do you think invented religion? Tax collectors!'

'I thought religion was invented by the arbitrary hierarchy obsessed with control and power to justify their elite eminence over their enslaved subjects.'

'Same people, Ackle.'

'I don't see you lording it over any of us here, Spilgit.'

'Because you refuse to accept my authority! And for that I blame Lord Fangatooth Claw!'

'Feloovil says that the manservant's masters are going to kill him.'

Spilgit leaned forward. 'Really? Give me that wood, damn you. Let's get some heat in here. Tell me more!'

With Sordid and Bisk Fatter working the oars, Wormlick was up at the prow, studying the beach ahead with narrowed eyes. 'He's a comber, I'd say,' he said in a hoarse growl. 'No trouble to us, and that's their boat, pulled up on the strand.'

There'd be words. There'd be answers, even if Wormlick had to slice open their bellies and pull out their intestines. Most of all, there'd be payback. He scratched vigorously through his heavy beard, probed with light fingertips the small red rings marking his cheeks. He'd have to cut them out again, never a pleasant task, and he never got them all out. The damned worms knew when they were under assault, and spat eggs out in panic, and before too long he'd have more rings on his face, and neck. It was all part of his life, like cutting his hair, or washing out his underclothes. Once a month, every month, for as long as he could remember.

But getting back the loot stolen from them, why, he could find a proper healer. A Denul healer, who would take his coin and rid him of the worms that had given him his name. Coin could pay for anything, even a return to beauty, and one day, he'd be beautiful again.

'Almost there!' he called back over his shoulder. The comber had carried a big rock down to one side of the crescent beach, where he'd left it lodged right where the waves thrashed the shore. Now he had walked back to await them, his sheep-skin cloak flapping about in the wind. 'He's old, this one. Was a big man once, probably trouble, but that was decades past. Still, let's keep an eye on him. We're too close to see it all go awry now.'

They had pursued the *Suncurl* since Toll's Landing. Left to drown only a rope's throw from the ship, they had seen their comrades, Birds Mottle, Gust Hubb and Heck Urse, looking back on them from the rail, doing nothing, just standing there watching them drown.

But we didn't drown, did we? No, we don't drown easily. We stole the Chanter's hoard together, with Sater running the plan, only to be betrayed, and now we want our take, and damn me, but we're going to get it.

Glancing to his left, he studied the wreckage of the *Suncurl*. He and his companions weren't the only ones chasing that doomed, cursed ship. There'd been a clash with the Chanters, but the storm had broken them apart and if the gods were smiling, those Chanters had all gone down to the black world of mud and bones, a thousand fathoms below. In any case, they'd seen no sign of the wretched bastards since the first night of the storm.

The longboat ground heavily into the sand, jolting them all.

Sordid rose, sweeping back her flaxen hair, and arched her back before turning round and eyeing the comber. She snorted. 'Nice hat. I want that hat.'

'Later,' Bisk Fatter said, pitching himself over the side and wading ashore.

Wormlick followed.

Walking towards the comber, Bisk drew out his two-handed sword.

The man backed up. 'Please, I've done nothing!'

'This is simple,' Bisk said. 'So simple you might even live. Heck Urse. Birds Mottle. Gust Hubb. Where are they?'

'Ah.' The comber gestured to where a trail was cut into the sloped bank above the beach, near a shack. 'Off to the village, I would think. Spendrugle, upon the mouth of the Blear and beneath Wurms Keep. It is likely they are warming themselves at the King's Heel, on the High Street.'

Bisk sheathed his sword and turned to Wormlick and Sordid. 'We're back on land,' he said, 'and I'm corporal again. I give the orders, understood?'

Wormlick eyed his companion. Bisk was barely the height of his sword, but he had the build of a rock-ape, and a face to match. Those small eyes so deep in their shadowy, ringed sockets were like the blunted fingernails of a corpse from a man who'd been buried alive in a coffin. When he smiled, which was mercifully infrequently, he revealed thick pointy teeth, stained blue by urlit leaves. In his life he had killed thirty-one men, seven women and one child who'd spat on his boot and then laughed and said, 'You can't touch me! It's the law!'

Bisk was a man pushed into military service, but then, so were they all, in the days when Toll and most of Stratem were waiting for the invasion. But the Crimson Guard landed only to leave again; and then the Chanters decided to take over everything, and life turned sour.

All behind them now.

'All right, sir,' Sordid said with a shrug, standing loose the way she did when she was thinking of stabbing someone in the back. It was a miracle they'd not killed each other, but the deal was a sure one. Get back the loot, and then the blades could clash. But not until then.

'Let's go,' said Bisk. He pointed at the comber. 'Good answers. You live.'

'Thank you, good people! Bless you!'

The three ex-guards of Toll's City made for the trail.

Whuffine Gaggs watched the three walk past his shack, leaving it undisturbed. At that, the comber sighed. 'That could have been trouble, that's for sure.' He eyed the fine longboat rocking on the beach, and went to collect up its bowline. The big blow was coming back, like a whore finding a wooden coin, and he wanted to batten things down and be sitting warm and cosy in his shack by the time the furies arrived. This boat was worth a lot, after all, and he wasn't expecting to see those three fools again.

But the boat wasn't the only task awaiting him. Indeed, he had plenty to do before nightfall.

Whistling under his breath, he tied the bow rope around his chest, looped his right arm under it and then leaned forward. A boat built for twelve was a heavy beast, and this one was solidly constructed besides. Back in his younger days, he'd have no trouble dragging the thing high onto the beach. Now, he had to dig his feet deep into the sand and heave with all his strength.

Age was a demon, a haunting that slipped into the bones whispering weakness and frailty. It stole his muscles, his agility, and the quickness of his wit. It seemed a miserable reward for surviving, all things told, which was proof enough that life was a fool's bargain.

Maybe there was a god out there, somewhere, who'd decided that life was a good thing, and so made it real, like blowing on a spark to keep it going until it was nothing but ash, then sitting back and thinking, *Why, that was a worthy thing, wasn't it? Here, let's make lots more!* But a man's spark, or a woman's for that matter, had to be worth more than just a brief flicker of light in the darkness.

Behind him, as he pushed forward step by step, the boat ground its way up from the waves.

The muscles remembered younger, bolder days, and the bones could mutter all they wanted to, and if the haunting aches returned on the morrow, well, he would damn that day when it came.

His back to the sea, working as he was, Whuffine did not see the bloodred sail appear on the southern horizon.

'The challenges of governance,' said Bauchelain, studying the wine in the crystal goblet he held up to candlelight, 'pose unique travails that few common folk have the intelligence to understand. Would you not agree to this, sir?'

'I have said as much many times,' Fangatooth replied, glancing over at Coingood. 'As you have noted in my Tome of Tyranny, Scribe. Do you see, Bauchelain, how he writes down all that we say? I am assembling a book, you see, a work of many parts, and now, with this night, you yourself enter the narrative of my rise to power.'

'How congenial, sir,' Bauchelain said, raising the goblet in a toast.

'And if your companion would deign to speak, then he too would be rewarded with immortality, there upon the vellum of my virtues – Coingood, note that one! My vellum of virtues! It's my gift for the turn of phrase, you see, which I am adamant in preserving for posterity. "Preserving for posterity!" Write that, Scribe!'

'Alas,' said Bauchelain, 'Korbal Broach's talents lie elsewhere, and as a dinner guest he is often noted for his modesty, and his evident appreciation of fine food. Is that not so, my friend?'

Korbal Broach glanced up from his plate. He licked his greasy lips and said, 'Those bodies I left outside should be frozen by now, don't you think, Bauchelain?'

'I imagine so,' Bauchelain replied.

Grunting, Korbal returned to his meal.

Fangatooth gestured and a servant refilled his goblet. 'It always astonishes me,' he said, 'that so many common people look with horror and revulsion upon a corpse, when I admit to seeing in its lifeless pose a certain eloquence.'

'A singular statement, yes.'

'Precisely. Flesh in its most artless expression.'

'Which transcends the mundane and becomes art itself, when one considers its ongoing potential.'

'Potential, yes.' Fangatooth then frowned. 'What potential do you mean, Bauchelain?'

'Well, take those bodies you suspend upon hooks on your keep wall. Are they not symbolic? Else, why display them at all? The corpse is the purest symbol of authority there is, I would assert. Proof of the power of life over death, and in the face of that, defiance loses all meaning. Resistance becomes a pointless plunge into the lime pit of lost causes.'

Throughout this, Fangatooth was making rolling gestures with his hand, almost in the scribe's face, and Coingood scratched away as fast as he could.

'The corpse, my friend,' continued Bauchelain, 'is the truth of power laid bare. Undisguised, stripped away of all obfuscation. Why, the corpse exists in all forms of governance. May it rest beneath soft velvet, or perch gilded in gold, or hold aloft gem-studded swords. It remains a most poignant, if silent, rebuke to all those absurd notions of equality so common among trouble-makers.' Bauchelain paused and sipped at his wine. 'The corpse can only be the friend of the one in power. Like a bedmate, a cold lover, a bony standard, a throne of clammy flesh.' He lifted his goblet. 'Shall we toast the corpse, my friends?'

From the far end of the table, Emancipor belched and said, 'Aye, Master, that's one to drink to, all right.'

Fangatooth paused with his goblet almost touching his lips, and turned to eye Emancipor. 'Good Bauchelain, you permit your manservant such crass interruptions?'

'I do indulge him, it is true,' Bauchelain replied. 'With respect to the subject at hand, however, Mister Reese is something of an expert. Among the sailing community, he is known as Mancy the Luckless, for the misfortune that plagues his maritime ventures. Is that not so, Mister Reese?'

'Aye, Master. Me and the sea, we're uneasy bedmates all right. I'll have some more of that wine there, if you please.'

'Yet,' Bauchelain resumed, 'you do seem out of sorts, Mister Reese. Have you caught a chill, perhaps?'

'Chill? Aye, Master, down to the white roots of my hoary soul, but it ain't nothing a little drink won't fix. Lord Fangatooth, thank you for the escort you provided me up here. I doubt I would have survived otherwise.'

'Trouble in the village?' Bauchelain inquired.

'Some, Master, but I got away and that's all that counts.'

'Dear Mister Reese,' said Fangatooth, 'I do apologize if you have been in some manner inconvenienced in Spendrugle.'

'Milord, some things no man should ever see, and when he does, why, decades of his life are swept away from his future. This is the shiver that takes the bones, the shadow of Hood him-self, and it leaves a man stumbling, for a time. So, for the warm fire and the full belly, and all this wine here, I do thank you.'

'Well said,' Bauchelain added, nodding.

Seemingly mollified, Fangatooth smiled.

Emancipor leaned back, as the conversation at the other end of the table returned to its discussion of tyranny and whatnot. Against his own will, he thought back, with a shiver, to what he had seen in Feloovil's bedroom. Those mouths had to have come from other people, other women. Cut off and sewn back on . . . but then, he'd seen teeth, and tongues. No, he decided, something wasn't right there.

Pulling out his pipe, he tamped rustleaf into the bowl. Moments later, through clouds of smoke, he studied the scribe, Coingood. Scratching and scribbling, working through one wax tablet after another, the contents of which he'd then, presumably, transfer onto his lord's vellum of virtues. A life trapped in letters seemed a frightful thing, and one at the behest of a madman probably had few high points. No, Emancipor was glad he was not in Coingood's place.

Far better, obviously, this life of his, as manservant to a madman and his equally mad companion. Frowning, Emancipor reached for the nearest decanter of wine. *That's what's wrong with everything. It's the mad who are in charge. Who decided that was a good idea? The gods, I suppose, but they're madder than all the rest. We live under the jumpy heel of insanity, is what we do, and is it any wonder we drink, and worse?*

At the far end of the table, the madmen were smiling, even Korbal Broach.

I think I want to kill someone.

'. . . a most fascinating principle,' his master was saying. 'Are you absolutely consistent, sir, in hanging every stranger who visits your demesne?'

'For the most part,' Fangatooth replied. 'I do make exceptions, of course. Hence your presence here, as my guests.'

'Now, sir,' said Bauchelain with a faint tilt of his head, 'you are being disingenuous.'

'Excuse me?'

Through his smile, Korbal Broach said, 'You poisoned our food.'

'Yellow paralt,' said Bauchelain, nodding. 'Fortunately, both Korbal and I are long since inured to that particular poison.'

Emancipor choked on his wine. He struggled to his feet, clutching the sides of his head. 'I'm poisoned?'

'Relax,' said Bauchelain, 'I have been lacing your rustleaf with various poisons for some months now, Mister Reese. You are quite hale, as much as a man who daily imbibes all manner of poisons can be, of course.'

Emancipor fell back into his chair. 'Oh. Well, that's all right then.' He puffed hard on his pipe, glaring at Fangatooth.

The lord was sitting rather still. Then he slowly set his goblet down. 'I assure you,' he said, 'I had no idea. I will have words with my cook.'

'As you must,' said Bauchelain, rising. 'But not before, I hope, I am able to visit this fine kitchen of yours. I still wish to do some baking tonight, and I do promise you, I have no interest in poisoning such efforts, and indeed will prove it to you at first opportunity, by eating any morsel you care to select from my plate of delectable offerings.' He rubbed at his hands, smiling broadly. 'Why, I feel like a child again!'

'Alas,' said Fangatooth, and there was sweat on his high brow, 'I regret this breach of trust between us.'

'No need, sir. It is forgotten, I assure you. Is that not correct, Korbal?'

'What?'

'The poison.'

'What about it? I want to go look at the bodies now.' He paused and sniffed, and then said, 'A witch used to live here.'

Fangatooth blinked. 'Indeed, some while back. Witch Hurl was her name. How extraordinary, Korbal, that you can still detect some essence of what must be the faintest of auras.'

'What?'

'That you can still smell her, I meant.'

'Who? Bauchelain, will there be icing on the cookies?'

'Of course, my friend.'

'Good. I like icing.'

Moments later, a shaky Lord Fangatooth escorted Bauchelain

to the kitchens, while Korbal Broach drew on his heavy cloak and set out for the gates, still smiling.

Emancipor poured some more wine and eyed the scribe. 'Coingood, is it?'

The poor man was rubbing his writing hand. The glance he shot at Emancipor was guarded. 'Your masters – who in Hood's name are they?'

'Adventurers, I suppose you could call them. There's others names for them, of course, but that's of no matter to me. I get paid, I stay alive, and life could be worse.'

Abruptly the scribe thumped the table. 'My thoughts exactly! We got to do what we got to do, right?'

'Aye. It ain't pretty, but then, we'd never say it was, would we?'

'Precisely, friend, precisely!'

'Join me, will you? Here, some more wine, assuming it's not poisoned, too.'

'Of course not! That would be a terrible waste. Why, I will join you, friend. Why not? Let them bake, or whatever.'

'Aye, bake. My master does indeed love to bake.'

Shuffling over, Coingood shook his head. 'Seems an odd thing to me, I admit.'

Oh friend, that makes two of us, believe me. 'He is full of surprises, is Bauchelain.'

'Fangatooth will draw and quarter the cook, you know.'

'For poisoning us, or failing at it?'

Coingood grinned, but said nothing.

Emancipor found a spare goblet and poured the man a glass. Then he lifted his own. 'Here's to minions.'

'Good! Yes! To minions!'

'The hapless and the helpless.'

They drank.

Vague motion through the iced-over window caught Spilgit's eye and he leaned closer.

'More guests?' Ackle the Risen asked, leaning from one foot to the other. The front of his body was warm to the touch, but the back of his body, so close to the misaligned door, was frigid. When Spilgit made no reply, Ackle continued, 'We're in the same boat, my friend. Simply, we need to get out of Spendrugle. Now, winter's a hard season in these here parts, I'll grant you. But one of the Carter's better wagons, a solid ox or two, and plenty of food, rum and furs, and we could make it to a city on the coast inside a week, or we head north, though the roads will be bad, and the winds—'

'For a supposed dead man, Ackle, you talk way too much.'

'What so fascinates you out there, then?'

'Three strangers.'

'They're back? From the keep? Why—'

'Not them, you fool. Three other strangers. One of them's all bandaged about the head, and limping. Another one's a woman, half naked and that's the half I can't take my eyes off.

Ackle swung round and tugged open the door. He peered out. 'A gull got one of her tits,' he said.

'That's a birthmark, idiot.'

'Too white for that.'

'Ain't no gulls, Ackle. Too cold for gulls. No, it's a lack of pigment. Seen the like before, only not there, on the tit, I mean.'

The three strangers continued on to stop in front of the King's Heel. They argued there for a moment, in some foreign language, and then went inside.

'Wonder if Hordilo's going to arrest them?'

Spilgit sat back in his chair and sighed, rubbing at his eyes. 'Might need a golem to do that. They were all armed.'

Ackle pushed the door shut as much as it was possible to do so, and then faced the tax collector again. 'We could buy us a wagon and an ox, and stores and all, even for three of us, Spilgit, if you want to take Felittle. We could leave in the morning.'

'Oh, and how will we pay for all that? Carter's no fool and won't give credit.'

Ackle smiled. 'Let's find us a pair of shovels, shall we?'

'Oh, not this buried treasure rubbish again!'

'I wasn't about to leave on my own, not with the cold and all.

But now, well, here you are, Spilgit, with Feloovil planning to kill you a hundred ways. It's only indecision that's stayed her hand so far. As for Felittle, well, you should've heard her have a go at her ma. Things were said. Things there's no going back on. If you want her, now's the time, friend.'

'Friend? You're not my friend.'

'Then partner.'

'I don't partner with men who think they're dead.'

'Why not? I imagine there's some tax break involved.'

Spilgit studied Ackle for a long moment, and then shook his head. 'Shovels. Fine, we'll get some shovels. We'll dig up your treasure and then snatch Felittle away and make Carter rich and then make our getaway. What a plan. Pure genius.'

'Genius isn't required,' Ackle replied, 'when it's all straightforward, like I've been saying.'

Spilgit rose and collected up his threadbare cloak. 'You never had the look of a wealthy man, Ackle.'

'Never got the chance, Spilgit. Now, where will we get some shovels?'

'Gravedigger's place,' Spilgit replied. 'We'll offer to dig him a few holes, what with all the strangers about, and we'll offer it cheap.'

Ackle hesitated. 'I don't like that man.'

'You should. You should bless the drunk every damned dawn and every damned sunset.'

'We're not on speaking terms, is what I mean.'

Spilgit stared. 'I'll get the shovels, then.'

'I appreciate it, Spilgit. I really do. I'll wait here.'

'If you're wasting my time, Ackle . . .'

'I'm not. You'll see.'

When Spilgit had left, Ackle moved round the small desk and sat in the chair. He spent a moment imagining himself as a tax collector, stuffy with official whatever, feared by all and charmed on every turn by those same horrible people. He let the scenes linger in his head, and then sighed. 'No, I'd rather be dead.'

*

Hordilo was sick of escorting fools up to the keep. He was sick, in fact, of the whole thing. His responsibilities, the blood on his hands, the pointless repetition of it all, and the way every day ahead of him, down to the last day of his life, was probably going to be no different from all the days already behind him.

Most men dreamed the same things: a warm body to lie against, echoing their animal grunts; company at mealtimes; decent conversation and the floor free of scraps. But few men imagined a woman might want the same things, and then find them in a dog.

Wives were a curse, no doubt about it. So Hordilo had learned to trim down his dreams, as befitted a man made wise by years of grief and blissful ignorance horribly shattered on a fateful day when the world turned on its head and blew him a mocking kiss. It all came down to avoiding the pitfalls awaiting a decent man wanting a decent life, but that was never as easy as it should be.

He sat glowering at the table, ignoring the moans and complaints from all the scratched-up fools who'd been too slow or too drunk to escape the claws of Red the lizard cat, and studied the three newcomers lined up at the bar.

Now, a woman like that one would do me fine. She don't mind her mostly nakedness, I see, and showing me that backside ain't no accident, since I'm the only good-looking man in here and she eyed me coming in. Too knowing to be cold. Why, she could thaw a snared rabbit under hip-deep snow. And make it jump, at least once.

But no, he'd have to arrest her. Along with her two companions, and then see them all hanged until dead. What lord made a law that said being a stranger was against the law? The death sentence for having an unfamiliar face seemed a little harsh, as far as punishments went.

The three were speaking with Feloovil, but she was only half-listening, dabbing a damp cloth against the rake of claw-marks running down her right cheek. Finally, with an irritated gesture, she indicated Hordilo, and the three strangers swung round.

The bandaged one limped over. 'You! You thook them up there? The keep? And they wath made guethth?'

Hordilo glared at the other two. 'You elected this one your spokesman?'

The woman scowled. 'Bauchelain and Korbal Broach, and Mancy the Luckless. They're all up at the keep, are they?'

'They are, and you're welcome to join them.'

'Thath awfully nithe of you,' the bandaged man said, nodding and smiling.

'Just take the track up to the gate and knock,' said Hordilo, waving one hand. Then he pointed at the woman. 'But not you.'

'Why not me?'

'Got to question you.'

'About what?'

'I'm the one asking the questions, not you. Now, get over here and sit. You two, go on, up to the keep. There'll be a fine meal awaiting you, I'm sure.'

'And her?' the third man asked, nodding at the woman.

'I'll send her up anon.'

'Go on,' said the woman to her companions. 'He's the law around here.'

'I uphold the law,' Hordilo corrected her. 'It's Lord Fanga-tooth's law.'

'Lord what?'

'Fangatooth. You all think that's funny? Go and tell him so, then.'

When the two men had finished their drinks and left, the woman carried her tankard over and sat down opposite Hordilo. She studied him with level eyes and that was a look Hordilo knew all too well.

'Is that what you think?' he asked in a growl.

'Why shouldn't I?' she retorted, slouching and setting her tank-ard down on the thigh of the lone leg she stretched out – the one bare and pale and with a delicious curved line where the meat of it slung down from the chair's edge, and the sight of that made Hordilo want to fall to his hands and knees and crawl up under that thigh, if only to feel its weight on the back of his neck. He shifted about, felt sweat everywhere under his clothing.

'I don't like it when women think that,' he said.

One brow arched. 'If you weren't that way then no woman would think it, would she?'

'I wasn't until some woman did me in, not that I was ever married, of course, but if I had been, why, she would've done me in, all because she was thinking what she was thinking.'

'You're blaming the water for the hole it fills.'

'I've just seen that too many times,' Hordilo said, feeling surly. 'Women thinking.'

'If that's what you think, why talk to me? You could've questioned Gust Hubb, or Heck, even. But you didn't. You picked me, on account of me being a woman. So let's face it, you keep making the same mistakes in your life and I ain't to blame for that, am I?'

'If we're talking blame here,' Hordilo retorted, 'then it was you that sat down thinking what you were thinking. I ain't blind and I ain't dumb and I don't take kindly to being thought of that way, when we only just met.'

'What's your name?'

'Hordilo. Captain Hordilo.'

'All right, Captain Hordilo, since you know what I'm thinking, what are we doing here?'

'Women always think I'm that easy, don't they.'

'Is that what I was thinking?'

'I know what you were thinking, so don't try and slip around it with all this talk of us taking a room upstairs to continue this conversation. I got laws to uphold. Responsibilities. You're a stranger, after all.'

'You only think I'm a stranger,' she replied, 'because you ain't got to know me yet.'

'Of course you're a stranger. I never seen you before. Nobody has, nobody around here, I mean. I don't even know your name.'

'Birds Mottle.'

'That hardly matters,' he replied.

'Yes it does. Strangers don't have names, not names you'd know, I mean. But I do, and you know it.'

'What were you thinking, showing me that leg of yours?'

She glanced down and frowned. 'I wasn't showing it to you. I was just letting it lie there, resting. It does that when I sit.'

'I ain't fooled by anything so obvious,' Hordilo replied. He reached down and held his hand under her thigh. He hefted it once, then twice. 'That's a decent feel, I think.'

'You think?'

'I know. Decent weight. Solid, but soft, too.' He moved it up and down a few more times.

'Looks like something you'd be happy doing all day,' Birds Mottle noted.

Sighing, Hordilo sat back. 'And you said you didn't think I knew what you were thinking.'

'Got me.'

He rose. 'All right, then.'

'Upstairs?'

'I get this all the time,' he said, 'for being so handsome.'

Her eyes widened. But he'd seen that look, too, plenty of times, and whatever she was thinking, why, she could keep it to herself.

Feloovil Generous watched the two head up to Hordilo's room. She shook her head. There was no telling the tastes of women, and of all the idiotic conversations she'd heard from Hordilo over the years, that one was close to tops. *Can't figure how he does it. How it works every damned time.*

We'll still see her hang, of course. So, I guess, everyone wins.

She patted the stinging slashes on her cheek, looked round to see if Felittle had cracked open the cellar door and slipped out, but even as her head turned she saw the door snap shut again, the latch thrown with a muted *thunk*. Good, that embarrassment from her own womb could rot down there, for all Feloovil cared.

In the rooms above – all the rooms barring the one now occupied by Hordilo and that slutty woman – all of her girls were weeping and trying to put together what was left of them. Someone would have to sweep up the clumps of hair and bits of skin, but that could wait on her lovelies repairing themselves with make-up and wigs and whatnot.

She'd warned her daughter about taking in that lizard cat. It might have shown up looking half-dead and with a witless look in its wandering eyes, but a wild creature was just that. It belonged out among the rocks, sliming across the cliff-faces above the waves eating birds and eggs and stuff, instead of killing and eating the village cats and some of the dogs, too.

A spasm of grief clutched her at the thought of the two dogs Red had torn open. Scurry and Tremble had been decent hounds, a little fat and slow, true – fatally so, it turned out – and now Wriggle was all alone and pining under Ackle's table ... and where had that stinking man gone to? He should have been back by now, with Spilgit in tow, which would have given her the opportunity to turn this miserable day right around.

Throat-cut tax collectors stung no tears in any village. Questions of vengeance didn't need utterance, in fact, as it was more or less a given. She could picture a score of indifferent shrugs, and maybe a low quip about how Hood, Lord of Death, was the biggest tax collector of them all, or some such thing. A justifiable murder, then.

She should never have trusted Ackle with the task.

The door opened again and in strode three more strangers.

The man in the lead, carrying in both hands a huge sword, fixed Feloovil with a glare and in a ferocious accent said, 'Where are they, then?'

'Up at the keep,' she replied. 'Everyone's up at the keep, and there they'll stay, for as long as the Lord wants to entertain 'em. Now you three, you look worn out and all. So put those weapons away and sit down and I'll check the cookpot.'

They stared at her for a moment, and then the man with the sword sheathed it and turned to his companions. 'Like Wormlick said, we're almost there. Time for a celebratory drink.'

The other man – the third one was a woman, slinky and evil-looking – edged up to Feloovil where she stood behind the bar. His beard could not hide the mottled rings on his face, and he was eyeing the stairs and licking his lips.

The first man asked, 'You got girls for hire, then?'

'For you, aye,' she replied. 'But not the one with ringworm. Got to take care of my girls, right?'

The man glanced over at his companion and shrugged.

'Always the way,' the ringwormed man said in a grumble. 'Never mind. You go on, Bisk. Take two and think of me.'

The man named Bisk made a face. 'Thinking of you won't do me any good, Wormlick, if you know what I mean.' He then strode to the stairs and clambered up them as if he was one short cousin away from an ape.

The woman sidled up beside Wormlick. 'Don't get down on yourself,' she said to him. 'Things could always be worse.'

'So you keep saying,' Wormlick replied, and then caught Feloovil's eye. 'You, ale and food, like you promised!'

'And here I was starting to feel sorry for you,' Feloovil said, heading off to check the new pot of stew on its hook above the hearth.

'Yeah?' Wormlick called out behind her. 'Maybe I'll just take what I want and damn to you, then! What do you think of that?'

'Go ahead and try,' she replied, 'and you'll never leave the Heel alive.'

'Who'd stop me?'

She faced him. 'I would, you rude pocked oaf. Don't test me 'cause I ain't in the mood. Now, d'you want to eat and drink in here? Fine, only pay up first, on account of you not being local and all.' She collected up a couple of bowls, filled them both with broth and then spat in one before turning to walk back to the strangers.

But the woman was standing right in front of her. She took up the bowl not spat in and said, 'This one will do me fine, love, and wine if you have it.'

Feloovil watched the woman sway her way back to the bar. *Now that's what a good daughter should be like. Except for the evil eyes, of course. But then, at least evil implies some kind of intelligence. Ah, Felittle, it's all your father's fault, may his bones rot.*

Smiling, she carried the other bowl to Wormlick.

*

Whuffine sat back down in his chair, listening to the wind start its moan outside. Beneath lowered lids he studied the hunched lizard cat in the cage. 'So you ran to the old cave, did you? Made a mess of your cosy life in the tavern and had to get out quick.' He shook his head. 'But that cave ain't yours no more,' he told the creature. 'It's mine, for my stores. Not even consecrated any more, since I made a point of breaking the idols and scattering the offerings into the sea. It's . . . what's the word? Desecrated.'

The cat glared at him in the manner of all cats, its scaly tail twitching like a tentacle.

'So I set the trap,' he continued, 'knowing you'd be back sooner or later. Now here you are,' he finished with a sigh, 'the ninth. The last of you.'

Red hissed at him.

'Enough of that, Hurl. Your witching nights are done with, now. For good. You was killing too many locals, not to mention their livestock. It couldn't go on. I'm a patient man, a tolerant man, even, and minding my own business *is* my business. But you went and got greedy.' He shook his head. 'Now it's the cliff for you, Witch.'

He rose, pulling on his fox-fur hat and collecting up his walking stick and then, in one hand, the chains looped through the bars of the cage. Kicking open the door, he dragged the cage outside, and onto the cliff trail that climbed to the lesser of the two promontories. The light was fading but the air had grown wild and he could hear the frenzy of the waves as they pounded the rocks down and to his right.

As the cage scraped and growled its way up the trail in Whuffine's wake, Hurl lunged against the sides, spat and bounced and cracked its head; its limbs shot out between the iron bars and slashed at Whuffine, but the chains were long and he remained beyond the lizard cat's reach.

He was breathing hard by the time he reached the half-floor of tiles that marked the summit of the promontory – the other half had tumbled down to the broken shore below a century back, maybe more, and nothing else remained of the temple that had once commanded this grisly view. But he remembered that ghastly edifice, and the way it crouched like an ape, its gnarled face peering across the bay's surly waters to Wurms Keep. He doubted even Hood knew the name of the temple's long-forgotten god or goddess.

The windswept floor of worn tiles bore the faded, tessellated image of something demonic, its horror peculiarly blunted by the seemingly laughing cherubs half-hanging out of its fanged mouth. Miserable faith for a miserable place: it was hardly surprising how those two meshed with such perfection, and could make nightmares out of what could have been simple lives. He suspected that bad weather was the cause of most evil in the world. Gods just showed up to give a face to the foul madness. People had the need for such things, he knew, the poor fools.

He dragged the cage round until it balanced precariously on the cliff's edge. Dropping the chains and keeping his distance, Whuffine walked out to look down at the thrashing chaos of the rocks and spume below. 'Your sisters and brothers are waiting down there,' he said to the cat. 'Or at least their bones are. I never liked shapeshifters, you know, and D'ivers are the worst of them all. But I would've tolerated you, darling. I would have. So it's just too bad you got to end like this.'

The lizard cat wailed.

'I know,' he said, nodding, 'you've barely the wits left to even know who you was. Not my problem, of course, but I think it makes this something of a mercy, at least for the witch, if not for the brainless cat.' He looked down at the caged creature. 'So long, Hurl.'

He went round until the cage was between him and the cliff edge, and then jumped forward and gave it a hard kick.

The cat howled.

Chains whipping across the tiles, the cage slipped from sight and plunged to the rocks far below.

Whuffine stepped closer to the edge and peered down in time to see it strike. In the instant before the mangled cage slid down beneath the waves, he saw that its door was swinging wildly.

There was a flash of motion, weasel-like, and then nothing. 'Ah,' murmured Whuffine. 'Shit.'

Glancing up, he saw a huge, battered ship lunging into the bay, appearing so suddenly he would have sworn it had been conjured by the storm itself. Racing past the cut, it churned through the swells and, with a terrible sound that reached Whuffine atop the cliff, the hull drove into the sand. Waves exploded over its stern. The masts snapped and on their red billowing sails lifted into the air as the gale sought to carry everything into the sky. A moment later, amidst whipping lines, the rigging fell like a crimson shroud into the foaming seas.

Upon the canted deck, figures were swarming.

Whuffine sighed. 'What a busy day.' Picking up his walking stick, he set out on the trail, down to meet these newcomers.

Gust Hubb sat on a rock, hands over his bandaged ears as he rocked back and forth. He made low moaning sounds that the wind answered with glee.

Heck scowled at the man for a moment longer and then turned to look up at the keep. 'I don't like the looks of that place,' he said. 'And somehow, Gust, now it's just you and me, I'm thinking the farther away we are from those necromancers – and Mancy the Luckless – the safer we'll be.'

'They owe uth!' Gust said, looking up, his working eye wild with the whites showing all around. 'They owe me a healing! Ath leatht that! Look at me, Heck! Lithen to me! I want my tongue whole athain! It wath all their faulth!'

The wind was fierce and bitterly cold. Rain filled with sea spray was spitting into their faces: proof to Heck's mind that the world didn't think too much of them, and didn't give a Hood's heel about justice and making things right. It was all one long slog up some damned storm-whipped trail to some damned tower with some damned light shining and offering the false promise of warm salvation. That was life, wasn't it? As pointless as praying. As meaningless as dying when dying was all there was, some-where up ahead, maybe closer than anyone'd like, but then, wasn't it always closer than anyone'd like, no matter when that was? Well, it felt close enough right now, and if Gust was aching and moaning and too gimpy to finish this cursed climb, why, Heck wouldn't complain too much, and might even secretly confess – to someone, but no one nearby – that it was a whisker's trim from death where they were right now, and one step up the wrong way would see their bodies cold and lifeless before the dawn.

No, he wasn't sorry Gust was all done in, the poor man. Taking those necromancers aboard in Lamentable Moll had been the worst decision in Sater's life, and the captain had paid for it with that life, and now the *Suncurl* was a gnawed, burnt and chewed-up wreck, a sad end for the only ship to ever mate with a dhenrabi. *Some things, it has to be said, just aren't worth seeing close up, and that's all I'll say on the matter.*

'Whereth Birdth?' Gust asked.

'Probably rolling in the furs with that sheriff,' Heck said, and just saying those words out loud made him feel suicidal. 'She's a love no man can hold on to,' he said morosely. 'It's my curse – maybe yours, too, Gust, the way she was eyeing that split tongue of yours – to love the wrong woman.'

'Oh, thut up, Heck.'

'No, really. I wish I was the kind of man who could look at a woman's naked body and say, "nice, but it ain't enough, 'cause you ain't got the rest, so whatever it is you want from me, why, you ain't gonna get it." If I was a man like that, appreciative and all, but with, well, with *standards*, I bet I'd be a happier man.'

Gust had dropped his hands and was staring up at Heck with his one good eye. 'We need to thave her.'

'From what? She's exactly where she wants to be!'

'But thath theriff wuth ugly!'

'Aye, ugly in that gods-awful lucky way some ugly men have, when it comes to women. Now, good-looking men, with those winning smiles and good skin and whatnot, well, I wish 'em all the evil luck the world can bring, but luckily, we're not talking about them.' He shook his head. 'It don't matter anyway, Gust. She's happy and it's a happy without you or me and that's what stings.'

Hearing boots crunching on the trail below, both turned, momentarily hopeful, until it was clear that there was more than one person coming up on them, and as the newcomers came round a twist in the trail, stepping out from behind an outcrop, Gust rose to stand beside Heck, and both men stared in disbelief.

'You're alive!' Heck shouted.

Bisk Fatter drew out his sword. 'Aye, and we got a thing about being betrayed, Heck Urse.'

'Not uth!' Gust cried.

Wormlick asked, 'That you, Gust Hubb? Gods below, what happened to you?'

'Forget it,' snapped Bisk, hefting the sword. 'We ain't no Mowbri's Choir here, Wormlick, so save the songs of sympathy.'

'I'll say,' said Sordid, revealing a thin-bladed dagger in one hand and setting its point to the nails of the other in quick succession. 'You never could sing, anyway.'

Wormlick glared at her. 'What would you know about it? I wouldn't sing for you if you held my cock in one hand and that knife in the other!'

She laughed. 'Oh yes you would, if I asked sweetly.'

'How did you survive?' Heck asked them.

'We shucked off our armour and swam to the damned surface, you fool! But you were already under way, vanishing in the night!'

'Not that,' Heck said. 'I meant, how did you survive in each other's company since then? You all hate each other!'

'Treachery carves a deeper hate than the hate you're talking about, Heck. Now, we're here for our cut and then we're cutting you.'

'Ththill the idiot, eh, Bithk? Why would we cut you in on anything if you're then going to kill uth?'

'That's just talk,' said Sordid. 'He wasn't supposed to tell you we're going to kill you until *after* you gave us our cut. That's what you get from a fifty-six-year-old corporal.'

'And you take my orders!' Bisk retorted. 'Making you even dumber!'

'I'll accept that for the truth you just admitted to, sir.'

As Bisk Fatter frowned and tried to work out what she'd just said, Heck Urse cleared his throat and said, 'Listen, there wasn't no cut. We lost it all.'

'We never had ith in the firthth plathe,' Gust added, sitting back down and clutching the side of his head again.

'Sater's dead,' Heck continued.

'Birds?' Sordid asked.

Heck's shoulders slumped. 'Not you, too?' He sighed. 'She's alive, down in that inn down there.' He gestured at the keep. 'We picked up a cargo of trouble in Lamentable Moll, and we were just on our way to demand, er, compensation. Look at Gust. That's what those bastards did to us.'

'What bastards?' Sordid asked, her sleepy eyes suddenly sharp.

'Necromanthers,' said Gust. 'And if thath wuthn't enouthff, they got Manthy the Thluckthleth with 'em!'

'And you want compensation?' Sordid laughed, sheathing her knife. 'Corporal, we chased these idiots across the damned ocean. It really is a contest in stupidity here, and this squad you're now commanding could crush an army of optimists with nary a blink.' Turning, she stared out to sea, started and then said, 'Oh, look, here come the Chanters.'

Her next laugh shrivelled Heck's sack down to the size of a cocoon.

With two ashen-faced servants dragging the dead cook away by the feet, Lord Fangatooth grasped hold of Coingood's arm and pulled him out through the doorway, leaving Bauchelain and his manservant in the steamy kitchen.

'Did you write it all down?'

'Of course, milord—'

'Every word? And who said what?'

Coingood nodded, trying to keep from trembling while still in the clutches of his lord, and the hand encircling his upper arm was spotted with blood, since it was the hand that had driven a knife through the cook's left eye.

'Find the clever things he said, Scribe, and change them around.'

'Milord?'

'I'm the only one who says clever things, you fool! Make it so I said them – is that too complicated an order for you to comprehend?'

'No, milord. Consider it done!'

'Excellent!' Fangatooth hissed. 'Now, walk with me. Leave them to their baking—'

'He'll poison it, milord—'

'No he won't. He's too subtle, and that's what all this was about – making me look clumsy and oafish. That damned cook! Well, he won't be messing things up anymore, will he?'

'No, milord. But . . . who will make the meals?'

'Find someone else. None of that matters now. We need to devise a way of killing them. But cleverly, just to show them. We need genius here, Scribe!'

'But milord, it's – well, it's not in my nature to think diabolically.'

Fangatooth shook him. 'You think the way I tell you to think!'

'Yes, milord!'

Lord Fangatooth held up his fist and said, 'This is a game of murder, my friend, and I mean to win it or die trying!'

Emancipor found a jug, the contents of which smelled vaguely alcoholic. He downed a mouthful, and then another. The taste was sweet, cloying, and it burned his throat and made his sinuses drain down the back of his mouth, and then his eyes started watering fiercely. Grunting, he drank some more.

'Power that lacks subtlety,' said Bauchelain as he gathered and began lining up a half-dozen wooden bowls of varying sizes, 'betrays a failure of the intellect. Do you think, Mister Reese, it is safe to say that our host lacks certain nuances, degrading the very notion of tyranny? The veil is absent. Sleight of hand unimagined. The obfuscation of language and the unspoken threat are revealed as, well, let's be honest, as unexplored realms in this lord's mind. All of this, I must admit, is disappointing.'

'Well, master, this is a backwater holding, after all.'

'There is grit in this flour,' Bauchelain said. 'A millstone needs replacing. I am afraid I made no note of the dentition of our host or his servants, but I imagine we would see teeth worn down, chipped and gouged. Backwater indeed, Mister Reese, as you say.' Dusting his hands, he stepped over to Emancipor and gently prised the jug from Reese's hand. 'Extract of the vanilla bean, Mister Reese, is rather expensive. I believe you have already drunk down a month's wages, so it is well that the cook is no longer alive to witness such sacrilege.'

'Master, my stomach is on fire.'

'I imagine it would be. Will you survive?'

'No.'

'Your pessimism has lost whatever charm it once possessed, Mister Reese.'

'Must be all the poisons, Master, squirrelling my brain. Thing is, everywhere I look, or even think of looking, I see doom and disaster, hoary and leering. Shades in every corner and heavy clouds overhead. I ain't known good luck in so long I'd not know the lad's face if it up and kissed me.' He set about finding another jug. He needed something to quell the fires in his gut.

'Do you like cookies, Mister Reese?'

'Depends, Master.'

'Upon what?'

'What I been smoking, of course.'

'I suggest that you constrain your blends, Mister Reese, to simple rustleaf.'

'You don't want me to eat your cookies, Master? I thought you said you weren't going to poison them.'

Bauchelain sighed. 'Ah, Mister Reese, perhaps I only wish to see them shared out fairly among our hosts. It is, after all, the least we can do for their hospitality.'

'Master, they tried to kill us.'

Bauchelain snorted. 'It is a kindness calling such crude efforts an attempt to kill us. Tell me, do you know how to make icing?'

Emancipor scratched at his whiskers, and then shrugged.

'Seen the wife do it enough times, so, aye, I suppose.'

'Ah, your wife baked?'

'No, she just made icing. In a big bowl, and then ate it all herself, usually in one night. Once a month, every month. Who can fathom the mind of a woman, eh, Master? Or even a wife.'

'Not any man, surely. Or husband.'

Emancipor nodded. 'That's a fact, Master. Mind you, I doubt most women can fathom each other, either. They're like cats that way. Or sharks. Or those river fish with all the sharp teeth. Or crocodiles, or snakes in a pit. Or wasps—'

'Mister Reese, do get on with that icing, will you? Korbal Broach so loves icing.'

'Sweet tooth, then.'

'I suppose it shows,' Bauchelain said in a tolerant murmur. 'So like a child, is my companion.'

Emancipor thought about that, conjuring in his mind Korbal's broad, round face, the flabby lips, the pallor and the small, shallow eyes. He then thought about children, envisaging a toddling Korbal Broach running in a pack of runts, big-toothed smile and a snippet of hair on that now-bald head. He shuddered. *The fools. They should've known. One look, and they should've known. Those kind you do away with, head in a bucket, left out in the snows overnight, accidentally mixed up with the dog food, don't matter how, you just do away with them, and if the world trembles to your crime, relax, that was the rattle of relief.* Aye, that boy running with his gang, a gang that kept getting smaller, with all those pale parents wondering where their children vanished to, and there stood young Korbal Broach, face empty and eyes emptier. *They should've known. Priests can't cure them, sages can't unlearn them, jailers don't want them.*

Bundle him in a sack of lard and raw meat and dump the whole mess into a pit of starving dogs, aye. But who am I fooling? Children like Korbal never die. Only the nice ones die, and for that alone the world deserves every damned curse a decent soul could utter. 'Master?'

'Mister Reese?'

'You done with that vanilla?'

*

'That's right,' said Spilgit, 'two shovels.'

Gravedigger looked up blearily from the heap of dead people's clothes that he'd sewn together to make a mattress and pillow. 'That's *my* job,' he said, reaching for the clay jug, his arm snaking out like a withered root to tangle hairy fingers in the jug's ear, then drag it across the floor back to his bed.

'You look settled in, friend,' said Spilgit. 'I've been temporarily barred from the Heel, you see, and well, a man needing to stay warm has to work. Physical work, I mean.'

'You gonna use a shovel in each hand, then?'

'That's a silly idea, isn't it?'

'Right. So the other shovel, what's that for? Taxes? You taxing my one shovel and claiming the other as payment?'

'I think you've had a bit too much to drink.'

'Too much and what you're saying might make sense. Too bad for you, then, isn't it?'

'Taxation doesn't work that way.'

'Yes it does.' Gravedigger drank.

'All right, it does work that way. You keep one shovel and the tax collector takes the other one, and uses it to build you a nice level road.'

'Oh yeah? So how come it's me building that road, breaking my back and using my own shovel to do it with? While you sit there doing nothing, but you got a key in your pocket, and that's the key to a giant vault full of shovels. So tell me again, what good are you to anyone?'

'This is ridiculous,' Spilgit said. 'People have different talents. You build roads, or in this case, dig graves, and I do the collecting, or in this case, er, dig the graves.'

'Exactly, so take one shovel and go to it.'

'But I'd like both shovels.'

'Once a tax collector, always a tax collector.'

'Listen, you drunk fool! Give me the shovels!'

'I ain't got two shovels. I only got the one.'

Spilgit clutched his head. 'Why didn't you say so?'

The man tipped the jug again, swallowed, and wiped his mouth. 'I just did.'

'Where is it?'

'Where's what?'

'Your shovel.'

'You tax that shovel away from me and I ain't got no more work, meaning I don't earn nothing, meaning you can't tax a man who don't earn nothing, meaning you're useless. But you know you're useless, don't you, and that's why you want to take up grave digging, so you got yourself a real job, but what about me?'

'Are you going to loan me your shovel or not?'

'Loan now, is it? You gotta pay for that, mister.'

'Fine,' Spilgit sighed. 'How much?'

'Well, seeing as I'm renting the shovel from Hallig the pig trencher, and he's charging me a sliver a dig, for you it'll have to be two slivers, or I don't see any profit for my kindness.'

'Kindness means you don't charge anything!'

'I'm a businessman here, Tax Collector.'

'If you rent me that shovel, I'll have to tax your earnings.'

'How much?'

'A sliver.'

'Then I make nothing.'

Spilgit shrugged. 'I doubt anyone'd ever claim renting shovels was a profit-making enterprise.'

'Hallig does.'

'Listen, that damned shovel is leaning outside your front door. I could have come up here and just taken it and you'd never have known the difference.'

Gravedigger nodded. 'That's a fact.'

'But I thought to do this legitimately, as one neighbour to another.'

'More fool you.'

'I see that,' Spilgit snapped.

'Now what, then, Mister Tax Collector?'

'I'm taxing you that shovel.'

Gravedigger shrugged. 'Go ahead, now it's Hallig's problem.

Only the next time you need to bury somebody, don't bother coming to me. I'm now unemployed.'

'I'll loan you a shovel from the vault.'

'Right, and I suppose you want me to be grateful or something. Is it any wonder tax collectors are despised?'

Spilgit watched the man take another drink, and then he left the shack, collected up the shovel, and then, noticing another shovel beside it, he collected that one too, and headed off.

Red huddled in the wet cave with nothing but bones for company. Just below, down a slant of bedrock, the seas surged with foam and uprooted trees from some tumbled cliff side; and with each thunderous wave Red's refuge grew more precarious as water rolled up and over the rock.

Amidst the racket, the bones jumbled around the cat seemed to whisper, in flinty voices, and he could almost make out the words as he crouched, trembling with fury. The low susurrations filled his skull. He glared at the bones, and saw in the gloom skulls among them. The skulls of lizard cats. They rustled and shifted before his eyes, and the whispering grew more urgent.

Red could smell a whiff of power, old power, and a need gripped his soul like a clawed hand about a throat.

Ssss . . . sssembling!

Semble! Semble you fool!

Yowling, the cat shook with tremors, and the bones crowded close, and things suddenly blurred.

The sorcery made the sweat on the cave walls steam and spit. Stone fissured and fell, shattering. In the miasma surrounding Red, old bones pushed into the cat's body. There was terrible pain, and then triumph.

'I am Hurl! Witch Hurl!'

She tottered to her feet, impossibly weak, and looked down at her naked form. Leathery skin stretched over bones, tendons like twine. Not enough flesh, not enough living tissue to make her whole, to make her as she once was. But, it was *enough*.

Hurl cackled. 'I have my mind back! My beautiful, perfect mind! And . . . and . . . I remember everything!' A moment later she slumped. 'I remember everything.'

She needed food. Fresh meat, hot, bloody meat. She needed to feed, and she needed it *now*.

Feeling frail, she ventured out from the cave, skirting the foaming tumult. It was almost dark, the storm coming in like a bruise on a god's forehead. There were corpses wedged among the rocks. Then she saw one lift an arm. Cackling, Hurl scrambled towards the hapless figure.

But when she crouched over him, she found herself looking down upon a dead man. Who then smiled. 'I was never much of a sailor,' he said. 'Tiny said: take the tiller. I tried to warn him, but the Chanters listen to nobody. I'm stuck. Will you help me?'

'You're dead!' she spat.

'I know, and that's the thing, isn't it? We're all cursed with our lot. I was probably alive once, but it's not like I can go back. No one can. Still, if you help me get out of this crevice, then I could walk home. It's somewhere across the ocean, but I'll find it, I'm sure. Eventually.'

'But I need warm flesh! Hot blood!'

'Don't we all, darling?'

She shook her head. 'You'll have to do, for now. It isn't much, but it's something.'

'A philosophy we share, my sweet. Now, about this help – oh, what are you doing? You're eating my thigh. That's not very nice, and you an old woman at that. Well, I suppose if you eat enough of me, I'll be able to squeeze free. So that's something. When you're dead, it pays to remain optimistic, or so I have found. Not too much on that one now, all right? Here, see, you can reach the other one, too. It's much fresher, I'm sure. Horrible weather we're having, isn't it?'

Tiny Chanter turned to survey his surviving siblings as they gathered on the beach, the icy water thrashing up round their ankles as the storm worsened. 'It's simple now,' he said. 'We kill everybody.'

90

The one sister among them, Relish, snorted. 'That's your plan, Tiny?'

'That's always my plan.'

'Exactly, and see where it's gotten us.'

Frowning, Midge said, 'It's got us on shore, Relish.'

'Like Midge says,' growled Tiny, 'it's got us here, and that makes it a good plan, just like it's always been a good plan, since it got us wherever we ended up, and we ain't ended up anywhere but where the plan meant us to end up, and if you think I'm going to keep on tolerating your bad moods and foul mouth, Relish, well, that ain't in the plan.' He turned to the others. 'Draw your weapons, brothers. There's killing to do, and that killing ends with those two sorcerers who stole our treasury.'

'They didn't steal our treasury,' said Scant. 'It was a squad of city guards and that treacherous captain, Sater.'

Tiny scowled. 'But she's dead, and we had nothing to do with that, meaning we're still hunting for justice, and punishment, and those sorcerers objected to us killing them and that's not allowed. We got to answer for things like that.'

Puny Chanter laughed. 'Sater got between a dhenrabi and his mate! That was funny!'

Sneering, Relish said, 'It's only funny to you, Puny, because you're sick in the head.'

'That's funny, too! Hah hah!'

'Be quiet all of you,' commanded Tiny. 'Draw your damned weapons and let's get on with it. Stint, Fren, Gil, you kill that man up at the shack. But don't mess up that fur cap of his. I want it. The rest of us, we go to the village. We get us a warm meal if we can find it, and maybe a few tankards, and then we kill everyone. Then we go up to that keep and kill everything there, too.'

'It's your genius what leaves me speechless,' said Relish.

'I wish,' Tiny replied. Then he pointed at two of his brothers who were both gripping the same huge sword. 'Flea, Lesser, what in Hood's name are you doing?'

'It's our three-handed sword, Tiny,' said Flea.

Tiny walked up to Flea and whacked him on the side of the head. 'Let go of that! There, take that axe, the five-bladed one. Let's go everyone, we're in for a bloody night.'

They set off up the beach, falling into single file on the trail, with Stint, Fren and Gil taking up the rear.

Leaning on his walking stick, Whuffine Gaggs stood beside his shack and watched the ten strangers approach. They were a big lot, he saw, each one with weapons bared and marching in a way that seemed ominous. Probably Tarthenal blood in the line, somewhere a few generations back. The sight of them made him feel nostalgic. The one woman among them was more reasonably proportioned. In fact, he saw as they drew closer, she had more curves than a clay ball, and knew how to use them as she bounced and rolled her way up the trail.

The one in the lead offered up a bright smile that didn't reach his eyes, and simply trudged past Whuffine, as did all the others barring the last three. They halted and readied their weapons.

Whuffine sighed. 'It's like that, is it?'

The one in the centre of the line shrugged. 'Tiny says we kill everybody.'

'You got me all over nostalgic here,' Whuffine said.

The man grinned and turned to the man on his right. 'Hear that, Stint? The old comber remembers better days.'

'A good way to go on your last day,' Stint replied.

Whuffine glanced back to see that the others had all vanished somewhere up the trail. He looked back at the three brothers. 'Tell you what,' he said, 'you go on, tell your brother you did me in like you were told to and leave it at that.'

'We don't lie to Tiny,' said the one named Stint.

The third man frowned. 'That's not true, Stint. Remember the porridge?'

Stint sighed. 'You still on about that, Fren?'

'It had to be you!' Fren shouted.

'Listen,' said the first brother, 'we're wasting time and it's cold, so let's just do this, loot the shack and get on our way.'

'Don't forget the hat, Gil,' said Stint. 'Tiny wants the hat.'

Whuffine nodded. 'It's a fine hat, isn't it? Alas, it's mine and I ain't selling it or giving it up.'

'That's all right,' said Gil, his grin broadening. 'We'll take it anyway.'

'You're making me defend my hat,' said Whuffine, raising his walking stick and gripping the silvered end with both hands.

The three brothers laughed.

They stopped laughing when the shaft shimmered, became a thick-bladed longsword, the blade of which then burst into flames.

A rather short time later, Whuffine stood amidst sizzling chunks of human flesh, from which wisps of smoke rose as if from candlesticks. He watched the last bits of gore burn crispy black and then flake off from the blade of his sword. A moment later the weapon shimmered again and once more he was holding his walking stick. He looked down at the remnants of the three brothers and sighed. 'It ain't good to get me all nostalgic.'

Adjusting his fur hat, he went back inside his shack. He sat down in his captain's chair and stretched out his feet. He looked round, studying his surroundings as if seeing them for the first time. The shark-jaws lining the slatted walls, the burst of dusty, curly hairs pushing out between the boards, the lanterns and brass fittings, the casks and skinning knives and shucking stones, the harpoon heads and bundles of netting, the dhenrabi spines and Jhorlick gills, the heaps of clothing and fine cloth, and the amphorae filled with oil or wine or dyes, the clay jar on the shelf with all the gold teeth, and the half-dozen Seguleh masks . . .

Whuffine grunted. All in all, he decided, this was a far finer abode than any chilly, draught-filled temple with muttering priests for company, and all the slippy pattering of bare feet in the dead of night, as cots creaked under unusual weight and unlikely forces made them sway and jerk. Better, indeed, than the dusty shadows of the alcoves smeared in old wax and crowded with pointless offerings, where spiders built webs only to die of starvation and their tiny shrivelled bodies crunched down to bitter nothing between the teeth.

But somewhere in that temple, it was held, there was faith, thick as curdled cream, upon which a god could grow fat. Well, he'd yet to see that happen. The corridors echoed with pointless hopes and muddled ambitions, with sordid crimes and petty betrayals. Faith was a claw hammer to prise loose the boards beneath the commonry's feet, an executioner's axe to lop off the heads of unbelievers, a flaring torch to set light to the kindling crowding a thrashing fool bound to a stake. Whuffine snorted. Why, a god could get sick with this lot, no doubt about it.

If it wasn't too much work, he would have ended this world long ago, and without much regret.

But I'll settle for what washes up every morning. The bodies and dead dreams, the brave and the insipid, the frightened and the belligerent, the wise ones – but oh how rare they are! – and the idiots, of which there are far too many.

'Ah, listen to me, all nostalgic again.'

Slithering with all the stealth she could muster, Witch Hurl moved among the chopped-up hunks of scorched meat outside the door to Whuffine's shack. She gathered a few clumps up and under one arm and continued on up the trail.

This meat was fresh. This meat wouldn't sour her stomach the way that dead man had, and she wouldn't have to listen to any endless nattering about crossing the ocean and getting home, when all he had left was his head, or his cry of thanks when she kicked it into the waves.

She tore off mouthfuls of the human flesh, swallowing without chewing.

Remembering everything gave her good reasons, now, reasons to continue on, up into the village, where she would deliver a night of vengeful mayhem that, by dawn, would see not a single villager left alive.

And you, Feloovil Generous, you I'll save for the last. You betrayed me when I needed you the most, and for that you will pay – by all the hoary pig-gods of the Hog Harbingers of Blearmouth – may their bones rot in their stupid little barrows – you will pay, aye, Feloovil.

Because, woman, I remember everything!

With every mouthful of bloody flesh she swallowed, she felt her strength returning.

Soon, everyone dies! She cackled, choked, and then spat out a sliver of shattered thighbone.

Behind her, the storm struck the shore, and its howl filled the air. Reaching the rise and coming in sight of Spendrugle, Witch Hurl paused. A single glaring light was visible in the distant keep tower. *My tower! My keep!*

Such a delicious night of slaughter awaited them all!

'We take the beach trail,' said Ackle, 'but then cut off from it while still on the rise. Then it's two hundred paces along the goat trail further down the coast. There's a cut that leads down to a secluded strip of sand.'

'If you say so,' Spilgit said. He was freezing, clutching his shovel in hands swiftly growing numb. The light was almost gone, the wind turning ferocious and it buffeted them as they trudged along. Keeping his head down against the sea spray slanting in almost horizontally, Spilgit stayed a step behind Ackle.

They were halfway along the coast trail when Spilgit heard the man grunt and saw him stagger to one side.

A wild-haired old woman was suddenly before him, shrieking and lunging with hands hooked like talons.

Spilgit swung the shovel and the clang when the flat of the blade struck the woman's forehead was like a hammer on an anvil. The impact sent her tumbling into the brush between the trail and the beach.

'Gods below! Who was that?'

Ackle reappeared and joined Spilgit as they peered into the tangled thicket. 'Did you kill her?'

Spilgit licked his lips, his heart pounding hard in his chest. 'I don't know. She attacked me!'

'Ever seen her before?'

'No, I swear it. I thought I knew everyone.'

'Maybe she came up from the sea. Another one from the wreck.'

Spilgit's sigh was shaky. 'I suppose so.'

'You're a murderer now, Spilgit.'

'No I'm not. It was an accident. It was self-defence.'

'She had spindly hands and you had a shovel.'

'She attacked me, you fool. You saw it.'

Ackle shrugged in the gloom. 'She didn't attack me. But then, I'm not a tax collector, am I?'

'Let's just get on with this, shall we? We're out here, might as well bring the nightmare to an end, though I'm beginning to think that end is a long way off. Don't look at me with those eyes, I'm an innocent man.'

Saying nothing to that, Ackle set off once more, and Spilgit quickly followed.

Lying on the bed, Hordilo watched her getting dressed. 'It's not going to happen,' he said. 'I mean, you were great and all, but I've had my fill of wives.'

Birds Mottle glanced briefly at him before shrugging into her quilted gambeson with the huge tear exposing one breast. 'Thought you never married.'

'Exactly, and I mean to stay that way.'

She faced him. 'I was great, was I?'

'That's what I said, but don't take it to heart.'

'I won't, and you know why? You weren't so great. You're so hairy I thought I was rolling with a dog.'

Hordilo scowled. 'I know what this is.'

'What is it?'

'It's you thinking you need to throw a knife or two, since I told you I wasn't interested. Making up insults ain't no way to make yourself feel better. Maybe for a moment or two, but it never lasts. Besides, women like dogs, and I should know. So,' he concluded, 'it didn't work.'

'Well now,' said Birds, studying him, 'you got all the answers, don't you?'

'I got the answers to the questions, which is better than answers to questions nobody asks, since those kind of answers are a waste of time. So, if you still got a question, ask it and I'll answer it, unless it ain't a question worth asking.'

'I don't,' she replied, collecting up her weapon belt. 'There comes a point in a relationship when it all goes past words, or talking, even. And in the heads of the woman and the man, even thoughts dissolve into a grey, formless haze. Time itself turns into an illusion. Days and nights meld, forward and backward, up and down, now and then – all vanishing into a muddle of pointless existence.' She faced him from the door. 'We've reached that point, Captain.'

'I ain't fooled,' he said.

'By what?'

'You'll step outside the door and close it softly behind you, and lean against the wall, with tears running down your cheeks. Then you'll take a deep breath and find, from somewhere deep inside, the resolve to go on, alone, abandoned and rejected. But really, what else is there to do? The shattered, wounded heart will mend, maybe, in a decade or two. That's how it is for women and it's too bad, you know? But a man's got a thicker hide, and well, that's just natural. Something we're born with.'

'How did you know?' she asked him.

He shrugged, sitting up on the bed and reaching for his trousers. 'It's all there, in your pretty face.'

She opened the door behind her and stepped out into the corridor. Hearing the latch drop in her wake, she made her way to the stairs. *Gods, when a woman needs a drink so soon after sex, that's a bad sign for everyone concerned.*

Reaching the top of the landing she heard a door open behind her and turned. A young woman was edging out, and there was enough about her that made it clear to Birds Mottle that this was Feloovil's daughter. Seeing Birds, the young woman hurried over. 'Who are they?' she asked in a whisper.

'Always a good question,' Birds replied. 'Who is who?'

'Those huge men coming up the street. And one woman. Friends of yours?'

'Huge?'

'Giant!'

Birds pushed past her and hurried back up the corridor. She threw open the door to Hordilo's room. 'You were right! I need you. I want you. Let's get married! Find us a shack somewhere out of the village, where we can hide away, making wild love for days on end!'

Hordilo stood, thumbs tucked into his sword belt. 'A shack? Somewhere remote? Secluded, private, where no one will disturb us? Sounds like my farmhouse. Ain't been there since, well, since a while now.' He smiled at her. 'Who's the man with all the answers?'

'You!' she cried, rushing into his arms.

Tiny Chanter threw open the inn door and stepped forward, only to bang his head on the jamb. 'Ow,' he said, ducking and continuing on. Over his shoulder he said, 'Lesser, Puny, fix that door, will you?'

Behind him the two brothers started hacking at the plastered beam with their axes.

'Hey!' Feloovil shouted from behind the bar. 'Stop that!'

'Needs doing,' Tiny said, glaring round. 'Too low for a proper man, anyway.'

'Then you duck!'

Tiny bared his teeth. 'Tiny Chanter don't duck for nothing.'

'Glad to hear it,' Feloovil said, throwing a tankard at his head. It cracked hard just above his left eye, fell to a table and bounced and then dropped to the muddy floor.

'For that you die!' Tiny bellowed, one hand to his forehead.

'Before or after I serve you?' Feloovil asked.

'Make it after,' said Relish, slipping past her brother. 'I'm thirsty and famished!'

Flea went to a table and dragged locals from their chairs and flung them into a corner, and then he turned to his siblings. 'Found us a table, Tiny!'

As Lesser and Puny, putting away their axes, hurried to join Flea, Scant and Midge, Tiny pointed a finger at Feloovil. 'Ale. Food. Now.'

'Pay. First.'

'Tiny Chanter don't pay for nothing.'

'Tiny Chanter gets hungry and thirsty, and so do his brothers and sister. Not only that,' Feloovil continued, 'they all get to sit outside, on the ground.'

'Gods below,' Relish said to Tiny, 'cough up some coin, brother, so she don't spit in our bowls.'

Snarling, Tiny pulled out a small pouch. He loosened the drawstrings and peered into it. He frowned, small eyes getting smaller.

Feloovil snorted, leaning her forearms on the counter. 'No wonder Tiny don't pay for nothing.'

Midge rose from the table and walked to the bar, shoving Relish to one side as he slapped down three silver coins.

Feloovil swept them up in one hand. 'Got pretty women upstairs,' she added.

'Really?' Relish asked.

Ackle led Spilgit down to a shelf of sand and crushed shells well back from the thundering surf, but spray engulfed them nonetheless, icy and fierce. Lightning flashed through the massive storm cloud roiling above the wild seas, thunder drumming through the howl of the wind, and Ackle was hunched over like an old man, prodding the ground ahead every now and then with his shovel. At last he halted and faced Spilgit. 'Here,' he said.

'Then start digging,' Spilgit replied.

'I'm freezing.'

'The exercise will fix that.'

'No, I mean I'm freezing solid. My arms barely bend. I can't straighten my legs. There's ice in my eyes and my tongue feels like frozen leather.'

Spilgit scowled. 'Stop pretending to be dead, damn you! You think I'm not cold? Gods below, go on, then. Freeze solid for all I care.' Pushing Ackle back, he set to digging in the heavy, ice-laden sand. 'If this is a waste of time,' he said in a snarl, 'you're not leaving this spot, Ackle. In fact, I'm digging you a grave, right here.'

'It's there, Spilgit. My haul. My hoard. Enough to buy a damned estate, maybe two, if one of them is run-down and occupied by an old woman who's half mad and eats bats for breakfast. The kind of woman you can push down the stairs and no servants to ask any questions, so the property just falls into your lap, because of debts or whatnot—'

'What in Hood's name are you going on about?' Spilgit demanded, glaring up at the man. 'What old woman? What debts?'

'I'm just saying. I was the last one to go, you see, and maybe bats were fine with her but I was down to making tea from cobwebs, and yet I stayed on as long as I could, and did I get a word of thanks? Not on your life. That hag spat on me and clawed my face, but the candlesticks were my severance pay – she promised them to me! Instead, she rips the pack and everything falls out, and then she kicks my shin and tries to sink her teeth in my throat. But she didn't have any teeth. She gummed my neck, Spilgit, and that wasn't a pleasant experience.'

Spilgit laughed harshly. 'You ran from an old woman. Gods, Ackle, you really are pathetic.'

'She probably poisoned me. Or cursed me. Or both. I was actually looking forward to a proper death, you know. Just an end to this whole miserable existence. I'd earned it, in fact—'

Something clunked under Spilgit's shovel. Breathing hard from the exertion, Spilgit worked the blade around the object, and moments later he could make out the curved lid of a banded chest.

'That's it,' said Ackle. 'I told you I wasn't lying.'

Spilgit set the shovel aside and pulled at the chest, working it free. It was heavy and he grunted lifting it from the hole. 'Hold on,' he said, eyes finding the seal over the lock, 'this is a Revenue Chest!'

'That's right,' said Ackle. 'I beat a tax collector senseless, on the Whitter Road just east of Elin. With a candlestick.'

'You stole tax revenue!'

'Just getting my own back, Spilgit. Anyway, you quit as a tax collector, so what difference does it make to you? You're getting half, besides.'

Spilgit climbed out of the hole, brushed sand from his hands, and then leapt at Ackle. 'Thief!' His hands closed on the man's twisted, scarred neck, and his weight drove Ackle down to the ground. Spilgit knelt on him, squeezing with all his strength, seeing the ugly eyes bulge, the deepening hue of the face going from blue to grey. 'This time you die for real! Just what you wanted!'

Ackle's struggles fell away, his kicking stilled, and all life vanished from his mottled face.

Still Spilgit gripped Ackle's throat, gasping out the last of his rage. 'Thief,' he said again, but this time without much feeling. 'Look at you. Got your wish, fool. This was punishment. Legal execution, in fact. I'm still a tax collector – it's in my blood, in my bones, gods, in my hands!' He pulled his grip free, crawled off the corpse.

Eyes falling to the chest, he frowned. 'Stolen revenues. For building better roads. Lanterns in the streets. Keeping the drains clear. But still, well, a man needs to get properly set up. It's not like they'll take me back, anyway. I could go into accountancy, use my skills for the other side. A nice office, in a decent neighbourhood, in a fine city, with proper clothes. Servants. It's what I deserve, after a year in Spendrugle. Year? Only a year? More like a century!' Reaching over he pulled close the chest, broke the seal and flipped back the lid.

The coins were properly columned, each column wrapped and sealed and marked with the total amount. They'd already been converted, meaning every damned coin was solid gold. *This wasn't no normal haul. Not some scrapings from villages, farms and hamlets. Gods below, this was a city's take. What in Hood's name was that tax collector doing with it on Whitter Road? Without an armed escort?*

Spilgit, you fool, the bastard was stealing it, of course!

He dropped the lid. He was getting cold again, now that he'd stopped digging and strangling Ackle. He had enough coin here to buy Spendrugle, all the lands surrounding it, and that damned Wurms Keep. He had the coin to hire an army and march back in the summer and lay waste to the whole place, and it was only what they all deserved.

Spilgit stood, staring down at the chest.

The shovel flattened the back of his skull and he toppled forward. His legs kicked a few times then went straight as spears. Ackle studied the sprawled corpse of the tax collector. 'I told you I was dead!' he shouted. 'You can't kill a dead man! I told you!'

Dropping the shovel, he fell to his knees and pushed the chest back into the hole. It could all wait until the spring, anyway. Too cold for travel. His joints were freezing solid, making every move a creaking ordeal.

Ackle filled in the hole again, and then took up Spilgit by the ankles and dragged him to the edge of the shelf. He kicked the body into the thrashing surf, watched as the corpse was tugged out to sea, sucked down and out of sight between two massive rocks.

'Killing tax collectors,' he muttered. 'I could make a living out of that.'

Picking up both shovels, he set off for the village.

Witch Hurl crawled up from the bushes and made it onto the trail on her hands and knees. Blood dripped sluggishly from her forehead, but the cold had frozen most of it. She had to hand it to Spilgit: the man's reflexes were like lightning. Still, no matter. Against nine of her, he would have no chance, and indeed the time had come.

Muttering under her breath, she sembled. Her form blurred, she yowled in pain, and moments later nine lizard cats emerged from the redolent, spicy haze. The wind whipped those scents away. Her bodies were scrawny, but filled with venomous hatred. She slipped forward, tails writhing, nine slinky forms rushing up the trail.

The King's Heel. It would all start there, with the conclusion of plenty of unfinished business. It was likely all the denizens of the village were in there, anyway, meaning she wouldn't have to do much hunting through houses and huts, pigsties and stables. No, they would all be crowded in the Heel tonight, sitting out the storm, warm in each other's stink.

She would make of that wretched inn a tomb, a haunted crypt, its walls sweating the blood of slaughter, the echoes running in all directions from the screams and shrieks and death rattles.

Racing closer, her gazes caught once more the glaring light from the tower of Wurms Keep. Her fury sizzled like fat in a pan, and she found her throats opening to hisses and then spitting, every scale upon her nine backs arching into serrated lines.

There, directly ahead, the entrance to the King's Heel.

Reaching it, she flung herselves against the barrier. And rebounded. Frustrated rage filled her bodies. Claws were unsheathed, lashing out at the wind, gouging deep furrows in the frozen mud. She glared at the door, willing it to explode. But it defied her power. Hurl screamed through nine throats.

At the high-pitched wailing from outside, Feloovil shivered. 'The wind's gone mad out there! Here, then, have another drink!'

Laughing, Relish held up her tankard, watching it weave before her. 'Brilliant idea,' she shouted. 'A tavern on a ship! We should've thought of that years ago!'

'You ain't on a ship no more,' Tiny said, his small red eyes tracking the room before returning to their concentrated fixation on Feloovil's breasts. 'You're drunk,' he explained. 'That's why you're all wavering back and forth, and the floor keeps tilting, and those lanterns swaying like that.' He belched then and leaned on the counter to get closer to those breasts, and then he addressed them. 'I know you're old and all,' he said, with a bleary smile, 'but that just makes you more desperate, and a desperate woman is my kind of woman.'

'The only kind, I would think,' Feloovil replied. 'And I'll have you know I'm only thirty-one years old.'

'Hah hah hah!'

'Now, if you had me some offerings,' she continued, ignoring his derision, 'I might show you the youth of my soul and all that.'

'Oh,' Tiny replied, 'I'll offer you something all right. Hah hah hah!'

'Listen to that wind!' Relish said, swinging round to face the door. 'Like voices! Screaming witches! Ugly hags riding the black winds!' She looked round, frowned at all the pale faces and the huddling forms at the tables. 'Wind's got you all terrified! You're all useless, the worst sailors I ever seen. All hands on deck! Stormsails, reef the jibe and trim the anchor!' She spun back to Feloovil. 'I want some women!'

'She can do that,' Tiny said, nodding, 'since it keeps her a virgin, and we promised old Ma we'd keep her virtue and dignity and stuff.'

Feloovil shrugged. 'Head on up and find one, then,' she said to Relish.

Weaving, Relish made her way to the stairs.

Feloovil eyed Tiny Chanter. 'You got small hands,' she said.

'They ain't small.'

'Too small for the rest of you, I mean. That's not too promising.'

'Tiny don't make promises,' he replied, nodding at her breasts. 'Tiny Chanter does whatever he wants to do, with anybody he wants to do them with, as long as they do what they're told, they'll do fine.'

'They'll do fine all right,' Feloovil said. 'And I bet you want to see them naked, don't you?'

He smiled.

'All right, then,' she said. 'Here's the deal. You all look tough and that's good. There's someone up at the keep needs killing.'

'I can kill,' Tiny said. 'Better than anybody. Just ask 'em, all those people I killed. I ain't just a sword, neither. I got sorcery. Necromancy. Jhistal, Demidrek, High Mage. Pick a title, I'm it.'

'Even better,' she said. 'Since that keep's full of sorcerers right now. Lord Fangatooth Claw, and his guests. Bauchelain and Korbal Broach.'

Tiny seemed to reel for a moment, and then his face darkened. 'Aye, them. Wait, who's Lord Fangatooth Claw?'

'The local tyrant,' she replied.

Tiny grunted. 'Nice name.'

'He thinks so,' said Feloovil. 'So, that's the deal.' She lifted her breasts. 'You get these, in all their glory. But you got to kill everyone in that keep first.'

'We can do that,' Tiny said. 'We was going to do it anyway.'

'Oh. Well, then—'

'After we killed all of you,' Tiny went on. 'But instead, we'll do it the other way round. Keep first and then everybody here, but not till after you and me do . . . you know . . . the stuff men and women do. The pinky stuff.'

'The what?'

Tiny reddened. 'Pinky naked, I mean. You know.'

'You ain't never done any of that before, have you?'

'Of course I have!'

But Feloovil shook her head. 'If you had, you'd know that what your sister's doing upstairs with one of my girls makes her no virgin in anyone's eyes.'

'Watch your mouth!' he snarled, reaching for his sword.

'Never mind what I just said, Tiny. Go on and kill them up there, if you think you can. Wurms Keep.'

'We will! And then we come back down and kill all of you!'

'The walk will sober you up, I hope,' she said, glancing over at Tiny's equally drunk brothers. 'You'll need your wits about you.'

'Tiny don't need no wits about him,' Tiny replied.

'You're giving me all the reasons I need know about why you're called Tiny,' said Feloovil. 'But I'm sure I'll get a few more by the time we're done.'

He jabbed a finger at her. 'Count on it!' Turning to his brothers he said, 'On your feet all of you! It's time! In the keep up there, we'll find Lord Fungaltooth and those two from the *Suncurl*!'

'Who's Lord Fingaltooth?' Midge asked.

'A dead man!' shouted Tiny.

Flea frowned and said, 'We gonna kill a dead man, Tiny? What for?'

'No, he ain't dead yet, Flea. But he's going to be, when he meets us!'

Midge laughed. 'And he won't be no Lord Fancytooth then, will he? Ha ha!'

'Fumbletooth,' corrected Tiny.

Feloovil watched the huge man draw his equally huge sword, and felt a brief wilting of anticipation. Shaking it off, she pointed at the door. 'On your way, Chanters. Destiny awaits!'

'Ha ha ha,' said Midge. 'Destiny's taking us up to the keep! Where is she, then?'

'Get the door, Puny,' commanded Tiny. 'We'll regroup in the street, and then begin our charge on the keep walls.'

'Up that hill?' Lesser asked.

'Tiny don't do hills,' Tiny said in a growl. 'We charge and that's that. We take the walls, and then we slaughter everyone!'

'Hey,' said Puny, 'where's Stint and Gil and Fren?'

'Probably ran off with your new hat, Tiny,' said Scant.

'We'll deal with them later,' Tiny snapped.

Puny walked to the door and swung it open.

'As far as stupid ideas go,' whispered Sordid, 'this is our worst one yet.' She was crouched with the rest of the squad, barring Birds Mottle, in the ditch beside the track, not thirty paces from the keep's gatehouse. From their hidden vantage point, they studied the lone guard standing in front of that gate.

'You got a bad attitude there, Sordid,' said Bisk Fatter in low tones. 'It's always been your problem, you know. You're always wanting to stand apart from the rest of us, as if you were special or something. Smarter, maybe.'

'Prettier, that's for sure,' Heck Urse said.

'Shut your mouth, Heck,' said Bisk in a growl. 'Listen, Sordid, it's bad for morale.'

She turned to study the man. 'Morale? Have you lost your mind, sir?'

'We can do this,' said Bisk, glowering in the gloom. 'He's just one guard, for Hood's sake.'

'But he'th juth sthanding there,' hissed Gust Hubb. 'Thorm'th

howling and wind'th blowing and thill he juth sthans there, holding tha' sthworth.'

Sordid saw Wormlick slide close to Gust, reach up with one
gloved fist, and knock on the side of the man's head.

Gust flinched away. 'I ain't thimple, you fool. Juth got a sth-
liced thongue.'

'And one eye, no nose and no ears, and bite marks on your
legs.' Wormlick laughed.

'Sthooth thoo clothe to Manthy, ith all.'

'Gave you the title, I'd say,' Wormlick went on. 'Gust Hubb the
Luckless. Sorry. The Luckleth.' He sniggered.

'Look whothe thalking, you pock-faced hog-butt.'

'Keep it down you two!' Bisk commanded in a rasp. 'Someone
throw a rock against the wall. Make the guard turn round, and
then we rush him.'

Sordid faced the guard again and shook her head. 'He ain't
right, sir. Too pale. Too bloated.'

Heck Urse pushed up beside her, squinting. 'Necromancy!
That man's dead. That's one of our shipmates from the *Suncurl*.
That's Briv, who drowned.'

Gust Hubb joined them on the bank. 'Briv the carpenter's
helper or Briv the rope maker?'

'That don't matter,' whispered Heck. 'This is Korbal Broach's
work.'

'So what?' Bisk said behind them. 'Dead or alive, it's just one
man.' He pulled up a stone from the ditch. 'Get ready.' He
straightened slowly, and then threw the stone. It sailed over the
guard's head and thumped high on the wooden gate.

The guard turned.

'Now!'

The squad rose from the ditch and rushed forward.

But somehow, still the guard faced them, and was now raising
his sword.

The charge slowed, wavered.

'How did he do that?' Wormlick demanded.

'It's not the same man!' Heck said. 'That's Briv, one of the other ones!'

'He thowed them thogether!' shrieked Gust Hubb.

The squad's charge dribbled away, and they stood staring at the new guard, with fifteen paces between them.

The dead man lifted his sword with some alacrity.

'A guard no one can sneak up behind!' cried Heck Urse.

'Gods below,' said Sordid. 'That's the stupidest thing I have ever seen.'

'You're only saying that,' retorted Heck, 'because you weren't on the *Suncurl*!'

'Wormlick, you and Bisk go to the right. Heck and Gust, to the left. Follow me.' She headed forward, drawing her fighting knives.

'I'm corporal here, Sordid—'

'Just follow, sir.'

The others fanned out while Sordid advanced on the guard. 'Hey!' she shouted.

As she suspected, the guard facing the gate sought to turn round. The other one resisted the effort and they stumbled.

Bisk howled and charged in from one side, trailed by Wormlick, while Heck attacked from the opposite flank. Gust Hubb stumbled on something and fell hard on the track. He cried out as he landed on his shortsword.

The guard tottered about, waving swords that kept clashing against one another.

Sordid came in low and hamstrung the creature. It fell over, just as Bisk shrieked and swung his huge two-handed sword. The heavy blade swished over the guard and flew from the corporal's hands. It sailed across the track and speared Gust Hubb through the right thigh. He loosed another howl.

Heck Urse reached the fallen guard and hacked at both heads. 'Briv and Briv! Die! Die and die and die again!'

Sordid backed away. 'Wormlick, check on Gust. See how bad it is.'

Wormlick laughed. 'How bad? The fool's skewered through the leg! And he fell on his sword! He's spurting blood everywhere!'

'Then bandage him up, damn you!'

'You ain't corporal—'

'No,' she snapped. 'Our corporal's the one who speared him! I'm busting him down right now. Whose plan was this? Did it work? Of course it worked. Why? Because it was *my* plan! Listen, all of you, I'm now Captain.'

'Sergeant, shouldn't it be?' Heck asked, still gasping from hacking open Briv and Briv's heads.

'Captain! Sater always had it in mind to promote me.'

'Since when?' Bisk demanded.

'Since I just said so.'

Gust's howls went on and on.

At that moment the gate swung open and there stood a tall man with a forked beard. 'Ah,' he said, eyes alighting upon Gust Hubb, 'the late Captain Sater's re-doubtable soldiers ... and friends. Well, your timing is impeccable. I have just made cookies.'

Emancipor Reese sat across from Korbal Broach, watching the huge, fat man licking the icing from one of Bauchelain's creations. His stomach rumbled and then gurgled. 'How is it you're allowed to eat them, then?' he asked.

Korbal blinked at him, said nothing.

There was a commotion from one end of the dining hall and a moment later, amidst clumping boots, gasps, whispers and moans, Bauchelain returned leading a woman and three men carrying between them a fourth, who had a massive sword thrust through one thigh, and a short sword driven up into an armpit. His bandaged form was splashed with blood.

Emancipor pointed a finger at one of the men helping this unfortunate comrade to a nearby bench. 'You was on the *Suncurl*,' he said. 'You led the charge onto the Chanters' ship during the mating and the battle and all. Then you stole one of their lifeboats and lit out.'

The man glared. 'Aye, Mancy. I'm Heck Urse. And this is the rest of Sater's squad. They chased us down, all the way from Stratem.'

'Very loyal of them,' said Bauchelain, resuming his seat. 'Korbal, my friend, will you do me a favour? This poor wounded man needs healing.'

At that the bandaged man suddenly sat up. 'No!' he cried. 'I'm bether!'

Korbal set the cookie – stripped clean of its covering of icing – down on the table, and then rose and walked over to the wounded man, who shrank back. When Korbal tugged the sword from the thigh, the man swooned, which made removing the shorter sword much simpler. Weapons clanging to the floor, Korbal Broach began peeling sodden bandages from the man.

Emancipor could see that this effort was going to take some time. He rose and reached out across the table for the cookie Korbal had left behind, only to have his hand slapped by Bauchelain.

'Now now, Mister Reese, what did I tell you?' Bauchelain then gingerly picked up the lone cookie, and slipped it into a pocket beneath his cloak, but not before Emancipor caught a glimpse of the pattern incised on the top of the flat cookie.

From somewhere below came a long, wavering scream.

The squad soldiers started.

'That would be our host,' Bauchelain said, smiling. 'I believe he is torturing prisoners in the cells below. However, I am assured he will be joining us soon, to partake of my baking.'

'He'll want a food tester,' Emancipor predicted, settling back and reaching for his goblet of wine.

'I sincerely doubt that,' Bauchelain replied. 'Lord Fangatooth is doomed to bravado, as we shall soon see. In any case, I shall be his food tester.'

'But with you immune to poisons, Master—'

'I assure you, Mister Reese, no poison is involved.'

'So how come the fancy patterns beneath the icing, Master?'

'My private signature, Mister Reese, that shall remain so, yes? Now, although I am not yet the host, permit me, if you will, to be

110

mother.' Bauchelain gestured with one thin, pale hand to the plate heaped with cookies. 'Do help yourselves, will you?'

The woman snorted and said, 'Wine will do for us, thank you. No, Heck, don't be a fool. Just wine.'

Bauchelain shrugged. 'As you wish. Of course, a lesser man than I would be offended, given my efforts in the kitchen and whatnot.'

'That's too bad,' the woman replied with all the sincerity of a banker. 'Heck was telling us about compensation. For injuries and all. Also, there's the whole matter of our cut in the haul from Toll's City, which Sater promised us.'

'Ah,' murmured Bauchelain, nodding as he sipped his wine, 'of course. It would be coin, wouldn't it, behind your impressive, if somewhat unreasonable, pursuit across an entire ocean. We are indeed driven to our baser natures in this instinctive hunger for ... well, for what, precisely? Security? Stability? Material possessions? Status? All of these, surely, in varying measures. If a dog understood gold and silver, why, I am sure the beast would be no different from anyone here. Excepting me and Korbal Broach, of course, for whom wealth is but a means to an end, not to mention cogently regarded with wisdom, with respect to its ephemeral presumption of value.' He smiled at the woman and raised his goblet. 'Coin and theft, then, shall we call them bed-mates? Two sides of the same wretched piece of metal? Or does greed stand alone, and find in gold and silver nothing but pretty symbols of its inherent venality? Do we hoard by nature? Do we invest against the unknown and unknowable future, and in stacks of coin seek to amend the fates? We would make of our lives a soft, cushioned bed, warm and eternal, and see a fine end – if we must – shrouded in the selfsame sheets. Oh, well.'

The woman turned to Emancipor. 'Does he always go on like this?' Without awaiting an answer she faced Bauchelain again. 'Anyway, cough up our share of the coin and we'll be on our way.'

'Alas,' said Bauchelain, 'we do not possess it. I imagine the bulk of the treasure will be found beneath the wreck of the *Suncurl*. That said, you are welcome to it all.'

Emancipor grunted. 'If that comber ain't collected it already.'

'Oh, I doubt that, Mister Reese, given the inclement weather. But the townsfolk, being wreckers, will of course contest any claim to that treasure.'

Sordid snorted. 'That's fine. Let them try.'

Bauchelain studied her for a moment, and then said, 'I am afraid you do not intrigue me in the least, which is unfortunate, as you are rather attractive, but by your tone and the cast of your face, I see both inclined to dissolution in the near future. How sad.'

She glared at him, and then slouched back in her chair, drew a knife and began paring her nails. 'Now it's insults, is it?'

'Forgive me,' said Bauchelain, 'if in expressing my disinterest you find yourself feeling diminished.'

'Not nearly as diminished as you'll feel with a slit throat.'

'Oh dear, we descend to threats.'

Korbal Broach returned to the table, sat and looked round for his cookie. Frowning, he reached out for another one.

'My friend,' said Bauchelain, 'I ask that you refrain for the moment.'

'But I like icing, Bauchelain. I like it. I want it.'

'The bowl awaits you in the kitchen, since I instructed Mister Reese to make twice as much as needed, knowing as I do your inclinations. Is that not so, Mister Reese?'

'Oh aye, Master, half a bowl in the kitchen. Ground powder of sugar cane, moderately bleached and with a touch of honey, too. Nice and cool by now, I should think.'

Smiling, Korbal Broach rose and left the dining hall.

Emancipor looked over at the bench to see that Heck had gone over to his companion, who was now sitting up. Divested of bandages, he was now recognizable as Gust Hubb, although one of his eyes was green while the other was grey, sporting a new pink nose that was decidedly feminine, and the ears were mismatched as well, but of scars and wounds there was no sign.

'High Denul!' hissed Heck Urse, shaking his friend by the shoulder. 'You're all healed, Gust! You look perf— as handsome as ever!'

'I'm marked,' groaned Gust. 'He marked me. Might as well be dead!'

'But you're not! You're healed!'

Gust looked up, wiped at his eyes and sniffled. 'Where's Birds? I want Birds to see me.'

'She will, Gust. Better yet, we're getting our cut! All we got to do is kill all the wreckers and go out to the *Suncurl* and collect it all up!'

'Really?'

'Really! See, it's all worked out for the best!'

Gust slowly smiled.

A moment later Lord Fangatooth Claw strode into the room, drying his hands with a small towel, and in his wake trailed Scribe Coingood, pale and sweaty and, as usual, burdened with wood-framed wax tablets. Eyes alighting on the heap of cookies on the pewter plate in the centre of the table, the lord nodded. 'My, don't those look tasty!'

'Oh they are,' said Bauchelain, reaching out without looking and taking one. He bit it in half, chewed and swallowed, and then plopped the second half into his mouth and followed that down with some wine. Sighing, he settled back. 'Delicious, but of course that does not surprise me. I speak not from a dearth of modesty, as the kitchen was impressively stocked, Lord Fangatooth. Most impressively.'

'It is nonetheless a shame,' said Fangatooth, 'that the sacred notion of host and guest must be dispensed with before the dawn.'

'I fully understand,' said Bauchelain. 'After all, we are two sorcerers under the same roof. High Mages, in fact, and so see in each other the deadliest of rivals. Like two male wolves in their prime, with but one pack awaiting the victor.'

'Just so,' Fangatooth said, pouring himself some wine – all the servants were gone, it seemed, or perhaps in hiding. The lord lifted the goblet and then made rolling motions with his other hand. 'Rivals indeed. Tyrants in the same bed. Rather, the blanket, only big enough to warm one of us. While in that bed. Two fish in the same basin, and only one rock to hide under.' He faltered for a moment, and then said, 'Oh yes, just as I said, Bauchelain. Rivals, in the midst of deadly rivalry. Foes, already locked in a contest of powers, and wits.' Then he blinked and looked round. 'Why, it seems we shall have ourselves an audience as well! Excellent. Dear strangers, make yourselves at home as my guests!'

'Right,' said the woman in a drawl, 'at least until you decide to kill us.'

'Precisely.'

She faced Bauchelain. 'Whereas you are prepared to let us go, is that right?'

'Why, so it is.'

'All right, then, we're with you, and not just for that, but for healing Gust, too.'

Smiling at her, Bauchelain said, 'Why, you grow warmer in my eyes, my dear.'

'Keep it up,' she said, 'and I might melt.'

'You do understand, don't you,' said Bauchelain, 'that I see little of the negative in dissolution?'

She grunted. 'Why, that makes two of us. Which is why you're too upright for me. Sorry, but we won't be rolling in a wedding bed anytime soon, I'm afraid.'

'Hence my earlier sadness.'

Fangatooth cleared his throat, rather loudly. 'I see, Bauchelain, that you have commandeered my chair at the head of the table.'

'My apologies, sir. An oversight. Or, perhaps, impatience?'

'No matter. In any case, you will not leave this room alive, I'm afraid. I have sealed the chamber in the deadliest of wards. Death awaits you at every exit. I note, of course, that your friend, the eunuch, is not here. But so too is the kitchen sealed, and should he endeavour to return here, intending to assist you once he hears your terrible cries, he will die a most terrible death.'

Bauchelain reached for another cookie. Bit, chewed and swallowed.

'The sorcery I have perfected,' Fangatooth continued, 'is solely devoted to the necessities of tyranny. The delivery of pain, the evocation of horror, the agony of agony – Scribe!'

'Milord?'

'Are you writing all this down?'

'I am, milord.'

'My last line, get rid of it. Devise something better.'

'At once, milord.'

Emancipor filled up his pipe and lit it using one of the candles on the table. He drew deeply and filled his lungs with smoke, and then frowned. 'Oh no,' he said. 'Wrong blend.' The scene sagged before his eyes. *Oh, and that was uncut, too.* His eyes fixed on the plate of cookies. Sweat sprang out under his clothes. He could feel his heart palpitating, and saliva drenched his mouth.

As Bauchelain reached for a third cookie, Fangatooth held up a hand and said, 'Please, you have well made your point, Bauchelain! I know well that these cookies are no more than a distraction, a feint, a not-so-clever attempt at misdirection! No, I imagine you have secreted about you an ensorcelled sword, or knife, as you clearly appraise yourself a warrior of some sort. But I am afraid to say, such things only bore me.' He reached out and collected up a cookie. Examined it a moment, and then used one fingernail to scratch loose some icing, which he then brought to his mouth, and tasted. 'Ah, very nice.' He bit the cookie in half, chewed and swallowed, and bit the next piece in half, and then the next, and so on until the cookie was gone, except for a single crumb on one finger, which he ate whole.

He sat back and smiled across at Bauchelain. 'Now, shall we begin?'

Bauchelain's brows lifted. 'Begin? Why, sir, it is already over.'

'What do you mean?'

'I mean that I have won, Lord Fangatooth.'

The man leapt upright. 'It was poisoned! A double-blind deception! Oh you fool, think you I am not also immune to all poisons?'

'I am sure that you are,' Bauchelain replied. 'But that will not avail you, alas.'

'Prepare to defend yourself!'

Bauchelain sipped at his wine.

Emancipor, trembling to keep from stealing a cookie, started as Fangatooth suddenly clutched his stomach and gasped.

'What? What have you done to me?'

'Why,' said Bauchelain, 'I have killed you.'

The lord staggered back, doubling over in pain. He shrieked. Then blood erupted from him, spraying out from his body. He straightened, arching as if taken by spasms, and his torso bulged horribly, only to then split open.

The demon that crawled out of Fangatooth's body was as big as a man. It had four arms and two bent, apelike legs with talons on the end of its toes. Beneath a low, hairless pate, its face was broad and dominated by a mouth bristling with needlelike fangs. Smeared in gore, it clambered free of Fangatooth's ruptured corpse, and then coughed and spat.

Lifting its ghastly head, the demon glared at Bauchelain, and then spoke in a rasping, reptilian voice, 'That was a dirty trick!'

Bauchelain shrugged. 'Hardly,' he said. 'Well, perhaps, somewhat unkind. In any case, you will be relieved to know that I am done with you, and so you may now return to Aral Gamelain, with my regards to your Lord.'

The demon showed its fangs in a bristling grimace or grin, and then vanished.

'Mister Reese!'

Bauchelain's hand slashed down, knocking the cookie only a hair's breadth from Emancipor's mouth.

'Beneath the icing, my friend, you will find pentagrams of summoning! Ones in which the demon so summoned is already bound by me, until such time that the pattern is broken by someone else! Now, step back, Mister Reese, at once. You were one cookie away from death, and I'll not warn you again!'

'I was just going to lick off the icing, Master—'

'You were not! And that is not rustleaf I am smelling from that pipe, is it?'

'My apologies, Master. It didn't occur to me to think.'

'Yes,' Bauchelain replied, eyeing him, 'upon that we are agreed.'

The dissolute woman stood. 'Glad that's all over with, then,' she said. 'Lord Bauchelain, would you be so kind as to disperse all those deadly wards surrounding this chamber?'

Bauchelain waved a hand. 'Korbal did so already, my dear. But will you not stay the rest of the night?'

She turned to her squadmates. 'Find beds, soldiers. A dry and warm night until we greet the new dawn!'

At that moment a loud crashing sound came from the stairs. Blearily, Emancipor turned to the doorway beyond which was the wide hallway that led to the staircase in time to see that door burst apart in splinters and shards, with a dented, broken golem tumbling into the chamber. Its bucket head rolled away from its leaking body, rocked back and forth for a moment and then fell still.

From somewhere atop the stairs came Korbal Broach's high, piping voice. 'It was an accident!'

Yowling in frenzy, Witch Hurl fought among herselves just outside the door to the King's Heel. She cursed that infernal barrier, and the pathetic claw-clattering paws sadly lacking in thumbs, a detail that made the door stand triumphant and mocking before her glaring, raging eyes.

The wind buffeted her writhing, spitting forms, forcing a few of her to slink low upon the frozen mud of the street. And still the fury within her burgeoned. Her serrated scales running the length of her spines were almost vertical; her tails whipped and reared like seaworms awaiting a fast-descending corpse. Her jaws stretched wide to lock the hinges of her canines, and that horrible wind whipped into the cavern of her mouths, cold and lifeless but hungry all the same. She slashed the ground with her claws. She leapt into the air in berserk rage, only to be flung sideways by the gusts storming down the street.

Murder filled her mind, a word that stood alone, that floated and surged up and down and slid to one side only to swim back to the centre of her thoughts. She could taste that word, its sweet roundness, its slithering tail of sound at the end of its utterance that stung like tart berries in a goat's belly. Fires licked around it, smoke curled from it, blackening the air. It was a word with a thousand faces and a thousand expressions displaying but the faintest variations of universal dismay.

She wanted to eat that word. Take it by the neck and hold on until all life left it. She wanted to leap upon it after a vicious rush low over the ground. She wanted to eye it venomously, unblinkingly, from nearby cover. She wanted it to stalk her dreams.

And in the midst of this mental tantrum of desire, the cruel door buckled, indifference torn away until its very bones of flat wood and banded bronze quivered as if with ague, and then it swung open.

Witch Hurl converged upon that misshapen eruption of light, and the figure silhouetted within it.

Murder!

Puny bellowed and staggered back. Scaly creatures clung to him, upon his chest, fighting to close jaws on his throat; upon his arms where they writhed like tentacles; another attempting to burrow into his crotch. Blood spurted. He batted at the things, tore them away, flung them in all directions.

His brothers roared. The patrons screamed.

Feloovil, standing behind the bar, hissed a vile curse under her breath.

Nine lizard cats and not one of them much bigger than a house cat, or a scrawny, worm-ridden barn mouser. But this did nothing to mitigate their viciousness.

Puny clambered back onto his feet. Tiny and the others began swinging their huge weapons. Blades crashed through chairs, tables. Shrieks ended in frothy gurgles as those weapons struck hapless locals. Severed skull-pates knotted with hair spun across the room; limbs flopped, bounced and twitched atop tables or on the muddy and now bloody floor. The lizard cats evaded every blow, spinning, leaping, darting, clawing at everyone.

Feloovil beheld utter carnage from her place behind the bar. She saw two of the brothers struggling to ready a three-handed sword, only to wither to an exploding tabletop, staggering apart, their faces and necks studded with splinters. A cat leapt to wrap itself around the side of one of the brother's heads, tearing the ear off with its jaws, while the other brother stumbled over a chair that collapsed under him, and as he thumped on the floor, four cats closed in. His scream became a spray.

Then, as if of one mind, the lizard cats spied Feloovil, and all nine suddenly rushed her, leaping over the counter. Their multiple impacts made her stagger back. She screamed as talons raked through her tunic, bit deep into her flesh. Clothes disintegrating under the assault, she was stripped naked in a welter of blood.

Until one cat, seeking to sink its fangs into one of her breasts, instead found savage teeth clamping about its throat. A moment later another cat howled as another mouth, this one from the other breast, caught hold of one of his forelimbs and bit down hard enough to break bones.

All at once, more mouths appeared upon Feloovil's ample form: upon her shoulders; upon her low-slung belly; her thighs. Another split open on her forehead. Each one stretched wide, bearing teeth sharp as knifepoints.

'You damned witch!' Feloovil shrieked from countless mouths. 'Get away from me! I am your goddess, you stupid fool!'

In the room before Feloovil and her snarling or yowling attackers, where only a few huddled figures still twitched amidst the wreckage, and only three of the Chanter brothers stood with heaving chests, with weapons draining blood and gore, with lacerations upon their bodies, faces turned, eyes fixed upon the battle on the other side of the bar.

A dead cat, its throat crushed and leaking, hung from Feloovil's left breast. The cat trapped by the other breast's mouth had clawed that swelling of soft flesh into ragged ribbons, and still the mouth held on, masticating to grind through the creature's forelimb.

The other cats withdrew, crowded on the blood-smeared countertop, and then from their throats came a wavering, shrill chorus of voices. *'She's mine! You promised! Your daughter is mine! Her blood! Her everything!'*

'Never!' Feloovil screamed.

Its ruined limb chewed through, the cat upon her right breast fell away, running three sets of claws down Feloovil's belly on its way to the floor. She glanced down and stamped on its head, making a crushed-egg sound.

The remaining cats all flinched, barring the dead one hanging from the other breast.

Feloovil's many mouths all grinned most evilly. 'I got rid of you once, Hurl, and I'll do it again! I swear it!'

'Not you, whore! Her father did that!'

A voice then spoke from the doorway. 'And it seems I shall have to do so again.'

The seven remaining lizard cats all spun round. *'Whuffal Caraline Ganaggs! Vile Elder! Leave me be!'*

The grey-haired man with the finely trimmed beard, moustache and eyebrows slowly drew off his fox-fur hat. 'I warned you, Witch. Now look what you've done. Nearly everyone is dead.'

'Not my fault! Blame the Tarthenal!'

'Lies!' bellowed Tiny Chanter. 'We was defending ourselves!'

Whuffine studied them. 'Begone,' he said. 'I have already slain three of your siblings and if necessary, I will do away with the rest of you. It's this nostalgia,' he added, with an apologetic shrug. 'It's not good me getting nostalgic, you see. Not good at all.'

Growling, Tiny glared about, and then said, 'Tiny don't do getting killed. Let's go.'

'What about Relish?' asked Midge.

Tiny pointed at Feloovil. 'Send her up to the keep after us.'

Feloovil's mouths twisted into sneers. 'Just be glad she ain't no virgin,' those mouths all said. 'Hurl wants herself a sacrifice.'

'No more sacrifices,' said Whuffine, leaning on his walking stick. 'It's my talents with stone what's done us in here, and so it's up to me to clean all this up.'

'Then kill that Fangatooth!' shrieked Feloovil.

'No need,' the comber replied. 'He's already dead.'

'Then kill the one who killed him! Away with all sorcerers! I will not again be bound to a witch or warlock!'

Whuffine sighed. 'We'll see. A word or two might be enough to send them on their way. I don't like violence. Makes me nostalgic. Makes me remember burning continents, burning skies, burning seas, mountains of the dead and all that.' He pointed at the D'ivers. 'Witch Hurl, best semble now.'

The lizard cats drew together, blurred and then, in a slithering of spicy vapours, transformed into a scrawny hag of a woman. 'Aagh!' she cried. 'Look at me! My beauty, gone!'

Feloovil cackled with many of her ghastly mouths, while the others said, 'You ain't worth nothing anymore, Witch. You're banished! Go on, out into the storm! And never come back!'

'Else I kill you for certain this time,' added Whuffine.

'I want my keep!'

'No,' said Whuffine.

'I hate you all!' Hurl hissed, rushing for the door. 'Murder will have to wait. Now it's the other sweet word! Now it's hate. Hate hate hate hate! This isn't over, oh no it isn't—'

An odd sound came from the doorway, where Hurl suddenly stopped, and then stepped back, but when she did so she had no head, only an angled slice exposing her neck, from which blood pumped. Her knees then buckled and she collapsed upon the threshold.

Tiny Chanter stepped over her and peered into the tavern, looking round with a scowl. Blood trickled rivulets down the length of his huge sword's blade. 'Tiny don't like witches,' he said.

'Begone,' Whuffine said again. 'My last warning.'

'We're storming the keep now,' Tiny said, with a sudden bright smile.

To that, Whuffine shrugged.

'Hah hah hah!' said Tiny, before ducking back outside and bellowing commands to his brothers.

Eyes fixing on Feloovil, Whuffine sighed and shook his head. 'All for a slip of the chisel,' he said.

Huddled at the top of the stairs, Felittle edged back. A muffled murmuring came from between her legs, to which she responded with: 'Shhh, my lovely. She won't last much longer. I promise.'
And then it's my turn!

Coingood broke the last of the manacles from Warmet Humble and stepped back as the broken form sank to its knees on the stained floor. 'It wasn't me,' the Scribe whispered. 'I'm a good scribe, honest! And I'll burn your brother's book.'

Warmet slowly lifted his head and looked upon Bauchelain. 'My thanks,' he said. 'I thought mercy was dead. I thought I would spend an eternity hanging from chains, at the whim of my foul, evil brother's lust for cruelty. His vengeance, his treachery, his brutality. See how broken I am. Perhaps I shall never heal, and so am doomed to shuffle about in these empty halls, muttering under my breath, a frail thing buffeted by inimical draughts. I see a miserable life ahead indeed, but I bless you nonetheless. Freedom never tasted as sweet as this moment—'

'Are you done now?' Bauchelain interrupted. 'Excellent. Now, good Scribe, perhaps the other prisoner as well?'

'No!' snarled Warmet. 'He cheats!'

The other prisoner weakly lifted his head. 'Oh,' he quailed, 'so not fair.'

Shrugging, Bauchelain turned to his manservant. 'By this, Mister Reese, we see the true breadth of honest compassion, extending no more than a single blessed hair from one's own body, no matter its state. Upon the scene we can ably take measure, indeed, of the world's strait, and if one must, at times, justify the tenets of tyranny, over which a reasonable soul may assert decent propriety over lesser folk, in the name of the threat of terror, then upon solid ground we stand.'

'Aye, Master. Solid ground. Standing.'

Bauchelain then nodded to Warmet. 'We happily yield this keep to you, sir, for as long as you may wish to haunt it, and by extension, the villagers below.'

'Most kind of you,' Warmet replied.

'Mister Reese.'

'Master?'

'Upon this very night, we shall take our leave. Korbal prepares the carriage.'

'What carriage?' the manservant asked.

Bauchelain waved a dismissive hand.

Warmet slowly climbed to his feet. Coingood rushed to help him. 'See, milord?' he said. 'See how worthy I am?'

Warmet grimaced with what few teeth he had left. 'Worthy? Oh indeed, Scribe. Fear not. I am not my brother.'

As the sorcerer and his manservant made their way to the steep, stone stairs leading up to the ground level, Warmet loosed a low, evil laugh.

Both men turned.

Warmet shrugged. 'Sorry. It was just a laugh.'

'Tiny never gets lost,' said Tiny, looking around with a frown on his broad, flat brow. The sun was carving its way through the heavy clouds on the horizon. Then he pointed. 'There! See!'

The keep's tower was perhaps a third of a league to the south. The brothers set out. Midge, Puny and Scant, and of course Tiny himself. A short time later, after crossing a number of denuded, sandy hills, passing near a wretched shack with thin smoke drifting from its chimney, they reached the track they had, somehow, missed last night.

At the keep's gate they found Relish sitting near a heap that consisted of one corpse lying atop another, with both heads caved in by weapon blows. Their sister rose upon seeing them. 'You useless twits,' she said. 'I saw what was left of the tavern, and Feloovil was wearing a shroud and didn't want to cook me any breakfast.'

'Be quiet,' Tiny retorted. He walked up to the door and kicked at it.

'It's open,' Relish replied.

'Tiny don't use his hands.' He kicked again.

Puny walked past and opened the heavy door. They all trooped inside.

They found servants huddled in the stables, their eyes wide and full of fear, and in the house itself there was little to see, barring a pair of broken iron statues lying in murky pools of some foul oily liquid, and the exploded body of some man in robes, lying in the dining hall with demonic footprints stamped in the man's own blood around the corpse.

'We'll have to search every room,' Puny said, 'and see what's been squirrelled away, or who's hiding.'

Tiny grunted, glaring about. 'The bastards fled. I can feel it. We're not finished with them. Not a chance. Tiny never finishes with anything.'

'Look!' cried Scant. 'Cookies!' And he and Puny rushed to the table.

From the dirty window, Birds Mottle had watched the Chanters walk past in the pale light of early dawn, and once they were out of sight she sighed and turned back to study Hordilo where he lay on the bed. 'Well,' she said, 'I'm heading into Spendrugle.'

'What for?' he demanded.

'I'm tired of this. I'm tired of you, in fact. I never want to see you again.'

'If that's what you think,' he retorted, 'then go on, y'damned gull-smeared cow!'

'I'd rather sleep with a goat,' she said, reaching for her weapon belt.

'We was never married, you know,' Hordilo said. 'I was just using you. Marriage is for fools and I'm no fool. You think I believed you last night? I didn't. I saw you eyeing that goat on the way here.'

'What goat?'

'You don't fool me, woman. There ain't a woman in the whole world who can fool me.'

'I suppose not,' she said, on her way out.

Down in Spendrugle she found the rest of the squad, and there was much rejoicing, before they all headed off to plunder the wreck of the *Suncurl*.

Feeling turgid and sluggish, Ackle walked into the tavern, whereupon he paused and looked round. 'Gods, what happened here? Where is everyone?'

From the bar, Feloovil lifted a head to show him a smudged, blotchy face and red eyes. 'All dead,' she said.

'I always knew it was catching,' Ackle replied.

'Come on in and have yourself a drink.'

'Really? Even though I'm dead, too?'

Feloovil nodded. 'Why not?'

'Thank you!'

'So,' she said as she drew out an ale from the tap, 'where's that tax collector hiding?'

'Oh, he's not hiding,' Ackle said. 'He's dead, too.'

Feloovil held up the tankard. 'Now,' she smiled, 'that's something we can both drink to.'

And so they did.

A little while later Ackle looked round and shivered. 'I don't know, Feloovil. It's quiet as a grave in here.'

On the road wending north, away from the coast, the massive, black-lacquered carriage rolled heavily, leaf-springs wincing over stones and ruts. The team of six black horses steamed in the chill morning air, and their red eyes flared luminously in the growing light.

For a change, Bauchelain sat beside Emancipor as he worked the traces.

'Such a fine morning, Mister Reese.'

'Aye, Master.'

'A most enlightening lesson, wouldn't you say, on the nature of tyranny? I admit, I quite enjoyed myself.'

'Aye, Master. Why we so heavy here? This carriage feels like a ship with a bilge full of water.'

'Ah, well, we are carrying the stolen treasure, so it is no wonder, is it?'

Emancipor grunted around his pipe. 'Thought you and Korbal didn't care much for wealth and all that.'

'Only as a means to an end, Mister Reese, as I believe I explained last night. That said, since our ends are of much greater value and significance than what might be concocted by a handful of outlawed sentries, well, the course ahead is obvious, wouldn't you say?'

'Obvious, Master. Aye. Still, can't help but feel sorry for that squad.'

'In this, Mister Reese, your capacity for empathy shames humankind.'

'Heh! And see where it's got me!'

'How churlish of you, Mister Reese. You are very well paid, and taken care of with respect to your many needs, no matter how insipid they might be. I must tell you: you, sir, are the first of my manservants to have survived for as long as you have. Accordingly, I look upon you with considerable confidence, and not a little affection.'

'Glad to hear it, Master. Still' – he glanced across at Bauchelain – 'what happened to all those other manservants you had?'

'Why, I had to kill them, each and every one. Despite considerable investment on my part, I might note. Highly frustrating, as you might imagine. And indeed, on a number of occasions, I was in fact forced to defend myself. Imagine, one's own seemingly loyal manservant attempting to kill his master. This is what the world has come to, Mister Reese. Is it any wonder that I envisage a brighter future, one where I sit secure upon a throne, ruling over millions of wretched subjects, and immune to all concerns over my own safety? This is the tyrant's dream, Mister Reese.'

'I was once told that dreams are worthy things,' said Emancipor, 'even if they end up in misery and unending horror.'

'Ah, and who told you that?'

He shrugged. 'My wife.'

The open road stretched ahead, a winding track of dislodged cobbles and frozen mud; on all sides, the day brightened with an air of optimism.

Bauchelain then leaned back and said, 'Behold, Mister Reese, this new day!'

'Aye, Master. New day.'

CRACK'D POT TRAIL

'There will always be innocent victims in the pursuit of evil.'

THE LONG YEARS ARE BEHIND ME NOW. IN FACT, I HAVE never been older. It comes to a man's career when all of his cautions – all that he has held close and private for fear of damaging his reputation and his ambitions for advancement – all in a single moment lose their constraint. The moment I speak of, one might surmise, arrives the day – or more accurately, the first chime after midnight – when one realizes that further advancement is impossible. Indeed, that caution never did a thing to augment success, because success never came to pass. Resolved I may be that mine was a life gustily pursued, riches admirably attained and so forth, but the resolution is a murky one nonetheless. Failure wears many guises, and I have worn them all.

The sun's gilded gift enlivens this airy repose, as I sit, an old man smelling of oil and ink, scratching with this worn quill whilst the garden whispers on all sides and the nightingales crouch mute on fruit-heavy branches. Oh, have I waited too long? Bones ache, twinges abound, my wives eye me from the shadows of the colonnade with black-tipped tongues poking out from painted mouths, and in the adjudicator's office the water-clock dollops measured patience like the smacking of lips.

Well I recall the glories of the holy cities, when in disguise I knelt before veiled tyrants and god-kissed mendicants of the soul, and in the deserts beyond the crowded streets the leather-faced wanderers of the caravan tracks draw to the day's end and the Gilk guards gather in shady oases and many a time I travelled among them, the adventurer none knew, the poet with the sharp eyes who earned his keep unravelling a thousand tales of ancient days – and days not so ancient, if only they knew.

They withheld nothing, my rapt listeners, for dwelling in a desert makes a man or woman a willing audience to all things be they natural or unnatural; while I, for all the wounds I delivered, for all the words of weeping and the joys and all the sorrows of love and death that passed my tongue, smooth as olives, sweetly grating as figs, I never let a single drop of blood. And the night would draw on, in laughter and tears and expostulations and fervent prayers for forgiveness (eyes ashine from my languid explorations of the paramour, the silk-drenched beds and the flash of full thigh and bosom) as if the spirits of the sand and the gods of the whirlwinds might flutter in shame and breathless shock – oh no, my friends, see them twist in envy!

My tales, let it be known, sweep the breadth of the world. I have sat with the Toblai in their mountain fastnesses, with the snows drifting to bury the peeks of the longhouses. I have stood on the high broken shores of the Perish, watching as a floundering ship struggled to reach shelter. I have walked the streets of Malaz City, beneath Mock's brooding shadow, and set eyes upon the Dead-house itself. Years alone assail a mortal wanderer, for the world is round and to witness it all is to journey without end.

But now see me in this refuge, cooled by the trickling fountain, and the tales I recount upon these crackling sheets of papyrus, they are the heavy fruits awaiting the weary traveller in yonder oasis. Feed then or perish. Life is but a search for gardens and gentle refuge, and here I sit waging the sweetest war, for I shall not die while a single tale remains to be told. Even the gods must wait spellbound.

Listen then, nightingale, and hold close and sure to your branch. Darkness abides. I am but a chronicler, occasional witness and teller of magical lies in which hide the purest truths. Heed me well, for in this particular tale I have my own memory, a garden riotous and overgrown yet, dare I be so bold, rich in its *fecundity, from which I now spit these gleaming seeds. This is a story of the Nehemoth, and of their stern hunters, and too it is a tale of pilgrims and poets, and of me, Avas Didion Flicker, witness to it all.*

There on the pilgrim route across the Great Dry, twenty-two days and twenty-three nights in a true season from the Gates of Nowhere to the Shrine of the Indifferent God, the pilgrim route known to all as Cracked Pot Trail. We begin with the wonder of chance that should gather in one place and at one time such a host of travellers, twenty-three days beyond the Gate. And too the curse of mischance, that the season was unruly and not at all true. Across the bleak wastes the wells were dry, the springs mired in foul mud. The camps of the Finders were abandoned, their hearth-ashes cold. Our twenty-third day, yet we still had far to go.

Chance for this gathering. Mischance for the straits these travellers now found themselves in. And the tale begins on this night, in a circle round a fire.

What is a circle but the mapping of each and every soul?

The Travellers Are Described

*I*N THIS CIRCLE LET US MEET MISTER MUST AMBERTROSHIN, *doctor, footman and carriage driver to the Dantoc Calm-positis. Broad of shoulder and once, perhaps, a soldier in a string of wars, but for him the knots have long since been plucked loose. His face is scarred and seamed, his beard a nest of copper and iron. He serves the elderly woman who never leaves the tall carriage, whose face is ever hidden behind the heavy curtains of the windows. As with others here, the Dantoc is on pilgrimage. Wealth yields little succour when the soul spends too freely, and now she would come bowl in hand to beg before the Indifferent God. On this night and for them both, however, benediction is so distant it could well be on the other side of the world.*

Mister Must is of that amiable type, a walking satchel of small skills, quick to light his pipe in grave consideration. Each word he speaks is measured as a miser's coin, snapping sharp upon the wooden tabletop so that one counts by sound alone even when numbers are of no interest. By his singular squint people listen to him, suspicious perhaps of his cleverness, his wise secrets. Whiskered and solid, he is everyman's footman, and many fates shall ride upon his shoulders anon.

The second circle is a jostled one, a detail requiring some explanation. There are two knights among the Nehemothanai, the stern pursuers of the most infamous dread murderers and conjurers Bauchelain and Korbal Broach, and close upon the corpse-strewn

134

trail of these two blackguards are these dangerous men and women, perhaps only days from their quarry. But there is more to their urgency. It is said a mysterious woman leads a vengeful army, also seeking the heads of Bauchelain and Korbal Broach. Where is she? None here know.

Tulgord Vise has announced himself the Mortal Sword of the Sisters, and he is purity in all but name. His cloak is lined in white fur downy as a maiden's scented garden. The bold enamelled helm covering his stentorian skull gleams like egg-white on a skillet. His coat of polished mail smiles in rippling rows of silver teeth. The pommel of his proud sword is an opal stone any woman could not help but reach out and touch – were she so brave, so bold.

His visage glows with revelation, his eyes are the nuggets of a man with a secret hoard none could hope to find. All evil he has seen has died by his hand. All nobility he has granted by his presence he has sired in nine months' time. This is Tulgord Vise, knight and champion of truth in the holy light of the Sisters.

Wheel now to the other knight, so brash as to intrude upon the Mortal Sword's winsome claim to singular piety. By title, Arpo Relent is a Well Knight, hailing from a distant city that once was pure and true but now, by the bone-knuckled hands of Bauchelain and Korbal Broach, a sunken travesty of all that it had once been. So does the Well Knight charge, and so too is announced the very heart of his vow of vengeance.

If blessed white bolsters the mien of Tulgord Vise, it is the gold of the sun to gilt Arpo Relent's stolid intransigence, and the concatenation of comportment between these two knights promises a most uncivil clash to come. Arpo is broad of chest. Sibling swords, long-bladed and scabbarded in black wood filigreed in gold, are mounted one upon each hip, with pommels like golden eggs that could hatch a woman's sigh, and proud indeed of these weapons is Arpo Relent, and most unmindful of sighs is this paragon of chastity, and what might we make of that?

With the company of three brothers who might well beat up gorillas for merriment, Relish Chanter could be destined to live a life *unplucked, and had not Tiny Chanter himself stared hard at the haggle of artists and said, clear as the chop of an axe, that any man who deflowered sweet Relish would get cut so clean not even a starving sparrow could find the worm?*

In the middle of this stark, blood-draining pronouncement from her biggest brother, Relish had wandered off. She'd heard it a thousand times, after all. But what is known at present and what is to become known are different things. For now, let us look upon this most charmingly witless woman.

Black silk, as all know, is the mourner's vanity, and one is reminded of such flowing tresses when looking upon Relish's hair, and in the frame of such dangerous honey there resides a round face with cheeks blushed like slapped buttocks, and raven feathered lashes slyly offering obsidian eyes to any who would seek to claim them. Fullest of bosom and pouched below the arms, sweetly round of belly and broad-hipped, this description alas betrays a sultry confession, as I am yet to note clothing of any sort.

But such brothers! Tiny's mother, lost in the forest of Stratem beneath a most terrible storm, found refuge in a cavern, plunging straight into the arms of a cave bear, but in the instant of crushing contact, all notions of culinary anticipation alighting fires in the bear's brain quickly vanished and in their place a sudden expostulation of amorous possibility lifted them both heavenward. Who would knuckle brow at the audacity of such claims, when the offspring of the wrestlers' pact stood solid and true before all witnesses? The giant man's eyes dispensed all confusion regarding the contrariness of his name, for they were beastly small and rimmed in lurid red with all manner of leakage milking the corners. His nose was a snubbed snout glistening at the scent of blood. His teeth had the busyness of rodents. He bore the muscles of three men misaligned upon his ursine frame and hair sprouted from unlikely places to match the unlikely cunning of the words trickled out from between curling lips.

His brothers held him in much terror, but in this detail's veracity one must roll in a bed of salt given the malice of their regards upon the turn of Tiny's montane back. Midge Chanter was twin to Flea Chanter, both being the get of their mother's misadventures upon a sea strand where walruses warred in the mating season and she had the tusk-gouged scars to prove it. Such origins are beyond argument, lest whiskers twitch and malodorous weights heave upward and close in deadly lunge. Unlike Tiny and his beastly cloak, Midge and Flea wore with brazen pride the hides of their forbearer.

Other siblings abound, t'was said, but mercy held them at bay with a beater's stick; elsewhere and of their grim tale we must await some other night here at the flames of poetic demise.

Among the circle of hardened hunters but one remains. Silent as a forest and professional as a yeoman, Steck Marynd is no boaster of past deeds. Mysteries hide in the crooks of roots, and if eyes glitter from the holes of knots their touch is less than a whisper upon death's own shadow. He is nothing but the man seated before us. His face is flat, his eyes are shallow, his lips thin and his mouth devoid of all depth. His beard is black but sparse, his ears small as an ape's and muscled as a mule's as they independently twitch at every whisper and scuff. He chews his words into leather strips that slap wetly at night and dry up like eels in the day's sun.

Upon the back of his shaggy horse he carries a garrison's arsenal, each weapon plain but meticulously clean and oiled. He has journeyed half the world upon the trail of the Nehemoth, yet of the crime to spur such zeal he will say nothing.

We now turn, with some relief, to the true pilgrims and of these there are three distinct groups, each group seeking blessing at a different altar (though in truth and as shall be seen, they are all one and the same). Sages, priests and scholars stiffen their collars to unwelcome contradictions that nevertheless speak true, but as I am none of these worthies, uncollared as it were, that which on the surface makes no sense disturbs me not. Thus, we have a host of parallel tracks all destined to converge.

The Dantoc Calmpositis, eldest among the venerable Dantocs of Reliant City, must remain a creature unknown. Suffice it to say she was the first to set out from the Gates of Nowhere and her manservant Mister Must Ambertroshin, seated on the high bench of the carriage, his face shielded by a broad woven hat, uttered his welcome to the other travellers with a thick-volumed nod, and in this generous instant the conveyance and the old woman presumed within it became an island on wheels round which the others clustered like shrikes and gulls, for as everyone knows, no island truly stays in one place. As it crouches upon the sea and sand so too it floats in the mind, as a memory, a dream. We are cast out from it and we yearn to return. The world has run aground, history is a storm, and like the Dantoc Calmpositis, we would all hide in anonymity among the fragrant flowers and virtuous nuts, precious to none and a stranger to all.

Among the pilgrims seeking the shrine of the Indifferent God is a tall hawk of a man who was quick to offer his name and each time he did so an expectant look came to his vultured eyes, for did we not know him? Twitches would find his narrow face in the roaring blankness of our ignorance, and if oil glistened on and dripped from the raven feathered hair draped down the sides of his pressed-in head, well, none of us would dare comment, would we? But this man noted all and scratched and pecked his list of offenders and in the jerking bobs of his rather tiny head anyone near would hear a grackling sound commensurate with the duly irritated; and off he would march, destination certain but unknown, in the manner of a cock exploring an abandoned henhouse.

Well attired and possibly famous and so well comforted by material riches that he could discard them all (for a short time, at least), he proclaimed for himself the task of host among the travellers, taking a proprietary air in the settling of camp at day's end beginning on that first night from the Gates of Nowhere, upon finding the oddly vacated Finder habitations past the old tumulus. He would, in the days and nights to come, grasp hold of this role even as his fine coat flew to tatters and swirling feathers waked his every step, and the cockerel eye-glint would sharpen its madness as the impossible solitude persisted.

Clearly, he was a man of sparrow fates. Yet in the interest of fairness, our host was also a man of hidden wounds. Of that I am reasonably certain, and if he knew wealth so too he had once known destitution, and if anonymity now haunted him, once there had roosted infamy. Or at least notoriety.

Oh, and his name, lest we forget, was Sardic Thew.

Seeking the shrine of an altogether different Indifferent God, we come at last to the poets and bards. Ahead, in the city of Farrog, waited the Festival of Flowers and Sunny Days, a grand fete that culminated in a contest of poetry and song to award one supremely talented artist the Mantle proclaiming him or her The Century's Greatest Artist. That this is an annual award, one might hesitantly submit, simply underscores the fickle nature of critics and humans alike.

The world of the artist is a warrened maze of weasels, to be sure. Long bodies of black fur snake underfoot, quick to nip and snick. One must dance for fame, one must pull up skirts or wing out carrots for an instant's shudder of validation or one more day's respite from the gnawing world. Beneath the delighted smiles and happy nods and clasped forearms and whatnot, resides the grisly truth that there is no audience grand and vast enough to devour them all. No, goes the scurrilous conviction, the audience is in fact made up of five people, four of whom the artist knows well and in so knowing trusts not a single utterance of opinion. And who, pray tell, is that fifth person? That stranger? That arbiter of omnipotent power? No one knows. It is torture.

But one thing is certain. Too many artists for one person. Therefore, every poet and every painter and every bard and every sculptor dreams of murder. Just to snap hand downward, grasp hard the squirming snarling thing, and set it among one's foes!

In this respect, the artists so gathered in this fell group of travellers, found in the truth to come an answer to their most fervent prayers. Pity them all.

But enough commiseration. The poet has made the nest and must squat in it whilst the vermin seethe and swarm up the crack of doubt and into fickle talent's crotch. Look then, upon Calap Roud, the elder statesman of Reliant City's rotundary of artists, each of whom sits perched in precarious perfection well above the guano floor of the cage (oh of course it is gilded). This is Calap's twenty-third journey across the Great Dry of inspiration's perdition, and he is yet to win the Mantle.

Indeed, in his wretchedly long life, he draws close upon the century himself. One might even claim that Calap Roud is the Mantle, though none might leap for joy at the prospect of taking him home, even for a fortnight. There is a miserable collection of alchemies available to the wealthy and desperate (and how often do those two thrash limbs entwined in the same rickety bed?) to beat off the three cackling crows of old age, death, and ambition's dusty bowl, and Calap Roud remains a sponge of hope, smelling of almonds and cloves and lizard gall-bladders.

And so with the miracle of elixirs and a disgustingly strong constitution, Calap Roud looks half his age, except for the bitter fury in his eyes. He waits to be discovered (for even in Reliant City his reputation was not one of discovery but of pathetic bullying, backstabbing, sordid underhand graft and of course gaggles of hangers-on of all sexes, willing, at least on the surface, to suffer the wriggle of Calap's fickler every now and then; and worst of all, poor Calap knows it's all a fraud). Thus, whilst he has stolen a thousand sonnets, scores of epic poems and millions of clever offhanded comments uttered by talented upstarts stupidly within range of his hearing, at his very core he stares, mouth open, upon a chasm on all sides, wind howling and buffeting him as he totters on his perch. Where is the golden cage? Where are all the white-headed fools he shat upon? There's nothing down there but more down there going so far down there is no there at all.

Calap Roud has spent his entire albeit modest fortune bribing every judge he could find in Farrog. This was his last chance. He would win the Mantle. He deserved it. Not a single one of the countless vices hunting the weakling artists of the world dragged him down – no, he had slipped free of them all on a blinding road of virtuous living. He was ninety-two years old, and this year he would be discovered!

No alchemies or potions in the world could do much about the fact that, as one grew older and yet older, so too one's ears and nose. Calap Roud, as modestly wrinkled as a man in his late forties, had the ears of a veteran rock ape of G'danisban's coliseum and the nose of a probiscus monkey who'd instigated too many tavern brawls. His teeth were so worn down one was reminded of catfish mouths biting at nipples. From his old man's eyes came a leer for every woman, and from his leer came out a worm-like tongue with a head of purple veins.

Object of his lust, more often than not, was to be found in the Nemil beauty sitting languidly upon the other side of the fire (and if temptation burns where else would she be?). Purse Snippet was a dancer and orator famous across the breadth of Seven Cities. Need it be even said that such a combination of talents was sure to launch spurting enthusiasm among the heavy-breathing multitudes known to inhabit cities, towns, villages, hamlets, huts, caves and closets the world over?

Lithe was her smile, warm her midnight hair, supple of tongue her every curvaceous utterance, Purse Snippet was desired by a thousand governors and ten thousand nobles. She had been offered palaces, islands in artificial lakes, entire cities. She had been offered a hundred slaves each trained in the arts of love, to serve her pleasure until age and jealous gods took pleasure away. Lavished with jewels enough to adorn a hundred selfish queens in their dark tombs. Sculptors struggled to render her likeness in marble and bronze, and then committed suicide. Poets fell so far inside their poems of adoration and worship they forgot to eat and died at their garrets. Great warleaders tripped and impaled themselves on their own swords in pursuit of her. Priests forswore drink and children. Married men surrendered all caution in their secret escapades. Married women delighted in exposing and then murdering their husbands with ridicule and savage exposés.

And none of it was enough to soothe the unreasoning fires crisping black her soul. Purse Snippet knew she was the Thief of Reason. She stole wisdom from the wise and made them fools, but all that she took simply slid like lead dust between her amorously perfected fingers. She was also the Thief of Desire, and lust pursued her like a tidal surge, and where it passed, other women were left bloodless and lifeless. But with her own desires she was lost in frantic search, unable to alight long on any branch, no matter how inviting it had at first seemed.

So she had found a grey powder that she took in draughts of wine and this powder which had so blissfully taken her away from everything now revealed its true self. It was the Thief of her Freedom.

She would enter the famous shrine of the Indifferent God, seeking the blessing that none other had ever achieved. She believed she could win this, for she intended to dance and sing as she had never before danced and sang. She would steal the indifference from a god. She would.

She could not remember when last she had felt free, but she could not think of anything she wanted more.

Each night, alas, the powder beckoned her.

Arch rival to Calap Roud was the illimitable, ambitious, inexcusably young Brash Phluster. That he delighted in the old bastard's presence on this journey could hardly be refuted, for Brash so wanted Calap to witness youth's triumph in Farrog. With luck, it would kill him.

Seven years Calap had been defecating on Brash, trying to keep him down on the crusty floor, but Brash was not one to let a rain of guano discourage his destiny. He knew he was brilliant in most things, and where he lacked brilliance he could fill those spaces with bold bluster and entirely unfounded arrogance. A sneer was as good as an answer. A writhe of the lip could slice *throats across the room. He eyed Calap as would a wolf eye a dog, appalled at a shared pedigree and determined to tear the sad thing to pieces at the first opportunity.*

True talent was found in the successful disguise of genius, and Brash accounted himself a master of disguises. His future was glory, but he would reveal not a single hint, not one that some cragged critic or presumptuous rival might close in on, stoat fangs bared. No, they could dismiss him each and every day for the time being. He would unveil himself in Farrog, and then they would all see. Calap Roud, that stunning watery-eyed dancer, Purse Snippet, and the Entourage too—

The Entourage! Whence comes such creatures so eager to abandon all pretence of the sedentary? One envisages haste of blubbering excitement, slippery gleam in the eye, a lapdog's brainless zeal, as a canvas bag is stuffed full of slips and whatnot, with all the grace of a fakir backstage moments before performing before a gouty king. A whirlwind rush through rooms like shrines, and then out!

Pattering feet, a trio, all converging in unsightly gallop quick to feminize into a skip and prance once He Who Is Worshipped is in sight. The Entourage accompanies the Perfect Artist everywhere, gatherings great and small, public and intimate. They build the walls of the formidable, impregnable keep that is the Perfect Artist's ego. They patrol the moat, flinging away all but the sweetest defecatory intimations of mortality. They stand sentinel in every postern gate, they gush down every sluice, they are the stained glass to paint rainbows upon their beloved's perfectly turned profile.

But let us not snick and snack overmuch, for each life is a wonder unto itself, and neither contempt nor pity do a soul sound measures of health, lest some issue of envy squeeze free in unexpectedly public revelation. The object of this breathless admiration must wait for each sweet woman's moment upon the stage in the bull's eye lantern light of our examination.

To begin, we shall name all three and attach to each select obtuberances in aid of future recollection. Sellup, first for no particular reason, has seen twenty-three summers and remembers in excruciating detail four of them, from the moment she first set eyes upon her beloved Perfect Artist to the very present found in this tale. Of her first eighteen years she has no memory whatsoever. Was she born? Did she possess parents? Did they love her? She cannot recall. Brothers? Sisters? Lovers? Offspring? Did she eat? Did she sleep?

Dark brown and springy was her hair, whirling in spirals down upon her shoulders. Singular was her eyebrow yet miraculously independent in its expressions at each end. Her nose, narrow and jutting, bore all the mars of inveterate ill-considered interjection. Her mouth cannot be described for it never ceased moving long enough for an accurate appraisal, but her chin jutted with blurred assurance. Of her body beneath her flowery attire, no knowledge is at hand. Suffice it to say she sat a saddle well with nary a pinch upon the horse's waist. Sellup of the blurred mouth, then.

Next was Pampera, linguistically challenged in all languages including her native one. Hers was the art of simpering, performed in a serried host of mannerisms and transitory parades from pose to pose; each pose held, alas, both an instant too long and never long enough. In the span of one's self settling into a chair, Pampera could promenade from cross-legged on a silk cushion with elbows upon inside knees and long fingers laced to bridge the weight of her chin (and presumably all the rest above it) to a sudden languorous stretching of one long perfectly moulded leg, flinging back her head with arms rising in rampant stretch to lift and define her savage breasts, before rising to her feet like smoke, swinging round with a pivot of her fine hips wheeling into view the barrel cask of her buttocks before pitching down on the divan, hair flowing like tentacles as she propped up her head with one hand whilst the other (hand, not head) endeavoured to reinsert her breasts into the skimpy cups the style and size of which she likely settled upon a month into puberty.

For Pampera, it must be noted, puberty was buried beneath virginity deep in a tomb long sealed by a thick mound of backfill, with the grass growing thick and high and all significance of the hump long lost to the memory of the local herders. Despite this, she was nineteen years old. Her hair, for all its tidal pool titillations, was the hue of honey though tipped with black kohl ink a finger's width at the ends. She had the eyes of a boy's fantasy, when eyes meant something, the two of them being overlarge and balanced just so to hint at warm scented boudoirs wherein things slid from mothering to something other with all the ease of a blinking lid (or two). Sculptors might dream of smoothing out her likeness in golden wax or creamy clay. Painters might long to lash her fineness to canvas or stuccoed wall, if not ceiling. But one could not but suspect the obsession was doomed to be short lived. Can an object of lust prove much too lust-worthy? Just how many poses are possible in the world and how did she come by them all? Why, even in sleep her repose palpitates in propitious perfection. The sculptor, looking upon this, would despair to discover that Pampera is her own sculpture and there was naught to be done to match or hope to improve upon it. Painters might fall into toxic madness seeking to match the tone of her flawless skin and it is to the toxic we will return to precipitate our reminding of dearest Pampera.

Could a poet hope to match her essence in words without an intermission of nausea?

To return to these three, then, we at last come to Oggle Gush, innocent of all depravity not through inexperience, but through blissful imperviousness to all notions of immorality. A slip of mere sixteen years since the day in wonder her mother issued her forth, as naturally unaware of her pregnancy as she was of the innocence her daughter would so immaculately inherit, Oggle Gush deserves nothing but forgiving accolades from paladins and scoundrels alike (excepting only Great Artists). Ever quick to smile even at the most inappropriate of times, shying like a pup from a master's twitching boot one moment only to cuddle in his lap upon the next, squirming as only a thing of claws, wet nose and knobby limbs can.

Not one of her deeds was ill-meant. Not one of the numerous fatal accidents trailing her could be set upon her threshold. When she sang, as she often did, she could not find a solid key if it was glued to her tongue, but all looked on in damp-eyed adoration – and what, perchance, were all thinking? Was this an echo of personal conceits crushed and abandoned in childhood? Was it the unblinking boldness of the talentless that triggered reminiscences of childish lavishments? Or was it something in her dramatic earnestness that disengaged some critical faculty of the brain, leaving only sweet-smelling mush?

Oggle Gush, child of wonder and plaything of the Great Artist, all memory of you is sure to remain immortal and unchanging. As pure as nostalgia, and the cold cruelty with which you were misused, ah, but does this not take us to the Great Artist himself, he with the Entourage? But it does indeed.

Nifty Gum has thrice won the Mantle of the Century's Greatest Artist. His Entourage of three as found upon the trail across the Great Dry, only a month past numbered six hundred and fifty-four, and if not for Oggle's well-intentioned house cleaning beneath the deck of the transport barge, why, they'd all still be with him. As if Oggle knew a thing about boats and whatnot. As if she even understood the function of hull plugs and drain holes, or whatever those things were called.

He looked taller than he looked, if one can say such a thing, and by the sure nods all round, it seems that one can. He wore his cloak and measured his stride as if he was a bigger man than he was, and not one of his even features could be said to be exaggerated yet neither were they refined. In gathered host they were pleasant on his face, but should one find them neatly severed and arrayed among rivals on a hawker's bazaar table, why, none would even so much as reach for them, much less buy them – except, perhaps, as curios of mundanity.

Of talent's measure Nifty Gum had an ample helping, nothing to overflow the brim, yet something, a fire, a wink, a perspicacity for promotion, the brazen swanning of his sweep and flurry in passage (trailed as ever by his giggling entourage), something or perhaps all these things and more, served him so well that his renown was as renowned as his songs and poems. Fame feeds itself, a serendipity glutton of the moment prescient in publicity.

For such a figure, no exaggeration can be overstated, and the glean of modesty rests in uneasily thin veneer upon a consummated self-adoration that abides the presumption of profundity with all the veracity of that which is truly profound. And to this comment my personal failure as a poet has no bearing whatsoever. Why, I have never viewed words as worthy weapons, having so many others of far more permanent efficacy at my disposal.

Indeed, as I look upon myself at this fire upon the twenty-third night, I see a young(ish) poet of modest regard, scant of pate and so casting nothing of the angelic silhouette upon yonder tent wall as Nifty Gum's cascading curls of thick auburn hair achieve without his giving it a moment's thought, as the gifted rarely if ever regard their gifts except in admiration, or, more deliciously, of admiration in witnessing the admiration of others for all that which is of himself, be it voice or word or hair.

No, I am retracted unto myself, as was my wont in those times, the adventurer none knew, a teller of tales to defy the seam of joinings between those I spun in the Great Dry all those years ago, and this tale that I spin now.

Lives hang in the balance at every moment, in every instant, for life itself is a balance, but sometimes the sky is bright overhead and brilliant with sun and heat and sometimes the sky is darkness with the cold spark of stars dimmed by mistral winds. We see this as the wheel of the heavens, when such a belief is only our failed imagination, for it is us who wheel, like a beetle clinging to a spinning ring, and we are what mark the passing of days.

I see myself then, younger than I am, younger than I have ever been. This is my tale and it is his tale both. How can this be?

But then, what is a soul but the mapping of each and every wheel?

*

Upon such stately musings rests lightly, one hopes, this adden-
dum. On the twenty-third day just past, the grim mottle of travellers
came upon a stranger walking alone. Starved and parched, Apto
Canavalian was perhaps in his last moments, and as such might
well have met a sudden and final demise at the hands of the Nehe-
mothanai and pilgrims, but for one salient detail. Through cracked
lips that perhaps only filled out with a steady diet of wine and raw
fish, Apto made it known that he was not a pilgrim of any sort.
No, more an adjudicator in spirit if not profession (aspirations
notwithstanding), Apto Canavalian was among the elite of elites
in the spectrum of intellectualia, a shaper of paradigms, a prog-
nosticator of popularity in the privileged spheres of passing
judgement. He was, in short, one of the select judges for The Cen-
tury's Greatest Artist.

His mule had died of some dreaded pox. His servant had stran-
gled himself in tragic mishap one night of private pleasuring and
now lay buried in a bog well north of the Great Dry. Apto had
made this journey at his own expense, the invitation from Farrog's
mystical organizers sadly lacking in remuneration, and had noth-
ing left of his stores save one dusty bottle of vinegarish plonk (and,
it soon became known, his dread state of dehydration had more to
do with the previous nine bottles than with a dearth of water).

If artists possessed true courage (and this is doubtful) their
teeth-bared defence of Apto's life in the moments following his
discovery would do well as admirable proof, but so often in life
does one mistake desperation and self-interest for courage, for in
mien both are raw and indeed, appalling.

Even venerable Tulgord Vise withdrew before the savage dis-
play of barely human snarls. In any case, the vote had already
been concluded.

The night is younger than you might think, and the tale now lies
before us, an enormous log of mysterious origins quick to drink
flames from the bed of coals, and the fat sizzles and the circle is
drawn tight save the Dantoc who remains, as ever, within her
carriage.

Let us, for convenience, list them once more. Apto Canavalian, newly arrived and perhaps more pallid than salvation would invite. Calap Roud, an artist with a century of mediocrity lifting him to minuscule heights. Avas Didion Flicker, venerable voice of this modest retelling. Purse Snippet, demure in the sultry flare of flames, her eyes haunted as dying candles. Brash Phluster, destined as first to speak in the circle only moments away, sitting like a man on an ant hill, feverish of regard and clammy with sweat. Nifty Gum, redoubtable in his reclination, polished boots gleaming at the ends of his outstretched legs upon which are draped two of his Entourage, Oggle Gush, her lashes brushing in every slow blink the precious bulb of Nifty's flower, and Sellup, brow awiggle like a caterpillar on a burning twig, whilst Pampera shifts to a new pose artful in breastly impression upon the side of Nifty's auburn-flowing head and what gurgling promise does that single imprisoned ear detect?

Tiny and Flea and Midge Chanter command the bulwark upon one side of the circle, a pugnacious wall wildly bristling and smelling like a teenaged boy's bedding, and close to Tiny's scabbed hand sits Relish Chanter, lips smeared in grease and casting hooded wanton but unwanted glances my way. Steck Marynd paces off to her right, ghostly in the faded glow of the hearth. Growl might his stomach but damned if he will soothe it in this company of beasts. Well Knight Arpo Relent sits in the shiver of firelit gold glaring at the Chanters while Tulgord Vise picks at his (own) teeth with the point of a dagger, poised as ever for a cutting remark.

At the last seat is our host, and lest we forget his name, it is suited to muscled sartorial commentary, thus stunning the memory to recollect Sardic Thew, avian in repose, cockerel in assuredness though perhaps somewhat rattled by this point in the proceedings.

Thus, and so well chewed this introduction not a babe would choke upon it, one tremulously hopes.

The tale begins with sudden words in the light of the fire, the heat laden with watering aroma, and in the gloom beyond, three horses shift and snort and the two mules eye them with envy (they look taller than they really are, and those brushed manes are an affront!). The Great Dry is a frost-sheathed wasteland beyond the fiery island, a scrabble of boulders and rocks and stunted shrubs. The carriage creaks with inner motion and perhaps one rheumy eye is pressed to a crack in the curtains, or an ear perched upon dainty hopes cocked in the folded crenellations of a peep-hole.

And of the air itself, dread is palpable and diluvian.

A Recounting of the
Twenty-third Night

'BUT LISTEN! WHOSE TALE IS THIS?' SO DEMANDED BRASH
Phluster, a man who was of the height that made short
men despise him on principle. His hair was natty and
recalcitrant, but fulsome. He had teeth aligned in a mostly even
row, full lips below a closely trimmed moustache and above a
closely trimmed beard. It was a mouth inclined to pout, a face
commissioned for self-pity, and of his nose nothing will be said.

Declamation ringing in the night air, Brash awaited a challenge
but none came. We may list the reasons, as they could be of some
significance. Firstly, twenty-three days of desperate deprivation
and then horror had wearied us all. Secondly, the pull-ward weight
of necessity was proving heavy indeed, at least for the more delicate among us. Thirdly, there was the matter of guilt, a most
curious yoke that should probably be examined at length, but
then, there is no need. Who, pray tell, is unfamiliar with guilt? In
punctuated pointedness, fat snapped upon coals and almost everyone flinched.

'But I need a rest and besides, it's time for the critical feasting.'

Ah, the critical feasting. I nodded and smiled though none noticed.

Brash wiped his hands on his thighs, shot Purse a glance and
then shifted about to make himself more comfortable, before saying, 'Ordig's only claim to artistic genius amounted to a thousand
mouldy scrolls and his patron's cock in hand. Call yourself an
artist and you can get away with anything. Of course, as everyone knows, shit's fertile soil, but for what? That's the question.'

151

The fire spat sparks. The smoke gusted and swung round, stinging new sets of eyes.

Brash Phluster's face, all lit orange and flush and lively, floated like a thing disembodied in the hearth's light; his charcoal cloak with its silver ringlets shrouded him below the neck, which was probably just as well. That head spouting all its words could just as easily be sitting on a stick, and it was still a wonder that it wasn't.

'And Aurpan, well, imagine the audacity of his *Accusations of a Guilty Man*. What a heap of tripe. Guilty? Oh, aye. Guilty of being utterly talentless. It's important – and I know this better than anyone – it's important to bear in mind the innate denseness of the common people, and their penchant to forgive everything but genius. Aurpan was mercifully immune to such risks, which was why everyone loved him.'

Flea Chanter grunted. 'Give that leg a turn, someone.'

Brash was closest to the spit but naturally he made no move. Sighing loudly, Mister Must Ambertroshin leaned forward and took hold of the cloth-wrapped handle. The crackling, sizzling haunch was weighty, inexpertly skewered, but he managed it after a few tries. He sat back, glanced round guiltily, but no one met his eyes.

Darkness, the flames' uncertain light and the smoke were all gifts of mercy this night, but still the stomach lowered heavy and truculent. No one was hungry. This cooked meat would serve the morrow, the aching journey through a strangely emptied Great Dry, the twenty-fourth day in which we travellers felt abandoned by the world, the last left alive, and there was the fear that the Indifferent God was no longer indifferent. Were we the forgotten, the sole survivors of righteous judgement? It was possible, but not, I fair decided as I eyed the leg over the flames, likely.

'So much for Ordig and Aurpan,' said Tulgord Vise. 'The question is, who do we eat tomorrow night?'

Critical feasting being what it is, sated and indeed bloated satisfaction is predicated upon the artist on the table, as it were. More precisely, the artist must be dead. Will be dead. Shall be naught else but dead. Limbs lie still and do not lash back. Mouth resides slack and rarely opens in affronted expostulation (or worse, vicious cut the razor's wit, hapless corpses strewn all about). The body moves at the nudge only to fall still once more. Prods elicit nothing. Pokes evoke no twitch. Following all these tests, the subject is at last deemed safe to excoriate and rend, de-bone and gut, skin and sunder. Sudden discovery of adoration is permitted, respect acceptable and its proud announcement laudable. Recognition is at last accorded, as in 'I recognize that this artist is dead and so finally deserving the accolade of "genius", knowing too that whatever value the artist achieved in life is now aspiring in worth tenfold and more.' Critical feasting being what it is.

Well Knight Arpo Relent was the first to speak on the matter (what matter? Why, this one). There had been desultory discussion of horses and mules, satisfaction not forthcoming. Resources had been pooled and found too shallow. Stomachs were clenching.

'There are too many artists in the world as it is, and that statement is beyond challenge,' and to add veracity to the pronouncement's sanctity (since the gaggle of artists had each and all shown signs of sudden alertness), Arpo Relent settled a gauntlet-sheathed hand upon the pommel of one of his swords. The moment in which argument was possible thus passed. 'And since we among the Nehemothanai, whose cause is most just and whose need is both dire and pure, so as to speak in the one voice of honourable necessity, since we, then, require our brave and loyal mounts, whilst it is equally plain that the Dantoc's carriage can proceed nowhere without the mules, we are at the last faced with the hard truth of survival.'

'You mean we need to eat somebody.' So said I at this juncture, not because I was especially dense, but speaking in the interest of pith (as one has no doubt already observed in the tale thus far). 'Say it plain' has always been my motto.

To my crass brevity Arpo Relent frowned as if in disappointment. What artist asks such a thing? What artist lacks the intellectual subtlety to stroke the kitty of euphemism? When the game shall not be played, fun shall not be had. The nature of 'fun' in this particular example? Why, the 'fun' of sly self-justification for murder, of course, and what could be more fun than that?

Tiny Chanter was the first to play, with a tiny grin and a piggy regard for the poor artists who now stood miserable as sheep in a pen watching the axeman cometh. 'But which one first, Relent? Fat to skinny? Obnoxious to useless? Ugly to pretty? We need a system of selection is what we need. Flea?'

'Aye,' Flea agreed.

'Midge?'

'Aye,' Midge agreed.

'Relish?'

'I like the one with the shaved head.'

'To eat first?'

'What?'

Tiny glared at me. 'I warned you earlier, Flicker.'

At some juncture in discourse with a thug, one comes to the point where any uttered word shall obtain as sole justification for violence. It is not the word itself that matters. It is not even the speaking thereof. Indeed, nothing of the world outside the thick skull and murky matter it contains is at all relevant. There is no cause and no effect. No, what has occurred is the clicking of a gear wheel, a winding down to the moment of release. The duration is fixed. The process is irreversible.

Resigned, I waited for Tiny Chanter's pique to detonate.

Instead, Relish said, 'They should tell stories.'

Steck Marynd took this moment to snort, and it was an exquisite snort in that it clearly counted as the first vote on the matter.

Tiny blinked, and blinked again. One could see the tumult of confusion whisk clouds over his brutal visage, and then his grin broadened, frightening away all the clouds. 'Flea?'

'Aye.'

'Midge?'

'Aye.'

'Knight Relent, you happy with that?'

'I am "Sir" to you.'

'Was that a "yes"?'

'I think it was,' said Flea. 'Midge?'

'Oh aye, that was a "yes" all right.'

At this moment Tulgord Vise, Mortal Sword to the Sisters, stepped into the understandable gap between the Nehemothanai and the limpid artists (of which, at this juncture, I blithely count myself). He blew out his cheeks (his upper ones) and stretched a measured regard upon all those gathered, including the host whose name momentarily escapes me, Mister Must, Purse Snippet and the Entourage (poor Apto was yet to arrive). One presumes this was meant to establish Tulgord's preeminence as the final arbiter in the matter (yes, this matter), but of course he too possessed but a single vote, and so the issue was perhaps, for him, one of moral compass. Clearly, he saw in this moment the necessity of justification, and upon ethical concerns who else but Tulgord Vise to dispense adjudication?

Well, how about the victims?

But the retort is equally quick, to be found in the puerile weaponry all within easy reach of those with nothing to lose and everything to gain. Since when do ethics triumph power? So uneven was this debate no one bothered to troop it out for trampling. Accordingly, Tulgord's posturing was met with all the indifference it deserved, a detail entirely lost on him.

The nightly procession was thus determined, as we artists would have to sing not to be supper. Ironically, alas, the very first victim had no tale to attempt at all, for his crime at this moment was to object, with all the terror of a lifetime being picked last in every children's game he ever played, and some memories, as we all know, stay sharp across a lifetime. 'Just eat the damned horses!'

But Arpo Relent shook his head. 'There is no question of any more votes,' he said. 'As anyone of proper worth would agree, a knight's horse is of far greater value than any poet, bard or sculptor. It's settled. The horses don't get eaten.' And he glowered as was his wont following everything he said.

'But that's just—'

It is safe to say that the word this nameless artist intended was 'stupid' or 'insane' or some other equally delectable and wholly reasonable descriptive. And as added proof when his severed head rolled almost to my feet following the savage slash of Tulgord Vise's blessed sword, the mouth struggled to form its thoughtful completion. Ah, thus did the memory stay sharp.

The first poet, having been killed so succinctly, was butchered and eaten on the eleventh night upon the Great Dry. The sixteenth night saw another follow, as did the twentieth night. Upon the twenty-second night the vote was taken following Arpo's raising of the notion of midday meals to keep up one's strength and morale, and so a second artist was sacrificed that night. At that time the ritual of critical feasting began, instigated by a shaky Brash Phluster.

Two more hapless poets, both bards of middling talents, gave the performance of their lives on that night.

At this point, listeners among you, perhaps even you, might raise an objecting hand (not the first one, you say? I wasn't paying attention). Thirty-nine days upon the Great Dry? Surely by now, with only a few days away from the ferry landing below the plateau, the need for eating people was past? And of course you would be right, but you see, a certain level of comfort had been achieved. In for a pinch, in for a pound, as some sated bastard once said. More relevantly, thirty-nine days was the optimum crossing, and we were far from optimum, at least to begin with. Does this suffice? No, of course it doesn't, but whose tale is this?

Ordig now resided in bellies with a weighty profundity he never achieved in life, while Aurpan's last narrative was technically disconnected and stylistically disjointed, being both raw and overdone. The critical feasting was complete and the artists numbered four, Purse Snippet being given unanimous dispensation, and by the host's judgement sixteen nights remained upon the Great Dry.

While talent with numbers could rarely be counted among the artist's gifts, it was nonetheless clear to all of us sad singers that our time upon this world was fast drawing to a close. Yet with the arrival of dusk this made no less desperate our contests.

Brash Phluster licked his lips and eyed Apto Canavalian for a long moment, before drawing a deep breath.

'I was saving this original dramatic oratory for the last night in Farrog, but then, could I have a more challenging audience than this one here?' And he laughed, rather badly.

Apto rubbed at his face as if needing to convince himself that this was not a fevered nightmare (as might haunt all professional critics), and I do imagine that, given the option, he would have fled into the wastes at the first opportunity, not that such an opportunity was forthcoming given Steck Marynd and his perpetually cocked crossbow which even now rested lightly on his lap (he'd done with his pacing by this time).

In turn, Brash withdrew his own weapon, a three-string lyre, which he set to tuning, head bent over the instrument and face twisted in concentration. He plucked experimentally, then with flourish, and then experimentally again. Sweat glistened in the furrows of his brow, each bead reflecting the hearth's flames. When those seated began growing restless he nudged one wooden peg one last time, and then settled back.

'This is drawn from the Eschologos sequence of Nemil's Redbloom Poets of the Third Century.' He licked his lips again. 'Not to say I stole anything. Inspired, is what I mean, by those famous poets.'

'Who were they again?' Apto asked.

'Famous,' Brash retorted, 'that's who they were.'

'I mean, what were their names?'

'What difference would that make? They sang famous poems!'

'Which ones?'

'It doesn't matter! They were the Redbloom Poets of Nemil! They were famous! They were from the time when bards and poets were actually valued by everyone! Not pushed aside and forgotten!'

'But you've forgotten their names, haven't you?' Apto asked.

'If you never heard of them how would you know if I knew their names or not? I could make up any old names and you'd just nod, being a scholar and all! I'm right, aren't I?'

Calap Roud was shaking his head but there was a delighted glimmer in his eyes. 'Young Brash, it serves you ill to berate one of the Mantle's judges, don't you think?'

Brash rounded on him. 'You don't know their names either!'

'That's true, I don't, but then, I'm not pretending to be inspired by them, am I?'

'Well, you're about to hear inspiration of the finest kind!'

'What was inspiring you again?' Tiny Chanter asked.

Flea and Midge snorted.

Our host was waving his hands about, and it was finally understood that this manic gesturing was intended to capture our collective attentions. 'Gentlemen, please now! The Poet wishes to begin, and each must have his or her turn—'

'What "her"?' demanded Brash. 'All the women here got dispensations! Why is that? Is it, perhaps, because everyone eligible to vote happened to be men? Imagine how succulent—'

'Enough of that!' barked Tulgord Vise. 'That's disgusting!'

Arpo Relent added, 'What it is, is proof of the immoral decrepitude of artists. Everyone knows it's the women who do the eating.'

Moments later, in the ensuing silence, the Well Knight frowned. 'What?'

'Best begin, Poet,' said Steck Marynd in a hunter's growl (and don't they all?).

A wayward ember spun towards Nifty Gum and all three of his Entourage fought to fling themselves heroically into its path, but it went out before it could reach any of them. They settled back, glowering at each other.

Brash strummed the three strings, and began singing in a flat falsetto.

> *'In ages long past*
> *A long time ago*
> *Before any of us were alive*

Before kingdoms rose from the dust
There was a king—'

'Hang on,' said Tiny. 'If it was before kingdoms, how could there be a king?'

'You can't interrupt like that! I'm singing!'

'Why do you think I interrupted?'

'Please,' said the host whose name escapes me again, 'let the Poet, er, sing.'

'There was a king
Who name was . . . Gling
Gling of the Nine Rings
That he wore—'

'On his bling!' Flea sang.

'That he wore one each day
Of the week—'

Apto broke into a coughing fit.

'Gling of the Seven Rings
Was a king whose wife
Had died and sad was his sorrow
For his wife was beloved,
A Queen in her own right.
Her tresses were locks
Flowing down long past
Her shapely shoulders and
Long-haired she was and
Longhair was her name
She who died of grief
Upon the death of their
Daughter and so terrible her grief
She shaved her head and was

Long-haired no longer
And so furious her beloved
Gling that he gathered up
The strands and wove a rope
With which he strangled
Her – oh sorrow!'

The 'oh sorrow' declamation was intended to be echoed by the enraptured audience, and would mark the closure of each stanza. Alas, no one was in a ready state to participate, and isn't it curious how laughter and weeping could be so easily confused?

Savagely, Brash Phluster plucked a string and pressed on.

'But was the daughter truly dead?
What terrible secret did King Gling
Her father possess
There in his tower
At the very heart
Of the world's greatest kingdom?
But no, he was a king
Without any terrible secrets,
For his daughter had been
Stolen, and lovely she was,
The princess whose name was
. . . Missingla
And this is her tale known to all
As Missingla's Tale
Beloved daughter of King Gling and
Queen Longhair,
A princess in her own right
Was Missingla of the shapely shoulders
Royal her eye lashes
A jewelled crown her sweet lips'

Oh dear, I just added those two lines. I could not help it, and so I do urge their disregard.

'Was Missingla of the shapely shoulders
Stolen by the king in the kingdom
Beyond the mountains between the lake
In the Desert of Death
Where almost nothing lived
Or could hope to live
Even should we live in hope'

Ah, and again.

'and this king his name was . . . Lope
Who bore a sword twice as tall as he
And the armour of an ogre made of stone
And cruel was his face, evil his eyes,
As he swam the lake at night
To scale the tower to steal her away
Missingla – oh sorrow!'

The Entourage cried, 'Oh sorrow!' and even Purse Snippet
smiled over her secretive cup of tea.

'But she was waiting oh yes, for
Cruel and evil as he was, so too rich
Beyond all measure ruling the world's
Richest kingdom beyond the mountains
And so not stolen at all, sweet daughter
No! Missingla Lope they swam away!'

In the chaos that ensued, Brash thrashed at the strings of the
lyre until one broke, the taut gut snapping up to catch him in the
left eye. Steck's crossbow, cursed with a nervous trigger, accidentally released, driving the quarrel through the hunter's right foot,
pinning it to the ground. Purse sprayed a startlingly flammable
mouthful of tea into the fire, and in the flare-up Apto flung himself backward with singed eyebrows, rolling off the stone he'd
been perched on and slamming his head into a cactus. The host's

hands waved frantically since he could no longer breathe. The Entourage was in a groping tangle and somewhere beneath it was Nifty Gum. Tulgord Vise and Arpo Relent were scowling and frowning respectively. Of Tiny Chanter, only the soles of his boots were visible. Midge suddenly stood and said to Flea, 'I pissed myself.'

By this extraordinary performance Brash Phluster survived the twenty-third night and so would live through the twenty-fourth night and the following day. And as he opened his mouth to announce that he wasn't yet finished, why, I did clamp my hand over the offending utterance, stifling it in the rabbit hole. Mercy knows a thousand guises, say you not?

Madness, you say? That I should so boldly aver Brash Phluster's suicidal desire to further skin himself? But while confidence is a strange creature, it is no stranger to me. I know well its pluck and princeps. It bears no stretch of perception to note my certain flair in the proceeding of this tale, for here I am, ancient of ways, and yet still alive. Ah, but perhaps I deceive you all with this retro-active posture of assuredness. A fair point, were it not for the fact of its error in every regard. To explain, I possessed even then the quiet man's stake, a banner embedded deep in solid rock, the pennants ever calm no matter how savage the raging storms of worldly straits. It is this impervious nature that has served me so well. That and my natural brevity with respect to modesty.

Upon recovery, whilst in relief Brash Phluster stumbled off to vomit behind some boulders, Calap Roud made to begin his tale. His hands trembled like fish in a tree. His throat visibly tight-ened, forcing squeaking noises from his gaping mouth. His eyes bulged like eggs striving to flee a female sea-turtle's egg hole. The vast injustice of Brash Phluster's dispensation was a bright sizzling rage in his visage, a teller's tome of twitches plucking at each and every feature so fecklessly clutched beneath his forehead. He was not holding up well to this terrible pressure, this twill or die. Unravelled his comportment, and in tumbling, climbing pursuit a lifetime of missed moments, creative collapses, blocks and heights not reached, all heaved up at this moment to drown him in a deluge of despair.

He was the cornered jump-mouse, the walls too high, the floor devoid of cracks, and all he could do was bare his tiny teeth in the pointless hope that the slayer looming so cruelly over him was composed of cotton fluff. Ah, how life defends itself! It is enough, oh yes, to shatter even a staked man's heart. But know we all that this modern world is one without pity, that it revels in the helplessness of others. Children pluck wings and when grown hulking they crush heads and paint rude words on public walls. Decay bays on all sides, still mourning the moon's tragic death. Pity the jump-mouse, for we are ourselves nothing other than jump-mice trapped in the corners of existence.

In his desperation, Calap Roud realized his only hope for survival would be found in the brazen theft of the words of great but obscure artists, and, fortunate for him, Calap possessed a lifetime of envy in the shadow of geniuses doomed to dissolution in some decrepit alley (said demises often carefully orchestrated by Calap himself: a word here, a raised eyebrow there, the faintest shakes of the head and so on. It is of course the task of average talents to utterly destroy their betters, but not until every strip of chewable morsel is stripped from them first). Thus lit by borrowed inspiration, Calap Roud gathered himself and found a sudden glow and calm repose in which to draw an assured breath.

'Gather ye close, then,' he began, in the formal fashion of fifty or so years ago, 'to this tale of human folly, as all tales of worth do so recount, to the sorrow of men and women alike. In a great age past, when giants crouched in mountain fastnesses, fur-bedecked and gripping in hard fists the shafts of war spears; when upon the vast plains below, glaciers lay like dead things, draining their lifeblood into ever-deepening valleys; when the land itself growled like a bear in the spring, stomach clenched in necessity, a woman of the Imass slowly died, alone, banished from her ken. She was curled in the lee of a boulder left behind by the ice. The furs covering her pale skin were worn and patched. She had gathered about herself thick mosses and wreathes of lichen to fight against the bitter wind. And though at this time none was there to cast regard upon her, she was beautiful in the way of Imass women, sibling to the earth and melt-waters, to the burst of blossoms in the short season. Her hair, maiden braided, was the colour of raw gold. Her face was broad and full-featured, and her eyes were green as the moss in which she huddled.'

A worthy theft to my mind, for I knew this tale. Indeed, I knew the poet whose version Calap was now recounting. Stenla Tebur of Aren managed to fashion a dozen epic poems and twenty or so hearth-tales (or garden-tales, as the Aren knew them, having long since abandoned such rustic scenes as sitting round a hearth beneath stars unmarred by city smoke and light), before his untimely death at the age of thirty-three. The altar upon which he breathed his last, I am told, was naught but grimy cobbles behind the Temple of Burn, and the breath whereof I speak was a wheezing one, thick with consumption. Alcohol and d'bayang had taken this young man's life, for such are the lures of insensate escape to the tormented artist that rare is the one who deftly avoids such fatal traps. T'was not fame that killed him, alas (for, I would boldly state, death in the time of fame is not as tragic as it might seem, for lost potential is immortal; far greater the sorrow and depression upon hearing of a once-famous life ending in the obscurity of the obsolete). Stenla had given up his siege upon the high and solid walls of legitimacy, manned as it was by legions of jaded mediocrities and coddled luminaries. Forays of vicious rejection had crushed his spirit, until senseless oblivion was all he sought, and found.

'What terrible crime had so cruelly cast her out from her own people?' Calap went on, quoting word for word and thus impressing me with his memory. 'The wind howled with the voices of a thousand spirits, each and all bemoaning this fair maiden's fate. Tears from the sky lost the warmth of life and so drifted down as flakes of snow. The great herds in the distance had wandered down to the valley flanks to escape the wind and its dread voices of sorrow. She curled alone, dying.'

'But why?' demanded Sellup, earning venomous glares from Pampera and Oggle Gush, for in showing interest in a tale not told by Nifty Gum she was committing a gross betrayal, and even the Great Artist himself was frowning at Sellup. 'Why did they leave her like that? That was evil! And she was good, wasn't she? A good person! Pure of heart, an innocent – she had to be! Oh, this is a terrible fate!'

Calap raised a hand in which was cupped borrowed wisdom. 'Soon, my dear, all will be known.'

'Don't wait too long! I don't like long stories. Where's the action? You've already gone on too long!'

And to that criticism Pampera, Oggle and Nifty all nodded. What is it to trust so little in the worth of a tale well and carefully told? What doth haste win but breathless stupidity? Details of import? *Bah!* Cry these flit-flies. Measures of pace and the thickening of the mat into which the awl must weave? Who cares? Chew into rags and be on to the next, spitting as you go! I look upon the young and see a generation of such courage as to dare nothing more than the ankle-deep, and see them standing proud and arrogant upon the thin shorelines of unknown seas – and to call this living! Oh, I know, it is but an old man's malaise, but to this very moment I still see Sellup and her wide-eyed idiocy, I still hear her impatience and the smack of her lips and the gulp of her breaths, a young woman who could pant herself unconscious in her haste to see her mind transported . . . elsewhere. A stutter of steps, a stagger of impetus, oh, so much she missed!

'Would she lie there unto death,' Calap asked, 'nameless and unknown? Is this not the darkest tragedy of all? To die in anonymity? To pass from the world unremarked, beneath the notice of an entire world? Oh, the flies wait to lay their eggs. The capemoths flutter like leaves in nearby branches, and in the sky the tiny spots that are ice vultures slowly grow larger with their cargo of endings. But these are the mindless purveyors of mortality and nothing more than that. Their voice is the whisper of wings, the clack of beaks and the snip of insect mouths. It is fey epitaph indeed.'

Steck Marynd limped close to the fire and set down another

branch collected from somewhere. Flames licked the hoary bark and found it to their liking.

'So we must turn back, outracing the cool sun of spring to the colder sun of winter, and we see before us a huddle of huts, humped upon the bones and tusks of tenag, thick bhederin hides stretched tight over the skeletal frames. The camp crouches not upon the highest hills overlooking the valley, nor upon the banks of the melt-water stream in the basin of the valley itself. No, it clings to a south-facing terrace a little more than halfway up the valley side. The wind's fiercest force is cut in this place and the ground is dry underfoot, draining well into the soggy flats flanking the stream. The Imass were greatly skilled at such things; perhaps indeed their wisdom was a bred thing, immune to true learning, or it may instead be true that those not yet severed from the earth know full the precious secrets of harmony, of using only what is given—'

'Get on with it!' shouted Sellup, the words jumbled by the knuckle bones she was sucking clean. Spitting one out she popped another one in. Her eyes shone like candle flames awakened by a drunkard's breath. 'It was a stupid camp. That's all. I want to know what's going to happen! Now!'

Calap nodded. Never argue with a member of one's audience.

Well, perhaps he believed that. For myself, and after much rumination on the matter, I would suggest the following qualifiers. If that member of the audience is obnoxious, uninformed, dim, insulting, a snob, or drunk, then as far as I am concerned, they are fair game and, by their willingness to engage the artist in said contest, should expect none other than surgical savaging by said artist. Don't you think?

'These Imass in this camp had suffered a terrible winter. Their hunters could find little game, and the great flocks of birds were still weeks away. Many of the elders had walked off into the white to save the lives of their children and grandchildren, for winter spoke to them in a secret language only the aged understand. "In life's last days, the white and the cold will lie in the bed of the old." So said the wise among them. Yet, even for this sacrifice, the others weakened with each day. The hunters could not range as far as once they could before exhaustion turned them back. Children had begun eating the hides that kept them warm at night, and now fevers raced among them.

'She was out, upon the high ridge overlooking the camp, collecting the last autumn's mosses where the winds had swept the snows away, and so was the first to see the approaching stranger. He came down from the north, thickly clad in tenag furs. The long bone-grip of a greatsword rose behind his left shoulder. His head was bared to the winds at his back, and she could see that he was dark, stone-skinned and black-haired. He dragged a sledge in his wake.

'In the time before he drew closer, hard thoughts rattled in her mind. They could turn no stranger away in times of need. This was a law among her kind. Yet this warrior was a big man, taller than any Imass. His hunger would be a deep pit, and weakened as her clan's warriors now were, the stranger could take all he wanted if he so chose. And more, she was troubled by that sledge, for bundled as it was, she knew it bore a body. If it lived it would need caring. If dead, the warrior was delivering a curse upon her people.'

'A curse?' Sellup asked. 'What kind of curse?'

Calap blinked.

Seeing that he had no specific response to this question, I cleared my throat. 'Death *leaves* such camps, Sellup, and that is well and as it should be. This is why the elders, when they decide it is time to die, walk out into the white. It is also why all kills are butchered well away from the camp itself, so that only meat, hide and bones intended to be made into tools – gifts to life one and all – enter the camp. Should death come *into* the camp, the hosts are cursed and must immediately make propitiations to the Reaver and his demon slaves, lest Death find the camp to his liking and so make it his home. When the Reaver finds a home, the living soon die, do you see?'

'No.'

Sighing, I said, 'It is one of those rules couched in spiritual guise that, in truth, has a more secular purpose. To bring some-one dead or dying into a small camp is to invite contagion and disease. Among such a close-knit clan, any infection is likely to claim them all. Thus, the Imass had certain rules to prevent such a thing occurring, yet those rules, alas, conflicted with that of never turning a guest away in times of need. So the woman was with troubled thoughts, yes?'

'But he's evil – he has to be! He's the Reaper himself!'

'Reaver,' I corrected, 'or so the citizens of Aren so call the Lord of Death.'

Calap flinched and would not thereafter meet my eyes. 'So she stood, trembling, as the stranger, who had clearly chosen her as his destination, now drew up to halt nine paces distant. She saw at once that he was not Imass. He was from the mountain heights. He was Fenn, a giant of Tartheno Toblakai blood. And too, she saw that he bore the marks of battle. Slash wounds that had cut through the woolly Tenag hide had encrusted the slices with the warrior's own blood. His right hand and forearm were black-ened with old gore, and so too was his face spattered in violent maps.

'He was silent for a time, his heavy eyes held upon her, and then he spoke. He said—'

'Finish this tomorrow night,' Tiny Chanter said, cracking a wide yawn.

'That's not how it works,' Tulgord Vise said in a growl. 'We can't very well vote if one of the tales remains incomplete.'

'I want to hear more, don't I?' Tiny retorted. 'But I'm falling asleep, right? So, we get the rest tomorrow night.'

I noticed that Nifty Gum was endeavouring to catch my eye. In response I raised my brows and shrugged.

Oggle Gush said then, 'But I want to hear Nifty's story!'

Nifty made to silence the girl, if the twitching of his hands and their spasmodic clutching (miming throttling a throat) was any indication, though who but Nifty could truly say?

'Tomorrow during the day then! Same for the other one – we got time and since there ain't nothing to see anyway and nothing to do but walk, let's have 'em entertain us till sunset! No, it's settled and all, ain't it, Flea?'

'Aye,' said Flea. 'Midge?'

'Aye,' said Midge.

'But the night is still young,' objected Arpo Relent, and one could tell from a host of details in his demeanour that the sudden dispatch of impending death-sentences had frustrated some pious repository of proper justice within his soul, and now in his face there was the blunt belligerence of a thwarted child.

Purse Snippet then surprised us all by saying, 'I will tell a tale, then.'

'My lady,' gasped the host, 'it was settled – there is no need—'

'I would tell a tale, Sardic Thew, and so I shall.' With this assertion muting us all she then hesitated, as if startled by her own boldness. 'Words are not my talent, I admit, so forgive me if I stumble on occasion.'

Who could not but be forgiving?

'This too belongs to a woman,' she began, her eyes on the flames, her elegantly fingered hands encircling her clay vessel. 'Loved and worshipped by so many—' She sharply looked up. 'No, she was no dancer, nor a poet, nor actress nor singer. Hers was a talent born to, yet not one that could be further honed. In truth, it was not a talent at all, but rather the gathering of chance – lines and curves, symmetries. She was, in short, beautiful, and from that beauty her life was shaped, her future preordained. She would marry well, above her station, and in that marriage she would be the subject of adoration, as if she was a precious object of art, until such time that age stole her beauty, whereupon her fine home would become a tomb of sorts, her bedroom rarely frequented at night by her husband, whose vision of beauty remained forever youthful.

'There would be wealth. Fine foods. Silks and fetes. There would be children, perhaps, and there would be something . . . something wistful, there in her eyes at the very end.'

'That's not a story!' Oggle Gush said.

'I have but begun, child—'

169

'Sounds more like an end to me, and don't call me child, I'm not a child,' and she looked to Nifty for confirmation, but he was instead frowning at Purse Snippet, as if seeking to understand something.

Purse Snippet resumed her tale, but her eyes were now bleak as she gazed into the fire. 'There are quests, in a person's life, that require no steps to be taken. No journey across strange landscapes. There are quests where the only monsters are the shadows in a bedroom, the reflection in a mirror. And one has no companions hale and brave to stand firm at one's side. This is a thing taken in solitude. She was loved by many, yes. She was desired by all who saw the beauty of her, but of beauty within herself, she could see nothing. Of love for the woman she was inside, there was none. Can the pulp of the fruit admire the beauty of its skin? Can it even know that beauty?'

'Fruits don't have eyes,' said Oggle Gush, rolling her own. 'This is stupid. You can't have quests without mountain passes and dangerous rivers to cross, and ogres and demons and wolves and bats. And there's supposed to be friends of the hero who go along and fight and stuff, and get into trouble so the hero has to save them. Everyone knows that.'

'Oggle Gush,' Apto Canavalian said (now that he'd done plucking cactus spikes from the back of his head), 'kindly shut that useless hole in your face. Purse Snippet, please, go on.'

Whilst Oggle gaped and mawped and blinked like an owl in a vice, Steck Marynd appeared to add more wood to the fire and it occurred to me that the stolid, grim ranger was indeed doing woodly things, which meant that all was well, though of greater tasks and higher import something must obtain with this personage, sooner or later. One hopes.

'She would stand upon a balcony overlooking the canal where the gramthal boats plied carrying people and wares. Butterflies in the warm air would lift as if on sounds to gather round her.' She faltered then, for some unknown reason, and drew a few breaths before continuing, 'and though all who chanced to look up, all who set eyes upon her, saw a maiden of promise, indeed, a work of art posed thus upon that balcony, why, in her soul there was war. There was anguish and suffering, there was dying to an invisible enemy, one that could cut the feet beneath every mustered argument, every armoured affirmation. And the dark air was filled with screams and weeping, and upon no horizon did dawn make promise, for this was a night unending and a war without respite.

'A lifetime, she would tell you, is a long time to bleed. There is paint for pallor, the hue of health to hide the ashen cheeks, but the eyes cannot be disguised. There you will find, if you look closely, the tunnels to the battlefield, to that unlighted place where no beauty or love can be found.'

The fire ate wood, coughed smoke. No one spoke. The mirror was smudged, yes, but a mirror nonetheless.

'Had she said but a single word,' muttered someone (was it me?), 'a thousand heroes would have rushed to her aid. A thousand paths of love to lead her out of that place.'

'That which cannot love itself cannot give love in return,' she replied. 'So it was with this woman. But, she knew in her heart, the war must end. What devours within will, before long, claw its way to the surface, and the gift of beauty will falter. Dissolution rots outward. The desperation grew within her. What could she do? Where in her mind could she go? There was, of course,' and inadvertently her eyes dropped to the cup in her hands, 'sweet oblivion, and all the masks of escape as offered by wine, smoke and such, but these are no more than the paths of decay – gentle paths, to be sure, once one gets used to the stench. And before long, the body begins to fail. Weakness, illness, aching head, a certain lassitude. Death beckons, and by this alone one knows that one's soul has died.'

'My lady,' Tulgord Vise ventured, 'this tale of yours demands a knight, sworn to goodness. 'Tis a fair damsel in deepest distress—'

'Two knights!' cried Arpo Relent, although with a zeal that sounded, well, forced.

Tulgord grunted. 'There is only one *one* knight in this tale. The other knight is the other knight.'

'There can be two knights! Who is to say there can't?'

'Me. I'm to say. I will allow two knights, however. The real one, me. The other one, you.'

Arpo Relent's face was bright red, as if swallowing flames. 'I'm not the other knight! You are!'

'When I cut you in two,' Tulgord said, 'you can be two knights all by yourself.'

'When you cut me in two you won't know which way to turn!'

Silence has flavour, and this one was confused, as follow certain statements that, in essence, make no sense whatsoever, yet nonetheless possess a peculiar logic. Such was this momentary interlude composed of frowns, clouds and blinks.

Purse Snippet spoke. 'She came to a belief that the gods set alight a spark in every soul, the very core of a mortal spirit, which mayhap burns eternal, or, in less forgiving eyes, but gutters out once the flesh has fallen beyond the last taken breath. To sharpen her need, she chose the latter notion. Now, then, there was haste and more: there was a true edge of possible redemption. If in our lives, we are all that we have and ever will have, then all worth lies in the mortal deed, in that single life.'

'A woman without children, then,' Apto murmured.

'What gift passing such beauty on? No, she was yet to marry, yet to take any seed. Only within her mind had she so aged, seeing an end both close and far off, ten years in a century, ten centuries in an instant. Resolved, then, she would seek to journey to find that spark. Could it be scoured clean, enlivened to such bright fire that all flaws simply burned away? She would see, if she could.

'But what manner this journey? What landscape worth the telling?' And upon that moment her eyes, depthless tunnels, found me. 'Will you, kind sir, assemble the scene for my poor tale?'

'Honoured,' said I mostly humbly. 'Let us imagine a vast plain, broken and littered. Starved of water and bare of animals. She travels alone and yet in company, a stranger among strangers. All she is she hides behind veils, curtains of privacy, and awaiting her as awaiting the others, there is a river, a flowing thing of life and benison. Upon its tranquil shores waits redemption. Yet it remains distant, with much privation in between. But what of those who travel with her? Why, there are knights avowed to rid the world of the unseemly. In this case, the unseemly personages of two foul sorcerers of the darkest arts. So too there are pilgrims, seeking blessing from an idle god, and a carriage travels with them and hidden within it there is a face, perhaps even two, whom none have yet to see—'

'Hold!' growled Steck Marynd, looming out of the gloom, crossbow held at rest but cocked across one forearm. 'See how the colour has left the face of this woman? You draw too close, sir, and I like it not.'

Mister Ambertroshin relit his pipe.

'Lacks imagination,' purred Nifty Gum. 'Allow me, Lady Snippet. The village of her birth is a smallholding upon the rocky shores of a fjord. Beyond the pastures of her father the king, crowded forests rear up mountainsides, and in a deep fastness there sleeps a dragon, but most restlessly, for she had given birth to an egg, one of vast size, yet so hard was the shell that the child within managed no more than to break holes for its legs and arms, and with its snout it had rubbed thin the shell before its eyes, permitting it a misty regard of the world beyond. And, alas, the egg monster had escaped the cavern and now roved down between the black trees, frightened and lost and so most dangerous.

'In its terrible hunger it has struck now in the longhouse of the king, rolling flat countless warriors as they slept ensorcelled by the child's magic. Woe, bewails the king! Who can save them? Then came the night—'

'What knight?' Tulgord demanded.

'No, night, as in the sun's drowning in darkness—'

'The knight drowned the sun?'

'No, fair moon's golden rise—'

'He's mooning the sun?'

'Excuse me, what?'

'What's the knight doing, damn you? Cracking that egg in half, I wager!'

'The sun went down – that kind of night!'

'Why didn't you say so?' Tulgord Vise snorted.

'And the monster set a deep magic upon the longhouse. Bursting down the stout door—'

'He ran into the knight!'

'No, instead, he fell in love with the princess, for as she was ugly on the inside, he was ugly on the outside—'

'I'd suspect,' Apto said, 'he'd be pretty ugly on the inside, too. Dragon spawn, trapped in there. No hole for the tail? He'd be neck deep in shit and piss. Why—'

Brash Phluster, working on his second supper, having lost the first one, pointed a finger bone at Nifty and, with a greasy smirk, said, 'The Judge is right. You need to explain things like that. The details got to make sense, you know.'

'Magic answers,' snapped Nifty with a toss of his locks. 'The monster walked into the main hall and saw her, the princess, and he fell in love. But knowing how she would view him with horror, he was forced to keep her in an enchanted sleep, through music piped out from the various holes in his shell—'

'He farted her a magic song?' Apto asked.

'He piped her a magic song, which made her rise as would one sleep-walking, and so she followed him out from the hall.'

'What's that story got to do with Purse Snippet's?' Was that my question? It was.

'I'm getting to that.'

'You're getting to the point where I vote we spit you on the morrow,' said Tulgord Vise.

Arpo Relent agreed. 'What a stupid story, Nifty. An egg monster?'

'There is mythical precedent for—'

'Make your silence deep, poet,' warned Steck Marynd. 'My Lady Snippet, do you wish any of these pathetic excuses for poets to resume their take on your tale?'

Purse Snippet frowned, and then nodded. 'Flicker's will suit me, I think. A river, the promise of salvation. Strangers all, and the hidden threat of the hunted – tell me, poet, are they closer to their quarry than any might imagine?'

'Many are the stratagems of the hunted, My Lady, to confound their pursuers. So, who can say?'

'Tell us more of this quest, then.'

'A moment, please,' said Steck Marynd, his voice grating as if climbing a stone wall with naught but fingernails and teeth. 'I see that unease has taken hold of Mister Ambertroshin. He gnaws upon the stem and the glow waxes savage again and again.' He shifted the crossbow, his weight fully on the one leg whose foot had not suffered the indignity of a quarrel through it only a short time earlier. 'You, sir, what so afflicts you?'

Mister Ambertroshin was long in replying. He withdrew his pipe and examined the chipped clay stem, and then the bowl, whereupon he drew out his leather pouch and pinched out a small amount of stringy rustleaf, which he deftly rolled between two fingers and a thumb before tamping it down into the pipe's blackened bowl. He drew fiercely a half-dozen times, wreathing his lined face in swirling clouds. And then said, 'I think I'm going to be sick.'

'Ordig was something sour, wasn't he?' Brash Phluster opined, and then he laughed in the manner of a hyena down a hole, even as he wiped grease from his hands.

Grunting, Steck Marynd limped away, and over one shoulder said, 'It's suspicious, that's all. Suspicious strange, I mean. Diabolical minds and appalling arrogance, aye, that spells them sure. I need to think on this.' And with that, off into the darkness he went.

Tulgord Vise was frowning. 'Addled wits. That's what comes of living in the woods with the moles and pine beetles. Now then, Flicker, you have a burden to bear with your tale, for it must carry this Lady's charge. Tell us more of the knights.'

'They number five in all,' did I respond, 'though one was counted senior by virtue of skill and experience. Sworn were they to the execution of criminals, and criminality in this case was found in the committal of uncivil behaviour. More specifically, in behaviour that threatened the very foundations of civilization—'

'Just so!' said Arpo Relent, fist striking palm, an unfortunate gesture in that he was wearing gauntlets with studded knuckles but only kid leather upon the palms. His eyes widened in pain.

'Tender pleasures this night for you,' commented Apto Canavalian.

Of course Arpo would not permit a single utterance of agony to escape him. So he sat, cringing, jaw muscles bulging, water starting in his eyes.

'As it is known to all,' I resumed, 'civilization lies at the very heart of all good things. Wealth for the chosen, privilege for the wealthy, countless choices for the privileged. The promise of food and shelter for all the rest, provided they work hard for it. And so on. To threaten to destroy it is, accordingly, the gravest betrayal of all. For, without civilization there is barbarism, and what is barbarism? Absurd delusions of equality, generous distribution of wealth, and settlements where none can hide in anonymity their most sordid selves. It is, in short, a state sure to be deemed chaotic and terrible by the sentinels of civilization, said sentinels being, by virtue of their position, guardians of property more often than not their own. To display utter disdain for civilization, as surely must be the regard of the two mad sorcerers, can only be seen as an affront and a most insistent source of indignation.

'Thus fired with zeal we see our brave knights, sworn one and all to destroy those who would threaten the society that has granted them title and privilege, and what could be more selfless than that?'

Purse Snippet, I saw in aside, was smiling, even as both Tulgord and Arpo made solemn their nods, Arpo having recovered to some extent from his foray into the melodramatic. Apto Canavalian was smirking. Brash Phluster was dozing, as were Nifty Gum's entourage of three, whilst their erstwhile paragon was hair-twirling (one of those habitual gestures that brings to mind the measured unravelling of intelligence or at least the appearance thereof) and, at the same time, seeking to catch the eye of Relish

176

Chanter, the last Chanter still awake this night. There are, it must be said, men of the world who, for all their virility, will at times confuse the gender of their flirtations. For it is in my mind the woman who twirls (for how wonderfully attractive is vacuousness, assuming natural affinities to knee-high morals and such), and bats lashes with coy obviousness, not the man. Nifty Gum, alas, having no doubt witnessed endless displays of said behaviour directed at him, now seemed to believe it was courting's own language; alas, in giving back what he so commonly received, he did little more than awaken Relish's sneer, Relish being a goodly woman and not inclined to mothering.

'I could speak now of the pilgrims,' said I, 'but for the ease of narrative, let it be simply said that all who seek to catch the eyes of a god, are as empty vessels believing themselves incomplete unless filled, and that said fulfilment is, for some reason, deemed to be the gift given by some blessed hand not their own.'

'Is there no more to it, then?' so asked Mister Ambertroshin, who seemed to have recovered his momentary disquiet.

My gesture was one of submission. 'Who am I to say, in truth? Even I can see the lure of utter faith, the zest of happy servitude to an unknown but infinitely presumptuous cause.'

'Presumptuous?'

'Anyone can fill silence with voices, kind driver,' I said in reply. 'We are most eager inventors, are we not?'

'Ah, I understand. You suggest that religious conviction consists of elaborate self-delusion, that those who hear the words of their god telling them to do this and that, are in fact inventing their certainty as they go.'

'I would hazard it all begins,' ventured I, 'with someone else, a priest or priestess, or the written words of the same, telling them first. The mission needs direction, yes? One serves a purpose, and in the god's silence, who is it that presumes to describe that purpose? If all are lost, the first to shout that he or she has found something will be as a lodestone to others, and their desperation will become the joy of relief. But who is to say that the one who shouted first was not lying? Or mad? Or possessing ambitions of a far more secular nature – to wit, how much can I bilk all these fools for?'

Mister Ambertroshin puffed on his pipe. 'You do indeed walk a wasteland, sir.'

'And does yours look so different?'

'We may agree on the rocks and stones, sir,' he replied, 'but not their purpose.'

'Rocks?' Tulgord said, eyes a little wild. 'Stones and purpose? Aye, give me a rock, something for you to trip over, driver, but for me, something to bash in your head.'

Mister Ambertroshin blinked. 'Why, Mortal Sword, why ever would you do that?'

'Because you're confusing things, that's why! Flicker's telling a story, right? By all meets he must now give voice to the evil whispers seeking ill of our heroes.'

'I think he just did,' the pipe-puffing old man said.

'The knights hold to honour and purpose and the two are one and the same,' proclaimed Tulgord Vise. 'While the pilgrims seek salvation. Now, who else travels with the worthy ones? Someone diabolical, no doubt. Speak on, poet, for your life!'

'I hesitate, good knight.'

'What?'

'Without the Chanters, there can be no proper vote, can there? And by their collective snores one can presume only that they are insensate to the moment. Lady Snippet, does your need devour all patience?'

She regarded me with some slyness. 'Do you promise redemption, poet?'

'I do.'

Sudden doubt in her eyes, perhaps even a trembling vulnerability. 'Do you?' she asked again, this time in a whisper.

I gave a gentle nod.

'It would seem most honourable,' suggested Apto, studying me grave and seriously, 'that your fate, Flicker, now be made to depend solely upon Purse Snippet's judgement. Should you achieve redemption of the woman in her tale, your life is secured. Should you fail, it is forfeit. This being said, and by all the nods I see it is a notion well-met, it would not do to string her along and so assure your survival. So I pose the following provision. Should she decide, at any time in your telling, that you are simply . . . shall we say, *padding* your narrative, why, one or both of the knights shall swing their swords.'

'Wait!' cried Calap Roud. 'I am not nodding and this is not well-met – not by me anyway. Can we not all see that Lady Snippet is a woman of mercy? And not such a soul as would so cruelly condemn someone? This is Flicker's devious mind at work here! He makes a promise he cannot keep, but only to win his life upon this terrible journey! Perhaps indeed they are in cahoots!'

At that the dancer straightened in perfect haughtiness. 'Bitter words from you, poet, dredged from a poor and squalid mind. I have performed before the most fickle tyrants, when it was *my* life that was at stake. Of harsh yet true adjudication, I have learned at the feet of masters. Do you think I would dissemble? Do you think I would not cast a most hardened eye upon this man who so boldly promises redemption? Be it understood to all, that Avas Didion Flicker chooses – if he dares – the deadliest of courses in the days ahead!'

So stark and shocking this bridling that all were humbled, and as all eyes now fixed upon me, I knew the truth of this bargain. Did my courage quiver? Did my bowels loosen more than a stomach full of human meat warranted (and yes, Ordig was indeed most sour)? Shall I take this instant to weave the woeful lie? I shall not. Indeed, I make no comment whatsoever, and before that sharp wealth of regard, I tilted my head a fraction toward the venerable dancer and said, 'I do accept.'

And to that she could only gasp.

Weariness soon landed on bat wings, ears twitching, flitting ghostly among us all, and this night was, by silent consensus, done. As I rose to walk watery into the darkness for a few moments of cold desert air and mocking stars, beyond all heat and light from the dying hearth, I drew close about me my threadbare cloak. It is the still moments in which doubts assail the soul. So I'm told.

The notion was untested as soft arms closed about my waist and two full and generous breasts spread across my back. A breathy voice then murmured in my ear, 'You're a clever one, aren't you?'

Perhaps not so clever as I believed, as my right hand dropped and stole back to find the outside of her thigh. What is it with men, anyway? To see is as good as to touch when seeing is all we can manage; but to touch is as good as to explode in milky clouds in the spawning stream. 'Oh,' murmured I, 'sweet Relish. Is this wise?'

'My brothers snore, do you hear them?'

'Alas, I do.'

'When they're snoring, you can drop rocks on their heads and still they won't wake. I know. I've done it. Big rocks. And when they wake up with knobs and bruises, I just tell them they all knocked heads together last night, and so they get mad at each other and that's that.'

'It would seem that I am not the only clever one here.'

'That's right, but then, maybe you ain't so smart after all. She'll see you killed, that bitchy dancer, you know that, don't you?'

'It is indeed quite possible.'

'So this could be your last night left alive. Let's make it a fun one.'

'Who saw you leave the camp?'

'No one. I made sure everyone was bedded down.'

'I see. Well, then . . .'

Shall we titter and wing gazes heavenward now? Shall we draw the veil of modesty upon these decorous delicacies? Is it enough to imagine and paint private scenes in the mind? A knowing smile, the flash of bared flesh, a subtle editing of grunts and pinches and shifts as elbows prod and jab? Dreamy our sighs, delicious our ponderings? What's wrong with you?

She straddled my face. The meaty flesh of her thighs closed like the jaws of a toothless leg monster, oozing with suffocating intentions. My tongue discovered places it had never known before, and partook of flavours I wish never to revisit. After some frenzied mashing of orifices that made the bones of my skull creak ominously, she lifted herself clear with an ear-crackling sucking sound, twisted round and descended once more.

There are places in the human body where no man's face belongs, and this fact found its moment of discovery for hapless Avas Didion Flicker at that precise instant. Well, once her fullest intentions were made evident, that is. The heave with which I freed myself was of sufficient vigour as to throw her over my feet and flat on her face upon the stony ground. Her grunt was most becoming. She endeavoured a vicious kick which I deftly dodged as I rolled up and onto her back, forcing both knees up between her legs. Twisting, she flung a handful of sand and gravel into my eyes. Ignoring this ambiguous gesture I took hold of her meaty thighs and lifted them off the ground, and then impaled her most mightily.

She clawed furrows in the hard ground as if swimming for shore, but the riptide of my lust held her fast. It was, assuredly, do or drown for Relish Chanter. Her gasps gusted clouds of dust round her face. She coughed, she hacked, she moaned in the manner of mothers behind the pantry door, and with her hips she bolted like a cow before the bull, only to lunge backward with small animal cries. I leaned forward and wrapped close my arms, hands finding her breasts. I took hold of full nipples and tried to twist them off, failing but not for want of trying to be sure.

As all know, lovemaking is the most gentle art. Sweet sensations, tender strokes of desire, the sudden nearness of hovering lips, a brush of cheeks, the sharing of wine breaths and so on. Clothes peel off languorous and sultry, shadows tease and warmth invites and then drips, and about all the bedding closes to enfold soft and fresh.

Lacking such amenities of the seductive, let the dogs howl. Beneath savagely cold stars, in beds of wiry stunted bushes, broken branches, rocks and buttons of cacti, this was the scrape and gouge of seed's wild spill, a life's banking in a dubious vessel of potential posterity, when said vessel is all there is on offer. Burgeon proud seed! Steal vigorous root in sweetest flesh! Bay with life's triumph! I held her very nearly upside down as I unleashed my hungry stream, and if she didn't weep white tears it is no small miracle.

The reparations that followed were conducted in sated silence. She combed through her hair to remove the bark, pebbles and saliva. I rubbed my face with sand and would have cut off my own left arm for a bowl of water. We hunted down our wayward clothing, before each in turn staggering off to find our bedding.

Thus ended the twenty-third night upon Crack'd Pot Trail.

A Recounting of the
Twenty-fourth Day

LIKE RUBBING A GLOSSY COAT THE WRONG WAY, SECRET amorous escapades can leave the elect parties stirred awry in the wake, although of course there are always exceptions to the condition, and it would appear that, upon the dawn of the twenty-fourth day, both your venerable chronicler and Relish Chanter could blissfully count themselves thus blessed. Indeed, I never slept better, and from Relish's languid feline stretch upon sitting up from her furs, her mind was as unclouded as ever, sweet as unstirred cream upon the milk.

Far more soured the dispositions of the haggard mottle of artists as the sun elbowed its way up between the distant crags to the east. Wretched their miens, woeful their swollen eyes. Harried their hair, dishevelled their comportment as sullen they gathered about the embers whilst Steck Marynd revived the flames with sundry fettles of tinder and whatnot. Strips of meat roasted the night before were chewed during the wait for the single small pot of tea to boil awake.

With bared iron fangs, the day promised torrid heat. Already the sun blazed wilful and not a single cloud dared intrude upon the cerulean sands of heaven's arena. We stood or sat with the roar of blood in our ears, the silty tea gritty upon our leathery tongues, our hands twitching as if reaching for the journey's end.

From somewhere close came the keening cry of a harashal, the cruel lizard vulture native to the Great Dry. The creature could smell the burnt bone, the ravelled flaps of human skin and scalp, the entrails shallowly buried in a pit just upwind of the camp. And with its voice it mocked our golden vigour until we felt nothing but leaden guilt. The world and indeed life itself lives entirely within the mind. We cast the colours ourselves, and every scene of salvation to one man shows its curly-haired backside to another. And so standing together we each stood alone, and that which we shared was unpleasant to all.

With, perhaps, a few exceptions. Rubbing a lump on his temple, Tiny Chanter walked off to fill a hole, humming as he went. Flea and Midge grinned at each other, which they did with unnerving frequency. Both had sore skulls and only moments earlier had been close to drawing knives, the belligerence halted by a warning grunt from Tiny.

Mister Ambertroshin filled a second cup of tea and walked over to the carriage, where a chamber pot awaited him set on the door's step. A single knock and the wooden shutter on the window opened a crack, just wide enough for him to send the cup through, whereupon it snapped shut, locks setting. He collected the chamber pot and set out to dispose of its contents.

Tulgord Vise watched him walk off and then he grunted. 'Looked to be a heavy pot for some old lady. See that, Steck? Arpo?'

The forester squinted with slitty eyes, but perhaps that was just the woodsmoke drifting up to enwreathe his weathered face.

Arpo, on the other hand, was frowning. 'Well, she took two helpings last night, so it's no wonder.'

'Did she now?' and Tulgord Vise glanced over at the carriage. He scratched at his stubbled jaw.

'Must get horrid hot in there,' Apto Canavalian mused, 'despite the shade. Not a single vent is left open.'

Arpo set off to see to his horse, and after a moment Tulgord did something similar. Steck had already saddled his own half-wild mount and it stood nearby, chewing on whatever grasses it could find. Mister Ambertroshin returned with the scoured pot and stored it in the back box, which he then locked. He then attended to the two mules. So too did the others address to sundry chores or, as privilege or arrogance warranted, did nothing but watch the proceedings. Oggle Gush and Pampera set about combing Nifty's golden locks, while Sellup bundled bedding and then laced onto Nifty's feet the artist's knee-high moccasins.

Thus did the camp break and all preparations were made for the trek ahead.

Calap Roud and Brash Phluster came up to me in the course of such readying. 'Listen, Flicker,' said Calap in a low voice, 'nobody's even told the Chanters about your deal last night, and I'm still of a mind to argue against it.'

'Oh, did the Lady's word not convince you then?'

'Why should it?' he demanded.

'Me neither,' said Brash. 'Why you anyway? She won't even look at me and I'm way better looking.'

'This relates to the tale, surely,' said I. 'A woman such as Purse Snippet would hardly be of such beggarly need as to consider me in any other respect. Brash Phluster, I began a tale and she wishes to hear its end.'

'But it's not a believable one, is it?'

To that I could but shrug. 'A tale is what it is. Must you have every detail relayed to you, every motivation recounted so that it is clearly understood? Must you believe that all proceeds at a certain pace only to flower full and fulsome at the expected time? Am I slave to your expectations, sir? Does not a teller of tales serve oneself first and last?'

Calap snorted. 'I have always argued thus. Who needs an audience, after all. But this situation, it is different, is it not?'

'Is it?' I regarded them both. 'The audience can listen, or they can walk away. They can be pleased. They can be infuriated. They can feel privileged to witness or cursed by the same. If I kneel to one I must kneel to all. And to kneel is to surrender and this no teller of tales must ever do. Calap Roud, count for me the times you have been excoriated for your arrogance. To be an artist is to know privilege from both sides, the privilege of creating your art and the privilege in those who partake of it. But even saying such a thing is arrogance's deafening howl, is it not? Yet the audience possesses a singular currency in this exchange. To partake thereof or to not partake thereof. It extends no further for them, no matter how they might wish otherwise. Now, Calap, you say this situation is different, indeed, unique, yes?'

'When our lives are on the line, yes!'

'I have before me my audience of one, and upon her and her alone my life now rests. But I shall not kneel. Do you understand? She certainly understands – I can see that and am pleased by it. How will she judge? By what standards?'

'By that of redemption,' said Calap. 'It's what you have offered, after all.'

'Redemption comes in a thousand guises, and they are sweetest those that come unexpectedly. For now, she will trust me, but, as you say, Calap, at any time she can choose to abandon that trust. So be it.'

'So you happily trust your life to her judgement?'

'Happily? No, I would not use that word, Calap Roud. The point is, I will hold to my story, for it is mine and none other's.'

Scowling and no doubt confused, Calap turned about and walked away.

Brash Phluster, however, remained. 'I would tell you something, Avas Flicker. In confidence.'

'You have it, sir.'

'It's this, you see.' He licked his lips. 'I keep beginning my songs, but I never get to finish them! Everyone just votes me dispensation! Why? And they laugh and nobody's supposed to be laughing at all. No, say nothing just yet. Listen!' His eyes were bright with something like horror. 'I decided to hide my talent, you see? Hide it deep, save it for the Festival. But then, this happened, and suddenly I realized that I needed to use it, use it to its fullest! But what happened? I'll tell you what happened, Flicker. Now I know why I was damned good at hiding my talent.' He clawed at his straggly beard. 'It's because I don't have any in the first place! And now I'm sunk! Once they stop laughing, I'm a dead man!'

Such are the nightmares of artists. The gibbering ghosts of dead geniuses (yes, they are all dead). The bald nakedness of some future legacy, chewed down illegible. The torture and flagellation of a soul in crisis. The secret truth is that every artist kneels, every artist sets head down upon the block of fickle opinion and the judgement of the incapable. To be a living artist is to be driven again and again to explain oneself, to justify every creative decision, yet to bite down hard on the bit is the only honourable recourse, to my mind at least. Explain nothing, justify even less. Grin at the gallows, dear friends! The artist that lives and the audience that lives while they live are without relevance! Only those still unborn shall post the script of legacy, whether it be forgotten or canonized! The artist and the audience are trapped together in the now, the instant of mood and taste and gnawing unease and all the blither of fugue that is opinion's facile realm! Make brazen your defiance and make well nested your home in the alley and doorstep or, if the winds fare you well, in yon estate with Entourage in tow and the drool of adoration to soothe your path through the years!

'Dear Brash,' said I after this torrid outburst, 'worry not. Sing your songs with all the earnestness you possess. What is talent but the tongue that never ceases its wag? Look upon us poets and see how we are as dogs in the sun, licking our own behinds with such tender love. Naught else afflicts us but the vapours of our own worries. Neither sun nor stone heeds human ambition. Kings hire poets to sell them lies of posterity. Be at fullest ease, is it not enough to try? Is desire not sufficient proof? Is conviction not the stoutest shield and helm before wretched judgement? If it is true that you possess the talent of the talentless, celebrate the singularity of your gift! And should you survive this trek, why, I predict your audience will indeed be vast.'

'But I won't!'

'You shall. I am sure of it.'

Brash Phluster's eyes darted. 'But then . . . that means . . . Calap Roud? Nifty Gum?'

Solemn my nod.

'But that won't be enough!'

'It shall suffice. We shall make good time today, better than our host adjudges.'

'Do you truly believe so?'

'I do, sir. Now, the others have begun and the carriage is moments from lurching forward. Unless you wish to breathe the dust of its passing, we had best be on, young poet.'

'What if Purse hates your story?'

I could but shrug.

Now, it falls upon artists of all ilk to defend the indefensible, and in so doing reveal the utterly defenceless nature of all positions of argument, both yours and mine. Just as every ear bent to this tale is dubious, so too the voice spinning its way down the track of time. Where hides the truth? Why, nowhere and everywhere, of course. Where slinks the purposeful lie? Why, 'tis the lumps beneath truth's charming coat. So, friends, assume the devious and you'll not be wrong and almost half-right, as we shall see.

Not twenty paces along, Tiny Chanter pointed a simian forefinger at Calap Roud and said, 'You, finish your story, and if it's no good you're dead.'

'Dead,' agreed Flea.

'Dead,' agreed Midge.

Calap gulped. 'So soon?' he asked in a squeak. 'Wait! I must compose myself! The Imass woman, dying in the cold, a spin backward in time to the moment when the Fenn warrior, sorely wounded, arrives, sledge in tow. Yes, there I left it. There. So.' He rubbed at his face, worked his jaw as might a singer or pugilist (wherein for both beatings abound, ah, the fates we thrust upon ourselves!), and then cleared his throat.

'He stood silent before her,' Calap began, 'and she made a gesture of welcome. "Great Fenn," said she—'

'What's her name?' Sellup asked.

'She has no name. She is Everywoman.'

'She's not me,' Sellup retorted.

'Just so,' Calap replied, and then resumed. '"Great Fenn" said she, "you come to the camp of the Ifayle Imass, the clan of the White Ferret. We invite you to be our guest for the time of your

stay, however long you wish it to be. You shall be our brother."
She did not, as you may note, speak of the dire state of her kin.
She voiced no excuse or said one word to diminish his expect-
ation. Suffering must wait in the mist, and vanish with the sun's
light, and the sun's light is found in every stranger's eyes—'

'That was stupid,' said Oggle Gush, her opinion rewarded with
a nod from Sellup. 'If she'd said "we're all starving," why, then
he'd go away.'

'If that happened,' said Apto Canavalian, 'there can be no
story, can there?'

'Sure there can! Tell us what she's wearing! I want to know
every detail and how she braids her hair and the paints she uses
on her face and nipples. And I want to hear how she's in charge
of everything and secretly smarter than everyone else, because
that's what heroes are, smarter than everyone else. They see clear-
est of all! They wear Truth and Honour – isn't that what you
always say, Nifty?'

The man coughed and looked uncomfortable. 'Well, not precisely. That is, I mean – what I meant is, well, complicated. That's
what I meant. Now, let Calap continue, I pray you, darling.'

'What do they look like?' Apto asked Oggle.

'What does what look like?'

'Truth and Honour. Is Truth, oh, fur-trimmed? Line stitched?
Brocaded? And what about Honour? Do you wear Honour on
your feet? Well tanned? Softened with worn teeth and the gums
of old women?'

'You do maybe,' Oggle retorted, 'wear them, I mean,' and then
she rolled her eyes and said, 'Idiot.'

Calap continued, 'To her words the Fenn warrior did bow, and
together they walked to the circle of round-tents, where the chill
winds rushed through the furs of the stretched hides. Three hunters were present, two men and another woman, and they came
out to greet the stranger. They knew he would have words to
speak, and they knew, as well, that he would only speak them
before the fire of the chief's hut. In good times, the arrival of a
stranger leads to delight and excitement, and all, be they children

or elders, yearn to hear tales of doings beyond their selves, and such tales are of course the currency a stranger pays for the hospitality of the camp.'

'Just as a modern bard travels from place to place,' commented Apto. 'Poets, each of you can lay claim to an ancient tradition—'

'And for reward you kill and eat us!' snapped Brash Phluster. 'Those horses—'

'Will not be sacrificed,' uttered Tulgord Vise, in a low growl of lifted hackles. 'That was settled and so it remains.'

Tiny Chanter laughed with a show of his tiny teeth and said to Tulgord, 'When we done ate all the artists, peacock, it's you or your horses. Take your pick.' His brothers laughed too and their laughs were the same as Tiny's, and at this moment the knights exchanged glances and then both looked to Steck Marynd who rode a few paces ahead, but the forester's back stayed hunched and if his hairs prickled on his neck he made no sign.

Tiny's threat remained, hanging like a raped woman's blouse that none would look at, though Brash seemed pleased by it, evidently not yet thinking through Tiny's words.

'The Chief in the camp was past his hunting years, and wisdom made bleak his eyes, for when word came to him that a Fenn had made entrance, and that he brought with him a sledge on which lay a body, the Chief feared the worst. There was scant food, and the only medicines the shoulder-women still possessed – after such trying months – were those that eased hunger pangs. Yet he made welcome his round floor and soon all those still able to walk had gathered to meet the Fenn and to hear his words.'

Clearing his throat, Calap resumed. 'The woman who had first greeted him, fair as the spring earth, could not but feel responsible for his presence – though she was bound to honour and so had had no choice – and so she walked close by him and stood upon his left as they waited for the Chief's invitation to sit. Soft the strange whisperings within her, however, and these drew her yet closer, as if his need was hers, as if his straits simply awaited the strength of her own shoulders. She could not explain such feeling, and knew then that the spirits of her people had gathered close to this moment, beneath grey and lifeless skies, and the strokes upon her heart belonged to them.

'It is fell and frightening when the spirits crowd the realm of mortals, for purposes remain ever hidden and all will is as walls of sand before the tide's creep. So, fast beat her heart, quickening her breath, and when at last a child emerged from his grandfather's hut and gestured, she reached out and took hold of the stranger's hand – her own like a babe's within it, and feeling too the hard calluses and seams of strength – and he in turn looked with hooded surprise down upon her, seeing for the very first time her youth, her wan beauty, and something like pain flinched in his heavy eyes—'

'Why?' Sellup asked. 'What does he know?'

'Unwelcome your chorus,' muttered Apto Canavalian.

Calap rubbed his face, as if in sudden loss. Had he forgotten the next details? Did the Reaver now stand before him, Death at home in his camp?

'Before the fire . . .' said I in soft murmur.

Starting, Calap nodded. 'Before the fire, and with the sledge left outside where the last of the dogs drew close to sniff and dip tails, the Fenn warrior made sit before the Chief. His weapons were left at the threshold, and in the heat he at last drew free of his wintry clothing, revealing a face in cast not much elder to the woman kneeling beside him. Blood and suffering are all-too-common masks among all people throughout every age. In dreams we see the hale and fortunate and imagine them some other place, yet one within reach, if only in aspiration. Closer to our lives, waking each day, we must face the scarred reality, and all too often we don our own matching masks, when bereft of privilege as most of us are.' It seemed he faltered then, as if the substance of this last aside now struck him for the first time.

Statements find meaning only in the extremity of the witness, else all falls flat and devoid of emotion, and no amount of authorial exhortation can awaken sincerity among those crouch'd in strongholds of insensitivity. No poorer luck seeking to stir dead soil to life, no seed will take, no flower will grow. True indeed the dead poet's young vision of masks of suffering and blood, but true as well – as he might have seen in his last days and nights – a growing plethora of masks of the insensate, the dead-inside, the fallow of soul, who are forever beyond reach.

Calap cleared his throat yet again. 'The Chief was silent and patient. Tales will wait. First, meagre staples are shared, for to eat in company is to acknowledge the kinship of need and, indeed, of pleasure no matter how modest.' And once more he hesitated, and we all walked silent and brittle of repose.

'Too grim,' announced Tiny. 'Brash Phluster, weave us another song and be quick about it.'

Calap staggered and would have fallen if not for my arm.

Brash weaved as if punched and suddenly sickly was his pallor. Drawing deep, ragged breaths, he looked round wildly, as if seeking succour, but no eyes but mine would meet his and as he fixed his terror upon me I inclined my head and gave him the strength of my assurance.

Gulping, he tried out his singing voice. 'Va la gla blah! Mm-mmmmm. Himmyhimmyhimmy!'

Behind us the harashal vulture answered in kind, giving proof to the sordid rumour of the bird's talent at mimicry.

'Today,' Brash began in a reedy, quavering voice, 'I shall sing my own reworking of an ancient poem, a chapter of the famous epic by Fisher kel Tath, *Anomandaris*.'

Apto choked on something and the host ably pounded upon his back until the spasm passed.

One of the mules managed a sharp bite of Flea's left shoulder and he bellowed in pain, lumbering clear. The other mule laughed as mules were in the habit of doing. The Chanters as one wheeled to glare at Mister Ambertroshin, who shook his head and said, 'Flea slowed his steps, he did. The beasts are hungry, aye?'

Tulgord Vise turned at that. 'You, driver,' he barked, 'from where do you hail?'

'Me, sir? Why, Theft that'd be. A long way away, aye, no argument there, and varied the tale t'bring me here. A wife, you see, and plenty of Oponn's infernal pushings. Should we run outta tales, why, I could spin us a night or two.'

'Indeed,' the Mortal Sword replied drily, one gauntleted hand settling on his sword's shiny pommel, but this gesture was solitary as he once more faced forward in the saddle.

'For your life?' Arpo Relent asked, rather bitingly.

Mister Ambertroshin's bushy brows lifted. 'I'd sore your stomach something awful, good sir. Might well sicken and kill you at that. Besides, the Dantoc Calmpositis, being a powerful woman rumoured to be skilled in the sorcerous arts, why, she'd be most displeased at losing her servant, I dare say.'

The host gaped at that and then said, 'Sorcerous? The Dantoc? I'd not heard—'

'Rumours only, I'm sure,' Mister Ambertroshin said, and he smiled round his pipe.

'What does "Dantoc" mean?' Arpo demanded.

'No idea,' the driver replied.

'What?'

'It's just a title, ain't it? Some kind of title, I imagine.' He shrugged. 'Sounds like one, t'me that is, but then, being a foreigner to it all, I can't really say either way.'

A tad wildly, Arpo Relent looked round. 'Anyone?' he demanded. 'Anyone heard that title before? You, Apto, you're from here, aren't you? What's a "Dantoc"?'

'Not sure,' the Judge admitted. 'I don't pay much attention to such things, I'm afraid. She's well known enough in the city, to be sure, and indeed highly respected and possibly even feared. Her wealth has come from slave trading, I gather.'

'Anomandaris!' Brash shrieked, startling all three horses (but not the mules).

'*Anomandaris!*' cried the vulture, startling everyone else (but not the mules).

'Right,' said Tiny, 'get on with it, Phluster.'

'I shall! Hark well and listen to hear my fair words! This song recounts the penultimate chapter of the Slaying of Draconus—'

'You mean "ultimate" surely,' said Apto Canavalian.

'What?'

'Please, Brash, forgive my interruption. Do proceed.'

'The Slaying of Draconus, and so . . .'

He cleared his throat, assumed that peculiar mask of perform-ance that seemed to afflict most poets, and then fell into that stentorian cadence they presumably all learned from each other and from generations past. Of what stentorian cadence do I speak? Why, the one that seeks to import meaning and significance to every damned word, of course, even when no such resonance obtains. After all, is there really anything more irritating (and som-nolent) than a poetry reading?

> 'Dark was the room
> Deep was the gloom
> That was Draconus's tomb
> Dank was the air
> Daunting the bier
> On which he laid eyes astare
>
> The chains not yet broken
> For he not yet woken
> His vows not yet revoken
> His sword still to awaken
> In its scabbard black oaken
> Cold hands soon to stroken'

'Gods below, Phluster!' snarled Calap Roud. 'The original ain't slave to rhymes, and those ones are awful! Just sing it as Fisher would and spare us all your version!'

'You're just jealous! I'm making Fisher's version accessible to everyone, even children! That's the whole point!'

'It's a tale of betrayal, incest and murder, what on earth are you doing singing it to children?'

'It's only the old who get shocked these days, old man!'

'And it's no wonder, with idiots like you singing to innocent children!'

'Got to keep them interested, Calap, something you never did understand, even with a grown-up audience! Now, be quiet and keep your opinions to yourself, I got a song to sing!

> *'And his head flew into the air*
> *On a fountain of gore and hair!*
> *And—'*

'Hold on, poet,' said Tiny, 'I think you missed a verse there.'
'What? Oh, damn! Wait.'
'And it better start getting funny, too.'
'Funny? But it's not a funny story!'
'I get his brain,' said Midge. 'All that fat.'
'You get half,' said Flea.
'Wait! Here, here, wait—

> *'Envy and Spite were the daughters*
> *To the Consort of Dark Fathers*
> *She the left breast and her the right*
> *Two tits named Envy and Spite!*
> *And deadly their regarrrrd!*
> *Cold the nipples' rewarrrrd!*
> *And when Anomander rose tall*
> *Between them so did they fall*
> *Sliding down in smears of desire*
> *Down the bold warrior's gleaming spire!*
> *And crowded the closet!*
> *Sharp the cleaving hatchet!'*

'Damn me, poet,' said Tulgord Vise, 'the Tomb of Draconus has a closet?'
'They had to hide somewhere!'
'From what, a dead man?'
'He was only sleeping—'
'Who sleeps in a tomb? Was he ensorcelled? Cursed?'
'He ate a poisoned egg,' suggested Nifty Gum, 'which was

secreted into the clutch of eggs he was served for breakfast. There was a wicked witch who haunted the secret passages of the rabbit hole behind the carrot patch behind the castle—'

'I hate carrots,' said Flea.

Brash Phluster was tearing at his hair. 'What castle? It was a tomb I tell you! Even Fisher agrees with me!'

'A carrot through the eye can kill as easily as a knife,' observed Midge.

'I hate witches, too,' said Flea.

'I don't recall any hatchet in Anomandaris,' said Apto Canavalian. 'Rake had a sword—'

'And we been hearing all about it,' said Relish Chanter, and was too bold in her wink at me, but for my fortune none of her brothers were paying any attention to her.

'I don't recall much sex either – and you're singing your version to children, Brash? Gods, there must be limits.'

'On art? Never!' cried Brash Phluster.

'I want to hear about the poisoned egg and the witch,' said Sellup.

Nifty Gum smiled. 'The witch had a terrible husband who spoke the language of the beasts and knew nothing of humankind, and in seeking to teach him the gifts of love the witch failed and was cast aside. Spiteful and bitter, she pronounced a vow to slay every man upon the world, at least, all those who were particularly hairy. Those she could not kill she would seduce only to shave clean their chest and so steal their power, which she stored in the well at the top of the hill. But her husband of old haunted her still, and at night she dreamed of warped mirrors bearing both her face and his and sometimes the two were one in the same.

'The city was named Tomb. This detail, by the way, is what confused legions of artists, including Fisher himself, who, dare I add, is not so nearly as tall as me. And Draconus was the city's king, a proud and noble ruler. Indeed he had two daughters, born of no mother, but of his will and magic gifts. Shaped of clay and sharp stones, neither possessed a heart. Their names they took upon themselves the night they became women, when each saw her own soul's truth and could not look away, could not lie or deceive even unto their own selves.'

Noting at last the host of blank expressions, he said, 'The significance of this—'

'Is a form of torture I will not abide,' said Tiny Chanter.

'Carrot through the eye,' said Midge. 'Anyone got a carrot?'

'Eye,' said Flea.

'Anomander kills Draconus and gets the sword!' shouted Brash Phluster. 'You never let me get to the funny bits – you can't vote, it's not fair!'

'Oh be quiet, will you?' said Tulgord Vise. 'Plenty of light left this day, and we've plenty of cooked meat from yesterday. No, what we need is water. Sardic Thew, what chance the next spring is dry?'

The host stroked his jaw. 'We've no more than trickles for days now, in every watering hole. I admit I am worried mightily, good sir.'

'Might have to bleed someone,' said Tiny, showing his tiny teeth again. 'Who's flush?'

His brothers laughed.

I spoke then. 'Vows are as stone, each a menhir raised like a knuckled finger to the sky. The knights who hunted the Nehemoth were not alone in such cold chisel. Another travelled in the group, a strange and silent man who walked like a hunter in forestlands, yet in his face could be seen the ragged scrawl of a soldier's cruel life, a past of friends dying in his arms, of the guilt of surviving, of teeth bared to fickle chance and a world stripped of all meaning. The gods are as nothing to a soldier, who in prayer only begs for life and righteous purpose, and both are selfish needs indeed. This is not reaching up to touch god. It is pulling the god down as if stealing a golden idol upon a mantelpiece. Begging voiced as a demand, a plea paid out as if owed, such are a soldier's prayers.

'Faith fell beneath his marching boots long ago. He knows the curse of reconciliation and knows too its falsity, the emptiness of the ritual. He has abandoned redemption and now lives to excoriate a stain from the world. That stain being the Nehemoth. In this, perhaps, he is the noblest of them all—'

'Not true!' hissed Arpo Relent. 'The Well Knight serves only the Good, the Wellness of the soul and the flesh that is its home! Not a single three-finned fish has ever passed these lips! Not a sip of wretched liquor, not a stream of noxious smoke. Vegetables are the gift of god—'

'Didn't stop you stuffing your maw last night though, did it?'

Arpo glared at Tiny who grinned back. 'Necessity—'

'Of which the hunter and soldier understood all too well,' I resumed. 'Necessity indeed. The vow stands tall upon the horizon, bold in bleak skies. Even the sun's light cringes from that dark stone. Has rock earned worship? Does a man so lose himself as to kneel before insensate stone? Does one cherish home or the walls and ceiling so enclosing? To see that vow each day, each night, season upon season, year upon year, is it any wonder that it becomes unto itself a god before the supplicant's eyes? In making vows we chisel the visage of a master and announce our abjection as its slave.

'Yet, does not the soldier now standing unmoving behind his eyes not see and understand the dissembling demanded of him, the bending of reason, the burnishing into blindness the madness of absurd conviction? He does, and is mocked within himself, and the god of his vow is a closed fist inside iron scales and those iron scales mark the lie of his own hand, there upon the saddle horn.'

At last, Steck Marynd did twist round in his saddle. 'You presume at your peril, poet.'

'As do we all,' I replied. 'I tell but a tale here. The hunter's face is not your face. The knights are not as travel here in our company. The carriage is nothing like the carriage in my tale. To noble Purse Snippet I paint a scene close enough to be familiar, indeed comfortable, as much as such luxury can be achieved here on this fatal trail.'

'Rubbish,' said Steck. 'You steal from what you see and claim it invention.'

'Indeed, by simple virtue of changing a name or two here and there, or perhaps it is enough to say that what I relate is not what you may see around you. Each listener crowds eager with an armful of details and shall fill in and buttress up as he or she sees fit.'

Apto Canavalian was frowning, as Judges are in the habit of doing when they can't really think of anything worth thinking. He then shook his head, casting off the momentary fug, and said, 'I see no real value in changing a few names and then making everyone pretend it isn't what it obviously is. How is this invention, or even creative? Where is the imagination?'

'Buried six feet down, I should think,' said I, and smiled. 'In some far off land in no way similar to any place you know, of course.'

'Then why bother with the pathetic shell-game, now you've shown us where the nut hides?'

'Did I really need to show you for you to know where it is?'

'No, which makes it even more ridiculous.'

'I most heartily agree, sir,' said I. 'Now, if you will permit, may I continue?'

Flitting eagerness in the Judge's eyes, as if at last he understood. It warms the soul when this is witnessed, I do assure you.

Before I could speak, however, Purse Snippet asked, 'Poet, how fares their trek, these hunters and pilgrims of yours?'

'Not well. In flesh and in spirit, they are all lost. The enemy has drawn close – closer than any among them is aware—'

'What!' bellowed Tulgord Vise, wheeling his horse around and half-drawing his sword. 'Do you glean too close to a secret here, Flicker? Dare not be coy with me. I kill coy people out of faint irritation, and you venture far beyond that! You sting like spider hairs in the eye! On your life, speak true!'

'Not once have I strayed from what is true, sir. Now you show us your clutter of details and would build us something monstrous! Shall I weigh upon your effort? Terrible its flaws, sir, set no hope or belief upon such a rickety frame. This tale is thin and clear as a mountain rook. Sir, the blinding mud so stirred resides behind your eyes and nowhere else.'

'You dare insult me?'

'Not at all. But may I remind you, my life is in the palm of Lady Snippet, not in yours, sir. And I am telling her a tale, and for this breath at least she withholds her judgement on its merit. In the Lady's name, may I continue?'

'What's all this?' Tiny demanded. 'Flea?'

Flea scowled.

'Midge?'

Midge scowled, too.

The host waved his hands. 'Whilst you slept—'

'While we sleep everything stops!' Tiny roared, his face the hue of masticated roses. 'No votes! No decisions! No nothing!'

'Incorrect,' said Purse Snippet, and so flat and so certain her tone that the Chanters were struck dumb. 'I am not chained to you,' she went on, her eyes knuckling hard as stone upon Tiny's faltering visage. 'And the blades with which you would seek to threaten me strike no fear in this breast. I have charged this poet to speak me a story, to continue what I so poorly began. If he fails in satisfying me, he dies. This is the pact and it does not concern you, nor anyone else here. Only myself and Avas Flicker.'

'And how does he fair so far, Milady?' Apto asked.

'Poorly,' she said, 'but for the moment I shall abide.'

The day was most desultory, in the manner of interminable treks the world over. Heat oppressed, the ground grew harder underfoot, stones sharp stabbed beneath soles already tender with threat. The ancient pilgrim track was rutted and dusty, repository of every discarded or surrendered aspiration and ambition. To journey is to purge, as all wise ancients know, and of purging the elderly know better than most.

But what burdens could be so cast off our straining shoulders here on Cracked Pot Trail? Crushing and benumbing this weight, that our art should have purpose, but dare I hazard that those of you who are witness to this grim tale who are neither poet nor musician, not sculptor or painter, you cannot hope to imagine the sudden prickling sweat that bespeaks performance, no matter its shaping. Within the heated skull vicious thoughts ravage the softer allowances. *What if my audience is composed of nothing but idiots? Raving lunatics! What if their tastes are so bad not even a starving vulture would pluck loose a single rolling eyeball? What if they hate me on sight? Look at all those faces! What do they see and what notions ply the unseen waters of their thoughts? Am I too fat, too thin, too nervous, too ugly to warrant all this attention?* The composing of art is the most private of endeavours, but the performance paints the face in most dramatic hues. Does failure in one devour the other? *Do I even like any of these people? What do they want with me anyway? What if— what if I just ran away? No! They'd hate me even more than they do now! Dare I speak out?* Ah, these are most unwelcome streams, swirling so dark and biting. Assume the best and let the worst arrive as revelation (and, perhaps, dismay). An artist truly contemptuous of his or her audience deserves nothing but contempt in return.

But, the razor voice inside softly whispers, *idiots abound*.

No matter. The rocky outcrops are patiently ticking, the blue sky egalitarian in its indifference, the sun unmindful of all who would challenge its stare. The story belongs to the selfsame world, implacable as stone, resistant to all pressures, be they breath's wind or rain's piss. The mules plod befuddled by their own weight and clopping strain. The heads of the horses droop and nod, tails flicking to keep the flies alert. The plateau stretches on into grainy white haze.

'I am not happy about this,' Tiny said in pique, his girthless eyes flitting. 'Special rules and all that. Once special rules start, everything falls apart.'

'Listen to the thug,' Arpo Relent said.

'Midge?'

Midge spat and said, 'Tiny Chanter is head of the Chanters, and the Chanters rule Toll's City of Stratem. We chased out the Crimson Guard to do it, too. Tiny's a king, you fool.'

'If he's a king,' Arpo retorted, 'what's he doing here? Stratem? Never heard of Stratem. Crimson Guard? Who're they?'

Calap said, 'Since when does a king wander around without

bodyguards and servants and whatnot? It's a little hard to believe, your claim.'

'Flea?'

Flea scratched in his beard and looked thoughtful. 'Well, me and Midge and Relish, we're the bodyguards, but we ain't servants. King Tiny don't need servants and such. He's a sorcerer, you see. And the best fighter in all Stratem.'

'What kind of sorcerer?' the host demanded.

'Midge?'

'He can raise the dead. That kind of sorcerer.'

At that the pace stumbled to a halt, and Steck Marynd reined in to slowly swing his horse round, the crossbow cradled in one arm. 'Necromancer,' he said, baring his teeth and it was not a smile. 'So what makes you any different from the Nehemoth? That is what I want to know.'

Midge and Flea stepped out to the sides, hands settling on the grips of their weapons as Tulgord Vise drew his sister-blessed sword and Arpo Relent looked around confusedly. Tiny grinned. 'The difference? Ain't nobody hunting me, that's the *difference*.'

'The only one?' Steck asked in a dull tone.

Was it alarm that flickered momentarily in Tiny's eyes? Too difficult to know for certain. 'Eager to die, are you, Marynd? I can kill you without raising a finger. Just a nod and your guts would be spilling all over your saddle horn.' He looked around, his grin stretching. 'I'm the deadliest person here, best you all understand that.'

'You're bluffing,' said Tulgord. 'Dare you challenge the Mortal Sword of the Sisters, oaf?'

Tiny snorted. 'As if the Sisters care a whit about the Nehemoth – a madman and a eunuch never destroyed the world or toppled a god. Them two are irritants and nothing more. If you truly was the Sisters' Mortal Sword, they must be pretty annoyed by now. You running all over every damned continent and what for? An insult? That's what it was, wasn't it? They made a fool of you, and you'll burn down half the world all because of wounded pride.'

Tulgord Vise was a most frightening hue of scarlet wherever

skin was visible. He stepped forward. 'And you, Chanter?' he retorted amidst gnashing teeth. 'Hunting down a pair of rivals? I agree with Steck, necromancers are an abomination, and you are a necromancer. Therefore, you are—'

'An abomination!' shrieked Arpo Relent, fumbling with his axe. 'Midge, pick one.'

'That girl there, the one with only one eyebrow.'

Tiny nodded. He gestured slightly with his left hand.

Sellup seemed to vomit something even as she pitched forward, limbs rattling on the sand before falling still. Face down on the ground, motionless in death, and all eyes upon her. Eyes that then widened.

'Beru bless us!' moaned the host.

Sellup moved, lifted to her hands and knees, her hair hanging down and clotted with – what was it, blood? She raised her head. Her visage was lifeless, the eyes dull with death, her mouth slack in the manner of the witless and fanatic fans of dubious sports. 'Who killed me?' she asked in a grating voice, tongue protruding like a drowning slug. A strange groaning noise from her nose announced the escape of the last air to grace her lungs. 'That wasn't fair. There was no cause. Pampera, is my hair a mess? Look, it's a mess. I'm a mess.' She climbed to her feet, her motions clumsy and loose. 'Nifty? Beloved? Nifty? I was always for you, only you.'

But when she turned to him he backed away in horror.

'Not fair!' cried Sellup.

'One less mouth to feed, though,' muttered Brash Phluster.

'You killed one of my fans!' Nifty Gum said, eyes like two dustbird eggs boiling in a saucer.

'It's all right,' simped Oggle Gush, 'you still have us, sweet-thumb!'

'Tiny Chanter,' said Steck Marynd, 'if I see so much as a finger twitch from you again you're a dead man. We got us a problem here. Y'see, I get hired to kill necromancers – it's the only reason I'm still hunting the Nehemoth, because I guarantee satisfaction, and in my business without my word meaning something I'm nothing.'

Tiny grunted. 'Anybody hired you to kill me?'

203

'No, which is why you're still alive. But, you see, over the years, I've acquired something of a dislike for necromancers. No, that's too mild. I despise them. Loathe them, in fact.'

'Too bad,' said Tiny. 'You only got one quarrel and you won't get a chance to re-load before one or more of us get to you. Want to die, Steck?'

'I doubt it will be as uneven as you seem to think,' Steck Marynd replied. 'Is that a fair thing to say, Mortal Sword?'

'It is,' said Tulgord Vise in a growl.

'And you, Well Knight?'

Arpo finally had his axe ready. 'Abomination!'

'This is great!' said Brash Phluster in what he likely thought was a whisper.

Tiny's tiny eyes snapped to him. 'For you artists, yes it's perfect, isn't it? It was your meddling that caused all this.' And with that he looked straight at me. 'Devious tale – you'll spin us all to death!'

Innocent my regard. 'Sire?'

'I don't know Flicker's game and I don't much care,' said Steck Marynd, his stony eyes still fixed upon Tiny Chanter. 'You claim to be hunting the Nehemoth. Why?'

'I don't answer to you,' Tiny replied.

'You killed one of my fans!'

'I still love you, Nifty!' Arms opening, Sellup made pouting motions with her dry lips and advanced on her beloved.

He howled and ran.

Oggle shot Sellup a vicious glare. 'See what you done!' she hissed, and then set off in pursuit of the Great Artist.

Pampera posed for an instant, arching to gather and sweep back her hair, her breasts pushing like a pair of seals rising for air, and then with an oddly languorous lunge she flowed into a fluid sprint, buttocks bouncing most invitingly.

> 'In the wayward seas
> My love rolls in heaving swells
> Can a man drown with a smile
> Plunging deep beneath the foam?'

To my heartfelt quotation, Brash Phluster gusted a sigh and nodded. 'Gormle Ess of Ivant, aye, he knew his art—'

'Sandroc of Blight,' Calap Roud corrected. 'Gormle Ess wrote the Adulterer's Lament.' He tilted his head back and assumed the orator's posture, hands out to the sides.

> *'She was beauty beheld*
> *In shadows so sweet*
> *Where the fragrant blossoms*
> *Could kiss the tongue*
> *With honey dreams!*
> *She was desire adamant*
> *So soft to quiver under touch*
> *Leaning close in heat*
> *All this she was and more –*
> *Last night – oh the ale fumes*
> *Fail to abide the mole's squint*
> *In dread morning light!'*

'*Oh sorrow!*' cried Sellup, clapping her hands and offering everyone a bright and ghastly smile.

Arpo, staring up the trail, suddenly spoke. 'Could be the coward's running . . . from us.'

'We got horses,' said Tulgord Vise. 'They won't get away.'

'Even so, we should resume our journey.' Arpo then jabbed a mailed finger at Tiny. 'I will be watching you, sorcerer.' Taking his horse's reins, he set off.

Tiny grinned at Steck Marynd. 'The Well Knight has the memory of a twit-bird. Leave off, Marynd. When we finally corner the Nehemoth, you'll want me at your side. In the meantime—'

'In the meantime,' Steck jerked his head at Sellup, 'no more of that.'

'I was only making a point,' Tiny replied. 'And I don't expect to have to make it twice. Midge?'

'Once will do.'

'Flea?'
'Once.'

The march resumed, because time yields to no reins, nor its plodding course turned aside by wishes or will. The mules cloppled, the carriage clattered, the horses snorted, and we who would claim to exception and privilege among all the things of this world, we measured each and every step in bitter humiliation. Oh, we stood taller in our minds, as is reason's hollow gift, but what do such conceits avail us in the end?

Sixty paces ahead rose the tumulus announcing the wellspring, the heap of stones fluttering with bleached rags stuffed in cracks like banners of the crushed. But of Nifty Gum and his Entourage of Two there was no sign.

Snarling under his breath, Tulgord Vise kicked his horse into a canter, riding for the spring. Dust swirled like a mummer's cape in his wake. With a click of his tongue Steck Marynd rode out to one side and stood in his stirrups, scanning the horizons.

Calap Roud and Brash Phluster drew close to me.

'This is bad, Flicker,' Calap muttered with low breath. 'We can maybe eat Sellup tonight, if she ain't gone foul by then.'

'We should eat her now,' Brash interjected. 'That'd save us all for another night, wouldn't it? Wouldn't it? We got to suggest it – you do it, Flicker. Go on—'

'Good sir,' said I, 'I am of no mind whatsoever to suggest such a heinous thing. Tell me, would you have her complain all the while? While a single piece of her flesh exists, the curse of the unliving remains – what eternal torment would you consign to the poor lass? Besides,' I added, 'I know little of the art of necromancy, but it occurs to me that such flesh is itself poison to the living. Will you risk becoming an undead?'

Brash licked his lips, his face white. 'Gods below!'

'What if Nifty got away?' Calap demanded. 'It's impossible. He must be hiding out there somewhere. Him and his women. His kind get all the luck! Think of it, he's got an undying fan! I'd kill for that!'

'Calap Roud,' said I, 'your tale of the Imass is cause for concern. Where it leads . . .'

'But it's all I got, Flicker! The only one I remember word for
word—'

'Hold on!' said Brash. 'It ain't yours? That's cheating!'

'No it isn't. Nobody said it had to be our own compositions.
This isn't the Festival. They just want to be entertained, so if you
need to steal then steal! Gods, listen to me. I'm giving you advice!
My rival. Both of you! Flicker, listen! It's your story that's going
to get us all killed. You're too close to what's really going on
here—'

'Am I? I think not, sir. Besides, my task now is quite different
from the one you two face.'

'That was some fancy trickery from you, too! She knows we
can do a day or three without food. She only has to make sure
you outlive me and Phluster, and then you can make the last long
run to the ferry landing. You're in cahoots, and don't deny it!'

Brash Phluster smirked. 'It don't matter, Roud, because Flicker's going to lose. And soon, before either of us.'

Arch did an eyebrow upon my benign demeanour. 'Indeed?'

'Indeed,' he mimicked, wagging his head. 'You see, I saw you,
last night. And I saw her, too.'

Calap gasped. 'He's rollicking Purse Snippet? I knew it!'

'Not her,' Brash said, his eyes bright upon me, 'Relish Chanter.
I seen it, and if I tell Tiny – and maybe I'll have to, to buy my life –
why, you're a dead man, Flicker.'

Calap was suddenly grinning. 'We got him. We got Flicker.
Hah! We're safe, Brash! You and me, we're going to make it!'

Did I quiver in terror? Did my knees rattle and bladder loosen
to the prickly bloom of mortal panic? Did I fling myself at Brash,
hands closing about his scrawny throat? An elbow to the side of
Calap's head? Did my mind race, seeking an escape? 'Good sirs,
more of this discussion anon. We have reached the spring.'

'Aye,' said Calap, 'we can wait, can't we, Brash?'

But Phluster grasped my arm. 'Your tale's going to go sour,
Flicker. I know, you was nice to me but it's too late for that kind

of stuff. You were only generous because you felt safe. I'm not such a fool as to take such patronization from one such as you! I *am* a genius! You're going to disappoint Snippet, do you understand me?'

'I shall resume my tale, then, once we have slaked our thirsts.' Brash's grin broadened.

'I always hated you,' said Calap, now studying me as he would a worm. 'Did you know that, Flicker? Oh, I saw the aplomb in your pertinence, and knew it as a fraud from the very first! Always acting like you knew a secret nobody else knows. And that smile you show every now and then – it makes me sick. Do you still think it's all so amusing? Do you? Besides, your tale's stupid. It can't go anywhere, can it, because what you're stealing from isn't done yet, is it? You're doomed to just repeat what's already happened and they won't take that much longer. So, even without Phluster's ultimatum, you're doomed to lose. You'll die. We'll carve you up and eat you, and we'll feel good about it, too!'

Ah, artists! 'The truth of the tale,' said I, most calmly, 'is not where it is going, but where it has been. Ponder that, if you've the energy. In the meantime, sustenance beckons, for I see that some water survives still, and Mister Must is already unhitching the mules. Best we drink before the beasts do, yes?'

Both men pushed past me in their haste.

I followed at a more leisurely pace. I have this thing, you see, about anticipation and abnegation, but of that, later.

Steck had ridden up and was now dismounting. 'Found their tracks,' he said, presumably to Tulgord. 'As we know they must stay relatively close to the trail; however, we need not worry overmuch. Deprivation will bring them back.'

'We can go hunting, too,' said Tiny. 'A bit of excitement,' and he smiled his tiny ratty smile.

'Drink your fill,' cried the host, 'all of you! Such benison! The gods have mercy, yes they do! Oh, perhaps this will suffice! Perhaps we can complete our journey without the loss of another life! I do implore you all, sirs! We can—'

'We eat the artists,' rumbled Tiny. 'It was decided and there ain't no point in going back on it. Besides, I've acquired a liking for the taste.' And he laughed.

Midge laughed too.

So did Flea.

Relish yawned.

'We rest here,' announced Steck Marynd, 'for a time.'

Purse Snippet was crouched down at the murky pool, splashing her face. I squatted beside her. 'Sweet nectar,' murmured I, reaching down.

'They're tyrants one and all,' she said under her breath. 'Even Steck Marynd, for all his airs.'

Cool water closed about my hand with a goddess touch. 'Milady, it is the nature of such paragons of virtue, but can we truly claim to anything nobler? Human flesh has passed our lips, after all.'

She hissed in frustration. 'Our reward for cowardly obedience!'

'Just so.'

'Where will your tale lead us, poet?'

'The answer to that must, alas, wait.'

'You're all the same.'

'Perhaps,' I ventured, 'while we may taste the same, we are in taste anything but the same. So one hopes.'

'You jest even now, Avas Didion Flicker? Will we ever see your true self, I wonder?'

Cupping water, I took a sip. 'We shall see, Milady.'

A woman I once knew possessed a Kanese Ratter, a hairy and puny lapdog with all sanity bred out of it, and hers was more crazed than most. Despite its proclivities, which included attacking in a frenzy overly loud children and stealing the toys and rattles of babies, the beast was entirely capable of standing on its hind legs for inordinate amounts of time, and its owner was most proud of this achievement. Training with titbits and whatnot was clearly efficacious even when the subject at hand possessed a brain the size of a betel nut.

I was witness to such proof again when, at a single jab of one finger from Tiny Chanter, Calap Roud sat straight, all blood rushing from his face. Sputtering, he said, 'But Flicker's volunteered—'

'Later for him. Tell us about the giant and the woman.'

'But—'

'Kill him?' Midge asked.

'Kill him?' Flea asked.

'Wait! The tale, yes, the tale. Now, when we last saw them, the Fenn warrior was seated before the chief and a scant meal was being shared out. Gestures are ever delicate among such tribes. Language speaks without a single word spoken. In this song of nuance, it was understood by all the Imass that a terrible fate had befallen the warrior, that grief gripped the Fenn's broad, wounded shoulders. He bled within and without. His troubled eyes found no other in their weary wandering over the wealth of the chief, the furs and beaded hides, the shell-strung belts and steatite pipes, the circle masks with the skins of beastly faces stretched over them – the brold bear, the ay wolf, the tusked seal. Of the meagre portions of rancid blubber, dried berries and steeped moss tea, he ate each morsel with solemn care and sipped the tea with tender pleasure, but all was tinged with something bitter, a flavour stained upon his tongue – one that haunted him.'

We were gathered, squatting or seated in the shade of the carriage and the stolid mules. The wellspring's basin trickled as it slowly refilled with water. Flies danced on the mud our passages had left behind. Steck Marynd had dismantled his crossbow and was cleaning each part with an oiled cloth. Midge had produced a brace of fighting knives and was making use of a large boulder bearing the grooves of past sharpening, the *whisk-whisk-whisk* sound a grating undercurrent grisly in its portent. The host, Sardic Thew, had built a small fire on which to brew tea. Brash Phluster sat leaning against one gouged carriage wheel, examining his fingernails. Purse Snippet had walked behind the carriage to prepare her small pewter cup a few moments earlier, and now sat on my left, whilst to my right was Apto Canavalian, surreptitiously sipping from a small flask every now and then. Flea and Relish had begun dozing, and Mister Must sat upon the driver's seat of the carriage, drawing upon his pipe. Arpo Relent and Tulgord Vise sat opposite each other, askance their mutually resentful glances. Thus, we were assembled to hear Calap's tale.

'The maiden, kneeling to the Fenn's right, could hear little more than the drum of her own heart. What flower this thing called love, to burst so sudden upon the colourless sward? Its seed is a ghost that even the wind carries unknowing. The blossom shouts to life, a blaze of impossible hue, and in its wild flush it summons the sun itself. So bright! So pure! She had never before known such sensations. They frightened her, stealing all control from her thoughts, from her very flesh. She felt swollen of spirit. She could feel the rough truth of his scarred arm against her own, though they did not touch. She felt herself swaying closer to him with every breath he drew into himself, only to sway back at his exhalation.

'In all things of self, she was still a child, and her soft cheeks glowed as if lit with the fire of the hearth, as if all coverings but the sky could not contain her heat. Softly, unnoticed by any, she panted, every breath shallow and making her feel half-drunk. Her eyes were black pools, the sweat swam upon her palms, and in the folds between her legs a coal fanned hot and eager.

'The flower is suffering's gift, its only gift. Did her kin see it? Did its sweet scent fill the hut? Perhaps, but the winter's cruel ways had stolen the warmth from their souls. They sat in misery, wilted with need, and as the Fenn ate all he was offered they saw the count of their days diminishing. Before their eyes, they witnessed his return to strength and hale vigour. When blood flows, the place it leaves becomes pale and weak, whilst the new home deepens rich with life. They could not shake the chill from their huddled forms, and outside the sun surrendered to the Blackhaired Witches of night, and the wind awoke with a howl than spun long and twisted into a moan. The hide walls rippled. Draughts stole inside and mocked the ashes that seek naught but contented sleep.'

Calap Roud licked his lips and reached for a gourd of water. He sipped with great care, making certain he did not disturb the settled silts, and then set the bowl back down.

The host poured tea into Snippet's cup.

'When spake the Fenn, his voice was the bundle of furs, soft and thick, tightly bound and barely whispering of life. His words were Imass, proof of his worldly ways despite his evident youth – although, of course, with the Fenn age is always difficult to determine.

' "I am the last of my people," said he. "Son of a great warrior cruelly betrayed, slain by those he thought his brothers. To such a crime, does the son not have but one answer? This, then, is my tale. The season was cursed. The horned beasts of the mountain passes were nowhere to be found. The Maned Sisters of the Iron Hair had taken them away—" '

'The who?' demanded Arpo Relent.

'Thus the Fenn named the mountains of their home, good Knight.'

'Why do people have to name everything?' Arpo demanded. 'What's wrong with "the mountains"? The river? The valley?'

'The Knight?' retorted Tiny Chanter. 'Aye, why not just "the idiot"?'

' "The brainless ox," ' suggested Midge.

' "The Bung-Hole Licker," ' suggested Flea.

The three men snickered.

'I never licked no—'

'Hood's breath, Relent,' growled Tulgord Vise. 'Details are abominations with you. Stopper your trap and let him get on with it. You, Calap. No game left in the mountains, right? Let's get on with the tale. Betrayal. Vengeance, aye, that's the making of a decent story.'

' "My father," said the Fenn, "was the Keeper of the Disc, the stone wheel upon which the tribe's life was carved – its past, its present and its future. He was, therefore, a great and important man, the equivalent of chief among the Imass. He spoke with wisdom and truth. The Maned Sisters were angry with the Fenn, who had grown careless in their rituals of propitiation. A sacrifice was necessary, he explained. One life in exchange for the lives of all."

' "The night's gathering then chose their sacrifice. My father's second son, my own brother, five years my younger. The Clan wept, as did my father, as did I. But the Wheel was certain in its telling. In our distress –" and at that moment the Fenn warrior looked up and met the Imass Chief's eyes – "in our distress, none took notice of my father's brother, my own uncle, and the hard secret unveiled in his face."

' "There is blood and there is love. There are women who find themselves alone, and then not alone, and there is shame held within even as the belly swells. Truth revealed can rain blood. She held to herself the crime her husband's brother had committed upon her. She held it for her love for he who was her husband."

' "But now, on this night, she felt cut in two by a ragged knife. One of her sons would die, and in her husband's eyes she saw tears from a love fatally wounded. Too late she cast her regard upon her beloved's brother, and saw only the mask of his indifference." '

'Wait, I don't understand—'

'Gods below!' burst out Tiny Chanter. 'The uncle raped the mother, you fool, and the boy chosen was the beget of that!'

'The mother's uncle raped the boy? But—'

'Kill him?' Midge asked.

'Go on, Calap,' Tiny commanded.

' "In the deep of night, a knife was drawn. When a brother slays a brother, the gods are aghast. The Maned Sisters claw through their iron hair and the earth itself shakes and trembles. Wolves howl in shame for their brothers of the hunt. I awoke to hard slaughter. My mother, lest she speak. My father, too. And of my brother and uncle, why, both were gone from the camp." '

'Vengeance!' bellowed Tiny Chanter. 'No man needs a god when vengeance stands in its stead! He hunted them down didn't he? Tell us!'

Calap nodded. 'And so the Fenn told the tale of the hunt, how he climbed mountain passes and survived the whelp of winter, how he lost the trail again and again, and how he wept when he came upon the cairn bearing the frozen carcass of his brother, half-devoured by his uncle – who had bargained with the darkest spirits of the shadows, all to purchase his own life. Until at last, upon a broad glacier's canted sweep, he crossed blades with his uncle, and of that battle even a thousand words would be too few. Beneath the cold sun, almost blinded by the snow and ice, they fought as only giants could fight. The spirits themselves warred, as shadows locked with honoured light, until even the Maned Sisters fell to their knees, beseeching an end.'

He paused again to sip water.

'And it was light that decided the battle – the sun's flash on the son's blade, direct into the eyes of the uncle. A deft twist, a slash, and upon the crushed and broken ice and snow a crimson stream now poured, sweet as the spring's thaw.

'And so the son stood, the slayings avenged, but a bleakness was upon his soul. He was now alone in his family. He was, he knew, also the murderer of kin. And that night, as he lay sleeping, huddled in a rock shelter, the Maned Sisters visited upon him a dream. He saw himself, thin, weak, walking into the camp of his tribe. The season had broken, the terrible cold was gone from the air, and yet he saw no smoke, and no fires. He saw no one and as he drew closer he came upon bones, picked clean by foxes and here and there split open by the jaws of rock leopards, wolves and bears. And in the hut of his father he found the Wheel, split down the centre, destroyed forever more, and in his dream he knew that, in the moment his sword took the soul of his uncle, the Wheel had been sundered. Too many crimes in a single pool of blood – a curse had befallen the tribe. They had starved, they had torn one another apart in their madness. The warrior awoke, knowing he was now alone, his home was no more, and that there was a stain upon his soul that not even the gods could wash clean.

'Down from the mountains he came, a vessel emptied of love. Thus he told his tale, and the Imass keened and rocked to share his grief. He would stay for a time, he said, but not overlong, knowing well the burden he presented. And that night—'

'That will do,' pronounced Tiny, grunting as he climbed to his feet. 'Now we walk.'

'It's Flicker's turn now, isn't it?' So demanded Brash Phluster.

'Not yet.'

'But soon?'

'Soon.' He paused and smiled. 'Then we vote.'

*

Strips of charred meat were apportioned out, skins filled one last time, the mules and horses brought close to drink again, and then the trek resumed. Chewing with an array of curious and disparate expressions, we trudged along the worn trail.

What fate had befallen this region? Why, nothing but the usual vagary. Droughts settled like a plague upon lands. Crops withered and blew away, people and beasts either died or moved on. But the track where walked pilgrims asserted something more permanent, immortal even, for belief is the blood's unbroken thread. Generation upon generation, twisted and knotted, stretched and shredded, will and desire set the cobble stones upon this harrowed road, and each is polished by sweat and suffering, hope and cherished dreams. Does enlightenment appear only upon the shadeless travail, on a frame of soured muscles and aching bones? Is blessing born solely from ordeal and deprivation?

The land trembles to the slightest footfall, the beetle and the bhederin, and in the charms of the wind one can hear countless cries for succour.

Of course, with all the chewing and gnawing going on, not one of us could hear a damned thing.

We are pilgrims of necessity, stumbling in the habits of privation.

'The Dantoc must have known a mighty thirst.' So said Apto Canavalian. 'Two heavy skins, just for an old woman hiding in the cool gloom.'

'Elderly as she is,' replied Mister Must from atop the carriage, 'the Dantoc Calmpositis holds to the teaching of Mendic Hellup, whose central tenet is that water is the secret of all life, and much physical suffering comes from a chronic undernourishment of water in our bodies.' He chewed on his pipe stem for a moment, and then said, 'Or something like that.'

'You're an odd one,' Apto noted, squinting up at the driver. 'Times you sound rolled up as a scholar, but others like a herder who sleeps under his cow.'

'Disparate my learnings, sir.'

*

215

Moments of malice come to us all. How to explain them? One might set hands upon breast and claim the righteous stance of self-preservation. Is this enough to cleanse the terrible bright splashes stinging the eye? Or what of simple instinctive retaliation from a kneeling position, bearing one's own dark wounds of flesh and spirit? A life lived is a life of regrets, and who can stand at the close of one's years and deny the twisted skeins skirled out in one's wake?

In this moment, as the burden of the tale was set upon me once more, could I have held up before my own visage a silvered mirror, would I recoil before a mien of vicious spite? Were all witness to something bestial, akin to a rock-ape's mad gleam upon discovering a bloated tick dangling from an armpit? Did I snarl like a hyena in a laughing pit? A sex-sodden woman with penis and knife in hand, or breasts descending as weapons of suffocation upon a helpless, exhausted face? Wicked my regard?

Or naught but a sleepy blink and the coolness of a trickling rill only moments from a poisonous chuckle? Pray, you decide.

'The mortal brain,' quoth I, 'is an amorous quagmire. Man and woman both swim sordid currents in the gurgling caverns of unfettered desire. We spread the legs of unknown women at a glance, or take possession of the Gila Monster's stubby tail in a single flutter of sultry lashes. Coy is our silent ravishing, abulge with mutual lust pungent as a drunkard's breath. In the minds of each and every one of us, bodies writhe slick with oiled perfumes, scenes flash hot as fire, and the world beyond is stripped naked to our secret eyes. We rock and we pitch, we sink fast and grasp tight. Our mouths are teased open and tongues find bedmates. Aftermaths wash away and with them all consequence, leaving only the knowing meet of eyes or that shiver of nearness with unspoken truths sweet as a lick.'

None interrupted, proof of the truth of my words, and each and all had slid into and far down the wet channel so warm, so perfect in base pleasure. Sweat beaded beneath napes, walks stiffened awkward. Do you deny? What man would not roger nine of ten women he might see in a single day? Ninety of a hundred? What woman does not imagine clutching a dozen crotches and by magic touch make hard what was soft, huge what was puny? Does she not, with a shudder, then dream the draining weakness of utter surrender? We are rutters of the mind and in the array of each and every pose can be found all the misery and joy of existence. History's tumult is the travail of frustration and desire, murder the slaughter of rivals, slaying the coined purse of the spurned. Children die . . . to make room for more children! Pregnant women swing wild their trophies of conquest pitched so fierce upon their creaking hips. Young men lock horns in swagger and brainless gnashing of eyes. Old men drool over lost youth when all was possible and so little was grasped. Old women perch light as ragged songbirds on brawny young arms not even hinting of blemishes to come. But do not decry such truths! They are the glory of life itself! Make wild all celebration!

Just be sure to invite me along.

'Among the pilgrims,' so I did resume after an appropriate duration to stir the stew, 'maelstroms raged in silent touch of glance and hungers were awakened and the conviction of terrible starvation sizzled with certainty, and for all the threats spoken and unspoken, ah, love will find a way. Legs yearn to yawn, thighs quiver to clamp hard. Snakes strain to bludgeon into ruin all barriers to sentinel readiness.

'There was a woman,' and if possible, why, even the mules and horses trod more softly to challenge not my words, 'a sister to three bold warriors, and desired by all other men in the company. Hard and certain the warnings issued by the brothers. War in answer to despoiling, a thousand legions upon the march, a siege of a hundred years and a hundred great heroes dead on the sand. The toppling of kings and wizards upon the rack. Heads on spikes and wives raped and children sold into slavery. The aghast regard of horrified gods. No less to any and all of these the stern threats from the brothers.

'But who could deny her beauty? And who could ignore the hooked bait in the net she daily cast so wide into her path and wake both?'

Did I risk a glance at Relish Chanter? I did not. But let us imagine now her precious expression at this moment. Eyes wide in horror? Lips slack? A rising flush? Or, and with surety I would cast my coin here, an odd brightness to her gaze, the hint of a half-smile, a touch wilder and wider the sway of her petalled hips. Perhaps even a deflagrant toss of her head. No young woman, after all, can be chained to childhood and all its perverse innocence, no matter how many belligerent brothers she has in tow. The flush apple beckons every hand, and the fruit in turn yearns to be plucked.

'Among the poets and bards,' said I then, 'there was a states-man of the tender arts, elder in his years, but creativity's flower (still so lush in his mind) proclaimed with blind lie a vigour long past. And one night, after days of effort growing ever more desperate, ever more careless, did he finally catch the maiden's eye. Whilst the brothers slept, heads anod and snores asnore, out they crept into the night—'

'But I—'

Poor Calap Roud, alas, got no further.

With a roar, Tiny Chanter lunged upon the hapless old man. The fist that struck the poet was driven hard as a mace, crushing visage and sending shards of bone deep into Calap's brain. In his collapse not a finger's breadth of his body evinced the remotest sign of life.

Oh dear.

Do the gods stand in wait for each and every one of us? So many do believe. Someone has to pay for this mess. But who among us does not also believe that he or she would boldly meet such immortal regard? Did we not drag our sack of excuses all this way? Our riotous justifications? Even death itself could not defy this baggage train chained to our ankles and various other protuberances. Truly, can anyone here honestly assert they would do other than argue their case, all their cases, that mountain heap of cases that is the toll of a life furtively lived?

'*Yes, oh Great Ones, such was my laziness that I could not be bothered to dispose of my litter in the proper receptacles, and a thousand times I pissed against a wall behind my neighbour's house, even as I coveted and eventually seduced his wife. And yes, I was in the habit of riding my horse through town and country too quickly, exercising arrogant disregard for courtesy and caution. I cut off other riders out of spite, I threatened to trample pedestrians at every turn! I always bought the biggest horse to better intimidate others and to offset my sexual incapacities! I bullied and lied and cheated and had good reasons every time. I long ago decided that I was the centre of all existence, emperor of emperors – all this to hide my venal, pathetic self. After all, we are stupider than we like to believe: why, this is the very meaning of sentience, and if you gods are not to blame for your own miserable creations, then who is?'*

Just so.

And, as poor Calap Roud's corpse cooled there on the hard ground, all the others stared in an array of horror, shock, sudden appetite, or mulish indifference, first upon Calap and then upon me, and then back again, deft in swivel to avoid the Chanters with their gnarly fists and black expressions (and Relish, of course, who stood examining her fingernails).

Yet t'was Relish who spoke first. 'As if.'

Extraordinary indeed, how two tiny words could shift the world about-face, the volumes of disdain and disgust, disbelief and a hundred other disses, so filling her breath by way of tone and pitch as to leave not a single witness in doubt of her veracity. Calap Roud in Relish's arms? The absurdity of that notion was as a lightning strike to blast away idiotic conviction, and in the vacuous echo of her comment, why, all eyes now fixed in outrage upon Tiny Chanter.

Whose scowl deepened. 'What?'

'Now we'll never hear what happened to the Imass!' So cried our amiable host, as hosts must by nature be ever practical.

The mood soured then, until I humbly said, 'Not necessarily. I know that particular tale. Perhaps not with the perfect recall with which Calap Roud iterated it, but I shall do my best to satisfy.'

'Better choice than your own story,' muttered Apto, 'which is liable to see us all killed before you're done with it.'

'Unacceptable,' pronounced Purse Snippet. 'Flicker owes me his tale.'

'Now he owes us another one!' barked Tulgord Vise.

'Exactly!' chimed Brash Phluster, who, though an artist of modest talents, was not a fool.

'I shall assume the added burden,' said I, 'in humble acknowledgement of my small role in poor Calap Roud's fate—'

'Small?' snorted Steck Marynd.

'Indeed,' I replied, 'for did I not state with sure and unambiguous clarity that my tale bears only superficial similarity to our present reality?'

As they all pondered this, Mister Must descended from the carriage, to get his butchering tools from the trunk. A man of many skills, was Mister Must, and almost as practical as Sardic Thew.

Butchering a human was, in detail, little different from butchering any other large animal. The guts must be removed, and quickly. The carcass must be skinned and boned and then bled as best as one is able under the circumstances. This generally involved hanging the quartered sections from the prong hooks at the back end of the carriage, and while this resulted in a spattered trail of blood upon the conveyance's path, why, the symbolic significance was very nearly perfect. In any case, Mister Must worked with proficient alacrity, slicing through cartilage and tendon and gristle, and in no time at all the various pieces that had once been Calap Roud depended dripping from the carriage stern. His head was sent rolling in the direction of the shallow pit containing his hide, organs and intestines.

Does this shock? Look upon the crowd that is your company. Pox the mind with visions of dressed and quartered renditions, all animation drained away. The horror to come in the wake of such imaginings (well, one hopes horror comes) is a complicated mélange. A face of life, a host of words, an ocean of swirling thoughts to brighten active eyes. Grace and motion and a sense that before you is a creature of time (just as you no doubt are), with past, present and future. A single step could set you in his or her sandals, as easy as that. To then jolt one's senses into a realm of butchered meat and red bone, a future torn away, and eyes made dull and empty, ah, is any journey as cruel and disquieting as that one?

To answer: yes, when complimented with the growling of one's own stomach and savoury hints wetting the tongue.

Is it cowardice to turn away, to leave Mister Must to his work whilst one admires the sky and horizon, or perhaps frown in vaunted interest at the watchful regard of the horses or the gimlet study from the mules? Certainly not to meet the gaze of anyone else. Cowardice? Absolutely.

Poor Calap Roud. What grief and remorse assails me!

Brash Phluster sidled close as the trek resumed. 'That was vicious, Flicker.'

'When the mouse is cornered—'

' "Mouse?" Not you. More like a serpent in our midst.'

'I am pleased you heeded the warning.'

'I bet you are. I could have blurted it out, you know. And you'd have been lying there beside Roud, and I'd be safe.'

'Do you wish me to resume my tale, Brash? Recounting all the other lovers of the woman with the brothers?'

'Won't work a second time.'

'You would stake your life on Tiny Chanter's self-control?'

Brash licked his lips. 'Anyway, now you have two stories, and Purse isn't happy about it. She's disgusted by what you did to Calap. Using her story like that. She feels guilty, too.'

'Why, Brash, that is most perceptive.'

'She won't be forgiving, not anymore.'

'Indeed not.'

'I think you're a dead man.'

'Brash!' bellowed Tulgord Vise. 'Cheer us up! Sing, lad, sing!'

'But we got our supper!'

Tiny Chanter laughed and then said, 'Maybe we want dessert. Midge?'

'Dessert.'

'Flea?'

'No thanks.'

His brothers halted and stared at him. Flea's expression was pained. 'I been bunged up now six whole days. I got bits of four people in me, and poets at that. Bad poets.'

Tiny's hands twitched. 'A dessert will do you good, Flea.'

'Honey-glazed,' suggested Midge, 'if I can find a hive.'

Flea frowned. 'Maybe an eyeball or two,' he conceded.

'Brash!' Tiny roared.

'I got one! Listen, this one's brilliant. It's called "Night of the Assassin"—'

'Knights can't be assassins,' objected Arpo Relent. 'It's a rule. Knights can't be assassins, wizards can't be weapon-masters and mendics got to use clubs and maces. Everyone knows that.'

Tulgord Vise frowned. 'Clubs? What?'

'No, "night" as in the sun going down.'

'They ride into the sunset, yes, but only at the end.'

Brash looked round, somewhat wildly.

'Let's hear it,' commanded Tiny.

'Mummumummymummy! Oolooolooloo!'

'Oh sorrow!' came a gargled croak from Sellup, who stumbled along behind the carriage and was now ghostly with dust.

'I was just warming up my singing voice,' Brash explained. 'Now, "Night of the Assassin", by Brash Phluster. An original composition. Lyrics by Brash Phluster, music by Brash Phluster. Composed in the year—'

'Sing or die,' said Tiny Chanter.

> *'In the black heart of Malaz City*
> *on a black night of blackness so darrrk*
> *no one could see a thing it was all gritty*
> *when a guard cried out "harrrrk!"*
>
> *But the darkness did not answer*
> *because no one was therrre*
> *Kalam Mekhar was climbing the tower*
> *instead of using the stairrr*

The Mad Empress sat on her throne
dreaming up new ways of torturrre
when she heard a terrible groan
and she did bless the mendic's currre

There was writing carved on the wall
great kings and mad tyrants wrote dire curses
there in the gloomy royal stall
so rank with smeared mercies—'

'She's sitting on a shit-hole?' Tulgord Vise demanded. 'Taking a dump?'

'That's the whole point!' Brash retorted. 'Everybody sings about kings and princesses and heroes but nobody ever mentions natural bodily functions. I introduced the Mad Empress at a vulnerable moment, you see? To earn her more sympathy and remind listeners she's as human as anybody.'

'People know all that,' Tulgord said, 'and they don't want to hear about it in a damned song about assassins!'

'I'm setting the scene!'

'Let him go on,' said Tiny. Then he pointed a culpable finger at Brash. 'But no more natural bodily functions.'

'Out of the dark night sky
rained down matter most foulll
and Kalam swore and wiped at his eye
wishing he'd brought a towelll

But the chute yawned above him
his way to the Mad Empress was a black hollle
could he but reach the sticky rim
he was but moments from his goallll

In days of yore she was an assassin too
a whore of murder with claws unfurlllled

but now she just needed hard to poo
straining to make her hair currrlll'

'I said—'
'It's part of the story!' squealed Brash Phluster. 'I can't help it!'
'Neither could the Empress, seems,' added Apto under his breath.

'*Kalam looked up then to see a grenado*
but swift he was in dodging its plungggge
and he launched up into the brown window
and in the narrow channel he thrashed and lunggged

And climbed and climbed seeking the light
or at least he hoped for some other wayyy
to end the plight of this darkest night
as he prayed for the light of daayyy

Through the narrowest of chutes
he clambered into a pink caverrrnnn
and swam among the furly flukes
"oh," he cried, "when will I ever learrnnn?"

'Tis said across the entire empire
that the Empress Laseen did give birrthhh
to the Royal Assassins of the Claw entire
you can take that for what it's worrthhh

But Kalam Mekhar knew her better than most
and he did carve his name on her wallll
and we'd all swear he got there first
because we never went there at allll!'

Imagine, if you dare, the nature of the silence that followed 'Night of the Assassin'. To this very day, all these years later, I struggle and fail to find words of sufficient girth and suitable precision and can only crawl a reach closer, prostrate with nary more

224

than a few gibbering mumbles. We had all halted, I do recall, but
the faces on all sides were but a blur, barring that of Sellup, who
marched in from a cloud of dust smiling with blackened teeth and
said, 'Thank you for waiting!'

It is said that as much as the dead will find a way into the ground,
so too will they find a way out again. Farmers turn up bones
under the plough. Looters shove aside the lid of the crypt and
scatter trucked limbs and skulls and such in their hunt for baubles.
Sellup, of course, was yet to be buried, but in appearance she was
quickly assuming the guise of the interred. Patchy and jellying,
her lone brow a snarling fringe above murky matted eyes, various
thready remnants of mucus dangling from her crusted nostrils,
and already crawling with maggots that had writhed out from her
ear-holes to sprinkle her shoulders or choke in the nooses of her
tangled hair, she was the kind of fan to elicit a cringe and flinch
from the most desperate poet (though sufficiently muted as to
avoid too much offence, for we will take what we can get, don't
you know).

The curious thing, from the point of view of an artist, lies in
the odd reversal a dead fan poses. For the truly adoring worshipper, a favourite artist cursed to an undying existence could well
be considered a prayer answered. More songs, more epics, an
unending stream of blather and ponce for all eternity! And should
the poor poet fall into irreparable decays – a nose falling off, a
flap of scalp sagging loose, a certain bloating of intestinal gases
followed by a wheezing eruption or two – well, one must suffer for
one's art, yes?

We artists who remained, myself and Brash and indeed, even
Purse Snippet, we regarded Sellup with an admixture of abhor-
rence and fascination. Cruel the irony that she adored a poet who
was not even around.

No matter. The afternoon stretched on, and of the cloudy
thoughts in this collection of cloudy minds, who could even
guess? A situation can fast slide into both the absurd and the tragic, and indeed into true horror, and yet for those in its midst,

senses adjust in their unceasing search for normality, and so on we go, in our assembly of proper motions, the swing of legs, the thump of heels, lids blinking over dust-stung eyes, and the breath goes in and the breath goes out.

Normal sounds comfort us. Hoofs and carriage wheels, the creak of springs and squeal of axles. Pilgrims upon the trail. Who, stumbling upon us at that moment, might spare us little more than a single disinterested glance? Walk your own neighbourhood or village street, dear friends, and as you see nothing awry grant yourself a moment and imagine all that you do not see, all that might hide behind the normal moment with its normal details. Do this and you will come to understand the poet's game.

Thoughts to ruminate upon, perhaps, as the twenty-fourth day draws to a close.

A Recounting of the
Twenty-fourth Night

'WE MADE GOOD TIME THIS DAY,' ANNOUNCED OUR
venerable host, once the evening meal was done and
the picked bones flung away into the night. The fire
was merry, bellies were full, and out in the dark something voiced
curdling cries every now and then, enough to startle Steck Marynd and he would stroke his crossbow like a man with too many
barbs on his conscience (What does that mean? Nothing. I just
liked the turn of phrase).

'In fact,' Sardic Thew continued, beaming above the ruddy
flames, 'we may well reach the Great Descent to the Landing within
a week.' He paused, and then added, 'Perhaps it is at last safe to
announce that our terrible ordeal is over. A few days of hunger, is
that too terrible a price to pay for the end to our dread tithe among
the living?'

Midge grunted. 'What?'

'Well.' The host cleared his throat. 'The cruel fate of these few
remaining poets, I mean.'

'What about it?'

Sardic Thew waved his hands. 'We can be merciful! Don't you
see?'

'What if we don't want to be?' Tiny Chanter asked, grinning
greasily (well, in truth he was most fastidious, was Tiny, but given
the venal words issuing from those lips, I elected to add the grisly
detail. Of course, there is nothing manipulative in this).

'But that – that – that would be—'

'Outright murder?' Apto Canavalian enquired, somewhat too lightly in my opinion.

Brash choked and spat, 'It's been that all along, Apto, though when it's not your head on the spitting block, you just go ahead and pretend otherwise.'

'I will, thank you.'

'Just because you're a judge—'

'Let's get one thing straight,' Apto cut in. 'Not one of you here is getting my vote. All right? The truth is, there's nothing so deflating as actually getting to know the damned poets I'm supposed to be judging. I feel like a far-sighted fool who finally gets close enough to see the whore in front of him, warts and all. The magic dies, you see. It dies like a dried-up worm.'

Brash stared with eyes bulging. 'You're not going to vote for me?' He leapt to his feet. 'Kill him! Kill him next! He's no use to anyone! Kill him!'

As Brash stood trembling, one finger jabbed towards Apto Canavalian, no one spoke. Abruptly, Brash loosed a sob, wheeling, and ran off into the night.

'He won't go far,' opined Steck. 'Besides, I happen to agree with our host. The killing isn't necessary any more. It's over—'

'No,' said an unexpected voice, 'it is not over.'

'Lady Snippet,' Steck began.

'I was promised,' she countered, hands wringing about the cup she held. 'He gave me his word.'

'So I did,' said I. 'Tonight, however, I mean to indulge the interests of all here, by concluding poor Calap Roud's tale. Lady, will you abide me until the morrow?'

Her eyes were most narrow in their regard of me. 'Perhaps you mean to outlast me. In consideration of that, I will now exact yet another vow from you, Avas Didion Flicker. Before we reach the Great Descent, you will satisfy me.'

'So I vow, Milady.'

Steck Marynd rose. 'I know the tale you will tell tonight,' he said to me, and to the others he said, 'I will find Nifty Gum and

228

his ladies and bring them back here, for I fear they must be suffering greatly this night.'

'Sudden compassion?' said Tulgord Vise with a snort.

'The torment must end,' Steck replied. 'If I am the only one here capable of possessing guilt, then so be it.' And off he went, boots crunching in the gravel.

Guilt. Such an unpleasant word, no doubt invented by some pious meddler with snout pricked to the air. Probably a virgin, too, and not by choice. A man (I assert it must have been a man, since no woman was ever so mad as to invent such a concept, and to this day for most women the whole notion of guilt is as alien to them as flicking droplets after a piss, then shivering), a man, then, likely looking on in outrage and horror (at a woman, I warrant, and given his virginal status she was either his sister or his mother), and bursting into his thoughts like flames from a brimstone, all indignation was transformed into that maelstrom of flagellation, spite, envy, malice and harsh judgement that we have come to call *guilt*. Of course, the accusation, once uttered, is also a declaration of sides. The accuser is a creature of impeccable virtue, a paragon of decency, honour, integrity and intransigence, unsullied and unstained since the moment of birth. Why, flames of purest white blaze from that quivering head, and some force of elevation has indeed lifted the accuser from the ground, feet alight on the air, and somewhere monstrous musicians pound drums of impending retribution. In accusing, the accuser seeks to crush the accused, who in turn has been conditioned to cringe and squirm, to holler and rage, or some frenzied cavort between the two, and misery must result. Abject self-immolation, depression, the wearing of ugliness itself. Whilst the accuser stands, observing, triumphant and quivering in the ecstasy of the righteous. It's as good as sex (but then, what does the virgin know about sex?).

What follows? Why, not much. Usually, nothing. He dozes. She starts chopping dirty carrots or heads out and beats stained garments against a rock (said gestures having no symbolic significance whatsoever). The baby looks on, eating the cat's tail and the cat, knowing nothing of guilt, stares with bemused regard upon the wretched family it has adopted, before realizing that once again the horrid urchin is stuffing it into its mouth, and once again it's time to use the runt as a bed-post. The mind is a dark realm and shadows lurk and creep behind the throne of reason, and none of us sit that throne for long in any case, so let them lurk and creep, what do we care?

'As night came to the Imass camp,' said I, 'she led the Fenn warrior towards an empty hut which he was free to use as his own until such time that he chose to depart. In the chill darkness she carried a small oil lamp to guide their way, and the flame flickered in the bitter wind, and he strode behind her, his footfalls making no sound. Yet she did not need to turn around to be certain he followed, for she felt the heat of him, like a kiln at her back. He was close, closer than he need be.

'When she ducked through the entrance and then straightened, his arms crept round her. She gasped at his touch and arched her back, head against his lowest rib, as his huge hands reached to find her breasts. He was rough in his need, burning with haste, and they descended to the heap of furs unmindful of the cold and damp, the musty smell of the old rushes.'

'That nastiness obsesses you!' said Arpo Relent.

'Nastiness, sir?'

'Between a man and a woman, the Unspoken, the Unrevealed, the—'

'Sex, you mean?'

Arpo glared. 'Such tales are unseemly. They twist and poison the minds of listeners.' He made a fist with one gauntleted hand. 'See how Calap Roud died. All it took was a hint of something—'

'I believe I was rather more direct,' I said, 'although in no way specific, as I had no chance—'

'So you'll do it now! Your mind is a filthy, rotted tumour of lasciviousness! Why, in the city of Quaint your skin would be stripped from your flesh, your weak parts chopped off—'

'Weak parts?'

Arpo gestured between his legs. 'That which Whispers Evil Temptation, sir. Chopped off and sealed in a jar. Your tongue would be cut into strips and the Royal Tongs would come out—'

'A little late for those,' Apto said, 'since you already chopped off the—'

'There is a Worm of Corruption, sir, that resides deep in the body, and if it is not removed before the poor victim dies, it will ride his soul into the Deathly Realm. Of course, the Worm knows when it is being hunted, and it is a master of disguise. The Search often takes days and days—'

'Because the poor man talked about fornication?'

At Apto's query the Well Knight flinched. 'I knew you were full of worms, all of you. I'm not surprised. Truly, this is a fallen company.'

'Are all poets filled with such corrupting worms?' Apto pressed.

'Of course they are and proof awaits all who succumb to their temptations! The Holy Union resides in a realm beyond words, beyond images, beyond everything!' He gestured in my direction. 'These . . . these sullied creatures, they but revel in degraded versions, fallen mockeries. Her hand grasping his *this*, his finger up her *that*. Slavering and dripping and heaving and grunting – these are the bestial escapades of pigs and goats and dogs. And woe to the wretched fool who stirs in the midst of such breathless descriptions, for the Lady of Beneficence shall surely turn her back upon They of Rotten Thoughts—'

'Is it a pretty one?' Apto asked.

Arpo frowned. 'Is what pretty?'

'The Lady's back, sir. Curvaceous? Sweetly rounded and inviting—'

With a terrible bellow the Well Knight launched himself at Apto Canavalian. Murder was an onerous mask upon his face, his hair suddenly awry and the gold of his fittings shining with a lurid crimson sheen. Gauntleted fingers hooked as they lashed out to clutch Apto's rather scrawny neck.

Of course, critics are notoriously difficult to snare, even with their own words. They slip and sidle, prance and dither. So elusive are they that one suspects that they are in fact incorporeal, fey

231

conjurations gathered up like accretions of lint and twigs, ready to burst apart at the first hint of danger. But who, pray tell, would be mad enough to create such snarky homunculi? Why, none other than artists themselves, for in the manner of grubby savages in the deep woods, we slap together our gods from whatever is at hand (mostly fluff) only to eagerly grovel at its misshapen feet (or hoofs), slavering our adoration to hide our true thoughts, which are generally venal.

Sailing over the fire, then, uttering animal roars, Arpo Relent found himself clutching thin air. His hands were still grasping and flaying when his face made contact with the boulder Apto had been leaning against. With noises that would make a potter cringe at the kiln, the Well Knight's steely visage crumpled like sheet tin. Blood sprayed out to form a delicate crescent upon the sun-bleached stone, a glittering halo until his head slid away.

Apto Canavalian had vanished into the darkness.

We who remained sat unmoving. Arpo Relent's fine boots were nicely settled in the fire, suggesting to us that he was unconscious, dead or careless. When the man's leggings caught flame our venerable host leapt forward to drag the limbs clear, grunting as he did so, and then hastily snuffed out the smouldering cloth.

Tiny Chanter snorted and Flea and Midge did the same. From somewhere in the darkness Sellup giggled, and then coughed something up.

Sighing, Tulgord Vise rose, stepped over and crouched beside the Unwell Knight. After a moment's examination, he said, 'Alive but senseless.'

'Essentially unchanged, then,' said Apto, reappearing from the night's inky well. 'Made a mess of my rock, though.'

'Jest now,' Tulgord said. 'When he comes to, you're a dead man.'

'Who says he'll come to at all?' the critic retorted. 'Look how flat his forehead is.'

'It was that way before he hit the rock,' the Mortal Sword replied.

'Was it leaking snot, too? I think we'd have noticed. He's in a coma and will probably die sometime in the night.'

'Pray hard it's so,' Tulgord said, looking up with bared teeth.

Apto shrugged, but sweaty beads danced on his upper lip like happy bottle flies.

'You, Flicker,' said Tiny Chanter, 'you was telling that story. Was finally starting to get interesting.'

'Sore stretched indeed,' said I, 'and maiden no longer—'

'Hold on,' Tiny objected, all the flickering flames of the hearth mirrored in his ursine mien. 'You can't just skip past all that, unless you don't want to survive the night. Disappointment's a fatal complaint as far as I'm concerned. Disappoint me and I swear I'll kill you, poet.'

'I'll kill you, too,' said Midge.

'And me,' said Flea.

'What pathetic things you Chanters are,' said Purse Snippet.

Shocked visages numbering three.

Starting and blinking, Relish squinted at her siblings. 'What? Someone say something?'

'I called your brothers pathetic,' explained the Lady.

'Oh.' Relish subsided once more.

Tiny jabbed a blunt finger at Purse Snippet. 'You. Watch it.'

'Yeah,' said Flea. 'Watch it.'

'You,' said Midge. 'Yeah.'

'The most enticing lure to the imagination,' said Purse, 'is that which suggests without revealing. This is the true art of the dance, after all. When I perform, I seduce, but that doesn't mean I want to ruffle your sack, unless it's the kind that jingles.'

'Making you a tease!' Tulgord growled. 'And worse. Tell me, woman, how many murders have you left in your wake? How many broken hearts? Men surrendering to drink after years of abstinence. Imagined rivals knifing each other. How many loving families have you sundered with all that you promise only to then deny? We should never have excluded you from anything – you're the worst of the lot.'

Purse Snippet had paled at the Mortal Sword's words.

I did speak then, as proper comportment demanded. 'A coward's ambush – shame on you, sir.'

The knight stiffened. 'Tread softly now, poet. Explain yourself, if you please.'

'The tragedies whereof you speak cannot be laid at this lady's delicate feet. They are one and all failures of the men involved, for each has crossed the fatal line between audience and performer. Art is not exclusive in its delivery, but its magic lies in creating the illusion that it has done just that. Speaking only to you. That is art's gift, do you understand, Knight? As such it is to be revered, not sullied. The instant the observer, in appalling self-delusion, seeks to claim for himself that which in truth belongs to everyone, he has committed the greatest crime, one of selfish arrogance, one of unrighteous possession. Before Lady Snippet's performance, this man makes the foulest presumption. Well now, how dare he? Against such a crime it falls to the rest of her adoring audience to place themselves between that man and Lady Snippet.'

'As you are doing right now,' observed Apto Canavalian (wise in his ways this honourable, highly intelligent and oh-so-observant critic).

Modest the tilt of my head.

Visibly flustered, Tulgord Vise grunted and looked away, chewing at his beard and biting his lip, shifting in discomfort and shuffling his feet and then suddenly finding a kink in the chain of his left vambrace which he set to, humming softly to himself, all of which led me to conclude, with great acuity, that his flusterment was indeed visible.

'I still want details,' said Tiny Chanter, glaring at me in canid challenge.

'As a sweet maiden, she was of course unversed in the stanzas of amorous endeavour—'

'What?' asked Midge.

'She didn't know anything about sex,' I re-phrased.

'Why do you do that anyway?' Apto enquired.

I took a moment to observe the miserable, vulpine excuse for humanity, and then said, 'Do what?'

'Complicate things.'

'Perhaps because I am a complicated sort of man.'

'But if it makes people frown or blink or otherwise stumble in confusion, what's the point?'

'Dear me,' said I, 'here you are, elected as Judge, yet you seem entirely unaware of the magical properties of language. Simplicity, I do assert, is woefully overestimated in value. Of course there are times when bluntness suits, but the value of these instances is found in the surprise they deliver, and such surprise cannot occur if they are surrounded in similitude—'

'For Hood's sake,' rumbled Tiny, 'get back to the other similitudes. The maiden knew nothing so it fell to the Fenn warrior to teach her, and that's what I want to hear about. The world in its proper course through the heavens and whatnot.' And he shot Apto a wordless but entirely unambiguous look of warning, that in its mute bluntness succeeded in reaching the critic's murky awareness, sufficient to spark self-preservation. In other words, the look scared him witless.

I resumed. 'We shall backtrack, then, to the moment when they stood, now facing one another. He was well-versed—'

'Now it's back to the verses again,' whined Midge.

'And though heated with desire,' I continued, 'he displayed consummate skill—'

'Consummate, yeah!' and Tiny grinned his tiny grin.

From the gloom close to the wagon came Mister Must's gravel-laden voice, 'And that's a significant detail, I'll warrant.'

So did I twist round then to observe his ghostly visage in its ghostly cloud of rustleaf smoke, catching the knowing twinkle that might have been an eye or a tooth. *Ah,* thinks me, *a sharp one here. Be careful now, Flicker.*

'Peeling away her clothing, unmindful of the damp chilly air in the guest hut, he laid her bare, his rough fingertips so lightly brushing the pricked awakening of her skin so that she shivered again and again. Her breaths were a rush of quick waves upon a rasping beach, the tremulous water sobbing back as she gasped to his touch where it travelled in eddying swirl about her nipples.

'Her head tilted back, all will abandoned to his sure embrace, the deep and steady breaths that made his chest swell and ease against her. Then his hands edged downward, tracking the lines of her hips, to cup her downy-soft behind, and effortlessly he lifted her—'

'Ha!' barked Tiny Chanter. 'Now comes the Golden Ram! The Knob-Headed Dhenrabi rising from the Deep! The Mushroom in the Mulch!'

Everyone stared for a moment at Tiny with his flushed face and puny but bright eyes. Even Midge and Flea. He looked about, meeting stare after stare, a little wildly, before scowling and gesturing to me. 'Go on, Flicker.'

'She cried out as if ripped asunder, and blood started, announcing the death of her childhood, but he held her in his strong hands to keep her safe from true injury—'

'How tall was she again?' Flea asked.

'About knee-high,' Apto answered.

'Oh. Makes sense then.'

Relish laughed, ill-timed indeed as her brothers suddenly glared at her.

'You shouldn't be listening to this,' Tiny said. 'Losing maidenhood ain't like that. It's all agony and aches and filth and slow oozing of deadly saps, and shouldn't be undertaken without supervision—'

'What, you think you're gonna *watch*?' Relish demanded, flaring up like the seed-head of a thistle in a brush fire. 'If I'd known brothers were like this, I would have killed you all long ago!'

'It's our responsibility!' snarled Tiny, that finger back up and jabbing. 'We promised Da—'

'Da!' Relish shrieked. 'Till his dying day he never figured out the connection between babies and what he and Ma did twice a year!' She waved her arms like a child sitting on a bee hive. 'Look at us! Even I don't know how many brothers I got! You were dropping like apples! Everywhere!'

'Watch what you're saying about Da!'

'Yeah, watch it!'

'Yeah! Da!'

Relish suddenly crossed her arms and smirked. 'Responsible, that's a joke. If you knew anything, well, ha ha. Ha!'

I cleared my throat most delicately. 'He left her exhausted, curled up in his arms, stung senseless with love. And much of the night passed unwitnessed for our lovely woman for whom innocence was already a fading memory.'

'That is the way of it,' Tulgord Vise said with solemn nod. 'When they lose that innocence to some grinning bastard from the next village, suddenly they can't get enough of it, can they? That . . . that other stuff. Rutting everything in sight, that's what happens, and that boy who loved her since they were mere whelplings, why, all he can do is look on, knowing he'll never get to touch her ever again, because there's a fierce fire in her eyes now, and a swagger to her walk, a looseness to her hips, and she's not interested anymore in playing hide and seek down by the river, and if she turned up all slack-faced and drowned down on the bank, well, whose fault was that? After all, she wasn't innocent no more, was she? No, she was the opposite of that, yes, assuredly she was. The Sisters smile at whores, did you know that? They are soft that way. Innocent, no, she wasn't that. The opposite.' He looked up. 'And what's the opposite of innocence?'

And into the grim silence, in voice cool and low did I venture: 'Guilt?'

Some tales die with a wheezy sigh. Some are stabbed through the heart. At least for a time. It was late and for some, dreadfully too late. In solitude and in times broken and husked and well rooted in contemplation, we find the necessity to regard our deeds, and see for ourselves all that which ever abides, this garden of scents both sweet and vaguely rotting. Some lives die with a sated sigh. Some are drowned in a river.

Others get eaten by the righteous.

At certain passages in the night the darkness grows vapid, a desultory, pensive state that laps energy like a bat's flicking tongue a cow's pricked ankle. Somnolent the wandering steps, brooding the regard, drowsy this disinterest. Until in the murk one discerns a tapestry scene of the like to adorn a torturer's bedroom.

A mostly naked woman stood in fullest profile, her arms raised overhead, balanced in her hands a rather large boulder, whilst directly below, at her very feet, was proffered the motionless head of a sleeping sibling.

Soft as my approach happened to be, Relish heard and glanced over. 'Just like this,' she whispered. 'And . . . done.'

'You have held this pose before, I think.'

'I have. Until my arms trembled.'

'I imagine,' I ventured, drawing closer, 'you have contemplated simply running away.'

She snorted, twisted to one side and sent the boulder thumping and bounding through some brushes in the dark. 'You don't know them. They'd hunt me down. Even if there was only one of them left, I'd be hunted down. Across the world. Under the seas. To the hoary moon itself.' She fixed wounded, helpless eyes upon me. 'I am a prisoner, with no hope of escape. Ever.'

'I understand that it does seem that way right now—'

'Don't give me that steaming pile of crap, Flicker. I've had my fill of brotherly advice.'

'Advice was not my intention, Relish.'

Jaded her brow. 'You hungry for another roll? We damned near killed each other last time.'

'I know and I dream of it still and will likely do so until my dying day.'

'Liar.'

I let the accusation rest, for to explain that the dream wasn't necessarily a pleasant one, would have, in my esteem, been untimely. I'm sure you agree.

'So, not advice.'

'A promise, Relish. To free you of their chains before this journey ends.'

'Gods below, is this some infection or something? You and promises to women. The secret flaw you imagine yourself so clever at hiding—'

'I hide nothing—'

'So bold and steady-eyed then, thus making it the best of disguises.' She shook her head. 'Besides, such afflictions belong to pimply boys with cracking voices. You're old enough to know better.'

'I am?'

'Never promise to save a woman, Flicker.'

'Oh, and why?'

'Because when you fail, she will curse your name for all time, and when you happen to succeed, she'll resent you for just as long. A fool is a man who believes love comes of being owed.'

'And this afflicts only men?'

'Of course not. But I was talking of you.'

'The fool in question.'

'That's where my theories fall apart – the ones about you, Flicker. You're up to something here.'

'Beyond plain survival?'

'No one's going to kill you on this journey. You have made sure of that.'

'I have?'

'You snared me and Brash using the old creep, Calap Roud. You hooked Purse Snippet. Now you shamed Tulgord Vise and he needs you alive to prove to you you're wrong about him.' She looked down at Tiny. 'And even him, he's snagged, too, because he's not as stupid as he sounds. Just like Steck, he's riding on your words, believing there are secrets in them. Your magic – that's what you called it, isn't it?'

'I can't imagine what secrets I possess that would be of any use to them.'

She snorted again. 'If anybody wants to see you dead and mute, it's probably Mister Must.'

Well now, that was a cogent observation indeed. 'Do you wish to be freed of your brothers or not?'

'Very deft, Flicker. Oh, why not? Free me, sweet hero, and you'll have my gratitude and resentment both, for all time.'

'Relish, what you do with your freedom is entirely up to you, and the same for how you happen to think about the manner in which it was delivered. As for me, I will be content to witness, as might a kindly uncle—'

'Did you uncle me the other night, Flicker?'

'Dear me, I should say not, Relish.' And my regard descended to Tiny's round face, so childlike in brainless repose. 'You are certain he sleeps?'

'If he wasn't, your neck would already be snapped.'

'I imagine you are correct. Even so. It is late, Relish, and we have far to walk come the morrow.'

'Yes, Uncle.'

Watching her walk off to find her bedding, I contemplated myriad facets of humanly nature, as I selected the opposite direction in which to resume my wandering. Capemoths circled over my head like the bearers of grim thoughts, which I shooed away with careless gestures. The moon showed its smudged face to the east, like a wink through mud. Somewhere off to my right, lost in the gloom, Sellup was singing to herself as she stalked the night, as the undead will do.

Is there anything more fraught than family? We do not choose our kin, after all, and even by marriage one finds oneself saddled with a whole gaggle of new relations, all gathered to witness the fresh mixing of blood and, if of proper spirit, get appallingly drunk, sufficient to ruin the entire proceedings and to be known thereafter in infamy. For myself, I have always considered this gesture, offered to countless relations on their big day, to be nothing more than protracted revenge, and have of course personally partaken of it many times. Closer to home, as it were, why, every new wife simply adds to the wild, unwieldy clan. The excitement never ends!

Even so, poor Relish. Flaw or not, I vowed that I would have to do something about it, and if this be my weakness, then so be it.

'Flicker!'

The hiss brought me to a startled halt. 'Brash?'

The gangly poet emerged from night's felt, his hair upright and stark, thorn-scratches tracked across his drawn cheeks, his tongue darting to wet his lips and his ears twitching at imagined sounds. 'Why didn't anyone kill him?'

'Who?'

'Apto Canavalian! Who won't vote for any of us. The worst kind of judge there is! He wastes the ground he stands upon!'

'Arpo Relent attempted the very thing you sought, dear poet, and, alas, failed – perhaps fatally.'

Brash Phluster's eyes widened. 'The Well Knight's dead?'

'His Wellness hangs in the balance.'

'Just what he deserves!' snarled the poet. 'That murderous bag of foul wind. Listen! We could just run – this very night. What's to stop us? Steck's lost somewhere – who knows, maybe Nifty and his fans jumped him. Maybe they all killed each other out there in the desert.'

'You forget, good sir, the Chanters and, of course, Tulgord Vise. I am afraid, Brash, that we have no choice but to continue on—'

'If Arpo dies, we can eat him, can't we?'

'I don't see why not.'

'And maybe that'll be enough. For everyone. What do you think?'

'It's certainly possible. Now, Brash, take yourself to bed.'

He raked his fingers through his hair. 'Gods, it's not fair how us artists are treated, is it? They're all vultures! Don't they see how every word is a tortured excretion? Our sweat drips red, our blood pools and blackens beneath our fingernails, our teeth loosen at night and we stagger through our dreams gumming our words. I write and lose entire manuscripts between dusk and dawn – does that happen to you? Does it?'

'That it does, friend. We are all cursed with ineffable genius. But consider this, perhaps we each are in fact not one, but many, and whilst we sleep in this realm another version of us wakens to another world's dawn, and sets quill to parchment – the genius forever beyond our reach is in fact his own talent, though he knows it not and like you and I, he frets over the lost works of his nightly dreams.'

Brash was staring at me with incredulous eyes. 'That is cruelty without measure, Flicker. How could you even imagine such diabolical things? A thousand other selves, all equally tortured and tormented! Gods below!'

'I certainly do not see it that way,' did I reply. 'Indeed, the notion leads me to ever greater efforts, for I seek to join all of our voices into one – perhaps, I muse, this is the truth of real, genuine genius. My myriad selves singing in chorus, oh how I long to be deafened by my own voice!'

'Yearn away,' Brash said, with a sudden wicked grin. 'You're doomed, Flicker. You just made me realize something, you see. I am already deafened by my own voice, meaning I already am a genius. Your argument proves it!'

'Thank goodness for that. Now, sing yourself off to sleep, Brash Phluster, and we will speak more of this upon the morning.'

'Flicker, do you have a knife?'

'Excuse me?'

'I'm going to make Apto vote for me even if I have to kill him to do it.'

'That would be murder, friend.'

'We are awash in blood already, you fool! What's one little dead critic more? Who'd miss him? Not me. Not you.'

'A dead man cannot vote, Brash.'

'I'll force him to write a proxy note first. Then we can eat him.'

'I sincerely doubt he would prove palatable. No, Brash Phluster, you will receive no weapon from me.'

'I hate you.'

Off he stormed, in the manner of a golit bird hunting snakes.

'His mind has cracked.' With this observation, Purse Snippet appeared, her cloak drawn tight about her lithe form.

'Will no one sleep this night?' I asked, in some exasperation.

'Our cruel and unhappy family is in tatters.'

To this I grunted.

'Do doubts finally afflict you, Avas Didion Flicker? I intend no mercy, be certain of that.'

'The burdens are weighty indeed, Lady Snippet, but I remain confident that I shall prevail.'

She drew still closer, her eyes searching mine, as women's eyes are in the habit of doing when close we happen to stand. What secret promise are they hoping to discover? What fey hoard of untold riches do they yearn to prise open? Could they but imagine the murky male realm lurking behind these lucid pearls, they might well shatter the night with shrieks and flee into the shelter of darkness itself. But this is the mystery of things, is it not? We bounce through guesses and hazy uncertainties, and call it rapport, bridged and stitched with smiles and engaging expressions, whilst behind both sets of eyes maelstroms rage benighted in wild images of rampant sex and unlikely trysts. Or so I fancy, and why not? Such musings are easy vanquish over probable truths (that at least one of us is either bored rigid or completely mindless with all the perspicacity of a jellyfish, and oft I have caught myself in rubbery wobble, mind, or even worse: is that intensity merely prelude to picking crabs from my eyebrows? Oh yes, we stand close and behind our facades we quiver in trepid tremulosity, even as our mouths flap a league a breath).

Where were we? Ah yes, standing close, her eyes tracking mine like twin bows with arrows fixed, whilst I shivered like two hares in lantern light.

'How, then,' asked Purse Snippet (eyes tracking . . . tracking – I am pinned!), 'do you intend to save me, noble sir? In the manner of all those others, in a tangle of warm flesh and the oblivion of sated desires? Have you any idea just how many men I have had? Not to mention women? And each time a new candidate steps forth, what do I see in those oh-so-eager eyes?' She slowly shook her head. 'The conviction writ plain that this one can do what none before was capable of doing, and what must I then witness?'

'I would hazard, the pathetic collapse of such brazen arrogance?'

'Yes. But here, and now, I look into your eyes and what do I see?'

'To be honest, Lady, I have no idea.'

'Really?'

'Really.'

'I don't believe you.'

Do you see? She had crowbar in hand, the treasure chest looms (mine, not hers, we're being figurative here. We'll get to the literal in a moment), and the lock looks flimsy indeed. And in her eyes what do I see? Why, the conviction that she and she alone has what it takes (whatever it takes, don't ask me), to crack loose that mysterious lockbox of fabulous revelations that is, well, the real me.

Bless her.

Do you all finally understand my angst? I mean, is this all there is? What is *this* anyway? I don't know. Ask my wives. They prised me loose long ago, to their eternal disappointment, of which they continually remind me, lest I stupidly wander into some impractical daydream (such as this: Is there some woman out there who still thinks me mysterious? I must find her! That kind of daydream). As tired old philosophers say, the scent is ever sweeter over the garden wall. And my, how we do climb.

What a tirade of cynicism! I am not like this at all, I do assure you. I have this lockbox hidden inside me, you see . . . do come find it, will you?

It is a sage truth that there can never be too many disappointed wives.

Her lips found mine. Have I missed something? I have not. Quick as a cat upon a mouse, a cock upon a snail, a crow upon a sliver of dead meat. And her tongue went looking for the treasure chest. She didn't believe me, recall? They never do.

In my weakness, which I call upon in times of need, I could not resist.

Was she the most beautiful woman I ever knowingly shared fluids with? She was indeed. Shall I recount the details? I shall not. In protection of her sweet modesty, of that luscious night my lips shall remain forever sealed.

Oh, forget that. I cupped her full breasts, which is what men do for some unknown reason, except perhaps that it has something to do with the way we gauge value, upon scales as it were, replete with aesthetic appreciation, engineering terminology and so on. With a dancer's grace (and muscle) she drew one meaty thigh up along my left hip, grinding her mound against my crotch with an undulating, circular gyration that snapped the buttons of my collar and burst seams everywhere. With nefarious insistence, that leg somehow wrapped itself to rest athwart my buttocks (*buttocks*, what a maddeningly absurd word), her taut calf appearing upon my right, curling round (was this even possible?) to hook over my hip. If this was not outrageous enough, the very foot at the end of that selfsame leg suddenly plunged beneath my breeches to snare the rearing tubeworm of my weakness, between big toe and the rest.

At this point, she'd already closed one hand about the bag and was rolling the marbles to and fro, whilst her other hand was driving a finger against previously unexplored areas of sexual sensitivity in that dubious crack people of all genders cannot help but possess.

And my thoughts at this stage in the proceedings? Picture, if you will, a newborn's expression of interminable stunned witless stupidity, wide as a bright smile following wind, eyes spread to the wonder of it all when every bit of that 'all' is entirely beyond comprehension. If you have reared children or suffered the fate of caring for someone else's, then you know well the look I faint describe herein. This was the state of my organ of thought. Immune to all intrusion as my clothing miraculously melted away and she mounted herself smooth as perfumed silk, only to suddenly pull free, unwind herself with serpent grace, and step back.

'You get the rest when I am redeemed.'

Women.

I am at a loss for words. Even all these decades later. At a loss. Forgive.

For all our conceits we are, in the end, helpless creatures. We grasp all that is within reach, and then yearn for all beyond that reach. In said state, how can we hope for redemption? Staggering off to my bedroll, I slept fitfully that night, and was started awake just before dawn when Steck Marynd returned on his weary horse, the trundled form of Nifty Gum straddling the beast's rump.

Mild and fleeting my curiosity at the absence of the Entourage, until exhaustion plucked me free of the miserable world one last time before the sun rose to announce the twenty-fifth day upon Cracked Pot Trail.

A Recounting of the
Twenty-fifth Day

HIS FACE BLEAK, STECK MARYND CROUCHED BEFORE THE ash-heaped hearth, and told his tale whilst we gnawed on what was left of Calap Roud. Bludgeoning the heat with the sun barely squatting on the eastern hills. Turgid the dusted air through which crazed insects flitted. Squalid and pinched these faces on pilgrimage to expressions of ecstatic release. Unmindful the implacable mules and unhampered the innocent horses.

The host sat in fret. Tiny, Midge and Flea crouched and picked like rock-apes over the last of the unspoiled meat. Relish braided blades of grass, making small nooses. Mister Must puttered about the carriage, pausing to scratch his backside every now and then, before adding more leaves to the pot of tea, stirring and whatnot. Apto Canavalian huddled beneath his threadbare blanket, as if withering beneath the murderous glares of Brash Phluster. Purse Snippet sipped at her steaming cup and a hand and a foot was visible from the ditch where Sellup was lying.

Tulgord Vise paced, fondling his pommel as knights will do.

Arpo Relent, alas, had not moved a single twitch from his face-down deliberations, and this was ominous indeed.

As for Nifty Gum, why, from what could be seen in that bunch and fold of cloak, that haystack of once glistening gold hair now as dishevelled as a hairball spat up by a dragon, he was at the very edge of gibbering unreason, as might afflict a famous person no-one wanted to know anymore. Buffeted by our disregard, he sat like an overgrown milestone, head lowered, hands hidden, his boots splashed with dark stains and churning with flies.

Steck Marynd prefaced his recount with a shudder and hands up at his face, as if in horror of memories resurrected. Then he lowered those weathered hands, revealing a visage of guttered faith, and began.

I am a man of doubts, though with eyes set upon me none would say such a thing. Is this not fair? Stalwart and firm, is Steck Marynd. Slayer of demons, hunter of necromancers, the very spine of the Nehemothanai – you will be silent, Mortal Sword, for even you must accept that this is a bloodied trail I have followed far longer than you. I am the cutter excising the cancer of evil, the surgeon setting blade to the tumour of cold malice. Such is the course of my life. I have chosen it and do not begrudge this nest of scars.

Yet, there are doubts within me, the begat of the very life I have chosen for myself. I tell you all this: when one looks into the eye of evil, one's very soul is shaken, and trembles but one tug from uprooted and forever lost. The ground becomes uncertain underfoot. Balance tilts awry. To then strike it down, to destroy it utterly, is an act of self-preservation. In defence of one's own soul. It is like that. Each and every time. But there are moments when it is not enough, not nearly enough.

Are we the children of gods? If so, then what god would so countenance such ignoble spawn? Why is the proper and good path so narrow, so disused, while the cruel and wanton ones proliferate in endless swarm? Why is the choice of integrity the thinnest branch within reach? While the dark wild tree is a mad web across half the sky?

Oh, yes, I know. You poets will sing to me of value gauged in the strain of the challenge, as if sheer difficulty is the meaning of worth. If righteousness was easy, you say, it would not shine like gold. And do not beggars dream of gold, just as the fallen dream of salvation, and the coward dreams of courage? But you do not understand anything. Do the gods exult in the temptations they fling before us? Why? Are they insane? Are they, in fact, eager to see us fall? Give us the clear and true path, and in the act of seeing the darkness falls away, the lures vanish, the way home beckons us all.

If you would awaken our souls, dear gods, be so good as to then sweep the shadows from the road ahead.

No, the gods have all the moral rectitude of children. They created nothing and are no different from us, knuckled to the world.

Listen! I have no faith in any of you. And naught in me either. Do none of you see how this pilgrimage has already failed? Oh, easy enough for the poets to comprehend that hoary truth – seeking fame we step into their path and cut them down, and then gnaw on their bones. And what of you, Sardic Thew? And you, Lady Snippet? And the Dantoc and her footman? You have eaten of the flesh and it was the easiest road of all, wasn't it? And who stood tallest with armoured excuses? Why, none other than Tulgord Vise, Champion of Purity, and indeed the Well Knight Arpo Relent, paladin of virtue.

One day I shall stand before the Nehemoth, before Bauchelain and Korbal Broach. I shall look upon true evil. And they will see in my eyes all the evil that *I* have done, and they will smile and call me friend. Companion. Cohort in the League of Venality. Could I deny them?

Faith? Look upon Nifty Gum, this broken thing here. An artist beloved, so beloved his retinue of worshippers would bare fangs against the envy of the gods themselves.

I found their trail, even as the shadows of dusk closed in. A rampant, rabid thing, skittering this way and that, a small herd led by a blind bull. Rocks overturned, plants torn loose – yes, they hungered. They thirsted. And suffered. Two women, the man they honoured with their loyalty.

In darkness I came upon their first camp, and from the scuffs and signs I was able to reconstruct the dreadful events with nary a test to my woodsmanship. See me claw my face yet again? The youngest was set upon, the other two in cahoots, a pact forged in a demon's hole, that one. The innocent child, strangled, all the soft parts of her sweet form torn away by savage teeth. *Teeth*. Ah, Midge, do I see you pause in your breaking fast? Well you should. You see, when those eager mouths drank and fed, poor Oggle Gush was not yet dead.

They ate themselves sick, did Pampera and Nifty. And they left the body in their wake, spoiled, rotting. I see your shock, Brash Phluster, and I do mock it. If you had but one adoring fan in your wake, and starvation loomed, you would not hesitate – deny it not! See Nifty Gum, huddled there. No hesitation stuttered his hands.

When I renewed my tracking, I admit my thoughts were black as a pauper's pit. Now, I did hunt. I believed I could forge this distinction, you see, between what they had done to that child, and all that we have done on this here trail. Is not the soul a thing of sweet conceit?

So now, consider this. He had but one worshipper left, and she was close in that she shared his crime, a murderess, a belly-bloated beauty he could touch with familiarity so absolute no mortal could step between them. You might think. And you might fold tight your arms and whisper easing words to yourself. She but followed his lead – what else could she do, after all?

Was it guilt, then, that launched her upon his back? That sank teeth into his shoulder, striving towards his throat? The mouthfuls of spurting flesh she gobbled down, even as he shrieked and thrashed? And what of Nifty Gum? That he should twist round and bite her in turn, fatally as it transpired, snipping through her jugular, whereupon he bathed and did drink deep. Even as she died, she gnawed upon his right calf, and so was left in a pose of blessed defiance.

I caught him twenty paces down from this final atrocity, limping and streaming crimson. Oh yes, all of you set eyes upon him now. This poet of appetites. Study him in your arrayed expressions of horror and disgust. Hypocrites one and all. You. Me. The wretched gods, too. Aye, I should have killed him then and there. A quarrel through the back of his head. I should have. But no. Why should the blood stain my hands alone? I give him to you, pilgrims. He is the end of this path, the one we have all chosen. I give him to you all. My gift.

As his last words drifted and sank into earth and flesh, Brash Phluster licked his lips and said, 'But, where is she? Can't we still—'

'No,' growled Mister Must, in a tone that stirred awake his soldier days, 'we cannot, Phluster.'

'But I don't want to die!'

And at that, Steck Marynd did weep.

For myself, I admit to a certain satisfaction. Oh, don't look at me like that! Given the chance, what artist wouldn't eat his fans? Think of the satisfaction! Far preferable than the opposite, I fervently assert. But let us skip and dance from such admissions, lest they unveil things even more unsightly.

Sellup crawled from the ditch, her split lips stretched back in a ghastly smile, her eyes fixing upon Nifty Gum. 'All for me!' she cackled, dragging herself closer. 'I won't eat you, darling! I'm not even hungry!'

The wretched poet, thrice named Artist of the Century, lifted his bedraggled head. The modest balance of his features was gone, each detail inexpertly reassembled into a pastiche of Gumdom. Old blood stained his chin, flaked the edges of his tunnelled mouth. Flanking the ill-ruddered nose, each eye struggled with the other, fighting over proper alignment, which neither could quite manage. And if a lockbox waited behind those orbs, it was kicked over, contents strewn in tangled heaps. From the weep of his crusted nostrils to the coagulated clumps in his stringy hair, he was indeed a man bereft of his Entourage, barring one dead hag avowing undying servitude.

'It was the eggs,' he whispered.

At this even Sellup paused.

'I was so hungry. All I could think of was . . . was *eggs*! Sunny side up, scrambled, poached.' Trembling fingertips touched his mouth and he flinched, as if those fingers did not belong to him at all. 'Those tales. A dragon spawn trapped in a giant egg – that's just *stupid*. I— I don't even like meat! Not real meat. But eggs, that's different. Like an idea not yet born, I could eat those. I so want to! It was the maiden he stole. The Egg Demon, I mean. Stole – stole away in the night! I tried to warn them, you see, I really did. But they wouldn't listen!' He stabbed a finger at Sellup. 'You! You wouldn't listen! I'm out of ideas, don't you see that!? Why do you think I plundered every fairy tale I could find? It's – it's – *all gone!*'

'I'll be your egg, sweetie!' She picked up a rock and rapped it against the side of her head, eliciting a strange muted thump. 'Crack me open, darling! See? It's easy!'

As one might imagine, we stared in morbid fascination at this tableau and all its bizarre logic, and I was reminded of that cabal of poets from Aren a few centuries back, the ones who imbibed all manner of hallucinogens in a misplaced search for enlightenment, only to get lost in the private weirdness that is the artist's mortal brain when it can discern nothing but its own navel (and who needs hallucinogens for that?).

'Get away from me.'

'Sweetie!' *Thump-thump.* 'Here, take my rock!' *Thump!* 'You can do it too!' *Thump!* 'It's easy!'

As it turned out, even Nifty Gum was of no mind to discover what hid inside the skull of one of his fans. Instead, he whispered, 'Someone end it. Please. Someone. Plea—'

I would hazard the notion that this heartfelt utterance referred to a wholly natural desire to see Sellup expunged from his (and everyone else's) sight, and in that regard Nifty won my sympathies entire. For reasons unknown, however (oh how I lie, don't I?), Tulgord Vise misinterpreted the Great Artist and in answer he thrust his sword between the poet's shoulder blades. The point burst from Nifty's chest in a welter of blood and splintered bone.

Nifty's eyes gave up the struggle, and he sagged, leaning heavily on the sword blade before, with a grunt, Tulgord heaved the weapon free. The poet fell back in a puff of dust.

Sellup moaned. 'Thumbsy?'

Seeing the man's lips moving, I edged closer – after a wary glance Tulgord's way, but he was already cleaning his blade in the sand beside the trail – and then I leaned close. 'Nifty? It is me, Flicker.'

Sudden horror lit up Nifty's eyes. 'The eggs,' he breathed. *The eggs!'*

Whereupon, with a strange, blissful smile, he died.

Is this the fate for all artists who wantonly steal inspiration? Certainly not, and shame on you for even suggesting it.

Our family was indeed in tatters. But this morning was yet to give up the last of its shocking revelations, for at that moment Well Knight Arpo Relent sat up, blinking the gobs of mucus from his eyes. The crack in his head dripped pink tears, but he seemed unmindful of that.

'Who dressed me?' he demanded in an odd voice.

Apto Canavalian lifted his gaze, and a most forlorn and dejected gaze it was. 'Your mother?'

Arpo stood, somewhat unsteadily, and tugged clumsily at the straps of his armour. 'I don't need this.'

Poor Sellup had resumed her crawling and was now curled up on Nifty's sundered chest, tentatively licking at the blood. 'Look at this,' she muttered, 'I have no taste at all.'

'Well Knight,' said Tulgord Vise, 'do you recall what happened to you?'

At that Apto Canavalian started, and then stared up at the Mortal Sword in horror commingled with blistering hatred.

'The blood dried up,' Arpo answered. 'Miserable shits, after all I did for them. Open the flood gates! Who pissed on that altar? Was that a demon did that? I hate demons. Death to all demons!' He succeeded in shucking off his coat of mail and it fell to one side with a golden rustle. 'All dogs must hereafter walk backwards. That's my decree and make of it what you will. Pluck one eye from every cat, bring them in buckets – of course I'm serious!

No, not the cats, the eyes. It's tragic the dogs can't see where they're going. So, we take those eyes and we—'

'Well Knight!'

Arpo glared at Tulgord Vise. 'Who in Farl's name are you?'

'Wrong question!' the Mortal Sword snapped. 'Who are *you*?'

'Well now, what's this?'

We all stared at what Relent now gripped in one hand.

'That's your penis,' said Apto Canavalian. 'And I say that advisedly.'

Arpo stared down at it. 'Kind of explains everything, doesn't it?'

Personally, I see no humour in that statement whatsoever. In any case, Arpo Relent (or whoever happened to be inhabiting his body at that time) now focused his entire attention upon his discovery, and moments later made a mess of things. His brows lifted, and then he smiled and started over again. 'I could do this all day. In fact, I think I will.'

With a disgusted grunt Tulgord Vise turned to saddle his horse.

Sardic Thew clapped his hands. 'Well! I think today's the day!'

Tiny Chanter belched. 'Better not be. Flicker's got stories to finish and he ain't getting away with not finishing them.'

'Dear sir,' said I, 'we have the breadth of the sun's passage, if our host's assessment is correct and why would we doubt it? Fear not, resolutions abound.'

'If I don't like what I hear you're a dead man.'

'Yeah,' said Fl— oh, never mind.

Studiously, I avoided Purse Snippet's piercing regard, only to be speared by Relish's. The maddening expectations of women!

As if chilled, Apto Canavalian drew tighter his cloak. He rose to stand close to me. 'Flicker, a word if you please.'

'You need fear nothing from Brash Phluster, sir.' I raised my voice. 'Is that not true, Brash?'

The young poet's face twisted. 'I just want things to be fair, Flicker. Tell him that. Fair. I deserve that. We both do, you and me. Tell him that.'

'Brash, he is standing right here.'

'I'm not talking to him.'

Apto was gesturing, clearly wanting the two of us to walk off a short distance. I glanced around. Mister Must had reappeared with his teapot. Sardic Thew held out his cup with shaky hands, whilst Purse Snippet offered the old man a frail smile as he went to her first. Our host's visage flashed dark for a moment. Relish was now braiding a whole string of nooses together, reminding me of the winter solstice ritual of an obscure Ehrlii tribe, something to do with hanging charms upon a tree in symbolic remembrance of when they used to hang bigger things from trees. Her brothers were throwing small rocks at Sellup's head, laughing when one struck. The deathless fan, however, gave no indication of noticing, busy as she was eating Nifty's heart out. Steck Marynd sat staring at the ashes of the campfire, and all the knuckle bones that glowed like infernal coals.

Arpo Relent had worked his penis into exhaustion and was now slapping the limp tip back and forth with all the hopeless optimism of an unsated woman on a wedding night.

'We have a few moments yet, it seems,' I conceded. 'Lead on, sir.'

'I never wanted to be a judge,' Apto said once we'd gone about twenty paces up the trail. 'I shouldn't be here at all. Do you have any idea how hard it is being a critic?'

'Why, no. Is it?'

The man shivered in the wretched heat, leading me to wonder if he was fevered. 'It's what eats at us all, you see.'

'No, I am afraid I don't.'

His eyes flicked at mine. 'If we could do what you do, don't you think we would?'

'Ah.'

'It's like the difference between a fumbling adolescent and a master lover. We're brilliant in squirts, while you can enslave a woman across the span of an entire night. The truth is, we hate you. In the unlit crevices of our cracked soul, we seethe with resentment and envy—'

'I would not see it that way, Apto. There are many kinds of

talent. A sharp eye and a keen intellect, why, they are rare enough to value in themselves, and their regard set upon us is our reward.'

'When you happen to like what we say.'

'Indeed. Otherwise, why, you're an idiot and it gives us no small amount of pleasure to say so. As far as relationships go,' I added, 'there is little that is unique or even at all unusual here.'

'All right, it's like this, this here, this very conversation we're having.'

'I'm sorry?'

'"Entirely lacking profundity, touching on philosophical issues with the subtlety of a warhammer. Reiterations of the obvious" – see my brow lifting to show just how unimpressed I am? So, what do you think I'm really saying when I make such pronouncements?'

'Well, I suppose you're saying that in fact you are smarter than me—'

'Sharper than your dull efforts to be sure. Wiser, cooler of regard, loftier, far too worldly to observe your clumsy maunderings with anything but amused condescension.'

'Surely it is your right to think so.'

'Don't you feel a stab of hate, though?'

'Ah, but the wise artist – and indeed, some of us *are* wise – possesses a most perfect riposte, one that pays no regard to whatever murky motives lie behind such attacks.'

'Really? What is it?'

'Well, before I answer let me assure you that this in no way refers to you, for whom I feel affection and growing respect. That said, why, we forge a likeness in our tale and then proceed to excoriate and torture the hapless arse-hole with unmitigated and relentless contempt.'

'The ego's defence—'

'Perhaps, but I am content enough to call it *spite*.'

And Apto, being a critic whom as I said I found both amiable and admirable (shock!), was grinning. 'I look forward to the conclusion of your tales this day, Avas Didion Flicker, and you can be assured that I will consider them most carefully as I ponder the adjudication of the Century's Greatest Artist.'

'Ah, yes, rewards. Apto Canavalian, do you believe that art possesses relevance in the real world?'

'Now, that is indeed a difficult question. After all, whose art?'

To that I shrugged. 'Pray, don't ask me.'

All chill had abandoned Apto upon our return to the others. Light his step and fair combed his hair. Brash Phluster bared his teeth upon seeing the transformation, and stewed to a boil of suspicion was his glare in my direction. Mister Must was already perched and waiting atop the carriage, small clouds of smoke rising from his pipe. Steck Marynd sat astride his horse, crossbow resting across one forearm. He wore his soldier's mask once again, angled sharp with a strew of discipline and stern determination. Indeed, backlit by the morning sun, the exudation surrounding this grim figure was an aura of singular purpose, a penumbra ominous as a jilted woman's upon the doorstep of a rival's house.

Tulgord Vise was in turn swinging himself onto his mount in a jangle of chain and deadly weapons. Stalwart in pose, vigorous in defence of propriety, the Mortal Sword of the Sisters cast grating eyes upon the much-reduced party, and allowed himself a satisfied nod.

'Is this my horse?' Arpo Relent asked, glaring at the beast that still stood barebacked and hobbled.

'Gods below,' growled Tulgord. 'You, Flicker, saddle the thing, else we linger here all day. And you, Phluster, give us a song.'

'Nobody has to die anymore!'

'That's what you think,' retorted Tiny Chanter. 'The Reaver himself is your audience, poet, as it should be. A blade hovers over your head. A sneer announces your death sentence, a yawn spells your doom. A modest drift of attention from any one of us and your empty skull rolls and bounces on the road. Hah, this is how performance *should* be! Life in the balance!'

'And if it was you?' snarled Brash in sudden courage (or madness).

'I wouldn't waste my time in poetry, you fool. Words – why, anyone can put them together, in any order they please. It's not like what you're doing is hard, is it? The rest of us just don't bother. We got better things to do with our time.'

'I take it,' ventured Apto, 'as a king you are not much of a patron to the arts.'

'Midge?'

'He arrested the lot,' said Midge.

'Flea?'

'And then boiled them alive, in a giant iron pot.'

'The stink,' said Midge.

'For days,' said Flea.

'Days,' said Midge.

'Now, poet. Sing!' And Tiny smiled.

Brash whimpered, clawed at his greasy mane of hair. 'Gotho's Folly, the Lullaby Version, then.'

'*The what?*'

'I'm not talking to you! Now, here it is and no interruptions please.

> '*Lie sweet in your cot, precious onnne*
> *The dead are risin from every graaave*
> *The dead are risin, I say, from every graaa-yev!*
> *Bright your little eyes, precious onnne*
> *Bright as beacons atop that barrowww*
>
> '*Stop your screamin, precious onnne*
> *The dead ain't deaf they can hear you fine*
> *Oh the dead ain't deaf I say, they hear you fiii-yen!*
> *Stop your climbin, precious onnne*
> *Sweet it's gonna taste your oozin marrowww*
>
> *Oh we never wanted you anywayyy—*'

'Enough!' roared Tulgord Vise, wheeling his horse round as he unsheathed his sword.

Tiny giggled. 'Here it comes!'

'Be quiet you damned necromancer! You—' Tulgord pointed his

sword at Brash, whose poor visage was pallid as, well, Sellup's (above her mouth, that is). 'You are sick – do you hear me? Sick!'

'Artists don't really view that as a flaw,' observed Apto Canavalian.

The sword trembled. 'No more,' rasped Tulgord. 'No more, do you hear me?'

Brash's head was bobbing like a turd in a whirlpool.

Done at last readying the horse I gave its dusty rump a pat and turned to Arpo Relent. 'Your charger awaits you, sir.'

'Excellent. Now what?'

'Well, you mount up.'

'Good. Let's do that, then.'

'Mounting up involves you walking over here, good knight.'

'Right.'

'Foot into the stirrup – no, the other – oh, never mind, that one will do. Now, grasp the back of the saddle, right, just so. And pull yourself up, swing that leg, yes, perfect, set your foot in the other – got it. Well done, sir.'

'Where's its head?'

'Behind you. Guarding your back, sir, just the way you like it.'

'I do, do I? Of course I do. Excellent.'

'Now, we just tie these reins to this mule's harness here – do you mind, Mister Must?'

'Not in the least, Flicker.'

'Good . . . there! You're set, sir.'

'Most kind of you. Bless you, and take my blessing with solemn gratitude, mortal, it's been a thousand years since my last one.'

'Then I shall, sir.'

'For that,' Tulgord said to me, 'it's all down to you for the rest of the day, Flicker.'

'Oh Mortal Sword, it is that indeed.'

I would at this moment assert, humbly, that I am not particularly evil. In fact, if I was as evil as you perhaps think, why, I would have killed the critic long ago. We must bow, in either case, to the events as they truly transpired, though it might well paint me in modestly unpleasant hues. But the artist's eye must remain sharp and unforgiving, and every scene's noted detail must purport a burden of significance (something the least capable of critics never quite get into their chamber-potted brains, ah, piss on them I say!). The timing of this notification is, of course, entirely random and no doubt bred and born of my inherent clumsiness.

Leapt past that passage? Good for you. (And I do so look forward to your collected letters of erudition, posteritally.)

'Just like the dog, tally ho!' shouted Arpo Relent as the journey resumed, and then arose a milked joccling sound followed by an audible shudder and visible moan from the Very Well Knight.

We set out, in the scuff of worn boots, the clop of hoofs and the rackle of carriage wheels, leaving in our wake Nifty Gum's corpse and Sellup who was now gnawing beneath the dead man's chin, in the works a love-bite of appalling proportions.

Shall I list we who remained? Why not. In the lead Steck Marynd, behind him Tulgord Vise and then the Chanters, followed by the host and Purse Snippet, then myself flanked by Apto upon my right and Brash upon my left, and behind us of course Mister Must and the carriage of the Dantoc Calmpositis, with Arpo Relent riding his mount off to one side at the trail's very edge.

Pilgrims one and all, and the day was bright, the vultures cooing and the bees writhing in the dust as the sun lit the landscape on fire and sweat ran in dirty streams to sting eyes and consciences both. Brash was gibbering under his breath, his gaze focused ten thousand paces ahead. Apto's mouth was also moving, perhaps taking mental notes or setting Brash's latest song to memory. Relish punched one of her brothers every now and then, with no obvious cause. Usually in the side of the head. Which the brothers endured with impressive indulgence, she being their little sister. Purse walked in a drugged daze which would not ebb until mid-morning, and bearing this in mind I pondered which of two tales would prove most timely at the moment, and, a decision having been reached with modest effort, I began to speak.

'The Imass woman, maiden no longer, awoke in the depths of night, in the time of the watch, which stretches cold and forlorn before the first touch of false dawn mocks the eastern sky. Shivering, she saw that her furs had been pulled aside, and of her lover no sign remained. Drawing the skins close, she drank the bitter air and with each deep breath her sleepiness grew more distant, and around her the hut breathed in its own dark pace, sighing its soot to settle upon her open eyes.

'She felt filled up, her skin tight as if someone had stuffed her as one would a carcass, to better stretch the curing hide. Her body was not quite entirely her own. She could feel the truth of this. Its privacy now a temporary condition, quick to surrender to his next touch. She was content with that, as only a young woman can be, for they are at their most generous at tender age, and it is only in the later years that the expanse contracts and borders are jealously guarded – trails carelessly trampled are by this time thoroughly mapped in her memory, after all.

'But now, this night, she is young still, and all of the world beyond this silent and unlit hut is blanketed in untouched snow, plush as a brold's virgin fur. The time of night known as the watch is a sacred time for many, and one of great and solemn responsibility. Malign spirits are known to stir in the breaths of the sleeping, seeking a way in, and so one of the tribe must be awake in vigil, whispering wards against the swollen darkness and its many-eyed hungers.

'She could hear nothing past her steady breathing, except perhaps something in the distance, out across the bold sweep of snow and frozen ground – the soft crackle from among trees, as frost tinkled down beneath black branches. There was no wind, and somehow she could feel the pressure of the stars, as if their glittering spears could reach through the layered hides of the hut's banked roof. And she told herself that the ancestors were protecting her with their unwavering regard, and with this thought she closed her eyes once more—'

I paused a moment, and then continued. 'But then she heard a sound. A faint scrape, the patter of droplets. She gasped. "Beloved?"

she whispered and spirits fled in the gloom. The hut's flap was drawn to one side, and the Fenn, crouched low to clear the doorway, edged inside. His eyes glistened as he paused.

' "Yes," said he, "It is I," and then he made a soft sound, something like a laugh, she thought, though she could not be certain for it left a bitter trail. "I have brought meat." And at that she sat up. "You hunted for us?" And in answer he drew closer and now she could smell charred flesh and she saw the thick strip bridging his hands. "A gift," he said, "for the warmth you gave me, when I needed it most. I shall not forget you, not ever." He presented her with the slab and she gasped again when it settled into her hands, for it was still hot, edges crisped by fire, and the fat streamed down between her fingers. Even so, something in what he had said troubled her and she felt a tightness in her throat as she said, "Why would you forget me, beloved? I am here and so are you, and with this food we shall all bless you and beg that you remain with us, and then we—"

' "Hush," said he. "It cannot be. I must leave with the dawn. I must hold to the belief that among the tribes of the Fenn, those beyond the passes, I will find for myself a new home."

'And now there were tears in her eyes and this he must have seen for he then said, "Please, eat, gain strength. I beg you." And she found the strength to ask, "Will you sit with me when I eat? For this long at least? Will you—" '

'That's it?' demanded Relish. 'She gave up that easily? I don't believe it.'

'Her words were brave,' I replied, 'even as anguish tore at her heart.'

'Well, how was I to know that?'

'By crawling into her skin, Relish,' I said most gently. 'Such is the secret covenant of all stories, and songs and poems too, for that matter. With our words we wear ten thousand skins, and with our words we invite you to do the same. We do not ask for your calculation, nor your cynicism. We do not ask you how well we are doing. You choose whether to be with us, word by word, in and out of each and every scene, to breathe as we breathe, to walk as we walk, but above all, Relish, we invite that you *feel* as we feel.'

'Unless you secretly feel nothing,' Purse Snippet said, glancing back at me and I saw dreadful accusation in her eyes – her numbness had been burnt away, making my time short indeed.

'Is this what you fear? That my invitation is a deceit? The suspicion alone belongs to a cynic, to be sure—'

'Belongs to the wounded and the scarred, I should think,' said Apto Canavalian. 'Or the one whose own faith is dead.'

'In such,' said I, 'no covenant is possible. Perhaps some artists do not feel what they ask others to feel, sir, but I do not count myself among those shameful and shameless wretches.'

'I see that well enough,' Apto said, nodding.

'Get back to the tale,' demanded Tiny Chanter. 'She asks him to stay while she eats. Does he?'

'He does,' I replied, my eyes on Lady Snippet's back as she strode ahead of me. 'The darkness of the hut was such that she could see little more than the glint of his eyes as he watched her, and in those twin flickers she imagined all manner of things. His love for her. His grief for all that he had lost. His pride in the food he had provided, his pleasure in her own as she bit into and savoured the delicious meat. She believed she saw amusement as well, and she smiled in return, but slowly her smile faded, for the glitter now seemed too cold for humour, or perhaps it was something she was not meant to see.

'When she had at last finished and was licking the grease from her fingers, he reached out and settled a hand upon her belly. "Two gifts," murmured he, "as you shall discover. Two."'

'How did he know?' demanded Relish.

'Know what?' asked Brash Phluster.

'That she was pregnant, Relish? He knew and so too did she, for there was a new voice inside her, deep and soft, the tinkle of frost in a windless night.'

'What then?' demanded Tiny.

'A moment, if you please. Purse Snippet, may I spin you a few lines of my tale for you?'

She looked back at me, frowning. 'Now?'

'Yes, Lady, now.'

She nodded.

'The brothers were very quick to act, and before a breath was let loose from their glowing sister, why, the man she had loved the night before was lying dead. In her soul a ragged wind whipped up a swirl of ashes and cinders, and she almost stumbled, and the tiny voice inside her – so precious, so new – now wailed piteously for the father it had lost so cruelly—'

Tiny bellowed and spun to Relish, who shrank back.

'Hold!' I cried, and an array of sibling faces swung snarling my way. 'Beneath that tiny cry she found a sudden fury rising within her. And she vowed that when her child was born she would tell it the truth. She would again and again jab a sharp-nailed finger at her passing brothers and say to her sweet wide-eyed boy or girl: "There! There is one of the men who murdered your father! Your vile, despicable, treacherous uncles! Do you see them! They sought to protect me – so they said, but they failed, and what did they then do, my child? *They killed your father!*" No, there would be no smiling uncles for that lone child, no tossing upon the saddle of a thigh, no squeals, no indulgent spoiling, no afternoons at the fishing hole, or wrestling bears or spitting boars with sticks. That child would know only hatred for those uncles, and a vow would find shape deep within it, a kin-slaying vow, a family-destroying vow. Blood in the future. Blood!'

All had halted. All were staring at me.

'She would,' I continued with a voice of gravel and sharp stones. 'She . . . *could*. If they would not leave her be. If they dogged her day after day. Her virginity was now gone. They had nothing left in her to protect. Unless, perhaps . . . an innocent child. But even then – she would decide when and how much. She was now in charge, not them. She was, and this was the sudden, blinding truth that seared through her mind at that instant: she was *free*.'

And then I fell silent.

Tiny gaped, at me and then at Relish. 'But you said Calap—'

'I lied,' replied Relish, crossing her arms and happily proving that she was not as witless as I had first imagined.

'But then you're not—'

'No, I'm not.'

'And you're—'

'I am.'

'The voice—'

'Yes.'

'And you'll tell it—'

'If you leave me to live my life? Nothing.'

'But—'

Her eyes flashed and she advanced on him. '*Everything*. The truth! Hate's seed – to become a mighty tree of death! Your death, Tiny! And yours, Midge! And yours, Flea!'

Tiny stepped back.

Midge stepped back.

Flea stepped back.

'Are we understood?' demanded Relish.

Three mute nods.

She whirled then and shot me a look of eternal gratitude or eternal resentment – I couldn't tell which, and really, did it matter?

Did I then catch a wondering smile from Purse Snippet? I cannot be certain, for she quickly turned away.

As we resumed our journey Apto snorted under his breath. 'Flick goes the first knife this day. Well done, oh, very well done.'

The first. Yes, but only the first.

A voice from back down the trail made us turn. 'Look everybody! I brought Nifty's head!'

There is a deftness that comes of desperation, but having never experienced desperation, I know nothing of it. The same woeful ignorance on my part can be said for the savage wall that rises like a curse between an artist and inspiration, or the torture of sudden doubt that can see scrolls heaped on the fire. The arrow of my intent is well trued. It sings unerringly to its target, even when that target lies beyond the horizon's swollen-breasted curve. You do not believe me? Too bad.

I imagine such flaws in my character are unusual, perhaps even rare enough to warrant a ponder or two, but to be honest, I can't be bothered, and if I must shoulder through jostling crowds of scepticism, suspicion and outright disbelief, then 'ware my spiked armour, for my path is ever sure and I will not be turned aside. Even when it takes me off the cliff's edge, I shall spare you all one last knowing nod. As is only fair.

Is this to also claim that I have lived a life without error? Ah, but recall the beginning of this tale, and find therein my answer to that. Errors salt the earth and patched, sodden and tangled is my garden, dear friends, riotous in mischance at every crook and bend. This being said, I find my confidence unsullied nonetheless, and indeed so replete my aplomb that one cannot help but see in the wild swirling cloak of my wake the sparkle and shock of my assured stride. Nary a tremulous step, do you see?

Not yet? Then bear witness, if you will, to the harrowed closing of this most truthful tale.

'I can't see where we're going. Someone make this horse walk backwards. A new decree, where are the priests? Those purple-lipped perverts fiddling under their robes – oh, damn me! Now I know what they were up to!'

Once more we walked Cracked Pot Trail, and somewhere in the distance awaited the Great Descent to the river and its ferry landing. By day's close, or so our increasingly agitated host had proclaimed. An end to this nightmare – the fevered hope was bright in Brash Phluster's eyes, and even Apto Canavalian's stride was a stitch quicker.

Still the heat tormented. Our water was almost gone, the pieces of Calap Roud bubbling in our bellies, and our dastardly deeds clung to our shoulders with talon and fang. It did not help that Sellup was scooping out handfuls of Nifty's brain and making yummy sounds as she slopped the goo into her mouth.

Tulgord Vise, glancing back and taking note of this detail, twisted round to glare at Tiny Chanter. 'By the Blessed Mounds, do something about her or I will.'

'No. She's growing on me, isn't she, Flea?'

'She is. Midge?'

'She—'

'Stop that too!'

The three brothers laughed, and Relish did, as well, stirring in me a few curdles of unease, especially the way she now walked, bold, swaggering the way curvy women did, her head held high and all those black tresses drifting around like ghostly serpents with glinting tongues testing the air. Why, I realized with a start, she really thought she was pregnant. All the signs were there.

Now, as any mother would tell you, pregnancy and freedom do not belong in the same sentence, except one indicating the loss of the latter with the closing pangs of the former. That being said, I'm no mother, nor was I in any way inclined to disavow Relish Chanter of whatever comforting notions she happened to hold at the time, and was this not considerate of me?

'Look at me! I'm Nifty Gum the famous poet!' Sellup had jammed her hand up inside the head and was moving the jaw up and down, making the teeth clack. 'I say poet things! All the time! I have a new poem for everybody. Want to hear? It's called The Lay of the Eggs! Ha ha, get it? A poem about eggs! I'm famous and everything and my brains taste like cheese!'

'Stop that,' Tulgord Vise said in a dangerous growl, one hand finding the grip of his sword.

'I have found ruts,' announced Steck Marynd from up ahead, reining in and leaning hard over his saddle as he squinted at the ground. 'Carriage ruts, and heavy ones too.'

Tulgord rode up. 'How long ago?' he demanded.

'A day, maybe less!'

'We'll catch them at the ferry! At last!'

'Could be any carriage, couldn't it?' so queried Apto Canavalian, earning vicious stares from Tulgord and the Chanter brothers.

'I mean,' he stumbled on, 'might not be those Nehemoth at all, right? Another pilgrim train, or—'

'Aye,' admitted Steck. 'Worth keeping in mind, and we're worn out, we are. Worn out. We can push, but not too hard.' He tilted his crossbow towards Sardic Thew. 'You, tell us about this ferry. How often does it embark? How long the crossing?'

Our host rubbed his lean jaw. 'Once a day, usually at dusk. There's a tidal draw, you see, that it needs to ride across to Far-rog. Reaches the docks by dawn.'

'Dusk?' Steck's narrow eyes narrowed some more. 'Can we make it, Thew?'

'With a decent pace and no halt for lunch . . . yes, woodsman, I would say it is possible.'

The air fairly bristled, and savage the smiles of Tiny, Midge, Flea and Tulgord Vise.

'What is all this?' demanded Arpo Relent, kicking his horse round so that he could see the rest of the party. 'Are we chasing someone, then? What is he, a demon? I despise demons. If we catch him I'll cut him to pieces. Pieces. Proclamation! The Guild of Demons is herewith disbanded, with prejudice! What, who set the city on fire? Well, put it out! Doesn't this temple have any windows? I can't see a damned thing through all this smoke – someone kill a priest. That always cheers me up. Ho, what's this?'

'Your penis,' said Apto Canavalian. 'And before anyone asks, no, I have no particular fascination for that word.'

'But what's it do? Oh, now I remember. Hmmm, nice.'

'We pursue not a demon,' said Tulgord Vise, straightening to assume a virtuous pose in knightly fashion. 'Necromancers of the worst sort. Evil, murderous. We have avowed that in the name of goodness they must die.'

Arpo blinked up from his blurred right hand. 'Necromancers? Oh, them. Miserable fumblers, don't know a damned thing, really. Well, I'm happy to obliterate them just the same. Did someone mention Farrog? I once lived in a city called Fan'arrogal, wonder if it's, uh, related. On a river mouth? Crawling with demons? Ooh, see that? Ooh! New building programme. Fountains!'

You will be relieved that I bit off a comment about pubic works.

Tulgord stared wide-eyed at Arpo, which was understandable, and then he tugged his horse back onto the path. 'Lead us on, Marynd. I want this done with.'

Mister Must then spoke from atop the carriage. 'Fan'arrogal, you said?'

Arpo was wiping his hand on his bared chest. 'My city. Until the demon infestation, when I got fed up with the whole thing.' He frowned, gaze clouding. 'I think.'

'After a night of slaughter that left most of the city in smouldering ruins,' Mister Must said, his eyes thinned to slits behind his pipe's smoke. 'Or so the tale went. Farrog rose up from its ashes.'

'Gods below,' whispered Sardic Thew with eyes bulging upon Arpo Relent, 'you're the Indifferent God! Returned to us at last!'

Brash Phluster snorted. 'He's a man with a cracked skull, Thew. Look what's leaking out now, will you?'

'I'd rather not,' said Apto, quickly setting off after the Nehemothanai.

I regarded Mister Must. 'Fan'arrogal? That name appears in only the obscurest histories of the region.'

Wiry brows lifted. 'Indeed now? Well, had to have picked it up somewhere, didn't I?'

'As footmen will do,' said I, nodding.

Grunting, Mister Must snapped the traces and the mules lurched forward. I stepped to one side and found myself momentarily alone, as the others had already hurried after the Nehemothanai. Well, almost alone.

'I'm Nifty Gum and I'll do anything she says!' *Clack-clack.*

Ah, a fan's dream, what?

'Kill some time,' commanded Tiny Chanter, once I had caught up.

'Her tears spilled down upon the furs when, with a final soft caress, he left the hut. The grey of dawn mocked all the colours in the world, and in this lifeless realm she sat unmoving, as a faint wind moaned awake outside. Earlier, she had listened for the sledge's runners scraping the snow, but had heard nothing. Now, she listened for the bickering among the hunting dogs, the crunch of wrapped feet as the ice over the pits was cracked open. She listened for the cries of delight upon finding the carcass of the animal the Fenn had slain.

'She listened, then, for the sounds of her life of yesterday and all the days before it, for as long as she could remember. The sounds of childhood, which in detail did not change though she was a child no longer. He was gone, a cavern carved out of her soul. He had brought dark words and bright gifts, in the way of strangers and unexpected guests.

'But, beyond this hut . . . only silence.'

'A vicious tale,' commented Steck Marynd. 'You should have let it die with Roud.'

'The demand was otherwise,' I replied to the man riding a few strides ahead. 'In any case, the end, as you well know, is now near. Finally, she rose, heavy and weightless, chilled and almost fevered, and with her furs drawn about her she emerged into the morning light.

'Dead dogs were strewn about on the stained snow, their necks snapped. To the left of the Chief's hut the remnants of a bonfire died in a drift of ashes and bones. The corpses of her beloved kin were stacked in frozen postures of cruel murder beside the ghastly hearth, and closer to hand laid the butchered remnants of three children.

'The sledge with its mute cargo remained where he had left it, although the hides had been taken, exposing the frost-blackened body of another Fenn. Dead of a sword thrust.

'A keening cry lifting up through the numbness of her soul, she staggered closer to that sledge, and she looked down upon a face years younger than that of the Fenn who had come among them. For, as is known to all, age is difficult to determine among the Tartheno Toblakai. She then recalled his tale, the battle upon the glacier, and all at once she understood—'

'What?' demanded Midge. 'Understood what? Hood take you, Flicker, explain!'

'It is the hero who wins the fated battle against his evil enemy,' said I, with unfeigned sorrow. 'So it is in all tales of comfort. But there is no comfort in this tale. Alas, while we may rail, sometimes the hero dies. Fails. Sometimes, the last one standing is the enemy, the Betrayer, the Kinslayer. Sometimes, dear Midge, there is no comfort. None.'

Apto Canavalian fixed upon me an almost accusatory glare. 'And what,' he said, voice rough with fury, 'is the moral of that story, Flicker?'

'Moral? Perhaps none, sir. Perhaps, instead, the tale holds another purpose.'

'Such as?'

Purse Snippet answered in the coldest of tones. 'A warning.'

'A warning?'

'Where hides the gravest threat? Why, the one you invite into your camp. Avas Didion Flicker, you should have abandoned this tale – gods, what was Roud thinking?'

'It was the only story he knew by heart!' Brash Phluster snapped, and then he wheeled on me. 'But you! You know plenty! You could have spun us a different one! Instead – instead—'

'He chooses to sicken our hearts,' Purse said. 'I said I would abide, Flicker. For a time. Your time, I think, has just run out.'

'The journey has not ended yet, Lady Snippet. If firm you will hold to this bargain, then I have the right to do the same.'

'Do you imagine I remain confident of your prowess?'

I met her eyes, my lockbox of secrets cracked open – just a sliver – but enough to steal the colour from her face, and I said this, 'You should be by now, Lady.'

How many worlds exist? Can we imagine places like and yet unlike our own? Can we see the crowds, the swarming sea of strangers and all those faces scratching our memories, as if we once knew them, even when we knew them not? What value building bitter walls between us? After all, is it not a conceit to shake one's head in denial of such possibilities, when in our very own world we can find a multitude of worlds, one behind the eyes of every man, woman, child and beast you happen to meet?

Or would you claim that these are in fact all facets of the same world? A man kneels in awe before a statue or standing stone, whilst another pisses at its base. Do these two men see the same thing? Do they even live in the same world?

And if I tell you that I have witnessed each in turn, that indeed I have both bowed in humility and reeled before witless desecration, what value my veracity when I state with fierce certainty that numberless worlds exist, and are in eternal collision, and that the only miracle worth a damned thing is that we manage to agree on *anything*?

Nothing stinks worse than someone else's piss. And if you do not believe me, friends, try standing in my boots for a time.

And so to this day I look with fond indulgence upon my memories of the Indifferent God, if god he was, there within the cracked pot of Arpo Relent's head, for all the pure pleasure he found in the grip of his right hand. Its issue was one of joy, after all, and far preferable to the spiteful, small-minded alternative.

The name of Avas Didion Flicker is not entirely unknown among the purveyors of entertainment, if not culture, throughout Seven Cities, and by virtue of living as long as I have, I am regarded with some modest veneration. This has not yielded vast wealth, not by any measure beyond that of personal satisfaction at the canon of words marking a lifetime's effort, and as everyone knows, satisfaction is a wavering measure in one's own mind, as quick to pale as it is to glow. If I now choose to stand full behind this faint canon and its even fainter reputation, well, the stance is not precisely comfortable.

And the relevance of this humble admission? Well now, that's the question, isn't it?

Mortal Sword Tulgord Vise had girthed himself for battle. Weapons cluttered his scaled hands, the pearled luminescence of his armour was fair blinding in the noble light. His eyes were savage arrow-heads straining at the taut bowstring of righteous anticipation. His beard bristled like the hackled rump of a furious hedgehog. The veins webbing his nose were bursting into crimson blooms beneath the skin. His teeth gnashed with every flare of his nostrils and strange smells swirled in his wake.

The Chanter brothers walked in a three-man shieldwall, suddenly festooned with halberds and axes and two-handed and even three-handed swords. Swathed in bear skin, Tiny commanded the centre, with the seal skinned Midge on his left and the seal skinned Flea on his right, thus forming a bestial wall in need of a good wash. Relish sauntered a step behind them, regal as a pregnant queen immune to bastardly rumours (they're just jealous).

Steck Marynd still rode ahead, crossbow at the ready. Two thousand paces ahead the trail lifted to form a rumpled ridge, and behind it was naught but sky. Flanking this ominously near horizon was a host of crooked, leaning standards from which depended sun-bleached rags flapping like the wings of skewered birds. Every dozen or so heartbeats Steck twisted round in his saddle to look upon the Chanters, who being on foot were dictating the pace of this avenging army. He visibly ground his teeth at their insouciance.

Purse Snippet, with visage fraught and drawn, cast pensive glances my way, as did Sardic Thew and indeed Apto Canavalian, but still I held my silence. Yes, I could feel the twisting, knotting strain of the Nehemothanai, possibly only moments from launching forward, but I well knew that neither Tulgord nor Steck were such fools as to abandon the alliance with the Chanters upon the very threshold of battle. By all counts, Bauchelain and Korbal Broach were deadly, both in sorcery and in hard iron. Indeed, if but a small portion of the tales we had all heard on this pilgrimage were accurate, why, the necromancers had left a trail of devastation across half the known world, and entire frothing armies now nipped at their heels.

No, the Chanters, formidable and vicious, would be needed. And what of Arpo Relent? Why, he could be host to a terrible god, and had he not promised assistance?

Yet, for all this, the very air creaked.

'Gods,' whispered Brash Phluster clawing at his hair, 'let them find them! I cannot bear this!'

I fixed my placid gaze upon the broad furry back of Tiny Chanter. 'Perhaps the enemy is closer than any might imagine.' So I spoke, at a pitch that might or might not reach that lumbering shieldwall. 'After all, what secrets did Calap Roud possess? Did he not choose his tale after much consideration? Or so I seem to recall.'

Apto frowned. 'I don't—'

Tiny Chanter swung round, weapons shivering. *'You! Flicker!'*

'Lady Snippet,' said I, calm as ever, 'There is more to my tale, my gift to you, this offering of redemption in this sullied, terrible world.'

Tulgord barked something to Steck who reined in and then wheeled his mount. The entire party had now halted, Mister Must grunting in irritation as he tugged on his traces.

Arpo looked round. 'Is it raining again? Bouncing cat eyes, how I hate rain!'

'Through gritted teeth and clenched jaws,' I began, eyes fixed upon Purse Snippet's, 'do we not despair of the injustice that plagues our precious civilization? Are we not flayed by the unfairness to which we are ever witness? The venal escape unscathed. The corrupt duck into shadows and leave echoes of mocking laughter. Murderers walk the streets. Bullies grow hulking and make fortunes buying and selling property. Legions of black-tongued clerks steal from you every last coin, whilst their shrouded masters build extensions to their well-guarded vaults. Money lenders recline in the filth of riches stripped from the poor. Justice? How can one believe in justice when it bleeds and crawls, when it wears a thousand faces and each one dying before your very eyes? And without justice, how can redemption survive? We are whipped round, made to turn our backs on notions of righteous restitution, and should we raise our voices in protest, why, our heads are lopped off and set on spikes as warnings to everyone else. *"Keep in line, you miserable shits, or you'll end up like this!"*'

Now that I had their attention, even Nifty's, I waved my arms about, consumed by pious wrath. 'Shall we plead to the gods for justice?' And I jabbed a finger at Arpo Relent. 'Do so, then! One is among us! But be warned, justice cuts clean, and what you ask for could well slice you in two on the backswing!' I wheeled to face Purse Snippet once again. 'Do you believe in justice, Lady?'

Mutely she shook her head.

'Because you have seen! With your own eyes!'

'Yes,' she whispered. 'I have seen.'

I hugged myself, wretched with all my haunting thoughts. 'Evil hides. Sometimes right in front of you. I hear something . . . something. It's close. Yes, close. Lady, to our tale, then. She walked in the company of pilgrims and killers, but as the journey went on, as the straits grew ever direr, she began to lose the distinction – there among her companions, even within her own soul. Which the pilgrim? Which the killer? The very titles blurred in blood-stained mockery – how could she remain blind to that? How could anyone?

'And so, as dreadful precipices loomed ever closer, it seemed the world was swallowed in grisly confusion. Killers, yes, on all sides. Wearing brazen faces. Wearing veiled ones. The masks all hide the same bloodless visage, do they not? Where is the enemy? Where? Somewhere ahead, just beyond the horizon? Or somewhere much closer? What was that warning again? Ah, yes . . . be careful who you invite into your camp. I hear something. What is it? Is it laughter? I think—'

Bellowing, Tiny Chanter pushed through our ranks and thumped against the carriage. 'Everyone quiet!' And he set the side of his head against the shuttered side window. 'I hear . . . *breathing.*'

'Yes,' said Mister Must, looking down, 'she does that.'

'No! It's – it's—'

' 'Ware off there, sir,' rumbled Mister Must, his stained teeth visible where they clenched the clay stem of his pipe. 'I am warning you. Back off . . . now.'

'An old woman, is it?' Tiny sneered up at the driver. 'Eats enough to shame a damned wolf!'

'Her appetites are her business—'

Steck kicked his horse closer. 'Flicker—'

'By my bloody altar!' cried Arpo Relent, 'I just noticed!'

Tulgord raised his sword, head whipping round. 'What? What did you just—'

The pipe stem snapped between Mister Must's teeth and he set most narrow eyes upon the Well Knight. 'Let the past lie, I always say. Deep in the quiet earth, deep and—'

'I know you!' Arpo roared, and then he launched himself at Mister Must.

Something erupted, engulfing the driver in flames. Arms out-stretched, Arpo plunged into that raging maelstrom. Braying, the mules lunged forward.

Tiny flung himself onto the side of the carriage, hammering at the door. An instant later Flea and Midge joined him, clambering like wild apes. Where Mister Must had been there was now a demon, monstrous, locked in a deathgrip with Arpo Relent, as flames writhed like serpents around them both.

The carriage heaved forward as the mules strained in their harnesses.

Everyone scattered from its careening path.

Tulgord Vise fought with his rearing charger, and the beast twisted, seeking to evade the mules, Arpo's tethered horse and the crowded carriage, only to collide with Steck Marynd's shaggy mare.

The crossbow loosed, the quarrel burying itself in the rump of Tulgord's mount. Squealing, the beast lunged, shot forward, col-liding with Steck's horse. That creature went down, rolling over Steck Marynd and loud was the snap of one of the woodsman's legs. Tulgord had lost grip on his reins, and now tottered peril-ously as his horse charged up alongside the carriage.

More flames ignited, bathing the front half of the rollicking, thundering conveyance.

Tulgord's mount veered suddenly, throwing the Mortal Sword from the saddle, and down he went, rolling once before the front left wheel ground over him in a frenzied crunching of enamelled armour, followed by the rear wheel, and then his weapon belt went taut in a snapping of leather, and off the man went, dragged in the carriage's wake, and in spinning, curling clouds of smoke, the whole mess thundered ahead, straight for the edge of the Great Descent.

Steck Marynd was screaming in agony as his horse staggered upright once more, and the beast set off in mindless pursuit of the carriage, Tulgord's mount and Arpo's falling in alongside it. Relish howled and ran after them, her hair flying out to surround her head in black fronds.

Mute, we followed, stumbling, staggering.

None could miss the moment when the mad mob plunged over the crest and vanished from sight. It is an instant of appalling clarity, seared into my memory. And we saw, too, when the horses did the same, and through drifting smoke and clouds of dust we were witness to Relish Chanter finally arriving, skidding to a halt, and her horrified cry was so curdling Nifty's head went rolling across our paths as Sellup clapped greasy hands to her rotting earholes. Relish set off down the slope and we could see her no more.

There are instances in life when no cogent thought is possible. When even words vanish and nothing rises to challenge a choke-tight throat, and each breath is a shocked torment, and all one's limbs move of their own accord, loose as a drunkard's, and a numbness spreads from a gaping mouth. And on all sides, the world is suddenly painfully sharp. Details cut and rend the eyes. The sheer brilliant stupidity of stones and dead grasses and clouds and twigs strewn like grey bones on the path – all this, then, strike the eye like mailed fists. Yes, there are instances in life when all this assails a person.

It was there in the face of Apto Canavalian. And in Purse Snippet's, and even in Brash Phluster's (behind the manic joy of his impending salvation). Sardic Thew's oily hands were up at his oily lips, his eyes glittering and he led us all in the rush to the trail's edge.

At last we arrived, and looked down.

The carriage had not well survived the plunge, its smashed wreckage heaped in the midst of flames and smoke at the distant base, three hundred steep strides down the rocky, treacherous path. Bits of it were scattered about here and there, flames licking or smoke twirling. Astonishingly, the mules had somehow escaped their harnesses and were swimming out into the twisting streams of the vast river that stretched out from a cluster of shacks and a stone jetty at the ferry's landing. Immediately behind them bobbed the heads of three horses.

Of the demon and Arpo Relent, there was no sign, but we could see Flea's body lying among boulders just this side of the muddy bank, and Midge's bloody form was sprawled flat on its face two-thirds of the way down the track. Tiny, however, seemed to have vanished, perhaps inside the burning wreckage, and perhaps the same fate had taken Tulgord Vise, for he too was nowhere to be seen.

Skidding and stumbling, Relish had almost reached Midge.

And the ferry?

Fifty or more reaches out on the river, a large, flat-decked thing, on which stood four horses, and a tall carriage, black and ornate as a funeral bier. Figures standing at the stern rail were visible.

Sardic Thew, our most venerable host, was staring intently down at the burning carriage. He licked his lips. 'Is she – is she?'

'Dead?' asked I. 'Oh yes, indeed.'

'You are certain?'

I nodded.

He wiped at his face, and then reached a trembling hand beneath his robes and withdrew a silk bag that jingled most fetchingly. He settled its substantial weight into my palm.

I dipped my head in thanks, hid the fee beneath my cloak and then walked a half-dozen paces away to settle my gaze on that distant ferry.

Behind me a conversation began.

'Gods below!' hissed Apto Canavalian. 'The Dantoc – an old woman—'

'A vicious beast, you mean,' growled Sardic Thew. 'Relations of mine got into financial trouble. Before I could assume the debts,

278

that slavering bitch pounced. It was the daughter she wanted, you see. For her pleasure pits. Just a child! A sweet, innocent—'

'Enough!' I commanded, wheeling round. 'Your reasons are your own, sir. You have said more than I need hear, do you understand?' And then I softened my eyes and fixed them upon a pale, trembling Purse Snippet. 'So few, Lady, dare believe in justice. Ask our host, if you must hear more of this sordid thing. For me, and understand this well, I am what I am, no more and no less. Do I sleep at night? Most serenely, Lady. Yes, I see what there is in your eyes when you look upon me. Does redemption await me? I think not, but who can truly say, till the moment of its arrival. If you seek some softness in your self-regard, find it by measure against the man who stands before you now. And should you still find nothing of worth within you, then you can indeed have my life.'

After a time, she shook her head. That, and nothing more.

Sellup arrived. 'Anybody see Nifty's head? I lost it. Anyone?'

'Do you believe that art possesses relevance in the real world?'
'Now, that is indeed a difficult question. After all, whose art?'
To that I shrugged. 'Pray, don't ask me.'

Knives, garrottes, poison, so very crass. Oh, in my long and storied career, I have made use of them all as befits my profession, but I tell you this. Nothing is sweeter than murder by word, and that sweetness, dear friends, remains as fresh today as it did all those many years ago, on that dusty ridge that marked the end of Cracked Pot Trail.

Did I receive my reward from Purse Snippet? Why, on the night of the tumultuous party upon the awarding of the Century's Greatest Artist to Brash Phluster (such a bright, rising star!), she did find me upon a private island amidst the swirl of smiling humanity, and we spoke then, at surprising length, and thereafter—

Oh dear, modesty being what it is, I can take that no further.

It was a considerable time afterwards (months, years?) that I happened to meet the grisly Nehemoth, quarry of ten thousand stone-eyed hunters, and over guarded cups of wine a few subjects were brushed, dusted off here and there in the gentle and, admittedly, cautious making of acquaintances. But even without that most intriguing night, it should by now be well understood that the true poet can never leave a tale's threads woefully unknotted. Knotting the tale's end is a necessity, to be sure, isn't it? Or, rather if not entirely knotted, then at least seared, with fingertips set to wet mouth. To cut the sting.

So, with dawn nudging the drowsing birds in this lush garden, the wives stirring from their nests and the moths dipping under leaf, permit me to wing us back to that time, and to one last tale, mercifully brief, I do assure you.

Thus.

'It is a true measure of civilization's suicidal haste,' said Bauchelain, 'that even a paltry delay of, what? A day? Two? Even that, Mister Reese, proves so unpalatable to its hapless slaves, that death itself is preferable.' And he gestured with gloved hand towards all that the passing of the dust cloud now revealed upon that distant shore.

Emancipor Reese puffed for a time on his pipe, and then he shook his head. 'Couldn't they see, Master? That is what I can't get. Here we were, and it's not like that old ferryman there was gonna turn us round, is it? They missed the ride and that's that. It baffles me, sir, that it does.'

Bauchelain stroked his beard. 'And still you wonder at my haunting need to, shall we say, *adjust* the vicissitudes of civilization as befits its more reasonable members? Just so.' He was quiet for a time until he cleared his throat and said, 'Korbal Broach tells me that the city we shall see on the morn groans beneath the weight of an indifferent god, and I do admit we have given that some thought.'

'Oh? Well, Master,' said Emancipor, leaning on the rail, 'better an indifferent one than the opposite, wouldn't you say?'

'I disagree. A god that chooses indifference in the face of its worshippers has, to my mind, Mister Reese, reneged on the most precious covenant of all. Accordingly, Korbal and I have concluded that its life is forfeit.'

Emancipor coughed out a lungful of smoke.

'Mister Reese?'

'Sorry!' gasped the manservant, 'but I thought you just said you mean to kill a god!'

'Indeed I did, Mister Reese. Heavens forbid, it's not like there's a shortage of the damned things, is there? Now then, best get you some rest. The city awaits our footfalls upon the coming dawn and not even an unmindful god can change that now.'

And we can all forgive their not hearing the muttering that came from the ferryman's dark hood as he hunched over the tiller, one hand fighting the currents, and the other beneath his breeches. *'That's what you think.'*

THE FIENDS OF NIGHTMARIA

PART ONE
One Night in Farrog

BEETLE PRAATA'S HORSE COLLAPSED UNDER HIM JUST outside the embassy's stables, making it easier to dismount. He stepped to one side to regard the fallen beast, and then gave one tentative kick to its lathered haunch, eliciting no response.

Puny Sploor, the groundskeeper and stabler, edged into view from the sentry cubicle, holding one flickering candle, his rheumy eyes blinking.

Beetle Praata gestured at the horse. 'Brush this down and drag it close to some hay.'

Puny rubbed at one skinny arm, as if the effort of holding up the candle had exhausted it. 'It's dead,' he observed.

Beetle frowned and then shrugged. 'You never know.'

Leaving the stabler and the horse in the small yard, the Imperial Courier of Nightmaria made his way into the embassy. Just outside the heavy bronze door he paused and squinted up into the night sky. The stars seemed to swim in a vast pool of black water, as if he had sunk to unimaginable depths, swallowed by a diluvian dream from which no awakening was possible. He drew a deep, cleansing breath, and then lifted the heavy iron ring, turned it until it clicked, pulled open the massive door, and strode inside.

The air within was redolent, thick with the pungent reek of decay. Offering bowls of green, slimy copper occupied flanking niches at eye-level to either side of the formal entranceway, filled with moss from which parasitic flowers spilled down to snake

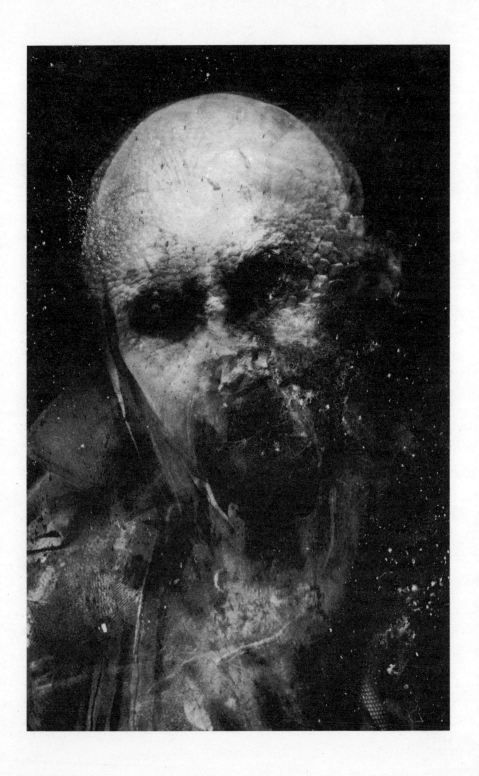

across the narrow ledges. A thick, loose rug underfoot made wet sounds beneath his boots, and from it arose the cloying smell of rot.

He unclipped his scaled leather highway cloak, shaking the dust from it before setting it on a hook. He plucked from his belt a pair of kid-skin gloves and methodically pulled them on, ensuring that each finger was snug. Satisfied, he continued on, exiting the entranceway to find himself in the vast audience chamber that had never known a foreign guest. The lush padding of the settees to either side of the Ambassador's Chair were now lumpy, the filling spilled out from rotted holes here and there, and in places where small creatures nested the humps in the fabric moved up and down every now and then. Overhead, a chandelier of roseate crystal was mostly obscured beneath frayed braids of moss and lichens, its hundred candles long since eaten by mice and whatnot. From somewhere nearby, water trickled.

Beetle Praata strode to one side and tugged on a ratty cord, somewhat gingerly lest it part, and upon hearing a distant chime, he nodded to himself and settled in to wait.

Motion from beneath one of the settees drew his eye and he observed as a slow-worm, with a blunt maw big enough to swallow the head of a small dog, slithered into view. Lifting its sightless muzzle, it quested from one side to the next, and then set out sliding directly towards Beetle.

From somewhere nearby, deeper into the sanctum, came a muted dragging sound, along with faint, meaty flops, and the hint of something scaly sliding across the damp tiles.

Beetle crouched when the slow-worm finally reached him. He patted its blunt head, lightly enough to keep the stains to his gloves to a minimum. The slow-worm circled him, its knobby tail twitching. As the other sounds drew closer, he straightened and turned in time to see a hunched, uneven form creep into view from a narrow passageway hidden behind a mouldy curtain.

Clad in green silks, Ambassador Ophal D'Neeth Flatroq seemed to hover a moment, and then began a rhythmic swaying, similar to a cobra with hood unfurled. The robe Ophal wore was high-cowled, framing a bald pate of glistening scales, strangely curled ears that ended at vague, possibly chewed points, eyes of murky green, pallid brows and cheeks the hue of a serpent's belly, and a toothless mouth of thick, flabby lips. One hand held up an open oil lamp, flames flickering, revealing fingers without nails and heavy scales upon the back of the hand.

A thin tongue slipped out and darted for a moment before retreating again.

Beetle Praata bowed. 'Ambassador.'

'Hissip svlah, thlup?'

'Alas, yes. As expected, I'm afraid.' The Imperial Courier reached beneath his tunic and drew out a wooden tube, its ends sealed in wax, the seals bearing the stamp of the Royal Signet Ring.

'Prrlll obbel lell,' Ophal sighed, placing the oil lamp on a nearby ledge and then accepting the king's command. Twisting one end of the tube broke a seal and the ambassador probed with a greenish finger until he was able to pull out the vellum. Unfurling it, Ophal peered close, eyes tracking the script. His tongue slithered out again, this time from one corner of his mouth, then retreated once more. 'Ahh, prrlll. Flluth villl rrrh na.'

Beetle's brows lifted. 'This very night? Very well. Shall I await the reply?'

Ophal nodded, and then sighed again. 'Mah yull thelff hathome.'

The courier bowed a second time.

The ambassador gestured down at the slow-worm, 'Eemlee, prrlll come!'

Ophal retreated from whence he came, the slow-worm slithering after him.

Beetle walked over to one of the settees and carefully sat down, ensuring that he crushed nothing. It was going to be a long night. He watched a spider chase a mouse across the floor.

'We do it tonight,' said Plaintly Grasp, leaning over the ale-stained table, the one always reserved for her at the very back of Pink's

Tavern. She ran a finger through a pool of ale, making a stream to the table's edge, and watched it drain.

'Hey,' growled Barunko, 'something's wet my crotch.' He straightened slightly, glaring about.

'You're always saying that,' observed Symondenalian Niksos – known to many as The Knife. He was playing with one of his daggers, the blade slipping back and forth and under and over his scarred, cut-up hand. The blade twisted and he winced, but continued his manipulations. 'Tonight, is it? I'm ready. I've been ready for a week.'

Scowling across at him, Plaintly said, 'She was arrested only two nights ago, you idiot. And stop that, you're dripping blood all over the table again.' She looked to the others. In addition to Barunko – their muscle – and Symondenalian Niksos, who couldn't recall seeing a back he didn't want to stab, there was Lurma Spilibus, who'd never met a lock she couldn't pick or a purse she couldn't snatch, her red tangle of curly hair piled high and wayward, her triangular face bulging at one cheek with a wad of pulped Prazzn, her eyes perpetually crossed as she squinted at the tankard cradled in her hands.

Beside Lurma and huddled together, Mortari and Le Groutt, master burglars who'd yet to meet a wall they couldn't scale. Mortari was the smaller of the two, with a pinched face and the manic eyes of a terrier needing to piss. He was panting slightly in the fug of the tavern. Leaning hard against his left shoulder was Le Groutt, swarthy and snaggle-toothed, showing his broad and possibly witless yellow grin, his head bobbing as he looked about, habitually assessing walls, railings, ledges and whatever else a man might climb.

She studied them all, gauging, and then nodded. 'So we're back together,' she said.

Le Groutt showed her his smile. 'The Famous Party of Five.'

'Infamous,' drawled Symon The Knife. He flinched and the knife clattered to the tabletop. Sucking at his thumb, he glowered at Plaintly but said nothing more.

'The Royal Palace,' mused Lurma. 'That won't be easy. Who

knows what that insane necromancer's let loose in the crypts.' She snapped up her crazed squint, shifted the wad in her mouth until it bulged the other cheek, and then said, 'Barunko, you up to this? Could be demons. Revenants. Giant snakes.'

'Unsubstantiated,' cut in Plaintly. 'He's a usurper. That and nothing more. And the new Grand Bishop is a drooling simpleton. All this talk of sorcery and necromancy is just propaganda, to keep away people like us.'

'Did I pee on myself?' Barunko asked.

'He's arrested the Head of the Thieves' Guild,' Plaintly went on. 'Our Mistress. Now maybe it's been a few years since we all worked together, but we ain't lost a step, not one of us. There's nobody better in Farrog, and now the usurper's declared war on our guild. We're getting her out and we're doing it tonight. One more time, the finest adventuring band of thieves this world has ever seen. So,' she leaned back baring her teeth. 'Is everyone ready for this?'

'I've been ready for a week,' said Symon The Knife, collecting up his blade and twirling it one-handed, until it slipped from his grasp and embedded itself in Barunko's meaty thigh.

The huge man sat up straighter, looking around. 'We in a fight? Is this a fight? Let me at 'im!'

The broad, blustery face of Grand General Pin Dollop, Commander of the Royal Farrogal Army, beamed. 'Say what you like about this new king,' he said in a voice that should have been low and throaty, perhaps even a growl, but was instead thin and reedy, 'he understands the importance of protecting our borders.'

Seneschal Shartorial Infelance paced before the General in the cluttered Strategy Room, her silk robes swirling with restless motion. 'I think you need to explain this to me one more time, Dollop. How is it that raiding beyond those borders constitutes a defensive gesture? Think well on your answer. These are the Imperial caravans of Nightmaria your troops are savaging. Granted, we don't know much about the Fiends but all that we've heard bodes ill. Stirring up that nest seems precipitous.'

'Nonsense,' Pin Dollop replied. 'It's been too long we let those inhuman spawn squat nice and cosy in those mountain keeps, watching our every move from on high. The old king flinched at his own shadow. It was all appease this and placate that. Concessions on the tolls and tithes, all that merchantware skipping right past poor Farrog, making the Fiends filthy rich and us scraping the coffers year after year.' His small eyes tracked Shartorial Infelance. 'Now, this new king of ours, he's got spine. And the Grand Bishop's just this evening signed the Proclamation of Holy War against the Fiends of Nightmaria.' He made a fist and ground it into the cup of his other hand. 'Scour the scum from their caves! Roast their lizard hides on spits!'

Shartorial sighed. 'They've always respected the closed borders between us, General, and have made a point of hiding their hideousness through intermediaries—'

'Barring that slimy Ambassador of theirs!' Pin Dollop shivered. 'Makes my skin crawl and creep. Well, enough of that. We got us a real king now and I don't care how he got to the throne – tell me, are you mourning the old king? Honestly?'

Frowning, she shook her head. 'Not much, granted. But,' and she halted her pacing to face Pin Dollop, 'something about this new one . . .'

'Give him time. Besides,' the General rubbed at his jowls, 'the man sports a very fine beard. Very fine indeed.'

Shartorial's frown deepened as she studied the man. 'Well,' she allowed in a neutral tone, 'there is that.'

'Precisely. Anyway, the army's chewing at the bit. We'll field the whole complement. Five Legions, four thousand soldiers who've been training for this for months.' He made stepping motions with one hand. 'Up into the mountains, killing every damned Fiend we come across! Investing the keeps, burning them out and if that doesn't work, starving them out! I've waited my whole life for this! Conquest!'

She cleared her throat. 'Our defensive strategy.'

'In the name of security,' Pin Dollop said, wagging a finger, 'all measures are justified. Fiends skulking in shrubbery. Unacceptable.

You don't tolerate a viper's nest in your backyard, do you? No, you burn it out, scour it clean, make the world a better place.'

'The citizens are certainly fired up,' Shartorial allowed.

'Exactly. Have we ever been so unified? No. Do recall, we came very near a civil war only three months ago! If not for the new king enforcing order, this city would be a shambles – and you can swear to the Indifferent God himself that the Fiends would have pounced!'

'General,' Shartorial Infelance said, 'I'd hardly call dissension over this year's Artist of the Century a civil war.'

'Anarchy in the streets, Seneschal! The new king's first act was decisive.'

'He arrested all the artists.'

'A brilliant move! Enough of these stupid festivals and all those snivelling poets! They didn't have much to sing about writhing on spikes on the city walls, oh no, hah!'

Shartorial sighed again. 'It's late. When do you march?'

'Soon,' Pin Dollop promised. 'Let the Fiends quiver and shake in their slimy holes!'

'Indeed,' she replied. She left the General at his map-table, his fist grinding rhythmically in the cup of his other hand.

'The world is so unfair,' moaned Brash Phluster, trying to loosen his shoulders, but with the rack on the third notch there was little give. He whimpered. 'What time is it? Where's that Royal Torturer? He's late! Why's he always late? He's forgotten me! How could he do that? Whose turn is it? Who's next? Someone bribed the bastard, didn't they? Which one of you? You disgusting pieces of filth! Every one of you! Oh, it hurts!'

'You've been there for less than half a bell,' said Apto Canavalian.

'It was you!' Brash accused, twisting about on the rack, turning his head in an effort to glare at the man chained to the wall to his right, but the angle was too sharp and spasms of agony lanced through his neck. 'Ow, you bastard!'

'I won't change my vote,' Apto taunted, rattling the chains.

'That's why I'm still alive. I'm too sane to kill, you see. For all the usurper's faults, he knows enough to admire a rational compatriot—'

'Shut your face,' growled Tiny Chanter. 'There ain't nothing rational about the Nehemoth. Tiny knows rational and this ain't it, they ain't it, you ain't it. Isn't that so, Midge?'

'It's so,' agreed Midge.

'Flea?'

'Yeah. So.'

'So shut your face, y'damned weasel. Besides, you know you're next on the rack, so it's not like you got no stake, is it? I know you're next 'cause I'm right after you—'

'No you're not,' said Midge. 'I am.'

'What? No, brother, I'm sure it's me. The fucking poet and then the fucking critic, and then Tiny Chanter.'

'I'm on the rack after Apto,' said Midge stubbornly. 'Then you, Tiny, and then Tulgord Vise—'

'What about me?' Flea demanded.

'You're after Steck Marynd, Flea, and he's not there long on account of his broke leg and all his screaming, and then it's back to the Century's Greatest Artist.'

'That title's a curse!' Brash Phluster hissed. 'Oh, this is what being an artist is all about, isn't it? You paying attention, critic? It's suffering, misery, torture! It's grief and pain and agony, all at the hands of people too dim-witted to appreciate talent, much less understand the sacrifices us poets make—'

'He hasn't killed you yet because he likes the joke,' cut in Apto Canavalian.

'*What joke?*' Brash screamed. 'Ow, it hurts to scream! Ow!'

'The joke,' the critic and short-lived guest judge in the Festival of Flowers and Sunny Days explained, 'that is you, of all people, winning the contest. Thief of talent, imposter and charlatan. This is the curse of awards. Their essential meaninglessness, their potential for absurdity and idiocy and crass nepotism—'

'Listen to you!' crowed Brash Phluster. 'Took so many bribes you bought a villa on the river-side!'

'That's right. I took them all, which in turn cancelled them all out, freeing me to judge on merit alone—'

'They arrested you before the vote! Before that necromancer murdered the king and took the throne!'

'And look at the hypocrisy of that fiasco!' Apto retorted. 'The same people calling for my head were the ones who bribed me in the first place!' He let out a long breath. 'Of course, it's my new-found wealth that permitted me to buy a day off from the rack. You've been doubled up, Poet. And why not? Like you said, art-ists suffer and so they should. Leeches on the ass of society, every one of you!'

'I knew it! Listen to him! Mister Bitter! Mister Envy!'

'Keep it up and I'll buy you another notch, Phluster.'

'You disgusting piece of filth! Death to the critic! Death to all the critics!'

'All of you,' grated Steck Marynd from across the chamber, 'be quiet. I'm trying to get some sleep here.'

Tulgord Vise cursed under his breath and then said, 'And so I am betrayed. By all of you! We should be planning our escape, not bickering about this and that. The Nehemoth now sits on the throne of this city, luxuriating in his evilness. We need to be devising our vengeance!'

'Tiny's got a plan,' said Tiny. 'Tiny goes on the rack all meek and nice. The Royal Torturer likes Tiny Chanter. It's all part of Tiny's plan.'

'Tiny's a nitwit,' said Apto Canavalian.

'When Tiny escapes,' growled Tiny, 'he leaves the critic behind.'

'Yes!' cried Brash Phluster.

'And the poet.'

'What? What have I ever done to you, Tiny? That's not fair!'

'We should've eaten you first on the trail,' said Tiny Chanter, shifting in his chains. 'Not those others. Instead, we'll just tighten things up another ten or so notches, ripping you apart. Pop! Pop, pop! Hah hah! Right, Midge?'

'Hah hah,' laughed Midge.

'Flea?'

'Why am I before the poet? I thought I was last!'

Emancipor Reese watched the headless corpse shuffle into the throne room bearing the gilded broken circle that symbolized the Holy Church of the Indifferent God, and a moment later the Grand Bishop strode in, dressed in heavy brocaded robes of vermillion and rose. He paused then, frowning as if ambushed by a sudden thought.

Clearing his throat, Bauchelain went on from his seat on the throne, 'Tyranny, as I was saying, Mister Reese, is a delicate balance between the surety of violence and the inculcation of passive apathy. The latter is presented as an invitation permitting a safe haven from the former. In short, keep your head down and your mouth shut, and you'll be safe. By this means once pacifies an entire population.'

Grunting, the Grand Bishop turned around and departed the chamber, the headless sigil-bearer turning and following.

Emancipor plucked a grape from the laden bowl beside his stool. He bit lightly and sucked out the juices before casting the wrinkled pulp into a spittoon at his feet. 'I get all that, Master. I was just saying how things have gotten kind of quiet, even boring, now that all the poets and singers and musicians and dancers are gone.'

'Art worthy of the name, Mister Reese, is the voice of subversion. Oh to be sure, there is a place for its lesser manifestations in the ideal civilization, as a source of mindless entertainment and indeed, eager escapism. One can appreciate the insidious denial promulgated by such efforts. Dance and sing whilst everything falls to pieces and the like. Have you ever perused – carefully and with diligence – the face of an ecstatic dancer or reveller? In some, Mister Reese, you will find the bliss of a trance state, an elevation of sorts you might say. But in most, you can see the glimmer of fear. Revelry is a flight, a frenzied fleeing from the misery of daily existence. Hence the desperate plunge into alcohol and drugs, to aid that escape.'

Emancipor squinted up at Bauchelain, eyes narrow. 'Is that so?' he said, reaching quickly for his goblet of wine.

'Maintaining a state of pensive terror of course has its limits,' the new king of Farrog went on. 'Hence the identification and demonization of an external threat. At its core, Mister Reese, the notion of "us" and "them" is an essential component in social control.'

Draining the goblet dry, Emancipor reached for his pipe and began tamping it with rustleaf and d'bayang. 'The Fiends,' he said.

'Just so. Convenient, wouldn't you say, that our kingdom borders a xenophobic but wealthy mountain empire of unhuman lizard people? Such an enemy obviates the convoluted abuse of logic required to differentiate and demonize neighbours who are in fact little different from the rest of us. Hair colour? Skin tone? Religious beliefs? Blue eyes? Yellow trousers? All patently absurd, of course. But unhuman lizard people? Why, could it be any easier?'

Emancipor lit his pipe and drew hard. 'No, Master, I suppose not.' He blew out a cloud of smoke. 'Mind you, sir, I've got some experience when it comes to peering at maps and whatnot.'

'Your point?'

'Well, Master, it's this, you see. Blank patches, on maps, make me nervous. The Unknown Territory and all that. I've sailed plenty of seas, come up on those patches, and well, usually they're blank for a reason, right? Not that they're unexplored – there ain't nothing in this world that ain't seen some adventurer creeping in to see what there is to see. So, blank patches, sir, are usually blank because whoever went in never came back out.'

'You certainly become voluble, Mister Reese, once the d'bayang floods your brain, diminishing, one presumes, its normal addled state. Very well, I do concede your point.'

Emancipor glanced again at Bauchelain. 'Aye? You do?'

'Let it not be said that I am unreasonable. We have travelled in step for some time now, haven't we? Clearly we have come to know one another very well indeed.'

'Aye, Master,' said Emancipor, quickly reaching for the carafe of wine and topping up his goblet again. He downed three quick mouthfuls and then resumed puffing the pipe. 'Very well, uh, indeed.'

'General Pin Dollop, however, being a native of Farrog, speaks with certain familiarity regarding the Fiends.'

'Aye, Master, he's a man full of opinions, all right.'

Bauchelain smiled from his throne. 'Ah, do I sense some resentment, Mister Reese? That he should have ventured so close in my confidence? Are you feeling somewhat crowded?'

'Well, Master, it's only that I share the Seneschal's caution.'

'Ah, the lovely Shartorial Infelance. Of course, caution is an essential virtue given her responsibilities.'

'Caution,' Emancipor said. 'Aye.'

'Mister Reese, the Royal Treasury is somewhat bare.'

'Well, sir, that's because we've looted it.'

'True. However, tax revenues are down.'

'Aye, we've squeezed them dry.'

'Just so. Hence the pressing need for an influx of wealth. Tyrannies are expensive, assuming the central motive of being a tyrant king is, of course, the rapid accumulation of vast wealth at the expense of the common folk, not to mention the beleaguered nobility, such as it is.'

'I thought it was all about power, Master. And control. And the freedom to frighten everyone into submission.'

'Well, those too,' Bauchelain conceded. 'But these are only means to an end, the end being personal wealth. Granted, there is a certain pleasure to be found in terrorizing lesser folk. In unleashing a torrent of fear, suffering and misery. And let it not be said that I have been remiss in addressing such pleasures.'

'No, Master, not at all. Who'd ever say something like that?'

'Precisely. In fact, I would proclaim such bloodlust a potent symbol of my essential humanity.'

'Well, Master, let's hope those lizards don't share that particular trait.'

The headless sigil-bearer returned, and behind it the Grand Bishop. 'Bauchelain,' said Korbal Broach in his high, thin voice, 'I just remembered what I was coming here to tell you.'

'Most excellent, Korbal. Out with it, then.'

'That ferryman, Bauchelain. The one we put in the deepest dungeon.'

'Our possessed prisoner, yes, what of him?'

'He's dead.'

Bauchelain frowned. 'Dead? How did that happen?'

'I think,' said Korbal Broach, 'death by masturbation.'

Emancipor rubbed at his face. 'Well, of all the ways to go . . .'

'Very well,' said Bauchelain. 'I see. Ah, of course.'

Korbal Broach nodded. 'Not possessed any more, Bauchelain.'

'In other words, old friend, the Indifferent God has escaped his mortal prison, and now runs free.'

Korbal Broach nodded a second time. 'That's bad.'

'Indeed, very bad. Hmm.' Abruptly Bauchelain rose to his feet. 'Mister Reese, attend me. We shall retire to my Conjuration Chamber. It seems that on this gentle night, we must summon and unleash a veritable host of demons. Korbal Broach, do you sense the god's presence in the crypts?'

'I think so. Wandering.'

'Then a most lively hunt awaits us, how delightful! Mister Reese, come along now.'

Trembling where he sat, Emancipor Reese tapped out his pipe. 'Master, you wish me to help you raise demons? You never asked that of me before, sir. I think—'

'Granted, Mister Reese, I may have been remiss in neglecting to mention the possibility in our employment contract. That said, however, these are most unusual circumstances, would you not agree? Fear not, if by some mischance you are rent limb from limb, be assured it will be a quick death.'

'Ah, thank you, Master. That is . . .'

'Of some comfort? Happy to set you at ease, as ever, Mister Reese.'

Korbal Broach said, 'I'll raise the rest of my undead, Bauchelain.'

Bauchelain paused and studied his old friend. 'Any risk that one might be suborned?'

'No, Bauchelain. None of them have any heads.'

'Very good then. Well, on a hunt such as the one awaiting us, the more the merrier. Mister Reese? Time's wasting!'

*

Mortari crouched in the shadows of the alley mouth, Le Groutt crowding his side. He peered at the high wall of Royal Palace. 'I see handholds,' he whispered.

'I see footholds,' Le Groutt whispered back.

'So, we got handholds and footholds.'

'Handholds and footholds.'

'Can't be done.'

'Not a chance.'

Together, they turned about and crept back to where waited the others. Mortari edged up close to Plaintly Grasp. He rubbed at his terrier face, scratched behind an ear, licked his lips and then said, 'Not a chance.'

'Not a chance,' chimed in Le Groutt, his large teeth gleaming.

'Unless Barunko can throw us high, up near one of the spikes,' Mortari said.

'Grab hold of the corpse's leg and hope it don't tear off,' added Le Groutt.

'Up past that . . .'

'Handholds and footholds.'

Sighing, Plaintly Grasp turned to Barunko. 'Well?'

'Throwing? I can throw. Give me something to throw.'

'You'll be throwing Mortari,' explained Plaintly. 'Up to one of those spikes.'

'Spikes?'

'The ones on the wall.'

'Wall?'

'Over there.' She pointed.

Barunko looked about. 'Wall,' he said, grunting. 'Show me.'

Symon The Knife spat onto the greasy cobbles. 'This is a problem,' he said.

'What is, Symon?' Plaintly demanded in a hiss. 'He said he can do it, didn't he?'

Drawing out a dagger, Symon gestured with it towards Barunko. 'Back when the Party of Five was the terror of the city's wealthy,' he said, 'our muscle here could still see past his own nose. Now, well . . .'

'It don't matter,' insisted Plaintly. 'We just point him in the right direction. Like we did on the last job—'

'Oh,' piped in Lurma Spilibus, 'the *last* job.'

'We survived it!' Plaintly snapped. She grasped Barunko by an arm and started dragging him towards the alley mouth. 'This way,' she said. 'You just grab Mortari and throw him as high as you can, right?'

'Throw Mortari,' Barunko said, nodding. 'Where is he?'

'I'm right here—'

Barunko spun, grasped hold of Mortari, and threw him across the street. The 2nd story man struck the palace wall with a meaty thud and then crumpled to the cobbles.

'No,' said Plaintly, 'that was too soon. Le Groutt, come here. Barunko, let Le Groutt take your wrist, yes, like that. He's going to lead you to the wall. When you get there, you throw him, upward. Straight up. Got it?'

'Got it. Show me the wall. Where's Le Groutt?'

'He's holding your wrist,' said Plaintly. 'Now, Le Groutt, lead him out there and quick about it.'

Lurma moved up alongside her and they watched Le Groutt pull Barunko towards the wall, close to Mortari's motionless form. 'Plaintly?'

'What?'

'I'm going to scout to the left there. Think I see something.'

'Go ahead, just be stealthy.'

She scowled above her crossed eyes. 'Don't patronize me, Plaintly.'

Shrugging, mostly to herself as she watched Lurma skitter one way and then that across the street, Plaintly returned her attention to Le Groutt and Barunko.

Symondenalian crept to her side, working his knife around one hand. 'More than Barunko's sight is dull,' he opined.

Plaintly Grasp turned on him. 'That's what I always hated about you, Symon. You're so judgemental.'

'What? That man made a habit of using his head to bash in doors!'

'And there wasn't a door that his head couldn't bash in!'

At the wall, Le Groutt had positioned Barunko beneath one of the spikes, in the dried puddle of all that had leaked out from the corpse speared on it, and was whispering in the man's ear. Nodding, Barunko grasped hold of Le Groutt, and in one swift surge, flung the man upward.

Le Groutt sailed up past the spike, scrabbled desperately at the wall, and then slid back down. The spike impaled his left thigh, arresting his fall. He dangled there for a moment, and then began writhing alongside the withered corpse.

'Come on,' hissed Plaintly and she and Symon hurried across to join Barunko.

Their muscle was crouched in a combative pose. 'Did I do it?' he asked when Plaintly and Symon arrived. 'I heard a whimper! Is he hanging on?'

'Oh,' said Symon, 'he is at that, Barunko.'

There was a groan from Mortari, and a moment later the man slowly sat up, one side of his head so swollen it seemed another head was trying to make its way out from his cheek and temple.

'What's leaking on me?' Barunko asked.

'That'd be Le Groutt,' said Symon. Then he dropped his knife. It landed point first on his right foot, sliding neatly through the leather of his shoe, slicing through everything else until it jammed in the sole. Symon stared down at the quivering weapon. 'Fuck,' he said, 'that hurts.'

'Stop pissing about, Symon,' hissed Plaintly. 'Barunko, that was a good throw. Honest. He just got hung up on the spike.' She squinted upward. 'Looks like he's trying to pull himself loose.'

Mortari used the wall to stand up. 'There were puppies,' he said. 'I never thought she'd have puppies. I should've guessed, the way she kept coming back and hanging around.'

Lurma Spilibus joined them. 'I found an old postern gate,' she said. 'Picked the lock. We're in.'

'Great work,' Plaintly said, and then turned back to Barunko. 'Barunko, you got to throw Mortari up there, so he can help get Le Groutt off that spike.'

'Throw Mortari,' Barunko said, nodding.

Plaintly pushed Mortari into Barunko's huge hands. 'Here he is—'
Barunko threw the man upward.

There was a thud, a scrape, and then a yelp.

Plaintly stepped slightly away from the wall and looked up. She
placed her hands on her hips, and then said, 'Okay, good throw.
Symon, get that knife out of your foot, you're next.'

Ambassador Ophal D'Neeth Flatroq exited the compound via
the back postern gate, creeping out into the alley. It was dark.
Just how he liked it. Hunched in his black snake-skin cloak he
peered up and then down the alley. A scrawny cat eyed him from
a heap of rubbish, hackles slowly lifting. Meeting its lambent
eyes, Ophal's tongue darted out and he blinked.

The cat fled in a scatter of dried leaves and pod husks.

Ophal crept deeper into the shadows, edging along a wall, his
broad, bare, nail-less feet silent on the grimy cobbles. There was
a route to the Royal Palace that never left alleys and unlit stretches
of street. He had made use of it many times in the decade or so of
his posting in the city of Farrog. Ideally, he would meet no-one en
route, but that was no certainty. Encounters were unfortunate,
but he had long since grown used to inspiring terror in the natives,
and without question some advantages accrued with the reputation now attending the lone Ambassador of Nightmaria.

His was the only embassy in existence, a concession to the
proximity of Farrog to the High Kingdom. As a general rule, his
people avoided contact with neighbouring realms. To be sure,
familiarity was the seed of contempt, and history was replete
with welcoming kingdoms suffering the eventual ignominy of
cultural degradation, moral confusion and the eventual, and
fatal, loss of self-identity.

All trade was strictly prescribed. No foreigner had ever managed to penetrate the kingdom beyond the trade posts situated
along the borders at one of the seven high-roads. The lands to
either side of the high-roads were a maze of gorges, sheer cliffs,
sink-holes and crevices, and even there, watchful wardens ensured

that no hardy adventurer or spy ever managed to slip into the high plateaus where the cities of the Imperial Kingdom thrived in their splendid isolation.

How he missed his home! And yet, necessities abided, responsibilities settled their burden, and besides, no-one back there much liked him, anyway.

Sighing, he continued on, creeping from alley to shadow, narrow wend to the twisted and foul trenches of the city's open sewers, his only company thus far resident rats, kilaptra worms, and three-eyed dart-snakes. Of these, he made an effort to avoid only the dart-snakes, as they were in the habit of trying to nest in whatever cracks and folds of the flesh a body might possess. For all his . . . eccentricities, Ophal was relieved that obesity did not count among them. Come to think of it, he could not recall the last time he'd seen an overweight citizen of Farrog. Mostly, from what he could discern from the high narrow windows of the embassy tower, the swarming figures below all shared a wretched hint of emaciation. It was, therefore, a mystery where the dart-snakes nested.

The question remained with him, gnawing away inside. An examination of the matter seemed worthy of some diligence, pointing at some treatise or at least a monograph. Assuming he'd find the time, and all things considered, the next while promised to be somewhat busy.

This new, belligerent and entirely unreasonable king of Farrog had made all too plain his venal desires, and now his wish would be answered. The Ambassador of Nightmaria was this night on his way to the Royal Palace, to deliver the official declaration of war between Nightmaria and Farrog.

His exploration of the nesting habits of three-eyed dart-snakes would, alas, have to wait.

As he made his way along a walled trench, ankle-deep in foul sewage, a kitten appeared on the ledge to his left, scampering along the narrow track. His hand snapped out, knobby, scaled fingers closing tight about the creature. It squealed, but the cry was short-lived, as he quickly broke its neck and then, disarticulating his lower jaw, began pushing the mangled furry carcass into his mouth.

In his wake but at a safe distance, a veritable carpet of dart-snakes slithered after him, enraptured by something like worship.

'Now's the time,' hissed Plaintly Grasp, glaring across at Lurma Spilibus, who scowled back at her.

They were all huddled against the wall, the gaping postern entranceway close by. Blood smeared the cobbles beneath Mortari and Le Groutt, while Symondenalian Niksos had pulled off his thin leather moccasin to tip it upside down so that it could drain. Barunko had just punched at his own shadow, thinking it was a guard, cracking two knuckles against the wall.

'But we're not even inside yet!' retorted Lurma.

'Getting in's always the hardest part,' Plaintly replied. 'Now we've done that and healing's needed. Le Groutt can't walk and Mortari's . . . well, Mortari's not all here.'

'Not one of them looked like me,' Mortari said, his swollen head tilted to one side. 'No matter what anybody said.' His tongue edged up to lick at the fluids draining from his nose. 'Besides, I'd been drinking all week and she had the cutest ears.'

'Lurma, get out that unguent, now.'

Snarling, Lurma, known to many as The Fingers, fumbled in her purse and then withdrew a gilded vial. 'It's my only one,' she said. 'For when things get really nasty. And now we're about to sneak into a Royal Palace crawling with demons and who knows what else. I'm telling you, Plaintly, this is a bad idea.'

'Hand it over.'

Lower lip trembling, Lurma passed the vial over. She and Plaintly struggled for a moment getting their hands to meet, as Lurma kept snatching the vial to the sides. 'Just take it already!'

'I'm trying! Hold still!'

Finally, with the vial in hand, Plaintly crouched beside Le Groutt. 'Here,' she said, 'one mouthful's all you need. This is potent stuff.'

Lurma snorted. 'Of course it is. Only the best for The Fingers. And now it's being wasted.'

'He's got a hole through his leg, Lurma,' said Plaintly, 'big enough for you to run your arm through.'

'I've seen worse,' Lurma replied, crossing her arms. 'I could run half a day with a scratch like that.'

Le Groutt gulped down his mouthful, and then settled back, sighing.

Turning to Mortari, Plaintly said, 'Now you, Mortari.'

'She howled outside my window for I don't know how many nights.'

'I bet she did. Here, drink. One swallow!'

Mortari drank down a mouthful and handed the vial back. 'A spike went through my shoulder,' he said. 'Not good.' He frowned. 'And my head. What's wrong with my head? Ma always said to let sleeping dogs lie, but did I listen? I must have. The puppies didn't look like me at all, not a chance.'

Le Groutt grunted. 'Healed the flesh wounds, but his brain's still addled.'

'It's not so bad,' said Mortari, blinking, 'being addled. She had this manic look afterwards, eyes all wild. Gave me the shivers. That's just how it is, all those regrets after you went and did it. Anyway, after dropping the puppies she just let herself go, you know what I mean? Udders dragging and all that. I was still young. I had a future!'

Plaintly handed the vial back to Lurma. 'See?' she said, 'there's some left.'

'Hey,' hissed Symon The Knife, 'what about me?'

'Not enough blood came out of that moccasin,' said Plaintly. 'You'll manage.'

'But I'm a knife fighter! I need to be light on my feet, dancing this way and that, dipping and sliding and weaving, a blur of deadly motion, blades flashing and flickering in the moonlight—'

'Just throw the fucking things and run,' muttered Lurma. 'It's what you always do.'

Symon twisted round to her. 'What's that supposed to mean?'

Plaintly Grasp, known to many as The Fence, held up her hands. 'Stop bickering, you two! Le Groutt, you up to taking point?'

'Point, aye. I got eyes like a cat. Handholds. Footholds.' He pulled from his bag a coil of rope. Seeing Plaintly's frown, he said, 'Might be traps.'

'Traps? This ain't some Jhagut sepulcher, Le Groutt. It's a fucking palace.'

Le Groutt's face turned stubborn. 'I don't go nowhere without my rope. And my ball o'wax. And my Cloak of Blending—'

'Your what?' Symon asked with a snicker. 'Oh, you mean that dusty poncho, right, sorry.'

'Dust, aye,' Le Groutt said in a half-snarl. 'To blend me into the walls and whatnot.'

'Just get going,' Plaintly said. 'Then you, Symon, followed by Mortari and then Lurma and then me. Barunko takes up the rear.'

'Up the rear,' said Barunko, 'Let me at 'im!'

Etched pentagrams of various sizes crowded the floor, with only a narrow path winding amongst them. Emancipor stood just inside the doorway, licking lips that seemed impossibly dry with a tongue that was even drier. His breathing was rapid, with shivers running through him, the sweat on his brow cold as ice.

'Mister Reese? Is something wrong?'

The manservant squinted across at Bauchelain, who stood near a long, narrow table crowded with phials, beakers, stoppered urns, small ornate boxes, clay jars, blocks of pigment, brushes and reeds of charcoal. Upon a shelf above this table was a row of raised disks, each one home to a tiny demon. Most of them squatted motionless in the centre of their modest prisons, eyes glittering, although a few paced like caged rats. All bore the smudged remnants of brightly coloured paint.

'Mister Reese?'

'Huh? Oh, no Master, I'm fine. More or less. Maybe something I ate.'

'Come along, then, and do recall, stay between the circles on the floor. There is a delicate art to conjuration. A mere misstep could prove disastrous. Now,' he clapped his hands, 'we'll begin with the most demanding of charges, the summoning of an

Andelainian Highborn Demon, perhaps even one of royal blood. Once we have compelled that worthy servant, we'll add in a few dozen lesser demons, each serving as bait for the voracious appetites of the Indifferent God. Ah, I tell you, Mister Reese, it has been years since I last felt so . . . enlivened.'

'Aye, Master, I see how excited you must be.'

Bauchelain paused, raising a brow. 'Indeed? Am I so obvious, then?'

'Your beard twitched.'

'It did?'

'Once.'

'Very well, I'll allow you the sharp observation. This time. Imperturbability and equanimity are of course virtues I hold dear, as befits a Master of Necromancy and Conjuration, not to mention a tyrant king – oh no, I shall not be of the frothing variety of the latter, whose antics I find utterly distasteful and, well, embarrassing.'

'Aye, Master, gibbering from the throne's bad form, as you say.'

Bauchelain raised one long finger. 'The illusion of control is essential, Mister Reese, at all times. Now, come along. I need you with me for the summoning.'

Emancipor approached. Carefully. 'What am I to do, Master? A demon prince, you said?'

'Yes. Who shall arrive ill of temper, disgruntled and perhaps even enraged.'

'And, uh, me?'

'You will stand . . . here, as close to the edge of the circle as you can manage, without touching it, of course. Come along, don't be shy. Yes, precisely. Now, don't move.'

'Master?'

'Mister Reese?'

'What do I do next?'

'Why, nothing. Now, the demon, upon seeing you, will naturally reach for you, intent on your messy death. Assuming the pentagram possesses no unseen flaws in its pattern, such as, perhaps, a single cat hair lying athwart the outer ring's line, the demon shall fail in grasping you.'

'Cat hair?' Emancipor turned to the other shelf, the one opposite the one bearing all the tiny demons, where a dozen cats were lying in solemn observation, tails twitching.

'Or some such thing,' Bauchelain murmured. 'Very well then—'

'Sir, if a single cat hair can break the circle, er, shouldn't those creatures be banned from this chamber? I mean, it would seem a reasonable precaution.'

'You might think that,' said Bauchelain, with a slight frown at being interrupted. 'There was a previous concern, you see. Mice.'

'Mice?'

'Many mice, Mister Reese. Possessing slithery tails, a common trait among mice specifically, and indeed, all rodents. A mouse that happens to find itself within or athwart a pentagram at the moment of conjuration, will often suffer the fate of possession. In fact, there are one or two mice still at large, somewhere in this chamber, that are in fact demonic.'

'Demonic mice?'

'Yes, alas. Which is why the cats are all up on that high shelf.'

'Oh.'

'Leaving me confident that no cat hairs mar the line of the outer circle.'

'Ah, right.'

'I trust my logic satisfies you, Mister Reese. Now, may I begin? Thank you. Oh, and say or do nothing that might distract me.'

'Master, I'm afraid I might scream.'

'Presumably, you would only be incited to such indelicacy following the demon's appearance, at which point the crucial moment of my concentration will have passed, leaving you free to scream. If you must.'

'I think, maybe, Master, I must.'

Bauchelain sighed. Adding nothing more, he moved to one side and faced the pentagram, raising both arms. Eyes narrowing to slits, he began muttering and mumbling an incantation.

This went on for some time. Restless, Emancipor shifted his weight from one foot to the other, and then scratched at his behind, which had become unaccountably itchy for some reason. Also, he needed to empty his bladder. All that wine, he supposed. Now his nose itched. He rubbed and pushed at it. Something tickled the back of his throat and he cleared it, which only made it worse, so he barked a cough—

'Mister Reese! If you please!'

'Sorry, Master. I'm trying!'

'Just . . . be still!'

Nodding, Emancipor settled. Or tried to. Instead, that itch in his bunghole intensified. Grimacing, he pushed his hand inside his breeches. Pushed with one finger this way and then that way. Now his left ear tingled. He reached up to push the same finger into that ear—

A deafening thunderclap made him jump.

Within the circle, so massive it filled the entire space, a demon twice Emancipor's height had suddenly appeared, standing in a strange crouch as if a moment earlier it had been sitting at a table. Knees momentarily buckling, it almost toppled backward, and then righted itself. Smoke pouring from its hairless blue hide, sparks raining down from its enormous iron torcs on its upper arms, in one hand it held a haunch of dripping meat and in the other a giant gold goblet now sloshing out burgundy wine.

Turning its blunt, broad, hairless head, its eyes flared bright emerald, fixing on Emancipor. 'You little shit—'

At which point, Bauchelain delicately cleared his throat.

The demon twisted round. 'Blast you to the Seven Fires of Kellanved's Maze! *Again?* And right at dinner . . . *again!* With the delicious High Concubine Allgiva sitting opposite me. *Again!* Scented candles, sweet wine, a priest of Dessembrae turning on the spit! *Again! Damn you Bauchelain and damn you again! Aaargh!*'

'Now now, Prince Flail Their Limbs, how am I to know your circumstances in the moment of summoning? You do me a disservice.'

'Oh, I'll disservice you, Conjurer. One of these nights—'

'Your threats are so tiresome, Prince Flail.'

The demon flung down the haunch of priest thigh, where it bounced, rolled and then spat and sizzled as it struck the invisible barrier of the pentagram. The demon then drained the last of his wine and crushed the goblet into a mangled ruin in his huge, taloned hand. 'This had better be good, and I don't mean hunting any fucking mice!'

Bauchelain smiled in seeming recollection. 'A mere lesson in whom between us has command of the situation, one that, I am sure, need not be repeated.'

'Fuck you, Bauchelain. And don't leave me anywhere near that creepy companion of yours—'

'I won't, although you may come across a few of his charges in the crypts below.'

'Fucking undead. How will I know them?'

'No heads.'

The demon subsided slightly, 'Well, that'll help.'

'Prince Flail Their Limbs, the Indifferent God haunts the levels beneath this palace. He has escaped his latest mortal prison and now seeks a new vessel.'

The demon grunted. 'Let him try me. I'll eat the bastard starting with his left little toe and finish him with the right little toe. I'll chew him into pulp so soft a newborn would think it sweet mother's milk. I'll peel his skin—'

'Yes yes, all that and more, I'm sure,' cut in Bauchelain. 'In the meantime, permit me to assemble for you a small army of minions—'

'But none of those ankle-high little shits you like to paint.'

'No, somewhat more impressive servants, I assure you.'

'They got under my clothes,' the Demon Prince continued in a low grumble. 'One of them tried climbing up my butt-hole, for fuck's sake.'

Flinching, Emancipor straightened, and then quickly reached back under his breeches.

Royal Torturer Binfun Son of Binfun played with his food on the plate before him, using the tip of his knife to prod the overcooked slab of meat this way and that. He poked it with the two-pronged fork, leaning closer to see if any juices bubbled up from the small punctures. Seeing nothing, he sighed and settled back. 'This is very disappointing,' he said to the desiccated head hanging from a hook opposite him. 'Cook does it deliberately, of course. She's singled me out, has it in for me for some reason. Women are a mystery. They hate for no reason, no reason at all.' Well, of course that was not true. She had a reason. Still, in the greater scheme of things, was he not entirely blameless?

He prodded the meat again. 'Nerve endings, Sire, are the source of all pleasure. This is simple fact. Dead flesh knows no joy, no delight, no sultry tickle of attention. It just . . . lies there. And where pleasure is not possible, why, neither is pain. And yet, does not history reveal a most sordid truth? That generation upon generation, we strive for insensitivity, the muffled simulation of death, benumbed, displaced, inured.'

The severed head of the old king said nothing, but then, he wouldn't, would he? He was dead. Indeed, grimly symbolic was the old king, reminding Binfun that death marked a failure of the torturer's art. Not that he'd had any opportunity to torture the old king. The Usurper's sword was very sharp and the cut beneath the old king's head was the cleanest Binfun had ever examined. A single slice – how he wished he'd seen it!

He stabbed the fork into the slab and left it standing there. 'I am losing weight. Unacceptable. Cook should pay me a visit, an invitation innocuous, beneath suspicion. An offering of wine, suitably drugged in her cup. Then, when she awakens gagged and trussed and utterly helpless . . . no no, I mustn't think such thoughts. Bad thoughts, bad imaginings. Fasting is good for me, so say the Purgists in the Herbmongers' Round. The stomach shrinks, impurities gush and spurt – one can tell they're impurities, given the wretched stench wafting up. And the lightheadedness that follows, why, such luminous clarity!'

He saw the reflected flicker of lamp-light in the old king's dull staring eyes, and twisted round in his chair in time to see Shartorial

Infelance stride into the chamber carrying an ornately jewelled oil-lamp. He rose quickly. 'Seneschal, good evening!'

'Sir Binfun, how are you this evening?'

The Royal Torturer bowed before responding. 'Milady, I suffer as it seems I must.'

The tall regal woman glanced down at the small table with its pewter plate and its lone slab of grey meat, and then set down the lamp. 'Ah, the Cook again, is it? Remind me to have another word with her.'

Binfun shrugged. 'I fear it will do no good, Milady, but I do appreciate the effort.'

'Well, I see now that I was not stern enough in reproaching her the last time. This vindictiveness is surely beneath her. Perhaps if I suggest that, should matters not improve, I may have a word with the king . . .'

'Oh, please, Milady, do not do that!'

Shartorial's delicate brows arched. 'An empty threat I assure you. It would be madness to invite the attentions of our liege in such matters. If Cook has any wits, however, the mere hint will set her aright.'

Binfun walked over to the severed head and gave it a light push to set it swinging gently back and forth. 'It's all down to a favourite actor of hers,' he admitted, 'that I had the pleasure of torturing. Or so I assume, since matters turned unpleasant immediately thereafter. But what was I to do? I am the Royal Torturer, and I obey my liege's commands!' The confession seemed to lighten his spirits and he luxuriated in the sensation of unadulterated relief.

'Indeed. Which actor was that?'

'Sorponce Egol, he of the Perfect Profile. Well, it was less than perfect when I was done with it, of course. And making him eat his own nose was perhaps excessive, I do admit.'

'Hmm, how long did he last?'

'Well, that's the thing, most curious. Not by a single instrument or exercise on my part did he give up living. Now, knowing how he used to preen, I set up a full-length mirror, exquisitely polished, so that he could regard himself day and night in the bright light of the dozen lanterns I kept lit. I believe that this broke his will to live. Fatal vanity!'

'I suspect you are correct, Binfun, and that was a most insidious torture, by the way.'

Binfun brightened. 'Yes it was, wasn't it? Thank you, Milady! Your observation has blessed me!' He interlaced his hands before him and smiled. 'Now, I imagine you wish to visit, once more, the one who most fascinates you.'

She shot him a look. 'You've not touched his face?'

'Not once, Milady. Indeed, apart from the rack, he is unmarred, as per your wishes.'

'Excellent.'

'Shall I lead you to the secret spy-hole now?'

'In a moment.'

He smiled. 'Of course. Anticipation is the sweetest nectar, is it not?'

'When are you due your report to the king?' she asked him.

His face fell slightly. 'Ah, I have delayed too long as it is, to be honest, in deference to your desires. Alas, Milady, your visits must soon come to an end, and this is truly tragic for all concerned. I must break the lot, in sessions most foul, and see to it that death delivers its soft kiss of release for each and every one of them. So the king commands.'

Shartorial stepped near the table. She picked up his dinner knife where he'd set it down beside the plate, and idly played with it.

Watching her fondling the knife, Binfun felt his loins stir. 'I will grieve,' he said huskily, 'the end of your visits down here, Milady.'

'Binfun, you say the kindest things. I am flattered.'

'I do regret what awaits the one who fascinates you,' he said. 'And I shall keep him until the last, and be uncommonly quick in taking his life. For you I do this, Milady, and not even the king's command will sway me in this.'

'Very sweet of you,' she said, turning about and plunging the dinner knife into his chest.

He staggered back, reaching futilely at the horn handle jutting from his chest, and then fell into his chair, making the wood creak. He gaped up at her and then frowned. 'Wrong side, Milady,' he gasped. 'This will take some time. Under the ... *cough* ... under the heart ... would have been better ...'

She looked down at him. 'Quick? I think not. Damn Cook and her petty vindictiveness! What use poison if you don't eat the damned shit?'

'I ... uh, *cough*, nibbled.'

'You are drowning in your own blood.'

He nodded. 'Subtle ... after a fashion. *Cough cough!* Unable to shout in alarm. *Cough cough cough!* Guards hear nothing and never *cough* come down besides. *Cough cough cough cough!* Clever, Milady. But, alas, not enough pain.'

'I take little pleasure in this.'

'Oh. Too bad.'

He wheezed, shuddered, and then sagged in the chair, head dipping until his chin rested on his sternum. Red bubbles slid down from his mouth for a few moments, and then the flow ceased.

Shartorial stepped closer and pushed a spiked heel down upon his left foot.

'Ow.'

'Fuck, just get it over with!'

'T-tell Cook ...'

'What? Tell her what?'

'Tell her ... *cough, gasp!* Next time ... medium rare.'

'I can't help it if every woman finds me desirable,' Apto Canavalian was saying. 'There's something impish about me, or so I'm told. They fling themselves at me, to be honest. I have to beat them off. Personally, I think it's down to me being a critic, an arbiter of taste, if you will. Such talent demands a high intellect and that becomes pretty obvious, I suppose, even after the briefest of conversations—'

'Gods below,' moaned Brash Phluster, writhing feebly on the rack, 'somebody kill him. Please.'

'I'm just explaining why I got invited to all the soirées and fêtes, and how all those lovely women ended up dangling on my arm. You know, all things considered, it was almost worth it.'

'Tiny will put him on the rack,' said Tiny Chanter. 'Notch him up until he's dangling from everywhere.'

'I've saved up my biggest bribe,' said Apto, smiling across at Tiny. 'Next time the Royal Torturer comes, I'm offering him my villa. To just let me slip away. The rest of you are dead anyway, so it's not like anyone will know, and I'll hightail it out of Farrog that very night. I hear there's a festival looking for judges down the coast, in Prylap.'

'Tiny's got a better bribe,' said Tiny, his small eyes glinting in the gloom. 'Tiny promises not to tear the torturer's head off. Beats a villa, doesn't it, Midge?'

'Beats it clean.'

'Flea?'

'No head tear beats a villa every time,' said Flea.

'You're in magicked chains, Tiny,' Apto pointed out. 'No shapeshifting crap from you. Your nemesis necromancer's got you all figured out.'

'Torturer has to unchain Tiny to get him on the rack.'

'I'll warn him this time. Besides, he puts that collar on you first, and it's magicked, too.'

'Tiny will bite out his throat when he gets close.'

'Right,' snapped Apto, 'and *then* you'll threaten not to tear his head off, right?'

'Exactly. Tiny's got it figured out.'

Apto looked over to Midge and then Flea. 'And you let this brainless dolt stay in charge? No wonder you're all in chains and about to die. Your sister had it right – run off with the Assassin and fuck you all.'

Tiny strained at his chains, glaring at Apto. 'We don't talk about her!'

'Well, I am! Listen! Relish Chanter is the smartest Chanter of them all! Smart enough to lose all you dead-weight brothers! Relish Relish Relish! She slept with me, you know? Jumped me right here in Farrog, before running off with Flicker. She was wild, an animal of lust! I needed a healer after she was done with me!'

'Lies!' roared Tiny Chanter. 'Lies and lies and more lies!'

Midge was crying, Flea glowering in deadly silence. A sudden shiver took Apto Canavalian and he decided he'd said enough. Maybe too much. He waved a hand, weakly as the shackles were heavy. 'I'm kidding. I was lying. Just teasing you. She never jumped me, and for all I know, the Assassin kidnapped her—'

'Of course he did!' Tiny bellowed.

'Besides,' added Apto, 'I was thinking, a whole damned villa should be enough to get us all out of here.'

At that, Tulgord Vise straightened in his chains. 'That had better not be a tease, Critic,' he said in a growl.

'It's not,' Apto promised. 'I mean, think on it. We all survived the journey here. We even survived the Assassin's treachery. Like it or not, a bond has formed among us all. It's always that way with survivors. We're inextricably linked because of what we all shared and in case you've forgotten, that journey was one long nightmare.'

'It wasn't so bad,' grumbled Tiny.

'Well, for those of us under threat of getting eaten—'

Brash Phluster lifted his head. 'But that wasn't you, was it, Apto the Corrupt Critic from the Squalid Pits of Evil Betrayal? No! It was us artists! Us ones with, with *talent*! No, not you! You cheated your way out of that, too, like the cheater you are!'

'Perhaps,' said Apto, 'but then, we had to suffer your singing, Phluster. And let's face it, even this Royal Torturer's got nothing on that.'

Tiny laughed. 'Hah hah hah!' and then glared at his brothers, who then laughed, too.

'Hahah!'

'Hah! Hah!'

And now sudden lamp-light lit the corridor beyond the barred door.

Apto straightened. 'All right, friends,' he whispered. 'It seems he's early but no matter. This is the moment. Wish me the Lady's Pull of Luck, wish it for all our sakes!'

The light brightened, and then suddenly dimmed as a hooded face appeared in the door's barred window.

Not the Royal Torturer after all. Some instinct told Apto that this was a woman, a beautiful woman who now watched them from the impenetrable shadows of the hood. He managed a bow. 'Milady,' he said in a soft murmur.

'I have been watching you all,' came the sibilant reply.

'Ah,' smiled Apto. 'I admit, on occasion, that I sensed hidden eyes, a certain fixation of attention, vision's lingering caress—'

'I looked upon the one with the broken leg.'

'I'm sorry, what?'

Keys ground in the lock and then the door squealed open.

Steck Marynd had sat up straighter at the back of the cell, an expression of curiosity upon his craggy and singularly unattract- ive features. Apto looked at the backwoods simpleton and felt a flood of acidic venom.

Dressed in opulent silks, the woman seemed to whisper into the chamber, floating like a dream. She crossed straight over to stand before Steck Marynd. 'Your leg, has it healed, sir?'

'I tend to think so,' he replied, 'until I'm on the rack.'

'Yes, that was most cruel. But no more will the Royal Torturer have his way with you. Indeed, even now his corpse grows cold. I am here, sir, to free you.'

Struggling, Steck regained his feet. 'Milady, that is most kind. Perhaps you could start with the poor man on the rack.'

She seemed to tilt her head. 'I said "you", sir, and I meant just that.'

Steck frowned, and then crossed his arms. 'I'm afraid I must decline your invitation, Milady. These are my companions, after all. Should you unlock my shackles, nothing can prevent me from doing the same to theirs.'

'Ah, I see. Well, why should I be surprised? I could see your innate nobility, and the bright virtue that is your loyalty. Still, your fellow prisoners spoke derisively of you, sir, without pause.'

'Theirs is a gruff camaraderie, Milady.'

'Tiny loves Steck,' said Tiny, and then he scowled. 'Not like

that. Tiny loves women, lots of women, more women than Tiny can count. Right, Midge?'

'That would be seven women,' said Midge, 'since you can't count past six.'

'Flea loves Steck, too,' said Flea. 'Flea loves Steck more than he loves his brothers. More than he loves women. More even than he loves Relish, his sister. More even—'

'For the love of decency,' said Apto, 'stop now, I beg you.'

Sighing, the woman lifted up the ring of keys. 'Very well, sir, you shall have your wish.'

'Milady, have you planned for us a way out? There are many guards in the level above us.'

'Unaccountably,' she replied, 'none were present.'

Steck frowned. 'None? But—'

At that moment an inhuman scream howled through the corridors, ending in a strangled snarl. Someone then shrieked, and that cry ended much more abruptly.

'Gods,' moaned Brash Phluster, 'what was that?'

With trembling hands, the woman set to Steck's bindings. 'We need to get out of here!'

'Tiny's not afraid,' said Tiny in a thin voice.

'Midge is,' said Midge.

Mute and pale, Flea nodded. 'Afraid. Eek!'

The forgotten postern gate cut through the outer wall of the palace, but doors to the right and the left in the wall itself opened into narrow cavities, with steps going down. As the palace's main gate was to the right, Plaintly Grasp decided that the left passage was likely the one they desired, so down they went, Le Groutt in the lead with a stubby candle in one hand and a coil of rope in the other.

'This just goes round and round the outer wall,' hissed Symondenalian Niksos. 'We should have gone further in, Plaintly, down through the coal cellar, or maybe the courtyard well.'

'I used to swim in my Pa's well,' said Mortari. 'That's how I found all the drowned cats. Those cats must've been the clumsiest cats in the world, and all drowning in a single night like that. I

figure one fell in and the others tried to help. Anyway, the worst bit was bumping into them, or getting a mouthful of manky fur. The water tasted of them for weeks, too.'

'Mortari,' whispered Plaintly, 'can you save the tales for some other time? We don't want anyone hearing us.'

'Pa never liked cats. He liked lizards, you see, and the cats kept killing the lizards, or eating their tails, so Pa would beat the cats back and rescue them. The lizards, I mean, even the ones without tails.'

'Symon,' said Plaintly, 'we're not going round and round. We're well under the wall's foundations now. We've been going down forever. This used to be a citadel, remember, the whole damned hilltop. Look! Le Groutt's found us a side passage and it's heading the right way.' She pushed up past Lurma and then Mortari and then Symon The Knife until she could rest a hand on Le Groutt's shoulder. Together, they peered into the narrow crack that led off from the rough staircase.

'Scout it out some,' she said to Le Groutt. 'Twenty paces, then come back.'

'Twenty paces,' he said, nodding. 'That'd be ten paces in, ten paces back, right? Got it.'

'No. Twenty paces in, twenty back.'

'That's forty paces, Plaintly. You said twenty.'

'I meant twenty in. I don't care how many to get back.'

'Well, it'd be twenty, wouldn't it? Unless I only came back half-way, or if I took long jumps. Could be any number then, between one and twenty, I mean. Or baby steps could make it, like, fifty!'

'That's all very true. Good points, Le Groutt. But let's make it as easy as possible. Twenty paces in, see if it goes past that, and then come back and tell us.'

'I won't be able to see if it goes past twenty, Plaintly, unless I go and find out.'

'Okay, stop at twenty and then do ten more. If that ten was the same as the first twenty, then come back.'

'Now we're talking upwards of sixty paces if you count both ways, and then another thirty if we decide to go that way.'

'Your point?'

Le Groutt bared his teeth. 'I get a bigger cut for doing more pacing than any of you.'

'Cut? What cut? We're trying to free the Head of the Thieves' Guild.'

Le Groutt frowned. 'Oh, right.' He then brightened. 'But there's bound to be treasure squirrelled away down here, a vault or something! A Royal Vault! We could clean it out once we've sprung the old hag—'

'Old hag? That's Mistress Dam Loudly Heer you're talking about!'

'She doesn't like me,' said Le Groutt. 'I only came for the loot.'

'There won't be any loot!'

'And you still expect me to walk an extra nine hundred paces?'

'Nine hundred? What are you talking about? Just scout the damned passage!'

'I'm a 2nd story man, Plaintly, not a scout.'

'So you won't do it?'

Le Groutt crossed his arms. 'No. I won't.'

Sighing, Plaintly turned and took Symon by the arm. 'You, take that candle and scout this passage.'

'Ten per cent extra on my cut.'

'Finc! Now go!'

Symon snaked past Le Groutt, reached back to snag the candle, and then set off.

'That's not fair!' hissed Le Groutt, 'I was only gonna ask for five per cent!'

'That's what you get for arguing,' said Plaintly. 'Now The Knife gets ten per cent of your cut.'

'*What?*'

'Shhh!'

'Ever had lizard tail soup?' Mortari asked. 'Ma used to make the best lizard tail soup. Boiled up in cat water. Even Pa couldn't complain.'

After some scrabbling sounds, and then a low yelp, the faint candlelight from the passage winked out.

Plaintly held up a hand when Le Groutt was about to speak. She listened, and then shook her head. 'That's not good. I don't hear anything.'

'Of course you don't,' said Le Groutt, 'you told me to shut up.'

'Not you,' she said. 'Symon.'

'Where is he?'

'He went down this passageway, remember?'

'It was a well,' Mortari said behind them. 'Full of drowned cats, floating and bobbing and smelling bad. That's when I found Granma.'

'I don't see any passageway,' said Le Groutt.

'Light another candle,' said Plaintly.

Le Groutt fidgeted in his bag for a few moments, and then he said, 'I only brought the one.'

Plaintly twisted round. 'Anyone else bring a candle?'

'I knew Le Groutt had one,' said Lurma.

'We only had the one candle?' Plaintly asked.

'I had one,' said Barunko. 'Then I took it in my hand and crushed it like it was melted wax. Ha!'

'Where is it now, Barunko?' Plaintly asked.

A moment of silence, and then Barunko said, 'I don't remember. It was years ago.'

'Le Groutt,' said Plaintly, 'you're going to have to creep along in the dark. You need to find Symon and that candle.'

'Where?'

'Down this passageway.'

'Here,' said Le Groutt, 'take this end of the rope.'

Plaintly took it and handed it to Mortari, who moved up to lean close to Le Groutt. They whispered back and forth for a bit and then with a grunt Le Groutt clambered into the passageway.

A short time later there was a cry, the sound of falling rocks, and then silence.

Plaintly sighed. 'Mortari, give me the end to that rope.'

Mortari held up both hands. 'Which one?'

'What? He gave you the other end, too?'

'Just to make sure, he said,' explained Mortari.

'Lurma,' said Plaintly, 'you've got the sensitive touch. Get down this passage, feel your way, and be careful!'

'Should've sent me to start with,' said Lurma. 'I was offering four per cent. Not that anyone bothered asking me. No, it's just "pick that lock, Lurma!" and "Listen at that door, Lurma!" and "Lift that key ring from his belt, Lurma!"'

'Okay okay,' said Plaintly, 'sorry.'

She wriggled past and then slipped into the crack in the wall. They waited.

'She gave me the clap, too,' said Mortari. 'The bitch.'

'Who?' asked Barunko.

'I told you. The bitch.'

'But who?' Barunko demanded.

'I told you!'

'No you didn't!'

'Be quiet, both of you! I hear something!' Plaintly edged into the passageway. 'Voices. Faint. Wait, I can almost make them out.'

'What are they saying?' Mortari asked.

'They're arguing . . . about . . . about, uh, who's got the end of the rope. Wait! Symon's found the candle! Come on you two, let's go. They've found a genuine tunnel!'

'A tunnel!' exclaimed Barunko. 'Here? Underground?'

'Plaintly?' asked Mortari.

'What?'

'What should I do with these rope ends?'

'How many have you got?'

'Two.'

'Bring 'em,' she said. 'Might come in handy.'

The passageway was narrow, the footing treacherous, but the sudden flare of candlelight ahead helped them reach the others. There was a ledge and then a drop of perhaps half a man's height, and sitting on the floor of the tunnel below were Symon, Le Groutt and Lurma.

Plaintly clambered over the ledge and dropped down, Mortari and Barunko following.

The tunnel was wide, low-ceilinged, the ceiling being the

narrow top of converging planes of set stone blocks. Brightly painted friezes covered the walls to either side, and the floor was made of shiny marble tiles. Plaintly took the candle from Symon and brought the light close to one of the paintings. 'I don't recognize any of this – must be thousands of years old – no, wait, is that the new king?' She brushed a finger against the frieze. 'Paint's still wet!'

Barunko sniffed. 'I smell shit.'

Lurma rolled one of her eyes. 'The word is "shitty", Barunko.'

'No,' said Symon The Knife, 'he's right! It's coming from down this way.' And he set off down the tunnel.

'We're tracking shit smells now?' Lurma asked.

Symon had disappeared behind a bend and now they heard his low cry. Plaintly in the lead, they hurried over.

Two bodies were lying on the floor at Symon's feet.

'Fast work, Symon!' said Lurma around her wad of Prazzn. 'Those painters couldn't paint worth crap!'

The Knife spun round. 'Wasn't me! Look at them! They've been torn apart!'

'Besides,' said Plaintly, 'if you'd bothered looking as carefully as I did, you'd have seen that the painters were just painting over some ancient king, replacing it with the Usurper's face. Desecrating historical artefacts! Skewing the timeline for generations of historians to come! I told you he was evil!'

'Skewing the what?' Symon asked as he drew his knife. 'Listen! Some wild beast is prowling these tunnels. Look at that smear of shit there – it's still fresh! We're not alone, is what I'm saying.'

'Symon's right,' said Le Groutt. 'There's me and Mortari and Plaintly and Lurma and—'

Lurma took a swing at Le Groutt's head and missed. 'He means there's a fucking demon down here is what he means, Le Groutt!'

'A demon! Where?'

'Close,' hissed Symon, tossing his knife from one hand to the next. A moment later it clattered to the floor.

Everyone tensed but thankfully, the skidding knife missed the smear of shit.

Sighing, Plaintly said, 'Pick that up, Symon, you might need it. I want you on point—'

'Me? Why not Barunko?'

'Yes,' said Barunko, 'why not Barunko, and where is he, anyway?'

'He's right here,' said Plaintly. 'You're Barunko, Barunko.'

'That's right! I'll take point! Where's point?'

Plaintly pushed him forward. 'We go this way,' she said.

'Why that way?' Symon demanded.

Plaintly grasped Barunko and spun him round. 'All right, we go that way!'

'That's better,' grunted Symon. 'Unless the other way's better.'

'It isn't,' snapped Plaintly. 'We're looking for the crypts.'

'So how do you know the crypts are that way?' demanded Symon, wiping blood from his hands.

'I don't.'

They set out, Barunko in the lead, his hands held out to make sure he didn't walk into a wall. Behind him, Lurma carried the candle and weaved from one side of the tunnel to the other and then back again, as was her wont. Behind her, Mortari walked with his swollen head tilted to one side, the strange bulges resting on his left shoulder. On his heels was Le Groutt, rope coiled in one hand. Then came Plaintly with Symon The Knife right behind her.

'Keep an eye out behind us,' Plaintly whispered to Symon.

'I'm trying,' he replied, 'only, it's dark back there, and I swear, that darkness is following us! Like some creeping tide of doom!'

'Just be ready in case something jumps us. Where's your other knife, anyway? I haven't seen it.'

'I lost it. Last week.'

'Oh, too bad. How'd you lose it?'

'It got stuck through the ear of a mule and the mule ran off.'

'You tried to assassinate a mule?'

'It seemed an easy twenty Broaches. That was one stubborn mule and the farmer was fed up having to carry all the bundles to market every day.'

'The bundles weren't on the mule's back?'

'Like I said, it was stubborn, and cranky.'

'So why did the farmer keep dragging the mule back and forth to market if it wasn't carrying anything?'

Symon snorted. 'I didn't say he was a smart farmer, did I? Twenty Broaches!'

'But you failed.'

'He paid me anyway, for the lost knife.'

Plaintly smiled and nodded. 'Clever, Symon. Seems you've learned from me after all and it only took how many years?'

'Not really. That knife was worth fifty.'

'Better twenty Broaches back than a kick in the head, though.'

'Well, it was the kick that messed up my aim.'

'Oh.'

Le Groutt twisted round to glare at them. 'Are you two done?'

'We're just passing the time,' hissed Symon The Knife. 'What's your problem, Le Groutt?'

'You getting ten per cent of my take! That's my problem!'

Up ahead there was a loud thump. Barunko had run into a door. Everyone clumped up behind him while he searched for the latch. After a few moments of this, Lurma snarled and pushed past the Muscle. 'Here, let me.' After a few tries, she clasped hold of the latch, turned it, opened the door, and glanced back triumphantly at Plaintly.

But no-one was really paying her any attention, for on the other side of the doorway crouched an ape-like demon with both hands savagely working its engorged penis. Glancing up, it blinked and then smiled, revealing a row of sharp fangs.

Symon's knife hissed through the air, but from long experience everyone had already ducked, even Barunko. The weapon flew past the demon to land far down the corridor.

Ignoring the demon, whose rocking had not abated, Mortari bolted after it.

'Attack, Barunko!' cried Plaintly. 'Straight ahead! Attack!'

As Barunko surged forward, the demon shuddered and then spurted all over the huge man. Who reeled back. 'Aagh! My eyes!'

Squealing, the demon rushed off down the corridor, barrelling over Mortari who had retrieved the knife with a wild, excited grin. He leapt back to his feet and scurried towards Symon. 'I got it!' he cried. 'Throw it again!'

Plaintly snapped, 'Forget all that! Lurma, help get Barunko cleaned up, will you?'

'What? Have you lost your mind?'

'Just use that flask of water and at least rinse out his eyes.'

'What if I get pregnant?'

'That would only happen,' Plaintly explained, 'if you wiped down his face with your crotch.'

'Crotch!' said Barunko, groping wildly. 'Face! Hurry!'

Scowling, Lurma drew out the flask. 'This was my special water,' she said.

'Why?' Plaintly asked. 'What's special about it?'

'It's the flask I drink from,' Lurma replied. 'Now I'm wasting it, on Barunko's face. I hope everyone's paying attention, because I'll be wanting compensation for everything I'm using up here.'

'I hope you get pregnant,' said Le Groutt.

'What?'

'You'd look pretty with that special glow.'

'Fuck off, Le Groutt.'

'Hey! I was complimenting you! Hood's breath, you're a sour one, aren't you? That's what happens when you ain't got that glow.'

Plaintly said, 'Just hurry up, will you? We've got to keep moving. It's not like we've got all night, is it?'

Symon frowned at her. 'Yes it is,' he said. 'We've got all night. What are you going on about, Plaintly?'

'Oh, just hurry,' she said, rubbing wearily at her face.

'You have a very wet crotch,' Barunko observed after Lurma sprayed his eyes with the flask. 'Are you peeing? You should have told me. I would've opened my mouth.'

In his years in the diplomatic service of Nightmaria, such as it was, Ophal D'Neeth Flatroq had become a man with far too much time on his hands, leading him to a more or less ongoing contemplation on the nature of political power in the modern age. He was not yet prepared to set forth anything like a theorem, since he remained in the stage of assembling a lengthy list of observations, characteristics and other such details as required prior to formulating any particular set of rules and such.

One obstacle to this process was a dearth of experience, since his only contact with such rulers amounted to the previous – now dead – King N'Gorm (the Lesser), and now the usurper, Bauchelain the First. Still, of histories there were plenty available in Farrog's Grand Library of the Arts, Alchemy, Nature and Divination, a small building off Harbor Square consisting of an imposing Archivist's Desk forming a barrier between the public and the collection, the latter of which consisted of twelve bound books, eighteen scrolls and seven stone tablets. As formidable as the desk was, it was the Archivist who naturally posed the greatest obstacle to perusing the Royal Collection of Letters. Fortunately, the poor man possessed a neurotic terror of snakes, lizards, toads and frogs: creatures either slimy or scaly or both, a descriptive that one could, without stretching, reasonably apply to Ophal himself.

In any case, certain arrangements had been reached between the Ambassador and the Archivist, permitting Ophal's access to the collection in the span of time between the midnight bell and dawn. As it turned out, the accumulated wisdom of the Farrogese had proved most illuminating, if somewhat depressingly limited.

Prior to King N'Gorm there had been a succession of mostly ineffectual rulers in Farrog. If this seemed a cruel assessment, it was nothing compared to Ophal's opinion of N'Gorm himself. In a cool and clinical state of mind, one might assert that the man had been excruciatingly useless, and indeed, that his ignominious assassination was in fact a mercy for all concerned (arguably including N'Gorm himself).

That said, as Ophal sat in the waiting room outside the Throne Room, the rule of King N'Gorm served a useful counterweight in Ophal's potential polemic concerning the art of political leadership, with the other end of the spectrum occupied by King Bauchelain the First.

Politically and under the present circumstances, of course, Ophal would rather N'Gorm had kept both his head and his throne, thus obviating the need for this fateful meeting.

Hearing a faint scuff from the doorway, Ophal glanced up and flinched back upon finding the Grand Bishop Korbal Broach standing there, small flat eyes fixed upon the Ambassador.

Clearing his throat, Ophal nodded in greeting. 'Prrlll ffllap—'

'Stop that,' said Korbal Broach.

'Ethcuse me, good ewening, Gwand Bithop.'

'I have proclaimed a holy war, Ambassador.'

'Yeth, why?'

Korbal Broach frowned. 'Because . . . I felt like it?'

'Aahh.'

The Grand Bishop stared down at him for a while longer.

Ophal fidgeted.

'I don't worship any gods,' Korbal Broach then said.

'Not ewen the . . . prrlll . . . Indifferent God?'

'Oh no. In fact, we're trying to kill him. He's hard to kill.'

'Yeth, I'm thure.'

'He's obsessed with sex.'

'Prrlll. Awen't we all?'

Korbal Broach blinked. 'No.'

All things considered, it was probably a requirement among all tyrants to possess a companion such as this Korbal Broach; indeed, Ophal was nearing the formulation of a truism regarding insanity as a prerequisite to tyranny. The absence of conscience, the curious shallowness of contemplation, a cool pragmatism leading to the justification of all manner of depravity, slaughter and inhumanity. Such individuals were clearly useful for the tyrant, assuming one appreciated a sounding board throwing back raving madness at every opportunity.

'I killed all my priests,' said the Grand Bishop.

'Aahh, how . . . thowough of you.'

'They talked too much.'

'Mhmm.'

Korbal Broach stared for a moment longer, and then departed.

Ophal allowed himself to relax. The kitten was coming back on him in a succession of furry burps. It had probably been infected with worms or something. That was the risk that came with unscheduled snacks, particularly in the alleys of Farrog. He was feeling decidedly queasy.

The King's manservant now appeared in the doorway. 'Ambassador? He'll see you now.'

Ophal rose from his seat. 'Prrlll, fflaapp, ethlenent!'

The old man grunted. 'Easy for you to say.' He hesitated, and then glanced back over a shoulder, before quickly stepping into the chamber. 'Listen, it's bad luck that you're, uh, lizard people. I mean, it's not your fault or anything, is it? It's just what you are, right? But you know, naming your kingdom Nightmaria, well, maybe that worked for old King N'Gorm, but for my master, well, that's more of an, uh, invitation.'

Ophal nodded excitedly. 'Yeth! I too have weathed this concluthion! Ethlenent! Go on, pweathe!'

'And calling yourselves Fiends, well—'

'Aahh! Prrlll! About that—'

Some noise made the manservant turn to the doorway. 'Oops, time to go, Ambassador. Please follow me – oh, you know the drill. Oh and remember, he likes genuflection, and obsequiousness. Grovelling is even better. Abject despair soothes him best of all – I've turned that into an art and, well, never mind. Come along.'

The manservant in the lead, they entered the throne room.

The headless corpse straddled Brash Phluster, both pallid hands slapping the artist across the cheeks, back and forth, back and forth. 'Aaagh!' Brash screamed, 'get it off of me! Please!'

For the moment, however, everyone else was too busy fighting off the dozen or so other headless undead crowding the narrow corridor, barring Apto Canavalian, who had found a niche that had, once upon a time, been home to a statue or some such thing, as he found himself on a raised pedestal. Remaining utterly motionless demanded all his nerve, but it seemed to be working, as the horrid decapitated figures seemed to be ignoring him.

In between his moments of utter terror, he found himself musing on how the damned things saw anything at all. The ways of sorcery and necromancy were indeed a mystery, were they not?

The Chanters were laughing as they waded in, stamping sideways into shins and snapping bones so that the undead monstrosities fell over, to flop about before starting to pull themselves along, resuming their pursuit and most of them, Apto saw, were converging on poor Brash Phluster, who had unfortunately fallen over and was now being swarmed.

Off to one side, Steck Marynd protected Shartorial Infelance, in that usual manly fashion of his. Apto knew it all to be an act. It must be. Selflessness was hardly a survival trait, was it? In fact, it was the very opposite.

'Self interest,' he whispered, trying not to move his lips since statues weren't in the habit of commentary. 'The rational course, first and foremost. Always. Who else matters more than me?'

Tulgord Vise was now dragging bodies off Brash Phluster, lifting them until they dangled, whereupon he snapped their spines over one thigh, like a man assembling firewood, before flinging them to one side to make a neat, tidy stack.

'A man without an axe, that is,' muttered Apto. 'And given how stupid he is, I doubt it's anything new on him. Firewood? Use an axe. No axe? Get someone else to do it. Someone like Tulgord Vise.' He almost snorted a laugh, coming ever so close to drawing the attention of the nearest headless undead.

Eventually, most of the creatures were little more than sacks of dead meat around broken bones, and Brash Phluster was at last able to scramble free, weeping uncontrollably, his cheeks bright red.

'Why?' he cried. 'Why did they do that?'

Deeming it safe at last, Apto stepped down from the pedestal, stretching to work out the stiffness that came with holding the same pose for so long. 'I recognize some of these bodies,' he said. 'They were judges.'

Brash stared at him, and then his swollen face twisted. 'You think you're funny? You're not. Whose idea was it to use that niche and that pedestal? Whose idea was to pose like a statue? Mine! Then you pulled me off and threw me to the ground!'

Apto shrugged. 'I know a good idea when I see it.'

'As Greatest Artist of the Century I was the better fit on that pedestal!'

'Fame is fleeting, isn't it? Us critics prop you up only to drag you down.'

Steck now limped forward. 'We need to keep moving,' he said. 'There's bound to be more of these things, and then there's the demons. We need weapons.' He turned to Shartorial, whose eyes gleamed in worshipful regard as she looked steadily upon Steck Marynd. 'We need to find the guards' armoury, Milady, and the lockers where our weapons are kept. Can you lead us there?'

She nodded.

'Tiny don't need weapons,' said Tiny, raising into view his battered fists. 'Tiny breaks bones. Bones go snap.'

'Crunch,' added Midge.

'Splinter,' said Flea, who then frowned.

'No,' rumbled Tulgord Vise. 'A Mortal Sword needs his sword. Otherwise he's just . . .'

'Mortal?' asked Apto.

'You begin to tire me, Critic,' said Tulgord, glowering. 'I am a Mortal Sword, blessed by a goddess, sworn to vengeance against the Nehemoth.' He made a fist. 'And they are almost within reach! This is our best chance!'

'I agree,' said Steck Marynd. 'The time has come to kill them. To finally rid the world of Bauchelain and Korbal Broach.'

Gesturing, Shartorial said, 'I will take you to your weapons! Come!'

They set off, stepping carefully to avoid all the grasping hands and reaching arms.

'All in all,' said Apto as they hurried down the corridor, 'those undead seemed pretty useless.'

Steck grunted. 'Aye. Distractions. Something else is down here in these crypts. I can feel it. Something truly nasty.'

'We've been hearing screams,' said Apto. 'That suggests that you are right, Steck Marynd, and the sooner all of you are armed the safer I'll – I mean *we'll* – feel.'

'Tiny feels safe,' said Tiny. 'Midge?'

'Safe,' said Midge.

'Flea?'

'Splinter,' said Flea. 'Bones go *splinter*! Like that, the sound. They go. The bones. Hah!'

Brash Phluster turned a glare on Apto. 'I'm putting you in my next epic poem. Where you're going to die most horribly, maybe more than once!'

'As a discerning scholar of art, Brash, I already die a thousand deaths with every song you sing, every tale you concoct, every mangled travesty of language you presume to call a poem.'

Brash made a fist, his puffy face working soundlessly, as he struggled through his fury to find words. In the end, he simply shook his fist in Apto's face.

'Oh dear,' said Apto. 'The artist waiting for inspiration ... wake me when you're ready, won't you?'

Tulgord Vise glanced back at them. 'Stop baiting the poor poet, Critic.'

'He just threatened to impugn my name and reputation!'

'No he didn't. Nobody's heard of you anyway.'

'I have a livelihood to protect!'

Tiny laughed his nasty laugh. 'Deadlihood, soon, if you don't shut your mouth.'

'Mouth,' said Midge.

'Bones,' said Flea.

'I will write an epic poem about all of you,' said Brash Phluster. 'The Nehemothanai, and their trek across half the world, hunting down the evil necromancers Bauchelain and Korbal Broach, slaying them at last in the cursed City of Farrog! I envisage at least twenty thousand stanzas—'

'As prologue, surely,' suggested Apto Canavalian.

Ignoring him, Brash continued. 'Every hero needs a poet, someone who witnesses them being, uh, heroes, and who can sing about them and make them famous, so their names journey down through the centuries.'

'Tiny needs no poet. Tiny journeys down the centuries himself.'

'That doesn't matter,' insisted Brash Phluster. 'Everything you do I'll make bigger, more amazing, more everything.'

'Everything Tiny does is already bigger and more amazing. Like when Tiny takes poet by the neck and twists off his head.'

'Now that's worth a poem all right,' said Apto.

'And then makes critic eat poet's head, so he chokes on poet's words, and hair.'

'You know, Tiny,' Apto observed, 'that quip would work much better with a little work. Might I suggest you delete the "hair" bit?'

'Tiny delete critic.'

'Hair,' said Flea.

Shartorial and Steck arrived at a narrow set of stairs leading upward, where they paused and Steck held up a hand. 'There's blood on these steps,' he whispered. 'Best you all be quiet now.'

'Tiny don't take orders from nobody.'

'Nobody,' agreed Midge.

Rubbing at his face, Steck said, 'Listen, it's just proper caution here. Remember, once we get our weapons, we become formidable and dangerous again, and we can carve our way up into the palace.'

'Tiny's not scared of anything.'

'Fine then,' growled Steck. 'Take the lead here, won't you?'

'You don't order Tiny. Tiny orders you, and you, and you, and you and you.' He pushed past Steck and Shartorial. 'Tiny goes first. You all follow and keep your mouths shut or Tiny shuts them for you, permanently if not forever.'

'You truly are obnoxious,' observed Tulgord Vise.

'That's right. Tiny kills ox with one hand, all the time. Tiny was an oxnobian before any of you were even born, or had mothers and shit.'

'Tiny pulled the legs off a mule when he was six,' said Midge.

'We're wasting too much time,' hissed Shartorial.

Tiny blew her a kiss that sprayed her face with spittle, earning a warning growl from Steck Marynd, but Tiny was already on the stairs and Shartorial reached out a hand to hold Steck back, while using her other hand to wipe at her face.

'Milady,' Apto heard Steck whisper, 'for that insult he'll die. This I swear.'

'It is no matter,' she replied. 'But do kill him at first opportunity anyway.'

'I shall.'

Apto glanced over at Midge and Flea. They stared back stonily. Apto smiled and waved.

Flea smiled and waved back.

Steck then took his new woman by one hand and led her up the stairs in Tiny's wake. Apto shoved Brash to one side to fall in directly behind Shartorial. Cursing, Brash scratched Apto's left ear, only to stumble and bark his shin on the first step. Midge then stepped on the artist, and Flea followed.

Tulgord Vise stopped to drag Brash to his feet. 'Stop being so clumsy, poet.'

'Don't let them kill me,' whimpered Brash.

The Mortal Sword said, 'Fear not, while I live. After all, a world without poets, sir, would be . . . would be . . . er, far less clumsy.'

'But—'

'Get moving and start acting like a man or I'll kill you myself.'

'You're all awful,' Brash Phluster hissed as he clambered his way up the steps. 'My epic poem won't lie about any of you! By the time I'm done *The Nehemothenai*, the audience will be cheering for the fucking necromancers!'

Hearing that, Apto twisted round, 'Now you're talking!'

Lurma Spilibus gently turned the latch and edged open the heavy door. A ribbon of light cut into the corridor, making everyone tense. She squeezed one eye into the crack, and then leaned back again, rubbing at that eye.

Plaintly whispered, 'What did you see?'

'A very narrow guard room. I couldn't see the walls but what I saw was empty. Except for the bits of flesh and bone and hair and ripped-up clothing.'

'Anyone see you?' Le Groutt asked.

'No,' said Lurma, 'I just told you.'

Plaintly nodded. 'Bits of flesh and bone and hair and ripped-up clothing.'

'That's what I said, isn't it? Bits of—'

'That must've been some party,' said Symon The Knife.

'Granma's wake was a damned good party,' said Mortari, 'even though she was just missing, but it'd been weeks and nobody takes that long drawing water from the well at the back of the yard. So we decided she was dead, and that was fair, wasn't it? And then, months later, I bumped right into her. In the well, I mean, with all those cats with their tails all tied together.'

Gesturing, Plaintly said, 'Go on, Lurma, check it out.'

But Lurma hesitated. 'Could be traps.'

'What kind of traps?'

'If I knew that they wouldn't be much good as traps, would they? No, leave this to me. Everyone else stay here, and be quiet while I check it out.'

'Good idea,' said Plaintly.

They remained crouched in the corridor, as Lurma Spilibus pushed the door open a bit more, and then slipped sideways into the guard room. A moment later her head popped back into view. 'It's wider that it was before, the room.'

'Anything else?' Plaintly asked.

'Wait.' The head popped out of sight again, and then they heard, 'Two doors in the opposite wall, identical, both ajar.'

'Room for all of us in there?' Plaintly asked.

A hand appeared and waved them in.

They quickly entered the guard room, and then stood around, amidst a knocked-over wooden table, shattered chairs, broken plates, dented tankards, bent knives and snapped swords, and an abattoir's worth of chopped-up meat and bone along with clumps of shredded, sodden clothing. Six crushed heads were piled up against a wall, along with twelve or so severed feet still wearing an assortment of cheap footwear.

Symon drew his knife. 'Should I check for survivors?' he asked.

'No,' said Plaintly, 'I think it's too late for any of these ones.'

'What do you think happened?' Le Groutt asked, his eyes slightly wild.

'That demon,' said Plaintly.

'The squirting one?' Symon then shook his head. 'Not a chance. That thing ran from us. It wasn't much taller than Mortari here.'

'Assuming I'm Mortari,' said Mortari.

'Well, who else would you be?'

'I don't know. It's a mystery.'

'Lurma,' said Barunko, 'more pee, please.'

'Listen,' said Plaintly, raising a hand to draw everyone's attention, 'something's wrong here.'

'What do you mean?' asked Le Groutt.

'Well, there was that demon, and now this room full of guards who've been torn to bits. It doesn't feel right. You all know to trust my instincts, and I'm saying . . .' she shook her head, 'the sooner we find the Head of the Thieves Guild and get out of here, the better.'

'So where do you think she is?' Lurma asked. 'Plaintly?'

'Plaintly's right here,' said Le Groutt. 'I'm looking at her, in fact.'

'Lurma meant our Mistress,' explained Plaintly, 'and I'm thinking in the cells down the hall, through that door there.'

'Which one?' Lurma asked.

'There's only one,' Plaintly said.

'What? I saw – oh, look at that! Only one door! The other one's vanished! I told you there were traps in here!'

'What kind of trap is a disappearing door?' Symon demanded.

'The kind that makes you go through the other one, of course. You'd better let me check it out first.'

'Symon,' said Mortari, 'let me borrow your knife.'

'What? Now?'

'Just for a moment, I promise.'

Symon handed over his knife. Mortari took it and popped the massive bulbous swelling projecting out from his temple. A stream of pink goo gushed out. 'Ah,' he said. 'That's better.' He handed the knife back, and then smiled his thanks at Symon.

A slimy puddle was fast forming on the floor at Mortari's feet.

Lurma stared down at it. 'You're going to clean that up, aren't you, Mortari?'

'Of course I am! On our way back, though. Anyone got a handkerchief we can throw over it in the meantime? Don't want any cat drowning in it or anything.'

'You're still leaking everywhere!' said Lurma. 'It's disgusting!'

'Everybody's squirted but me,' said Barunko, his lower lip trembling.

Plaintly moved close to The Muscle. 'It's all right, Barunko. You'll get your turn.'

'Really?'

'I promise,' said Plaintly, who then turned back to Lurma and gestured her towards the door.

Nodding, Lurma edged closer. She approached the door from one side, and then darted across to come at it from the other side. She reached the wall beside it and fumbled at the gore-spattered stones for a moment, before her fingers brushed the edge of the door and then she grasped it and pushed it open. Glanced through and then back. 'A corridor,' she whispered. 'Cell doors on both sides, all broken open.'

'And the other end?' Plaintly asked.

Lurma looked again. 'Two more doors.'

'Two?'

She looked back. 'One.'

'Just one? Are you sure?'

'Hold it, uhm, yes, the other one's vanished, just like the one in this room!'

'Is that one door busted open too?' Plaintly asked.

'Let's see,' said Lurma, looking yet again. 'No. But it's hanging from just one hinge.'

Symon grunted. 'Sounds busted to me.'

'That's because you can't see what I see,' Lurma snapped. 'I can see the latches. There's two of them and both look to be in perfect working condition. I'd have to pick them both if the door wasn't hanging from just one bent hinge. So don't go telling me my business, Symondenalian!'

'Sorry, Lurma,' said Symon. 'I'm just nervous, and why wouldn't I be, since I'm the only one armed, meaning you're all relying on me to cut through whatever comes at us. And that's my business, Lurma, so shut up about it!'

'All our talents are meshing perfectly,' said Plaintly. 'Okay, Lurma. Great work. Let's go check those open cells.'

'Cells? Who arrested me? I ain't going – oh, don't arrest me!' Barunko burst into tears.

Ophal glanced at the king's manservant, who wandered off to one side to pour himself a massive tankard of wine. He quickly downed three mouthfuls. Stood blinking, linking his lips, only to suddenly totter, reaching out to lean against the wall. Then he smiled, as if at some private joke.

King Bauchelain sat on his throne. 'Ambassador,' he said by way of greeting, 'are you well? Very good. So here we are again, another late-night meeting. Fortunately, it is my nature to prowl the span of night, although in this instance, and in the wake of conjurations, bindings and whatnot, I do admit to being somewhat weary. Given that, do be quick about it, will you?'

Tyrants, Ophal decided, loved to listen to themselves talk. 'Prrlll, gweetings, Thire.' He drew out his Imperial missive and began reading, 'To King Bauchelain and to the thitizens of Fair Farwog on the Wiver, after the untheasing prowocationth upon our peathful trade, carawanth and carawantherai, after the egwegiouth pwoclamation of Holy War upon the Wealm of Nightmawia, after the thucthethion of inthults and unwemitting therieth of hateful inthitationth, herrrwenow let it be known that a thtate of war exithth between Nightmawia and Farwog—'

'How delightful,' interjected the king. 'We were wondering

when you'd get around to it. I should inform you that Grand General Pin Dollop has assembled an elite force of formidable legions and is even now preparing to march to your mountain realm, there to slaughter and burn your civilization to ash.'

'Yeth,' Ophal nodded. 'However, prrllmit me to inforrrm you that our thpieth are well aware of your pwepawationth, and that Nightmawia, in antithipathion of thith impending *hsssp thvlah* conflict, hath not only athembled the Thoutherrrn Imperial Army, but ith awready on the march. *Fllapp prrlll thlup!*'

'Ah, well then, we shan't have to march as far then, to wipe out your measly horde of scaly lizards.'

Ophal frowned. 'Thcaly Withards?'

'Or is the epithet "Fiend" a more palatable descriptive?'

'Ahh, *prrrl*. Not "Fiend", Thire. "Firrrwend."'

Bauchelain frowned. 'Excuse me?'

'Firrwend, the name of the people of Nightmawia.'

From the wall, the manservant seemed to choke on his wine, hacking out a cough as his face reddened.

After a moment, Bauchelain waved a hand. 'Fiend or Firrwend. Unhuman either way.'

Ophal shook his head. 'Thadly, Thire, no.' He gestured somewhat embarrassedly at himself. 'Unfortunate thkin aiwlllment, awath, thuffithientwy abhorrwent to my fellow thitithenth that I wath thent to the motht wemote wethidence pothible. Thaddled with but one therwant, and but one Impewial Methenger.'

The manservant's coughing worsened and a glance over showed the old man sagging helplessly against the wall.

Ophal shrugged at the king. 'Mithchanth of birrrth, poor Ophal, cweft of pawate, dithjointed of jaw, thenthitive to wight and dryneth, thuth wequirrring thick humidity, dank and darrrk, forr comforrrt.' The Ambassador shrugged again. 'Motht twagic that I thould love petth in my company, ath I mutht thettle forr toadth, snakth, worrrmth and the wike. Of dethent company, ahh, *prrrl*, poor Ophal mutht make peath with thowitude.'

King Bauchelain had leaned back and was now stroking his

fine beard. 'I see,' he murmured. 'Now then.' He sat forward.
'This Imperial Army of yours . . .'

'Twenty-four wegionth, eighty thouthand heawy infantwy,
twellwe thouthand cavalllwy, twellwe thiege engineth, eighteen
twebuchetth, two wegionth Imperialll Thapperth, the Royalll
Cadwe of High Mageth and Withardth of the Ninth Orrrderrr.
Thith forrrce, conthituting the Thoutherrrn Awmy of Nightmawia,
ith ewen now cwothing yourrr borrrder and thould be at yourrr
wallth in two dayth. *Prrrl, flp!*'

'I take it, then,' said King Bauchelain, 'that reopening peaceful
negotiations are out of the question.'

'Alath, too wate, Thire. Motht unfortunate, yeth?'

Bauchelain then raised a long, thin finger. 'A question, sir, if
only to satisfy my personal curiosity. Your realm's name,
Nightmaria . . .'

'Yeth, welll, what betterrr name to keep unwanted foreigner-
rrth out of ourrr terrrwitowy?'

'So, in truth, you've been milking that dread reputation, and,
one might conclude, in no hurry to disavow the appellation of
"Fiend" either?'

Ophal shrugged for a third time. 'Wegretth arrre cheap.'

'Hmm, I see,' said King Bauchelain. 'Mister Reese?'

The manservant started slapping his own face. 'Aye, Master,
get the carriage ready. I'm on it.'

Tiny Chanter stepped around a corner and grunted as a man
nearly as big as he was stumbled into him. An instant later, with
an echoing bellow, the man swung his fist. The *crack* of that fist
impacting Tiny's prodigious jaw was a complicated mélange of
breaking bone, popping teeth, splitting lip and spraying blood.
Eyes rolling up to examine his own brain, Tiny collapsed.

Still bellowing, the stranger now ploughed down the steps, fists
flying. Shartorial's nose broke with a crunching sound. Steck
Marynd bulled forward, attempting to grapple, only to meet a
knee under his jaw that lifted him from his feet. In falling

backward, he landed on Apto Canavalian, thus sparing the critic any of the stranger's attention, as he leapt over the jumble of four tumbling, intertwined bodies, and hammered into both Midge and Flea. Biting, punching, kneeing, gouging, the three men fell in a heap, rolling down the stairs.

Shrieking, Brash Phluster leapt high. While this sent him above and thus clear of the tumbling bodies, it also slammed the top of his head into the ceiling. The impact closed his teeth about his tongue with a loud snap, cutting that tongue clean in half.

In the meantime, the wrestling mob reached Tulgord Vise, who had been staring slack-jawed. The impact took him across the shins, breaking both legs. Howling, he collapsed onto the others, although his interest in fighting was likely minimal at the moment.

Even as Apto pushed aside Steck Marynd's unconscious body and clambered upright, a knife hissed past, less than a hand's breadth from his face. It caught Brash Phluster on the way back down from the ceiling, sinking deep into his right shoulder. His scream was a throaty gurgle that erupted in a red cloud.

An instant later, strangers were rushing down the stairs, led by a cross-eyed woman who kept caroming off the walls to either side. They stepped on everyone in their mad rush down and past the escaped prisoners. Blinking, confused, Apto stared after them.

He saw the still-bellowing attacker now rise over the battered forms of Midge, Flea and Tulgord Vise, and then, with a blubbering bawl, set off after his friends.

Gasping, Apto sank down to sit on the steps.

Shartorial Infelance sat up opposite him, holding her mashed nose.

'That looks painful,' said Apto. 'Had I a handkerchief, Milady . . .'

She shook her head, gingerly, and then said, 'Most kind, sir.'

'Were they . . . guards?'

'I think not. But some were, uh, known to me. Thieves.'

'Thieves? Down here? Whatever for?'

'The King, he arrested Dam Loudly Heer, the Head of the Thieves' Guild. I suspect they have come to affect her rescue.'

'Right, but, uh, there's nobody down there. In the crypts, I mean.'

She nodded, but said nothing more.

Steck Marynd groaned where he was lying sprawled on the steps. Farther down, Brash Phluster had found his tongue and was cradling it in his lap as he wept. Someone had pulled the knife from his shoulder, but as there was no-one down there still conscious, Apto assumed that whoever had thrown the knife had retrieved it in passing.

Apto gestured, 'Look down there, Milady. At least one mercy in all this.'

'Excuse me?'

'That poet will never sing again.'

She frowned above her blood-smeared hand. 'You are most cruel, sir.'

'Me? Have you heard him sing?'

A voice quavered down from the stairs above. 'Is Tiny dead? Tiny feels dead. Are these Tiny's teeth? These look like Tiny's teeth.'

'Good thing you took point, Tiny,' called up Apto. 'Otherwise, who knows what might've happened!'

'Tiny hates critics.'

They stumbled into a room, collapsed exhausted to the floor. Barunko had ceased his blubbering, and now sat wiping his eyes and nose, his hands glistening in the faint torchlight.

Slowly regaining her breath, Plaintly set her back against a stone wall. 'Great work, Barunko,' she finally managed.

'They scared me,' said Barunko, knuckling his eyes. 'Came out of nowhere, right in front and there I was, right in front, too. It was like, the two of us, face to face, and his face was so . . . so ugly! I had to punch it, I couldn't help it!'

Lurma suddenly bumped against Plaintly. 'Shh!' she hissed. 'We're not alone!'

'What?' Plaintly looked up, and her eyes narrowed on the tall fat man in the brocaded robes who stood near a floor-to-ceiling cabinet on the other side of the chamber. The man was frowning as he studied the Party of Five.

Symon The Knife hissed, 'Mortari, give me my knife, damn you!'

'I got it,' said Mortari, crawling over. 'I took it out of that man's shoulder! Did you see me do that? Oh, throw it again!'

'Damn you, Symon,' said Lurma, 'if only you had two knives, you could take them both down!'

'There's only the one,' said Le Groutt.

'What? Is there? Oh! Where did the other one go?'

'It's the fucking Grand Bishop,' said Le Groutt.

Symon readied his knife and then threw it. The weapon struck the wall near the ceiling. It fell to the floor in two pieces.

'Shit!' cursed Symon.

'Here, try this,' said Le Groutt, pushing the coil of rope into The Knife's hands. 'Tie him up or something!'

The Grand Bishop then spoke, his voice thin and querulous. 'Who are you? What do you want?'

Plaintly climbed to her feet. 'We're the Party of Five, that's who we are!'

'But there's six of you.'

'What?' Plaintly looked at the others and then said, 'No, there's five, can't you count?'

'That's right,' said Le Groutt. 'Five. The priest's fucking illiterate.'

'No,' said Lurma, 'there's ten of us. I always thought it a strange title—'

'You're in my Chamber of Collections,' said the Grand Bishop. 'I didn't invite you.'

'Never mind that shit,' said Plaintly. 'We're here for the Head of the Thieves' Guild, and we're not leaving without her!'

The round-faced man's brow wrinkled slightly, and then with a shrug he turned and opened the cabinet and collected a severed head from one of the shelves crowded with dozens of other severed heads. Gripping it by the hair he held it out. 'Here, then.'

Plaintly gaped. 'But that's – that's – that's—'

'The head of the Thieves' Guild,' said the Grand Bishop. 'Wasn't that the one you wanted?'

'Hey!' cried Le Groutt, 'where's the rest of her?'

Squinting, Barunko added, 'She's shorter than I remember her. I think. I don't really remember her at all. Is that her? She's short!'

The Bishop frowned. 'Do you want it or don't you? Oh, and did you happen to meet a demon prince? We lost him down here. Him and the Indifferent God, and now we're running out of time.' He set the head down on a table and then brushed his pudgy white hands. 'I have to go.'

Plaintly licked dry lips and then looked about, quickly, before saying, 'Le Groutt, collect that head, will you? We're getting out of here.'

The Grand Bishop then departed through a secret door in the wall behind him.

Lurma leapt to her feet. 'Come on,' she said, 'let's take the other one!' And she sprinted forward until she slammed into a wall, where she slumped to the floor, unconscious.

Frowning, Plaintly said, 'Barunko, pick up Lurma. We can't be waiting around down here any longer, not with a demon prince wandering around!'

Barunko rose to his feet. 'Pick up Lurma. Where?'

'Mortari, guide him over, will you?'

Grumbling, Mortari walked up to Barunko, who grasped him suddenly and flung him into a wall. 'Did he reach the hook?'

'No,' said Plaintly, 'that was earlier, Barunko. Now we just need you to carry Lurma and Mortari.'

'Why, what's wrong with them? Are they dead?'

'Unconscious,' explained Plaintly. 'Le Groutt here will take you to them.'

'Okay,' said Barunko. 'Carry them out. Got it. Le Groutt? Who's got my wrist? Let go!'

'No!' cried Plaintly, 'don't—'

But it was too late, as Barunko punched Le Groutt, sending the man to the floor in a heap.

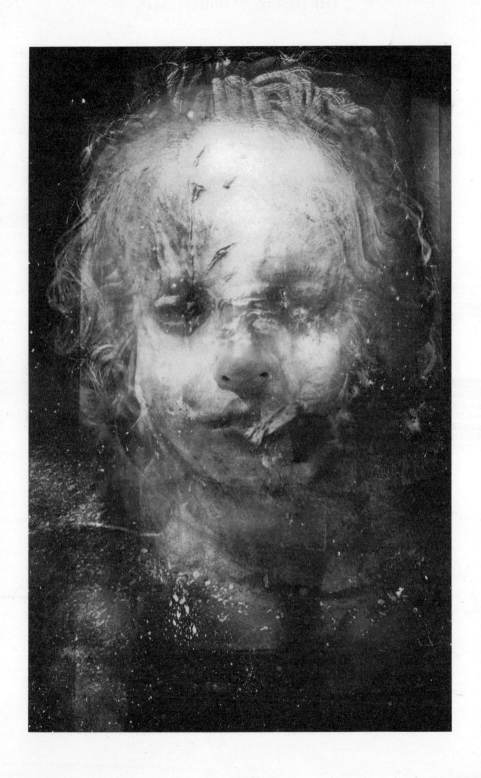

'Okay,' said Plaintly. 'Barunko, you just stand there, and Symon will drag them over to you, all right?'

'All right. Got it. Drag who?'

'Lurma and Mortari and, uh, Le Groutt. Think you can carry all three of them?'

'Carry? Not sure,' said Barunko. 'I mean, if Barunko was here, why, I bet he could!'

'You're Barunko, Barunko,' said Plaintly.

'Okay, good, hey there's bodies all around me!'

'That's Symon pushing them closer,' said Plaintly, 'so now all you have to do is pick them up one by one.'

Symon turned to Plaintly. 'Le Groutt can't carry the head anymore, Plaintly. Who should take it now?'

'Well,' said Plaintly, 'since you lost your knife, why don't you?'

'Damn,' said Symon, 'I should never have broken that knife.'

'That's how it goes on a mission like this one,' said Plaintly. 'Nothing seems to go as planned and then, all of a sudden, it's mission accomplished! Now all we have to do is evade the demon prince and the Indifferent God, and all those other demons and those headless things.'

'I've got three bodies here,' said Barunko. 'What do you want me to do with them?'

'Just carry them,' said Plaintly. 'Symon, you got her head?'

'I got it, and since her hair's real long, I could swing her like a weapon, maybe even spin round and round and throw her. You know, this could be better than any knife! Symondenalian The Head Niksos!'

'Smart thinking, Symon,' said Plaintly. 'All right then, take the lead, will you? Barunko's right behind you, and then it's me taking up the rear.'

'Watch out for that darkness behind you, Plaintly,' said Symon. 'It's been chasing us all night!'

'I will, Symon, thanks for reminding me. Now let's get going!'

Ophal D'Neeth Flatroq stepped out through the side postern gate and paused to brush at his green silks. All things considered, the audience had gone rather well, he decided. Formal proclamation announced and here he was, still in possession of his head. Indeed, it occurred to him that he might have to revise his notions regarding maniacal tyrants, as King Bauchelain had proved surprisingly polite, and not in any way inclined to either foam at the mouth or enact highly unjust but altogether expected punishment to the hapless messenger delivering unwelcome news.

Unfortunately for the citizens of Farrog, the approaching forces of Nightmaria weren't much interested in anything but the thorough sacking of the city, the slaughter of its modest army, and the ousting of both the Church of the Indifferent God and the new Royal Line of King Bauchelain, the latter two as messily as possible.

Of course, it seemed likely that neither the king nor his grand bishop would be found anywhere in the city once the defences collapsed and raging Firends ran amok through the streets. This at least was consistent with his assessment of tyrants. When the dung hits the wall, why, the source of all incumbent misery and suffering has long-since hightailed it out of harm's way.

Typical. He wondered, as he made his way back to the embassy, if there existed some high, impregnable keep, situated atop a mountain or on an isolated island in a sea swarming with savage beasts, where all tyrants fled to as soon as the inevitable occurred. If so, why, wouldn't it be a wonderful thing to, say, drop a whole other mountain on top of them? Crushing into paste every last one!

Slithering along dank alleys, creeping against moss-gummed walls, crossing foul trenches, he came at last to the embassy. Producing a key, he let himself in through the well-hidden back door, and then made his way to where waited the Royal Messenger.

The man was covered in spider's webs and dozing on a settee.

Ophal cleared his throat, although that merely produced a strange hissing sound. Still, that proved sufficient, as Beetle Praata flinched upright, blinking owlishly in the gloom.

He started clawing strands of web from his face. 'Ambassador! It is a relief to see you again.'

'*Prrlll*, yeth, fank you. Now, my fwend, we must pweepare to *prrllll* deparrrth, ath the wocalllth willl be motht angwy with uth, yeth?'

Beetle nodded. 'I shall inform the stabler, then, to ready us some mounts.'

'*Prrlll*, *flip thvlah!* Vewy good. In the meantwime, I thalll dethtwoy documenth and whatnot.'

'It is sad, is it not, Ambassador, that you must quit this city. Please, sir, do not deem this a failure on your part – the Council and the Emperor wish to make that as clear as possible. You did your best.'

'Fank you, sir. Motht kind of you. Thuch a welief!'

Beetle Praata dipped his head in a bow and then strode from the chamber.

In the yard outside, the Royal Messenger found Puny Sploor collapsed against the carcass of his horse. The man was weeping, his small hands curled tight into fists with which he beat weakly and futilely on the dead animal's well-groomed flank. A bucket of water had been dragged up beside the horse's mouth, along with a few handfuls of straw.

Beetle frowned down at the stabler. 'You should know by now,' he said, 'there's no point trying to feed and water a dead horse. Now then, Puny, we have to flee the city. Ready the remaining horses, with saddles upon three of them. The Ambassador will be here shortly.'

Puny Sploor blinked up at Beetle, and then with a shriek he launched himself at the messenger, fingers closing about Beetle's throat.

'Tiny can grow as many new teeth as he wants,' said Tiny, still sitting on the stone steps. 'Tiny has been attacked by demons before.'

'That wasn't a demon,' said Steck Marynd from two steps down, his hands at his temples and a pool of vomit between his feet.

'Tiny says it was a demon, so it was a demon, right Midge?'

'Demon,' said Midge, still trying to push his right eyeball back into its socket, but it kept popping back out. 'Midge can see up his own nose.'

Flea leaned close to his brother. 'Can you see up mine, Midge?'

'I could always see up yours, Flea.'

'But now it must be different, right?'

Midge nodded. 'Different.'

'Better?'

'Maybe.'

Flea smiled.

Apto had ripped a strip from his filthy tunic and given it to Shartorial, to help stop the blood flowing from her broken nose. Now he said, 'The problem is the Mortal Sword's broken legs. He needs splints, or at least binding, if Tiny or Flea are to carry him.'

'Tiny carries no-one,' said Tiny. 'Midge and Flea don't neither. The fool can crawl for all Tiny cares.'

'Fub fab bib,' said Brash Phluster, and then he burst into tears again.

'There is a cutter's room,' said Shartorial Infelance, 'containing the Royal Apothecary. Healing salves, unguents and some High Denul elixirs. It's not far.'

Brash leapt to his feet, eyes fervent with sudden hope. He still held his severed tongue.

Apto sighed, 'Right, I suppose we'll have to make for that then. But Tulgord still needs help to get him there, and I have a bad back and all. It's a chronic condition, had it since, uh, since birth.'

Groaning, Steck Marynd straightened. 'I will carry him, then. With luck, he'll pass out with the pain.'

'Pass out?' Tulgord glowered up at Steck. 'More like die!'

'Pray to your goddess for salvation, sir,' advised Steck, making his way down the steps. 'I'll be as gentle as possible, but I make no promises.'

'There is mercy in your soul, sir,' said Tulgord Vise, grudgingly.

'Tiny can grow as many new teeth as he wants. Tiny has been attacked by demons before.'

'You said that just a moment ago,' Apto pointed out.

'Tiny never repeats himself. Never.'

'I think you're addled.'

'Tiny's not addled. The world is addled. That's why the walls are leaking and his fingernails are buzzing.'

Amidst grunts, yelps, groans and moans, Steck Marynd worked Tulgord Vise onto his back, gripping the man's thick wrists. This meant the legs dangled and bounced along the steps, and after a few moments of this, Tulgord Vise passed out.

'Lead on, Milady,' rasped Steck Marynd.

Nodding, she resumed the journey up the stairs, Apto right behind her followed by the Chanters and then Brash Phluster behind them with Steck and Tulgord taking up the rear.

'Might get your tongue back, Phluster,' said Apto, 'proving the universe's essential indifference to justice.'

'Buh ovv,' the poet replied.

They reached a landing and Sharotrial led them through a doorway, down another passageway, through another doorway and then went left at a T-intersection, coming at last to a final door. 'We're here,' she said, turning the latch and swinging it open.

Crowded inside were thirty-two demons. Sixty-three eyes fixed upon the newcomers, and then in a collective roar, the demons attacked.

Apto grasped hold of Shartorial and pulled her behind the door as the swarm poured out in a shrieking, slavering mob.

Bellowing, the Chanters vanished beneath a mound of writhing, spitting, snarling, biting, clawing creatures. Farther down the corridor, Steck was dragging Tulgord into a side-passage, Brash Phluster trying to push past them.

Apto risked a peek into the chamber. 'It's clear!' he hissed, dragging Shartorial around and inside, whereupon he slammed shut the door. 'That was close!'

'But Steck—'

'Made his escape, Milady, I promise you! I saw it with my own eyes!' He paused, and then said, 'But if the demons followed, well, he's finished. Dead. The poet too. In fact, Milady, we're probably the last ones left.'

Beyond the door the demons were now screaming along with the Chanters. Bodies struck walls, the floor, the ceiling and the door itself, the meaty impacts rattling the thick planks and popping bronze rivets.

'Sounds lively out there,' said Apto, offering Shartorial a modest smile. 'But I judge us safe, at least for the next little while.'

The door opened and Tiny barged into the Apothecary with three demons clinging to him and more rushing in behind.

Apto shrieked, grasping Shartorial Infelance and pushing her forward. 'It's all her fault! Not me! Not me!'

'Ah,' said Bauchelain as he adjusted his cloak, 'here he is. Korbal Broach old friend, are you well?'

The Grand Bishop stepped into the courtyard and looked round. 'I think it's going to rain,' he said, peering up at the night sky and sniffing.

'Quite possible,' Bauchelain agreed.

'Your Demon Prince has escaped.'

'Yes well, these things happen. What of your god?'

'Gone, too.'

'No matter. As you can see, Mister Reese has made us ready to depart this ungrateful city and its humourless neighbours. Our carriage awaits, as it were.'

'There is an army coming,' said Korbal Broach. 'I can feel them. With many powerful sorcerers. They are all very angry. Why are they angry, Bauchelain?'

'Misapprehensions, alas, for which I have decided to blame Grand General Pin Dollop.'

'Shall I kill him for you?' Korbal Broach asked.

'Alas, he has already led his army out of the city and will momentarily march straight into the maw of the punitive Firrwend forces. I would imagine he'll not survive the encounter.'

'Oh. Good.'

'Indeed,' said Bauchelain as he drew on his leather gloves. 'It comforts, does it not, when justice is seen to be served. Mister Reese.'

Emancipor was leaning against the tall front wheel of the carriage. 'Yes, Master?'

'The Royal Treasury.'

'With all the other loot, Master, in that clever Warren you created beneath the floorboards. You know,' he added, 'I've been dumping stuff in there for years now.'

'Mmhmm, yes?'

'Well, I was just wondering, Master, when is enough enough?'

Bauchelain turned to face him, one thin brow arching. 'Dear me, Mister Reese. Very well, allow me to explain. Ideally, one – in this case yours truly – envisages a world with a single, indeed global, economy, wherein wealth flows from all quarters in a seemingly ceaseless river, or series of rivers, all gathering in one particular place, that place being, of course, my coffers.'

'Huh,' said Emancipor Reese.

'Like a massive body bearing a million small cuts, the blood draining into a single gutter.'

'And, er, you're the gutter then?'

'Precisely.'

'But what about everyone else, Master? The ones trying to make enough to live well, or even enough to eat and maybe raise a family?'

'Accord them no sympathy, Mister Reese. They make their own fate, after all, and if through incompetence, laziness or stupidity they must live a life of abject suffering and hopeless, despairing misery, why, no-one ever said the world was fair. In the meantime,' he added with a faint sigh, 'it falls to the capable ones, such as me, to bleed the suckers dry. And then to convince them – given their innate stupidity it proves rather easy, by the way – of just how fortunate they are that I am running things.'

'Aye, sir, sly as a fox you are, that's for sure.'

'I am not sure, Mister Reese, if I like the comparison. Foxes are often the prey of frenzied packs of dogs let loose by the inbred classes, after all. I do not see myself as the object of such sport.'

'Sport, huh? Aye, Master. My apologies, then.'

'Now, Mister Reese, I think it best we take our leave. Korbal, dearest, will you ensure the path before us is unobstructed all the way to the South Gate?'

'Okay.'

Emancipor prepared to climb up to the driver's bench, but then he glanced over at Bauchelain. 'Master, just one thing's got me wondering.'

'Yes?'

'All that loot, sir. You never seem to use any of it.'

'Well of course not, Mister Reese. I simply wish to *possess* it, thereby exercising my absolute power in preventing anyone else from ever using it. In fact, my special Warren is designed in such a manner that there are no exits from it. What goes in stays in. Unless I choose otherwise. I point this out to make certain you do not concoct any grand deception, or thievery, although I remain confident of your loyalty.'

'Uh, right. Thank you, Master. I had no plans in that direction.'

'I didn't think you had, Mister Reese. Now then, I believe Korbal Broach is ready?'

Korbal Broach nodded. 'Yes, Bauchelain. Everybody I've killed and worked on since we got here is now in the street outside.'

'Ah, excellent . . . yes, I think I hear the screaming begin. Mister Reese?'

Emancipor gathered the traces. The four black horses, their hides steaming as was their wont, lifted their heads, mouths opening as they sank their fangs into the bits, eyes flaring a lurid, blazing amber. He flicked the straps. 'Move along now,' he said, making clicking noises.

Mortari's head was now swollen on the other side, but Plaintly Grasp was relieved to see him smiling. Le Groutt's jaw had been unhinged by Barunko's punch and was shifted well off to one side, so that the lower half of his face was misaligned with the upper half. He could now close his mouth with nary a single clack of teeth, a trick that made even Barunko giggle.

Lurma Spilibus had also regained consciousness and was even

now creeping stealthily towards the postern door they had passed through earlier that night. Watching Lurma slip from side to side in the narrow corridor filled Plaintly with an almost overwhelming sense of well-being.

'Another successful mission by the Party of Five,' she said, glancing at Symon The Head Niksos. 'Into the very palace itself and back out again! Another legend to our name, friends. I don't know why we ever split up in the first place.'

'Artistic differences,' said Symon. 'Overblown egos, too much drugs and hard liquor.'

'No,' Plaintly said, scowling, 'that's what ruined The Seven Thieves of The Baker's Dozen and the Fancy Pillagers.'

'And the Masons, too,' added Barunko.

Symon frowned. 'What masons?'

'The Grand High Order of the Wax Masons,' said Barunko, rolling up a sleeve to reveal a tattoo of a bee on his forearm. 'I was Chief Rumpah of the Lavender Hive of the Full Moon.'

'You were a Honeymooner?' Symon asked, eyes widening. 'I never knew!'

'Once a month at the third bell before midnight,' said Barunko, 'I ate a basketful of lavender flowers and then bared my ass to the heavens, letting out aromatic farts – none of the others could fart as many times as me! That's when the jealousy started, and Borbos started sneaking in lima beans and cabbage to try and beat me so I had to kill him, right? Since he was a cheater! And besides, his farts were killing bees!'

'You had a whole secret life!' Symon accused Barunko. 'And you didn't tell any of us!'

Barunko blinked sleepily. 'Everything masons do is secret. That's the whole point of it. Being, uh, secret. And secretive, and keeping secrets, too. I drink a bottle of d'bayang oil every day to keep me from knowing my own secrets! I think,' he added, 'it's wearing off.'

'How can you tell?' Symon asked.

'Well, I can see straight, for one.'

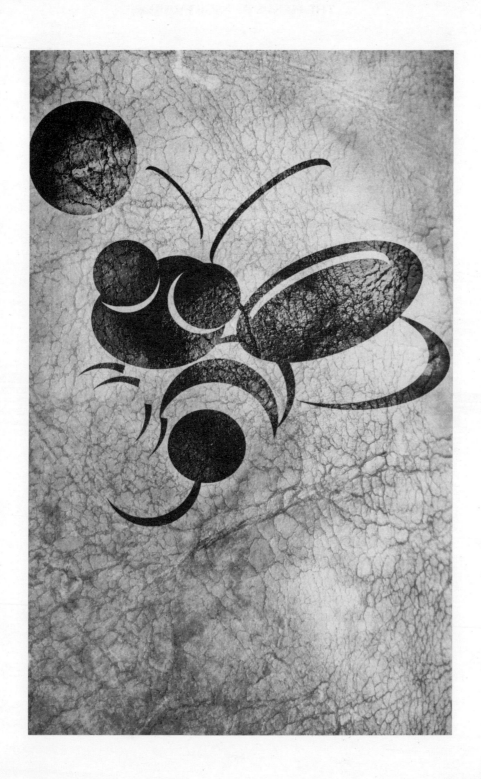

Lurma hissed impatiently from the door and then waved them over.

'Granma used to keep a kitten up her—'

'Not now, Mortari!' hissed Lurma, scowling, 'I can hear a crowd out there! In the street! They're partying or something – did we miss a fête? Never mind, we need to slink out, quiet like, so nobody notices us, and just blend in with the crowd, in case guards are watching or something.'

'Our last challenge,' said Plaintly. 'We can do it! The Party of Five went and retrieved the Head of the Thieves' Guild! Imagine that!'

'Actually,' said Barunko, 'There's six of us, provided you count yourself, too.'

'What?' Plaintly stared at Barunko.

'Never mind. Let's get out of here. I'm getting the shakes.'

Lurma fumbled for the latch for a moment, found it at last, and then edged open the door. Plaintly pushed Le Groutt forward, and then Mortari. 'Symon, have that head ready just in case,' she whispered, nudging him past her. 'Barunko, take up the rear.'

Barunko let out a loud fart, and then shrugged. 'Sorry, what you said was a code phrase. It's all coming back.'

Plaintly reeled against the wall. 'Hood's wind, Barunko, what have you been eating?'

'It's the d'bayang oil, Plaintly. You can't really drink it straight. Instead, you fill the bottle with slugs and let them soak it all up, then you swallow down the slugs.'

'That's what I'm smelling all right,' nodded Plaintly. 'Slug farts! I thought it was familiar. Now, stay right behind me, will you, as we make our way through the crowd.'

Barunko nodded.

Heart thudding with excitement, Plaintly slipped through the doorway after the others, and out into the street.

She caught a momentary glimpse of Symon, screaming soundlessly as he fought with a headless undead. Both had a grip on Dam Loudly Heer's head, and then Plaintly saw that the headless body was Dam Loudly Heer herself. Then she saw that almost the entire mob consisted of undead, most of them headless though a few sported two, even three heads, artlessly sewn onto shoulders. Still other figures were writhing jumbles of arms and legs, sprouting from mangled torsos. In the midst of this seething crowd were citizens shrieking in panic, along with palace guards busy getting their armour torn off, ears ripped off and eyes gouged from the sockets. Here and there swords swung, punctuated by meaty thuds or shocked screams; spears jabbed, fists flew, pitchforks stabbed – Barunko pushed past her. 'It's a fête!' he shouted, wading in.

'No, Barunko! Wait!'

To her utter astonishment, Barunko turned.

'We've got to gather the others! Get us all to cover! Anywhere! We've got to get out of this!'

He frowned, and then nodded. 'Okay. Follow me!'

There were dead demons everywhere. Bruised, bloody and exhausted, Tiny stood glowering, flanked by Flea and a one-eyed Midge, who now had a collection of eyeballs cupped in one hand and was poking them about, presumably looking for the right one.

Steck Marynd, with Tulgord Vise on his back, finally appeared in the doorway, and Shartorial – now mostly naked after her spat with a few demons – rushed towards him. Behind them all, Brash Phluster slipped round and stumbled into the Apothecary, heading straight for the shelves at the back of the room and their rows of phials, flasks, bottles and jars.

Apto straightened what was left of his prisoner's tunic. 'That was hairy,' he said. 'If not for my bad back I'd have joined in the slaughter. I'm sure you're all aware of that—'

Shartorial had said something – something probably unflattering regarding Apto – and now Steck Marynd carefully set Tulgord Vise down, straightened, and walked towards the critic.

Who backed away. 'What's wrong, sir? Look at us – we all

made it out alive! There's nothing – she's lying! Whatever she said is a lie!'

'Don't kill critic,' said Tiny. 'Tiny kills critic.'

Steck paused and glanced back. 'Not this time. This time, Steck Marynd will see justice done—'

'No! Tiny sees justice! Done!'

At the back of the chamber, Brash Phluster pushed into his mouth the piece of grey meat that had once been the front half of his tongue, and then started guzzling one bottle after another. He choked, gagged, coughed out the meat, stuffed it back in and resumed drinking.

'Look at the poet!' Apto cried.

Everyone turned.

Apto rushed past them all, back into the corridor, where he ran for his life. He heard angry shouts behind him. He found another corridor, pelted down it, and then, at the end of a short side passage, he found another set of stairs. At the threshold he paused. Up? No! They would expect that! Down! Down he ran.

Very faintly, from somewhere above, he heard Flea say, 'I thought he had a bad back!'

Apto laughed nastily. Then stumbled, fell, bounced and flounced wildly down the steps, and finally came to rest on a landing, or, perhaps, the lowest level. In agony, he lay gasping in the darkness, and then heard something shuffling towards him. Panic gripped him. 'What's that? Who's there? Leave me alone. I only ever speak the objective truth! Not my fault if I crushed your love of doing art, or whatever! Was it me who cut off your head? No! Listen, I own a villa and it's all yours! I promise!'

There was a low, weak chuckle, and then a demon's drawn, ashen face loomed over Apto Canavalian. The demon grinned. 'I remember you,' it said. 'From Crack'd Pot Trail.'

'No! Not possible! We've never met, I swear it!'

The demon's smile broadened. 'You've caught the attention of the Indifferent God. Very rare gift, this meeting here, oh, yes, very rare!' It held up a flaccid length of knobby, bruised meat that

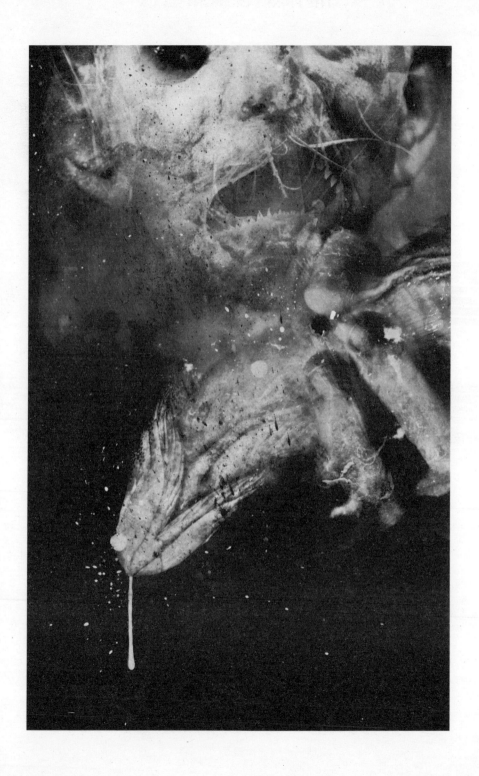

dripped from both ends. 'Look, I used it so much it fell off. Mother warned me but did I listen?'

'I'm sorry, what?'

'But I bet you have one. Should last me a week or two, easy.'

Apto suddenly laughed. 'You're wrong there! I've just broken my spine! I can't feel a thing from below the neck! Hah hah hah, you lose!'

The possessed demon scowled. 'Truly?'

'Truth! In fact, I've never been more spineless than I am right now!'

'Now you lie!'

'All right,' Apto admitted, 'that was perhaps an exaggeration. But that doesn't change anything. I broke my back, and I'll probably die right here, lost and abandoned by all my friends. It's a horrible way to go, and you know, if you were a merciful god, you'd—'

'Kill you? But I'm not a merciful god, am I?'

'You're not? Oh, damn. I'm doomed, then.'

The demon's face split into a wide grin again. 'Yes, you are. That's right, no audience for you! All alone! Forgotten! Discarded!' The demon pulled back, began shuffling away. 'Need,' it whispered, 'to find another. Another . . . oh me, oh my, Mother was right! Why didn't I listen? I never listen, oh why? Why?'

Apto listened to its whining dwindle, and then, finally, all was silence.

He sat up. 'Shit,' he muttered, 'that was close.'

'It worked!' cried Brash Phluster. 'It worked! I can talk again! And sing! Aaalahh la la lah leeee!'

'Tiny tear out his tongue again,' said Tiny. 'Everyone cheers. A standing ovation.'

Brash Phluster snapped his mouth shut and shrank back to cower beneath the shelves.

'We're forgetting why we're here,' said Steck Marynd. 'The Nehemoth.' He turned to Shartorial Infelance. 'Milady? Can you lead us to the throne room?'

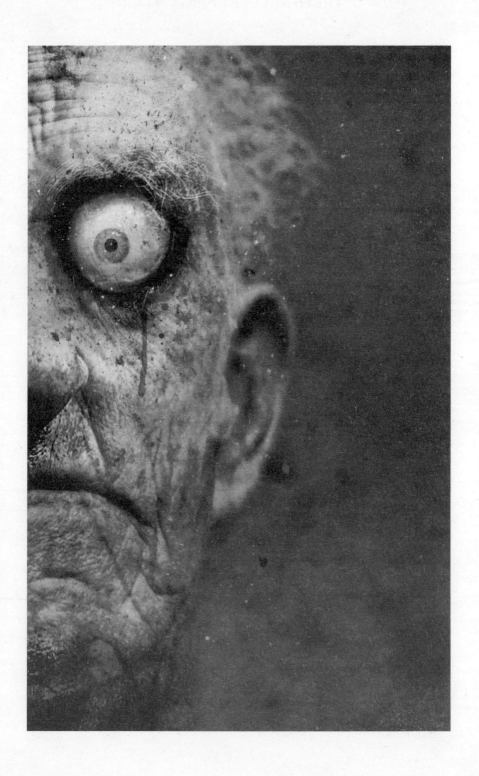

'Yes, of course, but I fear there will be many, many guards—'

'On your authority, however?'

She considered, and then nodded. 'Yes, a special audience. But I will need a change of attire if I am to be convincing.'

'I would advise,' said Steck, 'that you do so on your own, and then return here when you are ready.' He glanced at Tulgord Vise. 'That salve is working, but the bones still need more time to properly knit.'

'Soon,' promised the Mortal Sword. 'I can feel the heat of their mending!'

'Very well,' said Shartorial. She then leaned close and kissed Steck Marynd, before rushing out of the room.

Brash Phluster crept out a few steps. 'I will sing of this, Steck Marynd, the love that defied chains, and bars, and locked doors, and the fact that you haven't bathed in weeks and are pretty homely besides.'

'That's not his tongue,' said Midge, 'that's someone else's.'

Brash Phluster shrugged. 'What if it was? There were plenty lying about, and besides, look at that new eye of yours!'

Midge scowled. 'What about it?'

'Well, where did you find the dead goat? Is what I'm wondering.'

'It's a demon's eye!' said Midge. 'And with it I can see demon things!'

'What demon things?' Brash asked.

Midge waved about. 'Things demons can see, of course. That table there, and those chairs.'

'I can see those too.'

'But I see them the way demons do!'

'Well, with one eye at least.'

Midge made a fist. 'Not if I tear out my other eye and find another demon eye!'

'Possibly,' Brash said, and then shrugged, 'though I'm not convinced of that.'

Flea laughed and pointed. 'Look, Tiny, Midge has a goat eye! Ha ha!'

'It's not a goat! It's a demon!'

'Does it even work?' Brash Phluster asked.

Midge slumped. 'It will. Soon.'

'Tiny eats goats for breakfast and demons for lunch. Tiny eats dragons for supper.'

'And then sits on the shit bucket for the rest of the night,' said Brash Phluster.

Steck Marynd snorted, and then eyed the poet curiously. 'Most peculiar. I now wonder what potion you've swallowed, beyond the one miraculously mending your tongue.'

'The Make Tiny Kill Poet potion,' said Tiny.

Brash Phluster sneered. 'This is what an empowered artist is like, Tiny Chanter. No sharper weapon than talent, no crueller eye than that of an artist unleashed. Insult or threaten me again and I'll see you flensed alive, mocked in a thousand songs, aped by ten thousand mummers and twenty thousand clowns. I'll see you—'

'Better cease the threats,' advised Steck Marynd, 'before the witless thug does what all witless thugs do.'

'Which is?' Brash Phluster asked.

'Yes,' said Tiny, 'which is?'

'Why, kill the artist, of course.'

'Yes, this is what Tiny is going to do.'

Brash laughed, 'Really? So, Tiny Chanter, you're a witless thug, are you?'

'Tiny's not witless. Tiny's not a thug. Tiny's not a witless thug either.'

'So you won't be killing me after all?'

Tiny frowned, and then glanced at Midge, but Midge had one hand covering his good eye and was taking baby steps, his other hand held out lest he walk into something unexpected. Tiny then glanced at Flea, who looked back, smiled and waved.

Groaning, Tulgord Vise slowly regained his feet, wincing as he put his full weight on his legs. Then he straightened and let out a heavy sigh. 'Almost ready,' he said.

Shartorial Infelance rushed back into the chamber, wearing a new shimmery dress of creamy silk with rose petal patterns spilling down to the hem, which sat delicately above the tops of her small feet. Her hair was freshly coiffed, too.

'That was . . . amazing,' said Brash Phluster.

'We have a chance!' she said breathlessly, her cheeks pink, her eyes alight, 'there's no guards anywhere!'

Steck Marynd smiled. 'Necromancers garner little loyalty, it seems. As expected. To your weapons, friends, it's time to end this!'

Brash Phluster watched them all rush from the room, and then he turned back to the shelf and began pocketing as many phials and bottles as he could. He hummed under his breath as he did so, and it was a fine hum indeed.

Emancipor cursed as the mob seethed against one side of the carriage. He leaned down towards the speaking tube. 'It's no good, Master! The whole damned city's in the streets! They've torn apart all the monsters!'

The side door opened and out stepped Bauchelain. One gesture cleared a space as bodies went flying. He climbed up beside his manservant and stood looking at the mobbed street ahead.

'I see. How unfortunate. Can you see Korbal Broach?'

'He veered into a crow and flew away, Master.'

'Did he now? Well, to be expected, as he has every confidence in my ability to extricate ourselves from this situation.'

'Glad to hear it,' said Emancipor. 'Uh, exactly how do you plan on doing that, by the way?'

'Well, first of all, I shall set the horses on fire.'

'Oh.'

'Fear not, Mister Reese, they're used to it.'

'Right. That's good, then. And after that?'

'Well, as much as it offends my sensibilities, I shall have to walk ahead and clear for us a path. Shield your gaze as best you can, Mister Reese, as it shall be a messy traverse.' And from somewhere he drew out a midnight blue two-handed sword that then burst into flickering blue flames. 'In this blade,' Bauchelain said, 'are imprisoned a thousand hungry demons, and tonight, Mister Reese, they shall feed unto gluttony.'

'Right, good for them I say. Just get us out of here!'

Bauchelain smiled. 'Why, Mister Reese, whence the source of this admirable self-interest? Most enchanting.'

'Aye, Master, self-interest, that's me all over.'

Bauchelain brandished the sword, the gesture spraying out writhing tongues of blue flame – sufficient to draw some attention, as cries of terror arose on all sides. 'Now then, allow me some room, Mister Reese, and keep tight the traces as you follow along.'

'Aye Master, count on it!'

Bauchelain then leapt down.

And began the terrible slaughter.

Scratched, bitten, and battered, the Party of Five reached the back of the giant black carriage. Lurma Spilibus scrabbled at the latch of the storage trap and, eventually, found it. She then twisted the latch, only to turn her cross-eyed face at Plaintly. 'Locked!'

'Then pick it and hurry up!'

While she set to work, Barunko and Symon fended off wild, panicked citizens, most of whom seemed to be in a strange frenzy and disinclined to reason on this night, while Le Groutt scared people by leering with his misaligned jaw, and Mortari poked at his swollen head with a shard of broken glass, spurting goo at anyone who came too close.

'It's jammed!' said Lurma, 'and now I've broken the pick!'

With a bearish growl, Barunko stepped back, reached round and tore open the trap door.

Plaintly peered in. 'You won't believe this!' she hissed. 'It's full of gold coins and gems and diamonds and bolts of silk and—'

'Let's go!' cried Lurma, and she clambered inside. The others quickly followed. When Barunko, who was last, grunted his way into the narrow space, the trap door slammed shut, leaving them all in utter darkness.

Plaintly listened but only heard lots of harsh breaths and the

rustle of coins shifting under them. 'We all here?' she asked.
'Count off!'

Mortari said, 'Me!'

Le Groutt said, 'Eee!'

'I'm here,' said Barunko.

'So am I,' hissed Lurma Spilibus.

'That's it, then!' said Plaintly Grasp. 'We're all here! The Party
of Five!'

'No,' said Symon, 'you forgot me!'

'What? Oh, wait, we really *are* the Party of Six!'

'You counted wrong,' said Barunko, 'although you're right.
What I mean is, with Symon included, there's six of us, but only
if that includes you, Plaintly. Or in my case, me.'

'Why wouldn't you include me?' Plaintly demanded. 'Or you?
Anyway, until Symon spoke I counted five, so we must be the Party
of Six!'

'Unless,' said Mortari, 'someone else is in here with us!'

Plaintly Grasp tensed. 'Oh gods, we're not alone!'

'No,' said Mortari. 'There's me and Le Groutt and Lurma and . . .'

'I can't find the damned trap door,' said Barunko. 'It was right
behind me, I swear!'

'Everyone split up and start looking for the trap door,' said
Plaintly.

'Everyone?' asked Mortari.

'Everyone!'

'Even the one who's hiding in here with us?'

'Yes,' said Plaintly, fighting off her panic as she did not like
confining spaces. 'Even that one!'

'That means,' said Mortari, 'we're actually the Party of Seven!'

'No, six,' said Plaintly, who wasn't yet convinced of Barunko's
argument.

'Eleven,' said Lurma Spilibus.

'Seven,' said a voice no-one recognized.

Traversing empty corridors, crossing abandoned chambers
already looted and with stains of blood here and there on the

floor, Shartorial Infelance led them at last to the twin doors behind which waited the throne room.

The Nehemothanai began checking weapons, straps and fittings.

'Poet ran away,' said Tiny.

Grunting, Steck Marynd said, 'I'm not surprised. One can only hope that the potion that made him smarter than normal will wear off.'

'Why?' asked Tulgord Vise as he examined the longsword he'd found.

'A man with sufficient wits will likely escape this wretched night with his life,' Steck replied. 'A man with the normal wits of Brash Phluster is much more likely to die, and most horribly, too.'

'You reveal a cruel streak,' observed Tulgord Vise.

Steck Marynd shrugged. 'He'll survive the night, I'm sure. Beyond that, however, well, since when was an artist hard-eyed and silken-tongued enough to tell the truth, of any use to anyone? That man could become an icon of dissent, a lodestone to disenfranchised revolutionaries, the namby-pamby favourite of the worshipping classes of fawners, hangers-on and other assorted miscreants.' He paused as everyone was staring at him, Tiny with a frown, Midge with a scowl that made his demon eye glow, Flea with a wide smile, Tulgord Vise with a thoughtful expression, and Shartorial Infelance with an adoring one.

Suddenly uncomfortable, Steck said, 'I had aspirations to be a weaver of epics, once. It's said, after all, that there's an epic tale in each and every one of us. It's all down to just writing it down, and only the lucky few of us ever find the time away from the necessities of living, socializing, daydreaming and wishful thinking.' He grimaced and stared at a wall. 'Can't be very hard, anyway,' he muttered. 'Look at Brash Phluster, for Hood's sake!' Then, scowling, he shook his head and collected up his crossbow. 'Well, never mind all that shit. We've got some necromancers to kill!'

Shartorial Infelance flung herself onto Steck. 'I knew it!' she cried, loudly planting wet, sloppy kisses to his face. 'Oh, you could be the Century's Greatest Artist, I just know it!'

'Tiny wants to throw up.'

Swearing under his breath, Tulgord Vise stepped forward and kicked open the twin doors to the throne room.

One of the doors collided with something that made a crunching sound, followed by muffled curses, and an instant later an enormous demon bedecked in supple furs, oiled chain, iron torcs and assorted other accoutrements, staggered into view, clutching its nose which was now streaming blood.

'Bastard!' it groaned, glowing eyes bright with tears.

'Stand aside if you value your life!' Tulgord Vise bellowed.

Blinking, the demon stepped to one side, and then, as the Nehemothanai bulled into the room, it said, 'You're too late if you're after Bauchelain and Korbal Broach.'

'Not again!' cried Tulgord Vise.

Tiny laughed. 'Look! Tiny sees a throne for the taking! Hah ha ha! Hah! Hah ha!'

'Forget it,' said the demon. 'Tried that. It's no good.'

Tiny frowned up at the creature. 'You don't know Tiny Chanter.'

'That's true, I don't. Who is he?'

'This is Tiny Chanter,' said Tiny, thumping his own chest. 'High Mage! D'ivers! King of Toll City of Stratem! Leader of the Nehemothanai! And now king of Farrog, hah!'

'Leader of the Nehemothanai?' snorted Tuglord Vise. 'I take no orders from you, you brainless oaf!'

The demon pointed at the throne. 'We've all been played. Bauchelain left an heir, and woe to the fool who dares challenge him!'

Tiny squinted at the throne. 'Tiny sees nobody!'

'Draw closer, then,' the demon said, smirking.

Tiny crept gingerly forward, eyes darting, ears twitching at the slightest sound to the left and right, real or imagined. When he glanced back over a shoulder, Flea smiled and waved.

Six paces from the throne he halted, stiffened, and then slowly

straightened. 'I see a mouse on the cushion!' He looked back at the demon. 'Ha! Hah! Hah hah ha! Ha!'

'A demonic mouse,' said the giant demon. 'Oh yes, beware Bauchelain's sense of humour. The punchline of every one of his jokes is announced in a welter of blood, guts and messy death!' It gestured dismissively. 'You've been warned, the least I can do. Oh, and by the way, an army is about to crush this city. I wouldn't tarry overlong.'

The demon then fled the throne room.

Tiny continued eyeing the mouse, which in turn had lifted its cute little head, twitching with both its cute little nose and its cute little whiskers.

'Tiny can take it,' said Tiny in a quavering voice.

'Oh,' said Flea, 'it's so cute and little!'

'Heed that demon's words,' advised Steck Marynd. 'Milady,' he said, 'best step back.' He lifted his crossbow. 'This could get messy. But that said, is it not our duty to rid the world of the Nehemoth's minions, no matter where we find them?'

'Then we should all rush it as one,' suggested Tulgord Vise, hefting his sword.

'Once I loose my quarrel, aye,' nodded Steck Marynd. 'You listening, Tiny?'

'Tiny hears you,' said Tiny. 'Its eyes are glowing most fiercely. Do mouse eyes normally glow? Tiny's not sure. Tiny's not sure of anything anymore!'

Flea burst into tears.

Behind them all the double doors suddenly slammed shut, the sound so startling that Steck's finger instinctively flexed, releasing the quarrel.

Straight for the mouse.

Mayhem erupted.

A block away and traversing corpse-strewn streets, Brash Phluster flinched and turned at the sound of the palace's sudden, inexplicable collapse.

He paid the billowing dust and now flames only momentary

heed, his mind frantically occupied as it was on the Epic Lay of Brash Phluster, a ten volume, ten million word poem unwaveringly adhering to the classic iambic hexameter in the style of the Lost Droners of Ipscalon.

Visions of glory danced through his forebrain.

Twenty-four paces later, the Potion of Ineluctable Genius wore off. He looked round, shrieked and then ran for the nearest sewer hole.

PART TWO
The Next Day Outside Farrog

BENEATH THE BRIGHT LIGHT OF DAWN, GRAND GENERAL Pin Dollop cursed and then rode out in front of his legions. He wheeled his mount. 'This is our moment!' he cried in his thin, girly voice. 'Those numbers you see behind me are deceiving! Mere conscripts! A peasant army and never mind all that twinkly armour and those big shields! They'll shatter to our hammer blow! Run shrieking for the hills!'

'Shatter!' bellowed his army.

'Yes!' Pin Dollop screamed back.

'Run shrieking for the hills!'

'Exactly! Now, follow me, as we charge into legend!' And he dragged his horse round, set heels to its flanks, and led the wild charge into the mass of ordered legions directly ahead.

This was glory! This was jaw-dropping courage, breathtaking audacity, a charge not just into legend but into the hoary myths that crawled and stumbled their way down through all of history!

His horse tripped over a badger den, throwing the Grand General from the saddle. He landed in a perfect shoulder roll and lithely regained his feet even as he dragged free his shortsword.

Directly ahead, thirty thousand archers nocked arrows.

Laughing fearlessly, Pin Dollop glanced back—

To see his legions shattered, the soldiers flinging down their weapons and running shrieking for the hills.

384

He spun back round as thirty thousand arrows arced into the sky, all converging on Pin Dollop.

He ducked.

Well disguised beneath a heavy damp cloak, Ophal D'Neeth Flatroq sat perched upon the high saddle, stroking his pet slow-worm, which he kept covered up lest the sight of it frighten one of countless refugees lining the narrow road.

After some time, he sighed and twisted in the saddle. 'Willl you two thtop gwarrrwing at each other! It wuth awwrll a mithunderthtanding, yeth?'

'He tried to strangle me!' snapped Beetle Praata.

'And he made me groom and water and feed a dead horse!' retorted Puny Sploor.

'Oh, bother! Methenger Beetle, find uth a dank cave for the night, willll you? And you, Puny Thploor, clearrr uth a path thwough thethe wefugeeth!'

'Oh really? And how exactly do I do that?'

'I don't know why I keep you on, to be honetht.'

'You keep me on because I'm the only man in the world who doesn't throw up at the sight of you eating, oh Failed Ambassador of the Burning City of Farrog!'

Well, Ophal conceded, the man had a point there. He gestured with one gloved hand. 'Wellll, do the betht you can, then. And you, Methenger, why are you thtill here? A cave, I thaid!'

'Right,' Beetle growled, taking up his reins. 'Another fucking cave. Right. Got it.' He rode off.

Ophal sighed again. At least Eeemlee his pet slow-worm never complained. He resumed stroking it. Then glanced down to find that it was dead. 'Puny Thploor, betht look away, ath I am hungwy.'

A full day's travel from the city of Farrog and Emancipor could still see, when looking back, the pillar of black smoke. He wiped at his itchy, stinging eyes, and glanced at his master who sat

beside him on the bench. 'I have to admit, sir, that I'm glad you didn't have to kill and maim too many of them citizens before the rest broke and ran.'

'Mister Reese, your mercy remains a quaint if somewhat tiresome affectation. For myself, I confess to some disappointment. The demons bound in my sword are very frustrated indeed. We shall have to find us another city, or situation, in which to exercise my obligations to them.'

'Really? When?'

'Oh, not too soon, I assure you.' He lifted a hand and gestured ahead. 'Do you see Korbal there? He rides well the updraghts, wouldn't you agree?'

'I think he prefers being a crow to being a man.'

'On occasion, Mister Reese, I share his bias.'

'Ain't noticed that much of late, Master.'

'Well, it is easier keeping you company this way, Mister Reese, than being a crow balanced upon your rather thin shoulder.'

'All on account of me, huh? Well, I'm, er, flattered.'

'As you should be. That said, you must understand, frustration stalks us, alas. Oh, the endless wealth we steal soothes the soul, to be sure. But the true exercise of power, Mister Reese, ah, so fleeting!'

'Forgiving me being forward and all, Master, but what you two need is a keep somewhere. Impregnable, unassailable, forbidding, suitably haunted.'

'Hmm, a curious notion, Mister Reese. Mind you, do recall Blearmouth. Oh yes, it all started off well, and our wintering there was most enjoyable, until the infernal Nehemothanai caught wind of us. I admit that I grow weary of staying one step ahead of them, in particular that army and the Mysterious Lady commanding them.'

'A strong enough keep, sir,' ventured Emancipor, 'and you'd not have to worry.'

'You appear to share our weariness in this endless journey.'

'Well, Master, it's all the same to me, to be honest.'

'Perhaps if Korbal Broach assembled an army of undead . . .'

'That'd be fine, sir, if they weren't so, uh, useless.'

'Granted, although I warn you not to venture such opinions within hearing of my erstwhile comrade.'

'Not me, sir. Never. Not a chance.'

'Now, Mister Reese, I well see your exhaustion. Do retire to the confines of the carriage and get yourself some sleep. I can manage the traces for a time, I assure you.'

'Thank you, sir,' Emancipor said, handing the traces over to his master. He stretched out the kinks in his back. 'I'll just have me a pipe first, then, by way of relaxing and whatnot.'

'Best be quick,' Bauchelain advised. 'I am of a mind to take this carriage into a warren, to traverse the wild raging flames of some nether realm, if only to confuse our trail.'

Emancipor stuffed the pipe back into its pouch and made for the carriage door. 'I can smoke later,' he said hastily.

'As you will, Mister Reese. Now then, you may hear the horses screaming. Pay that no mind. They're used to it.'

Emancipor paused at the door. 'Aye, sir, and so am I.'

About the Author

Steven Erikson is an archaeologist and anthropologist – and the author of one of the defining works of Epic Fantasy: 'The Malazan Book of the Fallen', which has been hailed 'a masterwork of the imagination'. The first novel in this astonishing ten-book series, *Gardens of the Moon*, was shortlisted for the World Fantasy Award. He has also written a number of novellas set in the same fantasy world and *Willful Child*, an affectionate parody of a long-running science fiction television series. *Forge of Darkness* begins the Kharkanas Trilogy – a series which takes readers back to the origins of the Malazan world. *Fall of Light* continues this epic tale. Steven Erikson lives in Victoria, Canada.